DEMON BLADE

MARK A. GARLAND
CHARLES G. McGRAW

BAEN

DEMON BLADE

This is a work of fiction. All the characters and events portrayed in this book are fictional, and any resemblance to real people or incidents is purely coincidental.

A Baen Books Original

Baen Publishing Enterprises
P.O. Box 1403
Riverdale, N.Y. 10471

ISBN: 0-671-87610-4

Cover art by Larry Elmore

First printing, July 1994

Distributed by
Paramount
1230 Avenue of the Americas
New York, N.Y. 10020

Typeset by Windhaven Press, Auburn, N.H.
Printed in the United States of America

DEMON BLADE

MARK A. GARLAND
CHARLES G. McGRAW

BAEN

DEMON BLADE

A Baen Books Original

Baen Publishing Enterprises
P.O. Box 1403
Riverdale, N.Y. 10471

ISBN: 0-671-87610-4

Cover art by Larry Elmore

First printing, July 1994

Distributed by
Paramount
1230 Avenue of the Americas
New York, N.Y. 10020

Typeset by Windhaven Press, Auburn, N.H.
Printed in the United States of America

Prologue

Ergris stood close to the trunk of the massive old oak that marked the north edge of the clearing, watching. For many days there had been no sound or movement at the human's hut. No smoke rose from the morning's chill. The Old One could have been out in the wood gathering herbs or getting his walk, but the hut itself had a slightly tattered look; a scattering of branches from the roof lay at the base of the walls, and bits of wall lay with them. Most of all, the aura of the man was gone.

The Old One had always kept a tidy clearing. Now small seedlings grew everywhere about the yard and weeds choked the gardens. In all his years coming to visit here, with his elders or friends or even, in recent years, alone, Ergris had never seen this so.

He felt a pang of sorrow as his thoughts came round. The Old One had made the forest bloom where fires had touched it, had saved the dying bog during the dry years tenfold and tenfold years ago. And he told the most wonderful stories!

Too aged and frail to do any but the slightest physical tasks, it was the Old One's spell-weavings that had kept his home and land from the steady press of the living forest, and kept him hidden from the eyes of hunters and fools who wandered near these past few decades. Indeed, it was this talent with spells that had brought about the deaths of the first leshy to approach the hut, so many years ago. . . .

Ergris could not call out, leshy having neither the voice nor the disposition to allow such a thing in the quiet of the woods. He waited until the morning was nearly gone, eyeing every corner of the clearing, even circling it several times as he had done the day before, to be certain of things. Finally he made his way to the front door. He found it closed and boarded from the inside.

As he stood scratching his belly, dragging long sharp nails through the thin fur there, he decided that a simple favor was needed. He twitched his short muzzle, thinking his plan out exactly, then he cleared his throat, closed his eyes, and felt for the presence of the stout oak board on the other side of the door. He remembered the piece well; he had even placed it in the wooden brackets himself more than once, during evenings when he and the Old One would speak of man and leshy, of worlds long past and others to come—together alone, the two of them.

The oaken board was there, and Ergris began to woo it aside. Yet even as he did, the possibilities made him uneasy—magical traps, hidden deaths—humans had been known to lose their minds, or simply change them. Most of them were horrible creatures. He pressed on, caressing the wood with his mind.

Ergris knew no fear in his own forest, unlike human kings, who feared to go beyond their own bedchambers without armor and weapons. And Ergris considered himself the wisest, strongest leshy king of all. The Old

One—Ramins, as he called himself—was wise in many ways, and he had taught Ergris such things as no leshy king before him had been taught. But Ergris had initiated the talks knowing the risks were great. He still recalled the first two leshy who had tried to climb one on the other into the hut's only window, their petrified bodies lying piled up next to the wall for weeks, until Ergris had come with a party in the deepest depths of night to take them away.

But it was not curiosity, posturing, or even lack of good sense that finally brought Ergris out of the forest to confront old Ramins at the stream one day. In part the attraction was the wizard's own potent aura, but more, Ergris was drawn to the other aura that came from within the human's dwelling, that of something made by the gods themselves—a blade of some kind, Ergris was certain. He had sensed it with his leshy spirit the way one might smell ripe cherries on the mid-summer winds, incredibly sweet, alluring. He could not help his fascination any more than the leaves of plants could resist the sunlight. None of the leshy could, until two of them had been turned to stone.

The Old One had finally shown Ergris the Blade, even let him touch it several times—out of respect for Ergris' bravery, his wisdom, and, Ramins explained, out of gratitude for his good company. The sword's short blade shined with a glow that persisted, if faintly, even in darkness, at least to Ergris' leshy eyes. Its hilt was thick and black and smooth, too thick in fact for a leshy's tiny hands to properly wrap around. Ergris had never known or imagined the like of that magical blade, or the Old One, or the visits they had had together.

The brothers of the council had deemed the whole relationship utterly foolish and worthless—no good could ever come from contact with man, even this wizard-man. And the wizard had raised a dampening spell outside his house soon enough, which kept even leshy from sensing the Blade beyond the four walls that kept it. Without that subtle lure many others had begun to question Ergris's strange conduct as well. But Ergris was King, and Ergris had proven them wrong.

He cleared the past from his mind and focussed on the present as he leaned against the center of the cabin door. He smoothed his voice, adjusted his tone, caressing each band of the board's raw grain until it rose just high enough. Then he pushed the door open as the board dropped away; he picked it up, touching it gently with his hands now, then set the piece against the wall just inside the door.

Ergris stood still a moment, his eyes adjusting to the dimly lit interior of the hut. The Old One was seated in his chair at his table, head slumped forward onto the pages of an open book, a quill clutched in his bony fingers. His short staff of birch-wood lay on the floor beside him. The aura of power that had been Ramins' was gone, Ergris sensed, completely and forever.

I have lost a great companion, he thought, forcing himself to think it, since thinking such things of creatures like men was strange and difficult even now. But the Old One had come to treat the forest and its rightful occupants with the favor and regard they deserved, and was the only human any leshy now living had ever shared thoughts and fruit with, so far as Ergris knew. . . .

Ergris began to lose his thoughts, his nature overruling his mind as the sweetness of a very different aura, of something terrible and wonderful and potent, began pulling at him, growing stronger the longer he remained inside the hut. As he hurried to begin his search, his hide prickled with anticipation. *I have come in time,* he thought, following his senses, finding it at last. *The Demon Blade is still here!*

Chapter 1

Brittle shrieks broke the silence, filling the still night air from the high rock walls to the moonlit mountain slopes beyond. Voices echoed down the pass in a cold and grating chorus, building, burrowing into the brain until the mind could no longer endure the agony: the cry of the banshee was the sound of death.

Frost looked to his three Subartan warriors. In the deep shadows of the cliffs even the moon did not light their faces, but there was no doubt they understood. He watched their vague silhouettes move about him, forming a defensive triangle, leaving Frost at its center. This was the only arrangement possible; a big man by any measure, padded with far too much extra body fat and busy with his spells, he would make an easy target. Satisfied, he closed his eyes and drew on the strength of his body and his mind.

With that, the death wails seemed to grow more distant and less numerous. The light from the moon seemed to find its way a little farther into the depths of the rocky pass.

"Banshees can take no physical form," Rosivok, the oldest, largest Subartan said. "But they can use others. It is said they can control any creature at hand."

"Only those whose lives they have already stolen," Sharryl said, adjusting her stance just a bit, though she did not turn around. "Unless. . . ."

"The wolves," Jaffic, the youngest Subartan said for her. "I saw some yesterday, trailing us."

"It is true," Rosivok told Frost. "We all saw them. And they might make fine allies for a nest of banshees."

"Then beware wolves!" Frost told them. "I have the banshees to manage, and they are much stronger than I imagined. And many, I think. Not ten or twenty, as we were led to believe, but perhaps a hundred, and already they do not like the force of my will upon them." He paused, eyes closed, and spoke under his breath. Then he opened his eyes again and glanced up to the sky. *Good,* he thought, nodding to himself. "I have them subdued for the moment, but they may be holding back, plotting an answer. They have not survived death so long for lack of resource."

The banshee's faint wailing suddenly stopped altogether. Silence grew thick in the pass, though Frost took little comfort in it.

"What are they about?" Jaffic asked in a whisper.

"Let the master worry about that," Rosivok told the young warrior, a strict tone in his voice. Jaffic was not a true Subartan as Rosivok and Sharryl were—born and bred by the ancient desert tribes to be the most proficient fighters their land had ever known. But the other two had taught an eager Jaffic well in the use of the subarta blades, and the transformation of mind and body that was more important than mere weapons. He had been eager to learn, much more eager than he was to talk about his past, which remained a mystery; such mysteries, however, mattered little to Frost as long as the man performed his duties.

"It is all right," Frost told them. "In truth, I don't know what comes next. I have had very little experience with these particular creatures. Still, they have done their howling, and we have not given up our souls as yet."

"Are you so sure you have one?" Sharryl said, turning toward Frost, tossing her hair aside just enough to let her eyes find his in the faint light. The smile was implied; daylight would have shown nothing more.

"I do," Frost said. "I keep it well hidden. But I know where to find it if the gods or I should have need of it."

"I do not plan to need mine this day," Sharryl remarked.

"Nor I," Jaffic added.

"Enough," Rosivok snapped, and the others abruptly quieted. He held no rank or privilege over the other two, only experience and size and a proven talent for survival. Frost wasn't sure how Rosivok and Sharryl had met, though it was an alliance that had kept them both alive through travels that had taken years and covered half the continent. There was no lover's bond between them— between any two Subartans, so far as Frost knew—but another bond existed, which was to them much more important.

"Now, I only have one need," Frost said to them after a moment. Sharryl and Jaffic nodded only once, then focussed all their attention on the matter at hand, the darkness beyond them.

No breeze touched them, no creatures made their summer noises or rustled through the shadows. Frost heard Rosivok sniff at the cool air; he breathed in, as well, and his nose found the faint tinge of long-decayed animal flesh nearby.

"Something approaches," Rosivok said calmly, his voice low. "It does not smell of wolf."

"From this way as well," Sharryl agreed, poised in a

low stance, her subarta ready, her keen senses straining, like those of her warrior companions.

"Not the banshees," Frost remarked, "but they are still here, I assure you."

"What will you do with them?" Jaffic asked. A little out of line again, Frost thought, but he let it pass.

"I will ask them to leave, of course," Frost replied curtly, answer enough for now.

The moon had finally moved far enough over the high walls of the pass to cast some of its gaunt white light down into the narrows below. The wolves were clearly visible then, approaching slowly from both directions. Just ahead, in the wider section of the pass, the dried bones and carcasses of men and pack animals lay strewn about.

Abruptly the cries of the banshee colony rose anew, and kept rising to many times their former level. Frost tried to focus a part of himself on the two wolf packs even as he sought to turn back the songs of death that surrounded him, starting to violate his mind and body.

"These animals are not among the living," he said in a strained voice. This was what his Subartans needed to know: the dead were much harder to kill. The nearest wolf chose that instant to leap.

Sharryl lashed out with her subarta, the slicing blade flashed, then she turned and kicked. The first wolf's head tumbled left, while its body fell to the right. No fluids drained from the carcass; there was no sound, no twitching. Another animal took its place.

Sharryl dipped down, moving more quickly than eyes could follow. She gutted the beast as it lunged. This second butchered corpse fell inside the triangle, just short of Frost—who paid it little mind.

He was aware of the battle, or as aware as he dared to be, but he had more than enough to do just at the moment. The banshees were rallying, pressing on him with increasing force, pulling at him with a longing that seemed to have no hope of satisfaction other than the grave.

He saw Jaffic at Sharryl's side now, flaying another wolf as it tried to circle around. Ahead, Rosivok was busy carving more of the creatures into bloodless chunks. But on the rocky ground around them, the severed bodies of the fallen wolves stirred, anxious to rejoin the battle.

"Let the dead speak to the dead," Frost shouted, holding out both hands, summoning all his strength. In the ancient tongue he chanted the words that would bind the listening spell, then added further embellishments, a part of a deflection spell, and part of a spell usually used to bind a man to secrecy. Finally, he used a musical spell, a quaint incantation useful in helping singers reach their highest notes.

As he completed his work, the sounds of the banshees grew faint again, though they were rising in pitch this time, higher and higher, until human ears could no longer make them out. But as the sounds disappeared, the attacking wolves began to twitch and howl in terrible agony. Their dead eyes rolled back into their bony skulls, then a few turned and ran out of the pass. Soon the others followed, until the only things still moving were the twitching skulls of the beheaded.

A beginning, Frost thought, relaxing, easing the flow of energy into the spell. The immediate threat had ended. He and his Subartans could continue now, immune to the torturous screams of the banshees. But that was not what he had been paid to do. Highthorn Pass was the only way trade and travelers could pass through the Spartooth Mountains, the only path to the sea.

Shortages north of the mountains had become many, until they had lately begun to annoy even the richest lords, and Frost as well. His commission had been worthy, and the omens had all been good. He had every intention of completing his task in a proper fashion.

"You sing only to your own kind now," Frost shouted to the cliffs above. "But I can do more. You will sing only to yourselves if you do not leave this place."

He stepped forward, slightly unsteady at first, weakened by his efforts but growing stronger rapidly. As he moved with his Subartans into the open Frost could sense the spirits of the banshees all around them, closer now, gathering perhaps, he thought, to listen.

Frost had never heard of a colony of banshees as large as this, though there were legends from the time of the demons, centuries ago. He could not help but wonder why such a thing should occur now, though one could not ask questions of creatures that did not speak. In any case, why they were here mattered little—they had to leave.

"Go elsewhere!" he commanded. "Trouble another region. I have promised many safe passage though these mountains, and safe they will be."

He could sense their question, a tingle at the back of his mind: *Go where?*

"Go anywhere," he told them. "These mountains are filled with ravines and gorges seldom used by men. You will always find some, the unlucky and creatures that die from many natural causes, creatures whose spirits you can call to yourselves before they are gone. Enough, I think, to serve your needs."

He waited, letting his mind hear the faint reply.

"Hmmm, unfortunate," Frost said after a time.

"What?" Rosivok asked, speaking for the others.

Frost let slip a sigh. "They like it here." He turned to his Subartans. "Build a fire," he said.

They quickly gathered what twigs and brush they could from the sparse, stunted crop of bushes and trees that grew in the pass. In a moment, the smell and warmth of a small fire filled the air, and the bright light of its flames lit the darkness. Frost concentrated again.

He drew on his inner reserves, burning energy more quickly than the fastest runner, the strongest oarsman. He focused the spell and spoke to the fires.

The flames wavered, then left the pile of twigs and weeds and raced up through the pass, climbing the walls, leaping crevasses, crisscrossing the rocks until the entire chasm seemed to be engulfed. Even the corpses of banshee victims were consumed by the now too-bright, incredibly hot fires that changed colors as they burned in a rainbow spectrum. Inescapable, even for banshees. Yet nothing living was so much as singed.

After a moment Frost eased, and he began to smile. He stopped feeding energy to the flames and let them die away, until only the small circle of the original fire still flickered at his feet. He staggered and put one hand out to Rosivok, who quickly moved to steady the wizard.

"They did not like that at all," Frost said, a faint chuckle in his voice. "Especially the ones that perished."

The ones, he thought, that doubted he could threaten their existence. They had wagered far too much—*everything*—on that assumption. Such fools, he insisted, were a breed that fate was seldom kind to.

"We will make camp here," he added, straightening his stance. He moved slowly away and sat on a nearby rock, then took the very large drawstring pouch from his shoulders and began rummaging in it for food and a bladder of water. Thirst and hunger drove him now, an emptiness as deep as the mountain pass. He drank the water, then stuffed his mouth full of dried fish.

"Tomorrow, we go to Ikaydin," he said, adding nothing, content simply to fill his mouth again, though the thought of the journey made him smile. He had not been to that land in decades. Far too long. And he had every reason to believe that opportunity waited for him there, and just beyond.

"Ikaydin," Sharryl and Rosivok repeated, though Jaffic kept silent. An uneasy look seemed to cross his features, like the look of a man before a battle, but it faded before Frost could wonder at it long. The three Subartans gathered beside the firelight to open their own pouches. In the nearby hills, crickets began to chirp. Frost let his sight drift upward.

High above stars gathered around the moon, though there was a slight haze, Frost noticed, now that he looked more closely. Which was an omen not to be ignored, if memory served him now. An omen of stormy weather ahead. . . .

Chapter II

Madia fought to pull free of Jolann's clutches, but the woman was older, stronger and half again Madia's weight. She had hold of a handful of Madia's dress just behind the neck and was moving swiftly enough to keep Madia off balance, pulling her, walking her nearly backward. Jolann reached the end of the hallway and marched into the great entry hall. The hard soles of her shoes on the flat stones of the floor echoed off the high stone walls, a report surely heard throughout half the castle.

Lord Burtoll himself stood waiting by the open door. He seemed disinclined to look at Madia directly as Jolann placed her, swaying and ruffled, precisely in front of him. He was perhaps as old as Madia's father, though not as tall a man, nor as handsome, and not so fine a dresser in his unadorned tunic and leather bonnet. A good man who generally seemed to maintain a degree of humor under most circumstances, though these, Madia observed, were not such.

"Bring her," Burtoll said in a solemn mutter. He turned and the three of them went into the street, then made

13

their way briskly from the central keep to the manor's main gates. The king's carriage waited just off the bridge, escorted by two mounted men at arms, one on either side. The Lady Anna Renall stood waiting beside the open carriage door. Usually there were half-a-dozen carriages and wagons waiting for their charges, the daughters of the greatest lords of southern Ariman come to learn their lessons from Madam Jolann. This afternoon, however, having been held back until the others were gone, Madia had no company, or comfort.

"Why have I been forced to wait so long?" Lady Anna asked as they neared, in an aggrieved, demanding tone.

"Dear Anna," Lord Burtoll began, straightening his tunic with an air of purpose. "You must tell the king that while I will uphold my oath to him with my very life, and while I consider him the most worthy monarch in all the realm, I cannot allow his daughter to return within these walls!"

Lady Anna looked from Lord Burtoll to Madam Jolann, all insistence gone from her face, replaced by a painful, almost pleading expression. Jolann, for her part, was apparently in no mood to offer any help.

"She has disrupted lessons too many times to count," Jolann said, "as you and the king are both aware. She does poorly in her studies, much more poorly than the bright young girl that once graced these rooms, and she encourages others to do the same. Today, during lessons in caring for battle wounds, she explained that there would be no need for such learning if a knight inept enough to become wounded could only have the decency to finish the job and get himself killed! Task her on the ruling of a household, and she will say that is what people like myself are for. She will not read aloud without making up some of the words to suit her own humorous purposes, and she constantly conspires to mock not only myself but every lord and lady she—"

"She stirs the other girls, my daughter as well," Lord Burtoll said, interrupting Jolann, who was turning red and growing quite loud. "She refuses to quit with her stories of fortune and lust and strange adventures. She has listened well to the tales the minstrels and jongleurs tell in private company, to the boasting of troubadours and the knights of the castle, and I care not to speculate on how this has come to pass. I insist, however, that *my* daughter not be subjected to such, as do the lords who send the other girls."

Lady Anna stood stiffly, eyes avoiding everyone in the sudden silence. Then she glanced at Madia wearing a look less of pain and more of exhaustion, of defeat. Madia grinned in spite of herself. Lord Burtoll had never seen the wild looks on the other girl's faces; he didn't know how popular such tales and antics had made Madia. And probably Anna didn't, either. They never would.

"I will inform her father," Anna said, bowing her head, then taking Madia's hand. It wasn't fair to Anna, Madia thought, who lately had to endure such complaints on a regular basis, and who in turn had to endure the king's requests that Anna help do something about it. She was really the best lady Madia had had in recent memory, the only one Madia had been able to talk to since she was a child. Reform was something Madia had certainly considered, but it just didn't seem awfully practical. Not yet, anyway.

"What have you to add to this?" Anna asked, and Madia realized the question was addressed to her.

"I am sorry," Madia said, folding her hands in front of her, bowing her head.

"She said as much this Monday," Lord Burtoll grumbled. "Just the same way."

"And the week before *and* the week before," Jolann added.

The knight nearest the gathering chuckled softly.

Both women and Lord Burtoll glared up at him, and he reined his mount back just a step.

"I will inform the king," Anna said, curtseying abruptly and taking Madia by the arm. "In detail. Get in," she said.

As the carriage turned and headed out, not a word was said.

"I really am sorry. That I made the lord so mad, I mean," Madia said, noting how upset Anna continued to appear.

"Yes," Anna said, "so am I."

The coachman drove the carriage over the wide wooden bridge that crossed Lord Burtoll's dry moat, then he turned and headed down the road, toward the great walled city of Kamrit, and Lord Kelren Andarys, King of Ariman. The worst, Madia thought, was yet to come.

The city rose up over the fields before them, until its long stone walls and high towers eclipsed their view of the sea beyond. They passed by the main gateway, which consisted of portcullises and a drawbridge that stood between two massive towers, each with projecting becs. Instead, the carriage entered through the southern gate, part of the double walls and gates added by Madia's father some years ago. Here, away from the central market square and main guild halls, the streets were less busy.

Above them, on the second and third floors of houses, women with children beside them looked out to watch the small procession as it headed toward the castle. The children called out, and their mothers hushed them. Madia paid them little mind. She did not live among them; she lived just ahead, in the safety and seclusion of Kamrit Castle.

The castle itself was triangular in shape, with two of its

sides forming the city walls nearest the sea. Two separate wards stood within the walls, along with accommodations in the castle's six towers and four gate houses, and the great hall. Only once had the city come under siege, and never had the walls been breached.

As they drew nearer, freemen and serfs alike took pause, acknowledging the presence of their princess. Madia, for all the fuss, ignored them—all of them, that is, except a young knight on horseback, young Calif, son of Baron Durun and heir to his fair lands, a knight who until this coming winter served in King Andarys' army, and who was at the moment waiting just outside the castle's gate.

Sir Calif, dressed in full armor and carrying his helmet under one arm, nodded slowly from atop his mount. "Good day, my lady," he said, grinning too much like a boy.

Madia leaned out while the carriage waited for the gate to be drawn up. "Good day," she said, smiling precisely, winsomely. She had only met him two nights before, when they were introduced at the minstrel performances, though she had seen him about, his eyes set in her direction, several times before that. Their conversation that evening had done much to define the meaning behind his gaze.

"Have you nothing else to say to me?" she invited him.

He bowed. "You are the most magnificent woman in all Ariman," he told her. She had heard these words from other men many times before; still, from some men, they never seemed to grow stale. "Thank you," she said.

"I feared you would not speak to me," he replied, and Madia recalled the suggestions he had made late in the evening, both of them drunk on the king's best ale, suggestions no nobleman of any station should have made to the daughter of the king. There had been one particularly daring, inexcusable description involving several tender parts of her person and his deepest imaginings. But Madia could excuse a great deal under certain circumstances, and she found daring a stimulating quality in a man.

"Then you remember?" she said.

The coachman called the horses forward again.

"Need I apologize, my lady?" Calif asked, moving with the carriage.

He didn't look nearly so embarrassed as he should, Madia thought, though she knew she was guilty of the same. "Not as yet," she told him.

He nudged his horse again to keep along side. "Perhaps I will see you again." He grinned, dimples and all. "Perhaps tonight?"

"There is a chance we might happen upon one another, in the inner courtyard, just after the sun has gone—" She felt Anna's elbow nudge her ribs as Sir Calif nodded and turned his mount. The carriage passed behind the castle wall. When they stopped, the soldier on Madia's side dismounted and opened the carriage door. Lady Anna scowled at him and pulled it shut again.

"This is not wise," she whispered. "You would do well to keep your silence in public, even in front of your guards and the coachman. the king will not tolerate much more of this behavior, as he has made very clear. To both of us! He *cannot* tolerate it."

"We have had this talk before," Madia said, turning away from her.

"You choose not to see the position you are putting him in. But people ask how he can control a kingdom when he cannot control his own daughter. You have made your father a laughingstock. If you don't care what all Ariman thinks of you, you might at least consider him!"

"He can fend well enough for himself!" Madia said. "And I *don't* care what anybody thinks of me. They ought to learn what I think of them! Dullards, fools and cowards, all but a few. Followers of followers, with not a notion among them. I am not ready to choose their lives as mine."

"You have a duty, my lady. You owe—"

"All my life I have been told of my great, boundless debt, to the serfs and lords and barons and merchants and gentry, to the memory of a mother I never even knew, to my good and honorable father. But what of me, Anna? I owe something to myself as well. And that is the debt I chose to pay first." She fixed Anna with a straight look, one she knew would be understood. Lady Anna looked away, hands tight together on her lap for a moment.

"I must report what has happened at Lord Burtoll's house. Your father will want to speak to you."

"I know," Madia said, feeling a twinge of penitence, a feeling that did not bear close scrutiny; she had never been very close to her father—or he had never managed to become very close to her—but she bore him no ill will, and she liked the Lady Anna much more than she wanted to admit.

Still, doing anyone's bidding was something that worked much better as theory than practice. "He will get over it," she said, "as he always does."

"Not always," Anna said. She opened the door and got out without another word.

Madia arrived at her chambers alone and began sorting through clothing, looking for something appropriate to wear. She wanted to appear as sweet and charming as possible when her father summoned her to his chambers. She wished to avoid too childish a look, as he had recently made a habit of describing her actions as hopelessly immature, yet she could not appear too womanly, either, too old and . . . *responsible*. Or overripe, for that matter—at eighteen she was already past the age when most girls were wed, and she had no wish to remind him. She needed to look young and proper, shy and needing, yet somewhat sure of herself; she needed to look as much like her mother's paintings as she possibly could.

She chose a long burgundy-colored velvet tunic and skirt, embroidered and drawn at the waist, then chose a small veil. She undressed, washed her face and hands in the basin near her bed, and put scent under her arms and neck, then paused to check her body for bruises. She had taken a pair of awkward falls the day before during her lessons at swordsmanship. Inexcusable, both of them. Her talents with a short sword were legend, or at least she liked to think they were. But her latest tutor acted so differently from the last few that she had been unable to establish a rhythm; in fact, she'd been made a fool of—a condition made all the more untenable by this new instructor's lack of skills. He was no better than the last, and only barely capable of teaching others.

She would do better next time, of course. Truth be told, she could hold her own against all but the king's finest swordsman—a boast her father found of little value.

She looked over her legs and arms, then felt where she couldn't see and found a tender spot on her right buttock. A dark line, she saw then, turning back just far enough, straining her eyes and posture. The bruise ran horizontally across three or four inches to nearly her hip, the mark of her new tutor's sword. He had slapped her with the blade's flat side, laughing as he did, she recalled. A minor humiliation she would somehow repay. . . .

Minimal damage, she thought, straightening up, deciding the rest of her skin and figure was in order; this, too, was the stuff of legend, or at least that was what many of the king's finest knights and nobles had led her to believe. She had no wish to diminish herself in their eyes, or Sir Calif's eyes, in particular.

As she finished dressing, she heard a knock followed by the voice of Sir Tristan, the king's seneschal, just outside her door. "Speak," she said.

"You are to meet with your father prior to the meal," he said through the door. "Present yourself in the great hall at once."

"The great hall?" Madia said, looking up, staring at the door. There was no answer. The seneschal had gone, perhaps, or he had nothing more to say. He knew just as she did that there was no reason for her father to see her at court, in public. He never discussed personal matters in that way.

Unless there was some function she was not aware of. Visitors, possibly, or an outing? And if so, the evening might be consumed by related activities that would leave little time for private scolding and hand wringing. Tomorrow, the both of them about in the castle all day, she was sure to hear more than her fill, but by then her father would have softened at least somewhat on the matter of Lord Burtoll's complaints.

She really would have to hold her tongue a bit more in the future, she decided, or at least *try*. She opened the door and found the seneschal still there, tall and bearded, and old, though she was not sure of his age exactly; he had a low voice that he never raised, never seemed to need to. Tristan had been seneschal to Madia's grandfather, King Hual Andarys, when he brought peace to Neleva and conquered all the lands north to the Ikaydin Plateau. He had served Kelren since the old king's death and, as anyone would tell, had served him well. She looked at him now, his face firmly set with its common lines, eyes unreadable. "What is it?"

"I would have a word with you," he said, facing her now with a coldness she could not defend against. She was used to men looking at her, but not like this. There was nothing adversarial in his manner, past or present, more a silent lack of deference. He had never spoken much to little Madia; he had never been a friend.

"Is my father well?" she asked.

"Yes. I would speak of something else."

"Please."

"Were you to attend court more often, and take a proper interest in the daily affairs of your father, you would know that he is not without troubles these days. Messengers tell of the desert tribes massing beyond the Kaya Desert, of their preparations for a war that may come to us. And there is unrest in the north, talk of Lord Ivran of Bouren and his son secretly plotting with the other great lords against your father's crown, and for unknown reasons."

"But they have denied all that."

"True, but they would. Do not forget that Lord Ivran's men are suspected of taking part in the death of Sir Renall."

She had not forgotten, and there were constant reminders. Renall, Anna's husband, had been grand chamberlain to the king since before Madia was born. He had fallen prey to robbers on the road. Villagers found him with his sword still in his hand and many wounds to mark the fierceness of the battle, the valiant death he had finally suffered. But riders had been seen, heading north on the road that same day wearing armor bearing the crest of Bouren, the mark of Lord Ivran's crown and scabbards.

More than a year ago, she realized, recalling it now, since the Lord Ferris had taken his place.

For his part Lord Ferris seemed competent, though she thought he had changed somewhat along with his new status; he had never been a strong or influential individual in the past, or he hadn't shown it. Lately, he seemed to offer council constantly, and her father tended to listen.

"The king does not ask for my help, and I doubt he needs it," Madia told him.

"Perhaps, but he does not need a daughter who constantly insists on adding to his problems, who humiliates and embarrasses him repeatedly, despite his best efforts to reason with her. He does not need enemies. The lords, squires and gentry of the city are laughing at him. His detractors have begun to cast doubt on his ability to control nations when he cannot control one girl. He has never been tested in a great war as his father was. He is under constant scrutiny from all quarters and must continually prove himself a fitting leader in many small ways, lest he prove himself unfit."

"Oh, that's absurd!" Madia sneered. "He is easily as great a king as his father. Everyone from the ports of Neleva to Ikaydin knows that to be true. He has kept his father's word and law, and kept the peace. All the realm has prospered. I cannot believe that the northern lords would plot against him, or that I can so easily ruin him, and neither should you."

"Only yesterday," Sir Tristan said, "Lord Ferris spoke of robbers in growing numbers along many of our trade routes. He believes they are organized and owe their allegiance to the northern lords, or to the merchant guilds of Glister and Brintel, which grow more powerful every day. They breed fear and unrest throughout the land. Who do you believe militant villagers might side with if there is a war? If the desert tribes swept into eastern Ariman tomorrow, or if the fiefs revolt, would the people trust King Kelren to protect them?"

Madia said nothing. Sir Tristan somehow made his face even longer. "Your father has already called many of the men of Ariman to arms, and Ferris has begun hiring soldiers as an early precaution, but such men need a leader. Ariman needs an unblemished king to follow. A strong king. And one day, perhaps, a strong queen."

Madia clasped her hands tightly together, felt them shaking just slightly even so. She was a possible heir to the throne by birth, but she had never been able to imagine herself as any sort of queen! She knew that her blood was something she would have to face one day, like aging, like death, yet she had managed to put off the truth quite well for most of her life.

And there was her cousin, the young Duke Andarys, son to her father's long dead brother. He had always been seen as the more likely heir, and Madia had made no protest, but the fool had set out on a tour of the realm four years ago, the moment his uncle had deemed him old enough. Word of his adventuring had come from time to time, until two years ago, when he had been seen heading over the Spartooth Mountains toward the lands beyond. Another message arrived a year after that: news only that the duke was alive and well, and a promise to return in good time. But with the passage of yet another year and no further news, hopes had begun to dim.

Now, Madia's official destiny threatened to close in on her, to hunt her down. For in her cousin's absence, her father had grown older, and she had grown into a young woman. Madia loathed the thought of inheriting the throne.

"You have underestimated my father," Madia said, glancing at Tristan, fielding his stare as best she could.

"You have failed him."

She took a breath, mouth closed tight, nostrils flared as she stepped into the hall, then she reached out and pulled her door shut, cracking oak against stone with a jolt that echoed like cannon fire.

"My father is waiting," she said, and brushed past.

The day's gathering found the king's officials present in numbers: squires and lords, stewards, chancellors, men-at-arms and gentry, their silk or gold-trimmed tunics and embroidered dresses complimenting the silk and sendal hangings that adorned the high walls. Even the Holy Prelate from the city's Church of the Greater Gods was in attendance. Tristan took his place beside the chancellor and Grand Chamberlain Ferris. Lady Anna stood before the throne, waiting for Madia. She gestured, directing Madia to join her there.

Lord Ferris watched her unwaveringly, a face with too many wrinkles for an otherwise fit man of no more than forty, and eyes that never seemed to match his expression, eyes that made Madia feel physically uneasy, as if she were about to come down with some seasonal illness. She took comfort in the distance between them. A strange man, she thought, and no substitute for Anna's husband.

The crier announced Madia's presence. King Kelren Andarys, Lord Baron of all Ariman and the great northern fiefs, leaned forward and looked down at her for a moment, finding her with a scowl as intense as any she had seen before, but mixed with some newer—stress, perhaps.

Ferris whispered something in the king's ear. Kelren nodded but did not break his gaze.

"My daughter," the king said, loud enough that the words echoed back to Madia from behind, "this is to be the last time we will speak of your duties to the crown, and your duties to me. Today I make a proclamation: from the princess of Ariman there will be no further disobedience, no more reports of scandal or disgrace. Not from this day forward. As of this very moment!"

Kelren rose nearly out of his seat, the lines on his forehead growing dark with the redness that flushed his face. With age her father had grown anything but impulsive, was in fact known for an ability to control his temper in the most upsetting circumstances—usually, Madia reflected.

Earnest as she could be, she took one step forward. "I do apologize, Father. Of course I will make every effort to control my—"

"You have already made your efforts a hundred times, my daughter, as have *I*. And Lady Anna has made every effort as well, yet nothing works. Nothing lasts against your whims. No one seems able to reach your soul, if you still have one! Your teachers once spoke of a bright young girl, capable of mastering the sciences and the arts, medicine and philosophy, all as easily as she learned to charm her father. Yet this child-turned-woman now refuses to apply or control herself. Instead, she continually disobeys! She persists in disrupting not only her educators but her father's ability to rule!"

"My lord, I promise you," Madia replied quickly, somewhat stunned by her father's intensity, "as the Greater Gods are my witness, I have lately come to hold true remorse in my heart for my conduct." She gazed up at her father, making her eyes as big as possible, unblinking, so that the air would irritate them enough to bring a swell of moisture. "With the continued absence of my cousin, may the Gods keep and protect him, I have begun to see my station more clearly, and to recognize my many errors. In the future, I swear—"

Her father held his hand up, a command for silence. Madia had no choice but to comply.

"Whether the young duke returns or not, your actions undermine all I try to do," he said. "You have earned yourself a reputation that no one of royal blood would envy, yet for all your well-timed penitent moods, you do not seem to care. You say you are sorry day after day like a drunkard each morning, swearing off his ale."

He paused for breath and the edges on his face seemed to soften somewhat, though again, it was a look Madia was hardly familiar with. "I have finally come to believe that you hold no genuine regret in your heart at all. And therefore, no feelings for me."

"Not true!" Madia forgot herself. She stepped forward and up again until she stood nearly level to the throne. "You must not believe such things. Who fills your head with these lies?"

"My head can think for itself, just as my eyes can see. I am not blind, and not the idiot you take me for. Not completely. You, my daughter, have no right to speak of truth in this house."

"But I have every right! I *am* your daughter!"

"No daughter would continue to act as you have. For years I have believed you would finally grow up and come to good sense. But I have run out of time and patience and heart, and even hope. How long can a man love his own blood without any love in return?"

"Again you claim I do not love you. But I do!"

"Then prove it, Madia! Swear before your king and the court that you will bring no further disgrace upon yourself or this throne, upon your land. Swear it, and know that if you break your word, this time you will be sent away from this house and this city, cast out, until time and hardship have made you fit to return, or until a new life, or death, should find you. Rally the woman within you, if she is there at all!"

"I swear! I do swear!" Madia fell on both knees. She felt the blood ringing in her ears, heat flushing her face. She was blinking now, her sight blurred by genuine tears brought on by the sheer level of her emotions. She refrained from using her arm to wipe her cheek.

"Very well, but there will be no more discussion of this, my daughter. You have given your word to me and to all of Ariman, and I have given mine!"

King Kelren settled back into his throne. Grand Chamberlain Ferris leaned and whispered something in his ear again. The king seemed to nod. Madia bowed her head until her forehead touched the floor, then she slowly rose. There was nothing to say, nothing to do but turn and go. All eyes were upon her as she looked about. She wiped her face, then fixed her gaze on the stone beneath her feet as she paced slowly away, Lady Anna close behind her. Two young guards in gleaming, polished armor let them out of the hall. Madia knew one of the men well—but said nothing as she passed.

She could not eat with the rest of the house tonight, not after what her father had said to her, so Madia had food brought to her room. The bitterness of their meeting clung heavily, annoyingly to her. He was making too much of nothing, she reasoned, as kings sometimes did. He was losing his perspective, or didn't care to keep it. *He's getting old,* she thought. Her mother had died during childbirth, and Madia had always suspected that her father held her partly responsible in some way, though he would never admit to it. If he had found someone else these many years, a new queen to temper his moods and comfort him now and then, he might well act otherwise. *If my mother were alive, certainly. . . .*

As she ate her goose and bread and sipped a cup of wine, the thought of leaving Kamrit of her own accord crossed her mind. If her father did not love her, then how many others did? Or perhaps it simply didn't matter. He seemed determined to make the rest of her life the means of payment for all her past "sins." No longer the sweet, affable father of years gone by. *A tyrant now,* she thought. *The kingdom beware!*

She finished her meal and changed again into fresh undergarments and a deep claret-colored full dress with a low-cut bodice and tight sleeves. Then she plaited her hair and put it up under a short headdress and veil. When the chambermaid returned to take her plate, Lady Anna entered with her. The girl left quickly. Anna remained.

"You have somewhere to go?" she asked.

"A walk. I like to walk after I've eaten."

"Sometimes that is what you like to do."

Madia furnished the other with an abusive stare. Anna seemed to take it in stride. She reached out and touched the fine trim at the end of Madia's sleeve, then eyed the rest of the dress. "A bit snug at the waist, isn't it?" she asked. "And this," she added, waving at Madia's amply revealed neck and shoulders and cleavage.

"Not especially."

"Do not go to that young man tonight, Madia, please."

"But I make no such plans."

"You do, though I don't know why. Suppose you are caught? You heard your father! You saw the look on his face when he warned you. You swore an oath, Madia. He will hold you to your word, and he will keep his."

"I will not be caught! And my father would never truly banish me, not for any reason. Surely you can't believe otherwise. He is angry, yes, and apparently more upset than I imagined. But I am sure that's why he put on such a show, in order to frighten me into obedience. Wonderful theatrics, Anna, but little more. And frighten me he did! He may be losing his senses, but I am not. I *will* change. I will attempt to repair my ways." She closed her eyes and shook her head.

"I will conduct myself in a manner more fitting of my station, and all the rest. But if, just tonight, I happened to have an appointment with a perfectly lovely man, perhaps one last little adventure, then I would be most inclined to keep it. *If!* Tell me this, my lady, how will I ever marry if I do not see men?"

"Seeing them would be fine," Anna said, "if those visits were chaperoned, and if they stopped at that."

Madia grinned at her. "I remember wrestling with many of these same boys in the castle not so many years ago."

"I know," Anna said, "rough and tumble as any of them. But what has that to do with—"

"My father did not approve of that, either."

"This is different," Anna said.

Madia grinned all the more. "Oh, *I know* it is."

Anna frowned deeply. She looked about, as if searching for what to say next.

"Besides, any man, even someone like, for instance, Sir Calif, would have to live up to my expectations before he and I would engage in any . . . wrestling."

"Then I pray he is a dolt!" Anna snapped without a hint of humor. There would be no peace between them tonight.

"In the morning, we will talk more," Madia said. "And I will improve, you will see. I promise. But leave me now. I must go."

"You must not," Anna muttered.

"I already have," Madia replied, and whisked herself away, leaving Lady Anna alone in the chamber.

No one was about in the inner courtyard as darkness approached, except of course, Sir Calif. Wearing hose and a white shirt of fine linen, with blackwork at the neck and cuffs, and a short pourpoint coat over that, he looked as fine as any man Madia had known. He smiled warmly when he saw her approach, and Madia found the expression quite satisfactory.

"I was not sure I would find you out this evening," he said. "Word of your father's admonishments at court have spread to all the corners of the realm by now."

He was still smiling. Not an easily shaken man, Madia thought, appraising him further. He took her hand in his, bold again, then held it very gently. Young Calif had a great deal to live up to, Madia thought, recalling some of the men she had dallied with, the finest knights in all of Ariman. Though truly, he just might measure up.

She let him lead her on through the courtyard, and listened as he told her of his father's lands, of his own visions for the future. He had plans to clear more acres, and to enlarge his father's rather small manor, to make room for the family he would have. Some day. Then, as they arrived outside the king's stables, Calif began to talk about her, the way she looked in the moonlight, the way he imagined she must feel when properly held. Not awfully original any of it, Madia noted, but not bad, either. And she found herself wondering about him in that way as well.

She paused and stood close, facing him, just in front of one of the stable doors. "Then you must hold me," she said, "so that we will know."

After they had kissed, a long and passionate kiss, Madia let him lead her to the stable's ample supply of fresh August hay, where she let him hold her as he willed. In a few moments they were nearly naked, and locked in an evolving embrace of warmth and passion broken only by dry straw that nipped at Madia's fencing bruise. She ignored this almost completely. A moment later, she heard the metal rustle of armor, and the both of them sat up at attention.

They found themselves under the close scrutiny of four of the king's soldiers, and behind them, Lord Grand Chamberlain Ferris—and behind him, already turning away, the king.

The seneschal Tristan stood just outside the city's southern gates looking the girl over carefully. She appeared as much like a merchant's daughter as anything, thick woolen hose and a blouse of heavy linen, a dreary look, though her coat fit her snugly enough to make plain her femininity; it was made of fur and leather and covered her well to just above the knees, and was a bit too fine to be any but her own. A plain hood covered her head, her thick brown hair falling past her shoulders from underneath it.

Around her neck she wore a thin gold chain that bore a palm-sized circular gold medallion, its surface engraved with the king's mark and her own name, something Anna and her father had decided to give her, proof that she was who she claimed to be, should she need to present it. At her side hung a sheath filled with her favorite short sword, which the king had not objected to. Tristan handed her a leather drawstring pouch filled with food and necessities, and a few gold pieces. She hung it grimly around herself by the drawn cord.

"Keep the medallion under your blouse," Lady Anna suggested, taking hold of it and tucking it in. Madia stood limply, hands at her sides, allowing the intrusion.

"Your identity will bring you honor by some, but others might make a toy of you, or seek to ransom you back to your father," Tristan added. Then he tipped his head to her. "You have said nothing since we left your chambers, my lady." Madia only shrugged.

"Is there anything you would know, or anyone I should send word to?" Anna asked, her voice too thin, Tristan thought—not quite crying, but the woman was unable to still her chin.

Madia glared at Anna suddenly, a look that came from nowhere. "Word of what?" she asked wildly. "Would you tell others of your acts of betrayal?"

Anna shook her head. "I did not betray you, Madia."

"I am no fool! The fact is obvious, after all, despite what you say. My father *was* told of my rendezvous with Calif. We were followed, as well you know, whether you admit it or not. My own father has betrayed me—why shouldn't you?"

Anna stared at her, numb, or just weary of the argument, Tristan thought—just as he was. Madia had been at it for a day and a half, cursing everyone in memory, and the mothers that bore them. But especially cursing Anna. And with good reason, perhaps, Tristan speculated; Anna had quite possibly done exactly as Madia claimed.

"She means should we send word of your coming," the seneschal said, "to friends you might have elsewhere in the land."

"I—" She seemed to lose the words somewhere in her mouth for a moment. "I do not have . . . friends."

"Surely you have some destination in mind?" Tristan said.

"I have been to Kopeth before, several times. A busy city full of traders and adventurers. I may find I prefer such a place. Some will know me there. And I will make many friends. Perhaps the folk there will take pity on me, something no one in all Kamrit can seem to do. Indeed, a few might hold the thought that I may one day return to Kamrit and recall their kindness." She glared again at Anna. "Or their wickedness."

"How will you survive once your pouch is empty?" Tristan asked, hoping she might have an answer but doubting it.

"I have been taught many skills. I'm sure I will be of value."

Perhaps, the seneschal thought. Perhaps not.

"Kopeth may be sensible, but it is known for its dangers as well as its prosperity," Anna remarked.

"I can be sensible at times," Madia told her. "When I am allowed."

"He will relent, I think," Anna confided. "I believe that deep inside he still loves you. He will take you back, Madia, but many things must change first, and I think some time must pass."

"You must change," Tristan said.

"You must see that it is *you* who betrayed *him*," Anna said, starting in again. "And not—"

"My father is a heartless, evil man!" Madia screeched at her. "And you, Anna, are a traitorous, evil woman! The one friend I dared trust!"

"Enough, now," Tristan said, stepping between them. "It is time." He turned and took Lady Anna by the arm, then began to lead her back inside. Anna walked away, half turned around, looking back at Madia, all in tears now. Madia turned finally and started slowly up the road, headed north. Anna kept watching until Tristan was able to get her out of sight within the castle walls.

"They are both wrong," Anna said, straightening her dress, rubbing her eyes. "This is the worst that could happen to either of them. They need one another and yet—"

"Lord Andarys is king, my lady. He had no choice."

"I know." Anna turned away, quiet sobs beginning again. Tristan took a step toward her, then leaned very close. "We must trust in both of them."

"I did not betray her," Anna said, the tears flowing harder.

"I know," Tristan said, even though he didn't.

Anna nodded, then moved slowly away. Tristan waited patiently. When she was gone, he looked right and signaled forth a figure who waited there. Though a young man, and certainly a foolish one, Calif was a seasoned knight, Tristan thought. He wore light mail and battle leathers and the king's crested surcoat over that, and carried a leather traveler's drawstring pouch over his shoulder, as Madia had. His scabbard bore the same crest as his surcoat.

"The king puts great faith in you, Sir Calif. This is your only chance to redeem yourself in his eyes and, no doubt, those of your own father."

"He would have had me killed if I refused," Calif said grimly. "They both would have."

"Surely you don't want to see any harm come to the princess, all the same."

"Quite true, but she can get herself into a great deal of trouble, and I am not an army. Am I not even to be furnished with a mount?"

"The king wishes no one to know of his true concern for her welfare. A mounted knight would, you must agree, be rather conspicuous." Not quite true, of course, but Calif seemed to accept it. "Should I speak to the king of your misgivings?"

"No! Tell him I will guard Madia with my life, at the very least . . . and it will be our secret," Calif added a cordial bow.

"The king feels that a week or two at the mercy of the countryside will turn his daughter far enough around. She is your responsibility until then. Stay back so that she does not see you—which means making sure you don't catch up to her. But you are never to lose sight of her. When you reach a garrison, send a rider with word. At some garrisons, a rider will be waiting for you."

"I will, my lord."

"Then go."

Calif made haste, trotting out and making his way across the drawbridge, then he slowed and continued up the road. Tristan followed him to the walls. Madia was no longer in sight. He watched until Calif disappeared as well, then shrugged to himself. *You have served too long*, he reflected, finding himself unable to raise concern beyond a certain level, and deciding he didn't need to. He didn't have much faith in anyone at all these days.

Tornen approached from behind, leading his mount and followed some paces back by his squad of twenty men, hand picked. The seneschal turned and faced him. He was one of the most trusted captains in the king's guard. Today he would be entrusted with a part of the kingdom's future.

"Wait until young Calif is well on his way, give him perhaps half the morning, then follow along. The king wants you seen by neither the young lord or Madia, unless it becomes necessary."

"A distance may be sufficient for the road," Tornen said, "but what if she enters a village? How can we ensure her safety in a town from outside it?"

"You may have no choice but to show yourselves. It depends on the town, does it not? You know them all. Use your judgment."

"Of course," Tornen said, bowing his head slightly.

"No harm must come to her," Tristan reminded, staring into the captain's eyes.

"None will," Tornen replied, then he turned and walked away toward his waiting men.

They will all come back, or they will not, Tristan thought, *and the king will have to live with either end, just as Lady Anna will.* He walked back toward the castle, back to his duties.

Chapter III

In the fields, Madia saw families busy with the early harvest; men scything hay, women and children laying it out to dry or bundling that which the sun had already finished with. She saw people along the riverbank, bathing, washing their clothing, watering their livestock or fetching a bucketful. The waters flowed slowly south to Kamrit—welcome there, she thought, as she no longer was. Even the simplest peasant was welcome on his lord's manor, unless he'd committed the most terrible crimes. . . .

The truth of the matter was still almost impossible for her to accept, and yet here she was.

She kept walking, the sun high above her now. She watched women coming from a small manor house on a hill to the west, carrying pots of ale for the midday break. She had never observed such goings-on in detail before—never more than a passing glance from behind the king's swift horses. To Madia, the life of a serf seemed such a quaint and simple one, days filled with decent, productive work and plenty of the lord's ale, evenings

37

filled with family and village conversations, and a good deal more ale. Of course, she had often heard tell of some lords who were entirely without compassion, those that gave almost nothing to the villagers who bore them on their backs, but surely this was the exception. For most, as far as she had been able to determine, manor life was rather fair.

After all, the majority of barons treated their vassals and serfs reasonably well, awarding them land to grow what they needed to eat and even paying them enough to replace lost livestock. Some dreamed of freedom and saved enough to become freemen one day; perhaps many, she had never made a count. And these were all the dreams such people were capable of, certainly. All that they might require.

As she walked past pastures and small fields of crops she could not bring herself to imagine her own life coming to that. It was, after all, the same work, day after day, the same talk among the village huts each evening. A small existence with little sport or adventure. *Though your taste for adventure is what got you into trouble in the first place*, she reminded herself. That hunger was fading, but the idea still did excite her in a very real way. For the past two days, she had wondered how she would fare on the road, alone in the world, lost in the land. She did not see the situation as hopeless, having been well educated in spite of herself, and she still had her beauty—something a few men she'd known had valued more than gold. In the proper light, this could be seen as an opportunity for her to discover the world. Surely some wonderful things would happen, and just as surely, if trouble arrived, there would be a gentleman or two more than willing to come to her aid if she asked.

And her father, for all his ridiculous spit and rage, would not forsake her for long. *Anna was right about that*, Madia thought, *I am almost certain of it*. Without doubt this whole unfortunate affair was largely theatrics, all the result of an aging king's boyish posturing, of having too little to occupy his time—a king who would calm himself and come to his senses in due time. He had given her gold enough to live on for several weeks, if she spent it well, but no more. So he apparently planned to come for her long before winter spread across the land. She need only get by until then, prove herself somehow—whatever that involved—and then apologize again to His Pompousness like a good little girl when the time came, as it surely would.

The road curved away from the river then, branching off to the east. She kept to the main way, losing sight of the river as the country grew rocky and turned mostly to woodlands. As she walked in shade the air felt cool against her face, a breeze that came through the trees, free of the scent of livestock and cut hay, thick with the smell of moss. Many feared the forest, she knew, superstitious peasants who counted backward and hung garlic about and avoided stepping on each other's shadows—a whole parade of nonsense she had never understood. She had been through many a wood on royal hunts, and it seemed that no real or imagined menace dared so much as come near the king's knights and nobles, or his daughter.

Though, as she looked back and ahead at the road winding through the tall oaks, empty as far as she could see, as she listened to a silence touched only by the sounds of distant birds high in the forest's thick leafy canopy, she began to wonder what might be there, hidden, watching her even now? Who could say what mortal or mythical creatures existed in such deep, dark, silent places—afraid, perhaps, to confront a hunting party, but full of much sterner stuff where a single young girl was concerned?

She quickened her pace and tried to keep her eyes set

on the road ahead. She had never been much afraid of anything, and she didn't wish to start now.

The road turned again and rose up onto a knoll cast deep in shade, a place even farther removed from countryside and daylight than the rest of the woods. A small rocky hillside rose beneath the trees to her right, while on the left the edge of the road dropped away several feet into thick brush, then gave way again to the tall dark trees beyond. She began to wonder if she hadn't gone the wrong way back at the fork.

Move on, she thought. *Just get to someplace else.* A sudden rustling from behind startled her. She turned to find two figures approaching. The boy, a young man really, tall and stout, was staring at her with flat eyes set in a brutish, bone-heavy face; the girl looked about Madia's size and age, and her face made her the young man's sister. They were dressed in very plain shirts and tunics, dirty and worn, made of poor but sturdy linen. Each one wore a dingy white vest, possibly wool, Madia thought, though it was impossible to tell. They carried drawn ax and blade, crude rusted weapons, no doubt scavenged from some long forgotten battlefield, but sturdy enough that Madia knew her short sword would be a poor match.

Madia tried to draw her blade just the same, but the young man moved too quickly, laying his ax against her arm to stop her from bringing it up. The girl came slowly around to the right, extending her sword, and Madia feared she would simply run her through. *I may die*, she thought, tasting the idea like some new imported dish, finding little appeal. She felt her insides turning hard and cold, felt the blood pounding in her ears as sweat formed on her hands and face. An awful feeling, really, and getting worse. She noticed she was shaking. . . .

"A lady of some sort," the girl said, grinning a drunkard's grin. Madia could smell the ale on them now, overwhelming, and believed they would kill her for certain.

"We'll just see what you have in that purse," the girl said then. She slipped the edge of her sword blade under the leather cord on Madia's pouch and sliced back. The cord split and the bag fell to the ground. Next the girl leaned carefully and grabbed Madia's sword, then pulled it out and threw it down behind her. She sheathed her own sword and scooped up the bag.

"Gold," she said momentarily, plunging her hand into the bag, pulling out some of the coins. She grinned broadly and tossed a gold piece to her friend. He caught it with one hand, but kept his ax at the ready with the other.

"Best we've done in weeks," he said, looking the coin over. "How much have we got?"

"The king will have you killed for this!" Madia said, glaring at them, though she kept very still.

The girl barely glanced up as she rummaged in the bag. "Three handfuls at least," she announced—which Madia took to mean she couldn't count very high. Worthless folk, she decided, though they were experienced enough at robbery. And killing, no doubt.

Madia tried to think of something—any way to call attention to something else and grab the girl's sword, or lie that she had more gold in a pouch under her arm, and then, when the girl got close—but it all sounded so crazy! She knew none of that would work. These people knew what they were about, and she did not.

"Take the whole bag," the brother said, observing the food and change of clothes the girl was lifting out and examining, then putting back.

"And her jacket," the girl said, touching the leather of Madia's sleeve. "Take it off!" she snapped, the smile suddenly gone. And Madia saw a mood in the other's face that made her even more uneasy, a cold ire come to the surface that seemed more animal than human—something Madia knew she could not hope to fight. She tugged her coat off before the girl could force her and handed it over; she felt the cool air touch her as she did. The girl put the coat on, then ran her fingers over the front of it, grinning at the material.

"And see what's that little bit around her neck, too," the boy said, squinting.

The girl looked up and eyed Madia more closely. She stepped near again, then reached out and tugged at the thin gold chain that disappeared into the front of Madia's blouse. When the girl saw the medallion, her eyes went wide. She wrapped a fist around it and worked it up over Madia's head, yanking when it caught on one ear. Madia winced and tipped her head and the chain pulled free.

The girl looked her prize over thoughtfully a moment, then tossed the medallion to her friend. This too he caught in one hand, then held it up to the light. "The king's mark, I'd say."

The girl nodded.

"Gold dip, anyway," the young man added. "Bet she stole this off some other poor bastard!" He broke out laughing as he tossed it back to the girl. She slipped it over her head, centered it on her breast, then they laughed together, the two of them making enough noise that Madia didn't hear the sudden scuffle from the road behind them until her eyes called her to it.

A knight—wearing leather and mail armor, a mail coif over his head, and a surcoat which bore the mark and colors of King Andarys. His face was mostly obscured by the coif as he came near, rushing forward on foot, head down and sword drawn.

Which seemed odd, Madia thought. If her father had sent an escort after her, or someone to bring her back, surely he would have sent them on horseback—and certainly more than *one*. But if some dishonorable lord or paid knight from Kamrit had ransom or worse on their minds, they might come alone, hoping to catch up to her on the road. . . .

The others turned an instant later. The girl faced the attacker while the boy told Madia not to move. Madia watched the knight pause as he drew near, apparently looking things over, then he came forward again and prepared to strike the girl down. *She is dressed like me*, Madia realized. *He wants to kill me!* But the boy stepped up instead and stood before the girl—who seemed to understand. She turned and checked on Madia again. The knight took up with the peasant boy without protest. As the contest began, the other girl's eyes danced with the two men, following every move.

Madia stepped aside and scurried to pick her sword up off the ground. The girl saw the movement quickly enough and thrust her blade out straight ahead. Madia grasped her weapon and blocked the thrust, but felt her own narrow blade nearly give as it took the blow. *No match*, she thought again.

A few yards away, the knight and the boy traded a flurry of fierce blows, and the boy began falling back almost at once, his actions already purely defensive as he gave up ground. He called to the girl above the clang of steel, and she stepped back from Madia and turned toward him.

"Help me!" the boy yelled, then ducked as the knight's broadsword parted air where his head had been. "Kill the girl and get over here!"

Madia's eyes flashed from side to side—the girl, the two men, the near, inviting brush beside the road and the shadowy woods beyond. The girl glanced at Madia, then back again, taking another look at the two men as she readied herself for action. Madia turned and leaped, trying for a new advantage, but the other girl saw the move and swung hard. Madia pulled her sword back in time to shield herself, but at such an angle, and under such force, she could not hold onto it. The weapon left her hand and fell. She turned and leaped as high as she could, then leaped again.

She landed on her side at the edge of the road and rolled down the bank. Brush and rocks rose up, scratching her face and hands, bruising her back. At the bottom, she jumped up and felt pain lance through her right knee. She ran ahead, made it work anyway. The tall oaks waited there. She glanced over her shoulder as the leafy canopy cast cool shadows all around her. She could barely see the road now. No one followed.

She ran on all the same, stopping finally when she knew she could run no more. The quiet of the forest surrounded her, dark and thick and vast, like sleep. She stood till she caught her breath, until her heart had slowed down a bit. Finally she began to feel the chill of the damp air. Tiny jolts stabbed at her muscles like invisible pins, making them jerk.

You can't stay here, she told herself. Night would come in a few hours, and even the worst idiot knew not to be in the woods at night, at the mercy of animals or bandits or leshy—or worse. She began to recall in greater detail folk stories to do with the forest's penchant for swallowing unwary travelers, without leaving so much as a trace.

She felt an added chill sweep her spine, found herself glancing over her shoulder between tree trunks and seedlings. No doubt the scuffle was over already, the victors proclaimed. She could make her way back toward the road again, keep out of sight in the brush, get just close enough to glimpse the outcome. If the knight had killed the two robbers he might have left her bag, having little need of a few coins and women's clothing. Or the knight may have fallen and been carrying money that a wounded knave would overlook. She could at least attempt to learn who he was.

The combination of fear and curiosity began to overwhelm her. She felt nervous energy forming deep within her bruised and twitching body. *Go wide around to the south,* she told herself. *Approach from the higher ground, where the trees are closer to the road. Get up,* she insisted. *Quietly!*

She felt the bruised knee protest as she put weight on it. When she rubbed at a scratch on her cheek, she came away with blood on her sleeve. Her back ached in at least two places. She thought of her petty concern over the sword bruise on her backside; she wouldn't be anything so pretty to look at now, she guessed, though it didn't seem as important anymore. She started back through the trees toward the road.

"Someone ahead, Captain," the lead rider shouted back. Grear followed his line of sight. Three figures moved about in the road just at the bend. He pulled his horse up and ordered his men left toward the edge of the road, then waited until all five of them had come in line. Without the clamp of hooves and the rustle of battle dress, he could hear the metal ping of clashing sword blades, and he realized what the movement was about.

"Our friend Kaafk said she'd be alone," Grear said, mostly thinking out loud.

The man nearest to him shrugged. "Maybe it isn't her?"

"He did say she might be followed, which would explain at least a part of this mystery."

"If it be her, do we kill them all?"

Grear frowned. He had never taken a job quite like this before: payment in bits and pieces, no clear idea who he was ultimately working for, killing children. The entire arrangement had been conducted by a messenger sent to Ikaydin with a good deal of gold and just enough information—sent specifically to seek Grear out and bring him to southern Ariman. Since his work in the Dokany Wars, he had enjoyed a reputation as a trustworthy assassin, but he hadn't realized his name had come to command such a price!

The order to kill the king's daughter had come from a man who met them near the seaward swamps just south of Bail, a velvet and silk merchant calling himself Kaafk, and someone Grear did not especially care for. The merchant seemed a coldblooded man, even to Grear—a man whose round face and carnival manner very nearly concealed the look of poison Grear recognized in his eyes.

But the order had been accompanied by more gold, and the promise of still more afterward. Then came talk of additional, quite profitable work to come after that.

Grear had his questions, about why he was to report to no one else but Kaafk, about the Bouren surcoats the merchant had given him and his men to wear, and about this strange, somewhat distasteful task of killing the young Princess Madia—all questions he would ask the merchant when he and his men arrived back at Bail.

In the meantime, he had already collected more gold than he had ever imagined, a fortune that would buy himself and his comrades some glorious days in Kopeth while waiting for Kaafk and his purse to return as promised (and many good years afterward). To Grear's mind, that was answer enough for a while.

"Draw swords," he ordered. He heeled the horse forward, riding at a slow gallop until they were almost upon the others. The three were a peasant man and a soldier, King Andarys', at a guess, and with them a young girl wearing a coat of leather and fur and clutching a brown drawstring pouch. The girl and the knight had no doubt been set upon by a robber, or robbers—perhaps the knight and the other man were both opportunists, fighting over who would get to collect a bounty set on the girl's head?

It was difficult to tell who was fighting who, Grear thought, dismounting with a wave at his men to follow. No matter, he thought. The girl matched the description of the princess closely enough.

"Take him!" he shouted, pointing three of his men to the knight, certain that even in Bouren armor those odds would be enough. His other two men lunged at the highwayman, one fending off the young man's fatigued first swing of the ax, the other dodging to the opposite side and swinging his own ax with both hands. The ax ran through the boy's side and ripped out the front, and the boy's body fell almost at once. Grear saw the look in the girl's eyes as she turned toward him, the horror as he approached.

He stepped nearer and she raised her sword to defend herself, anticipating the need to block his attack. She turned her head wildly, searching for the two men circling behind her now, checking on Grear in front of her again. Grear took a stance and nodded, and suddenly advanced. She blocked his blade well enough, then jerked suddenly as the men behind her both thrust their blades into her and withdrew. She crumpled with a gasp beside the boy.

Grear looked over his shoulder. The knight lay dead, bleeding from both his arms and his abdomen. The men had tackled him, held him down and hacked through his mail with their battle-axes. One of Grear's troops had a bleeding gash in the vambrace protecting his arm—it looked as though the knight had cut it deep.

"All right, we're not through with this yet," Grear shouted. "Kaafk wants her to vanish." His men groaned in unison, but said nothing in particular. Grear bent over the girl, noticing the gold medallion she wore around her neck. "It's her all right," he said, nodding, working the chain over her head. He stood looking at the engraving. "We'll bring this, and the bag, to the meeting at Bail. But not until we've dug a quick and proper hole."

Grear put the medallion away, then grabbed one of the girl's arms. *Easy money*, he thought, *and more to come*. One of his men grabbed the other arm and together they dragged the body off.

Madia hid in a hollow in the center of a patch of sumac, peering through leaves. On the road she could see a half-dozen mounted men wearing armor and long tunics bearing what appeared to be the crest of Lord Ivran of Bouren. The girl and her brother lay dead on the ground, as did the knight that had come charging up on foot. Madia stayed very still, breathing quietly, watching as the soldiers dragged all three bodies behind thick brush. They dug a single large, shallow hole, pushed the bodies in and covered them up. They worked quickly, checking the road as they did, then they took to their horses again.

When they left she stayed, thinking, waiting for the courage or the inspiration to move again. Madia crouched on the one good knee with both arms wrapped around herself, shivering. Lord Ivran of Bouren had sent his men to kill her!

But why? What would Ivran or his son have to gain by killing me? Unless the rumors were true, and they really did want a war? Unless Lord Ferris was right. . . .

But that did nothing to explain the crazed knight from Kamrit—charging up all alone, obviously prepared to slay anyone in order to get at her. *Whoever was he? Whatever was he trying to do?*

How many people wanted her dead or captured? How many more? She felt a crushing urge to run home—to her father, to Anna—but they had both already betrayed her, and someone there certainly may have sent the dead knight!

She felt tears in the corners of her eyes and tried not to let them come; she didn't seem to have any choice.

After a moment she got the sobbing under control, sniffing it back, and felt a little bit better, though she soon noticed the air growing even colder, or so it seemed.

Time to get moving, she told herself. Already it was beginning to get dark. She scrambled from cover and searched the road for her shoulder bag and sword but found nothing. Then her eyes noticed the light color of something caught on a bush near the path the others had taken to the burial site. She hurried over, knelt and pulled it out: the peasant girl's worn vest. She put it on, ignoring the thick aroma that lingered in its weave. She was a little warmer, she decided.

As she started up the road she heard horses, many of them, approaching from behind. She left the road again and ran until she found another sheltered hollow in the trees and sumac, where she lay down and waited. Eventually the riders passed, perhaps two dozen in all, mounted soldiers from Kamrit. She thought she recognized the lead rider as Captain Tornen, though in the poor light of the setting sun it was difficult to tell.

She nearly cried out to them. Then she thought better of it and kept her mouth shut. When they had gone, she curled up, shivering. She fell asleep watching the moon rise in the sky.

Chapter IV

"Lord Ferris, the merchant has arrived!" the soldier announced. A second figure stood in the doorway behind him, a large man in a gold embroidered cape, a velvet coat and mullen cap.

The demon Tyrr made the body construct's head nod, made Ferris' voice say, "Let him enter, then leave us." The guard bowed, opened the door, then disappeared. The merchant Kaafk closed the heavy chamber door behind him.

"You will be pleased, my lord," Kaafk said demurely.

Tyrr went to one of the thick wooden chairs positioned about the single large table that dominated the room. A gold accented jug, filled with wine from the ports of Neleva, graced the table's center, accompanied by a pair of finely carved flagons. Wine was an economical device Tyrr had found handy when dealing with men. A bowl of sweet cakes rested there as well, quite useful in dealing with Kaafk in particular. "Sit," Tyrr said, "and specify."

"Grear and his men were successful." Kaafk smiled

51

broadly, as if telling a joke. "I met them as we arranged, near Bail, and completed payment. They were able to provide me with these."

Kaafk pulled a large leather drawstring travel pouch out from under his cape and opened it, then produced a bloodied fur and leather coat and a large gold medallion, all the Princess Madia's. "They buried the bodies, as I instructed."

"You know this?"

Kaafk paused, stuffing the coat back in the bag. He looked up, smiling again, his very fat face growing even wider. "I have found Grear to be a man who does what he says, or I would not deal with him. And on my trip home, I went by the site where they found her. The ground is stained, but that is all.

"When I met with them they still wore their Bouren surcoats and armor. I told them to put the clothes away, but to keep them about, for times to come. One never knows."

Kaafk paused again, tossed the bag on the table, then he sat down and tossed the medallion as well; it bounced twice before it came to rest near the table's center. "They took payment and departed without incident, and they've agreed to remain in the region, and at our service as we require. I told them we might also pay well for any useful information they come by." He filled a cup with wine and sipped it several times. As the drink settled, Kaafk's face went slack, then rebounded, another full grin, ears riding up above tight cheeks. "Grear and his men are a pleasure to deal with. As their reputation suggests."

A focused man, Tyrr thought, if rather pompous—a combination that made him both useful and annoying at the same time. This was a man unfettered by common regard, bound only to himself and his greed and, of course, to Tyrr. He watched the mood of the wine begin to spread over Kaafk's chunky features.

"I visited Kopeth as planned," Kaafk said, setting the empty flagon down. "I spent two days meeting with my messengers, who have been in Lencia. There is unrest, they say, even fear, though it is hard to tell what shape these things will take. They could not get anyone near King Ivran to talk, even for a sizable offer, though most may simply not have known very much." He leaned back, taking in a deep breath, expanding his great torso. His eyes sparkled.

Tyrr disliked the human affinity for making conversation a game, a petty, often wasteful practice, but it was just these sorts of weaknesses that, when kept in mind, made mankind so pliable. He took the bait: "Yes?"

"However!" Kaafk went on, tipping his head boyishly to one side. "I did personally manage to spend those nights with a most enjoyably unprincipled young girl who claimed she was somehow related to a Bouren lord, and who had recently been to Lord Ivran's castle. She told me Ivran's eldest son Jaran is calling in homages and training troops, though outwardly, neither Ivran nor any of the other northern kings seem to have any genuine plans to make war—perhaps only to guard against it. Which agrees with what my messengers said. The mood seems to be one of confusion."

"Confusion allows for manipulation," Tyrr said. *And on any level I desire.* Once King Andarys was dead, the vassals north of Ariman might let go of their loyalties to the old kings and give consideration to the new. In time they might serve Lord Ferris of their own accord. Though it was also possible, Tyrr believed, that they would raise objections, and might conceivably unite and turn against him. Tyrr did not intend to allow that progression. By one means or another, sovereignty would at least be maintained—at least. The four northern fiefs were too valuable to leave to their own lords for long in any case.

Forethought, Tyrr reminded himself. *Careful planning and execution. Flexibility, and above all, control!* These were the keys that would unlock the future and free him from the failures of the past—his own, and those of all the others. He must resist indulging in the hedonistic, reckless overconfidence that seemed to come so naturally to his kind. *Forethought, flexibility, control!*

Kaafk was nodding. "Manipulation is a fine thing, my friend," he said, chuckling now, an action Tyrr had not yet mastered, but one he was working on. "It allows us to do what we like." He leaned forward again, refilling his flagon. "I will admit, I feared the great kings of the north at first. The fool Andarys has let the fiefs have their way in recent years. I thought they would react to minimal pressure, and they have not. Your confidence amazed me at first, yet it is borne out! And my profits have already begun to soar. You are not the fool I took you for!" He laughed heartily now.

Tyrr felt a surging urge to recite an ancient chant adding poisons to the wine, so that he could watch this bloated impudent braggart twist in final agony. *Control,* he reminded himself again, *forethought!* How easily these things could be forgotten. He fought the impulse.

Tyrr had arranged for Kaafk to avoid paying most of the tolls imposed by the many vassals of Ariman and by the king's highway guards. Half of that windfall, of course, went directly to Tyrr—or rather, Tyrr thought, to the private treasury of Grand Chamberlain Ferris. The rest went to Kaafk, who was usurping trade territories and merchandise at an amazing rate. Which would likely be maintained, once King Andarys was removed and the existing tolls on regular trade and travel were raised, and once new ones were imposed, the situation would improve all the more.

"We have no room for fools," Tyrr remarked. "I foresee the prospect of many troubles, but by the time most of them arrive, great wealth and control will be mine. I plan to build armies to rival those of Hual Andarys. In the meantime, any trader who is not with us or cannot bear the expense will leave an opening which I expect you can easily fill."

Kaafk was still grinning, his servile mind easily following Tyrr's. "It will be my pleasure, my lord."

"Pleasure is something you think a great deal about, isn't it?"

"As anyone who can afford it will."

"I see." Tyrr waited while Kaafk again poured more wine. He would finish the wine jug and would be worthless for several hours after that, as was usual with men, especially Kaafk. No matter, their discussion was nearly through.

"So, what of old Kelren Andarys?" Kaafk asked then. "Why have I heard no new news? You speak of his death, and yet there is no death. What would you—"

The body shook. "Enough!" Tyrr sought control yet again. Kaafk looked up, then seemed to shrug Tyrr off. The tone of Kaafk's voice had soured notably, something that could well be considered disrespectful, foolishly self-important, quite stupid. Something Tyrr or any of his brethren would have killed a man for once. But this was a new Tyrr, a wiser being, splendid, evolved! Tyrr stopped shaking and slowly absorbed the comment. "Kelren Andarys will soon be gone," he explained.

"You said he'd be gone by *now,* long dead, yet he lives."

"He is gravely ill," Tyrr said, still holding back.

"Still, he lives," Kaafk repeated.

Tyrr felt the pull grow more unyielding. The topic was a frustrating one, and he required no criticism regarding it. But even a splendid Tyrr couldn't do business with dead men. And Kaafk, after all, was right about Kelren.

"Something keeps the king alive," Tyrr made the voice say. "I have tried many spells. If you have seen the king lately, you know of their effects. He is nearly gone; he simply has not died *yet*. He will."

"What else do you plan to do?" Kaafk asked, chewing sweet cakes now, obviously enjoying them.

Tyrr hated this minor interrogation enough to feel an enormous, fully renewed, urge to annihilate the merchant. Yet again he thought better of it, insisted on it, and noted that the task was getting somewhat easier with practice. *I must stick to my plan,* he repeated in his mind, *to that which sets me apart from the many that have gone before me—from Tybree!* "That," he stated, "is my concern."

Kaafk shrugged, downed another sweet cake, then swilled his wine a third time and set the flagon on the table. He sat there a moment, cheeks slightly rosied, immense calm in his eyes as his mind apparently wheeled in random directions.

The man was both a tool and a weapon, a poisonous thing in his own right, Tyrr thought, yet yielding when the need arose. Not that pliable men or women were in short supply—quite the contrary—but it was Kaafk's peculiar effectiveness that made him such an asset.

Abruptly Kaafk seemed to snap out of his trance. He took a deep breath and hoisted himself out of the chair. "Well," he said, letting his lungs deflate with a low sigh, "I'll just be on my way. Finest wine I've had in ages," he added. "Am *I* bringing that into Kamrit?"

"I have another source, but you may have the business if you wish."

"Certainly. What do I have to do?"

"Nothing. I will arrange for the current merchant to be charged and executed."

"I see," Kaafk said, eyes going wide, then normal again. He looked away, staring at the walls for a moment, at nothing. "What would the present merchant be charged with?" he asked.

"What does it matter?"

Kaafk stared at another piece of the wall, then looked up and shrugged. "Very well." He turned toward the door, then paused, glancing back. "My lord," he said, "do you mind if I take that gold trinket with me?" He came back and picked the medallion up, looking it over. "It'll bring a fair price in certain markets!"

Tyrr, whole and perfect sovereign of the dark eternal realm, made the construct's lips smile, made the voice say, "Come to me again in a week's time, and of course," he added, nodding at the medallion in Kaafk's hand, "what's mine is yours." *And what's yours is mine.*

Tyrr waited until evening, then made his way to the king's chambers and hovered there beside Kelren's bed, watching the ailing ruler sleep. His plan was still a good one, and Tyrr was reluctant to consider the possibility that something was going wrong so early on. The sickness should have taken Andarys by now, or at the very least, lack of food and water, which Tyrr had managed to keep to nearly nothing, should have done the trick—yet somehow the man held on.

Still, there was time, Tyrr reminded himself again. And with time could come new thoughts, new events, new spells, untold surprises and fortunes. With time he would prevail! Tybree had been wrong!

Tyrr had been right!

How many were there like Tybree? Doomsayers, cowards, fools who hid in the endless darkness even now, insisting that this world was not a thing that demons could ever again possess, not since they had been driven from it. The pain of that time was still burned into their consciousness, as were the many failures since then. But they were old, much too old to think clearly of such things. Memory had made of the past and those who inhabited it something larger than the truth. And Tybree was older than most. But Tyrr was young!

The old could not change, could not easily learn from the past and adapt to the present, or toward the future. In this world, the ancient wizards who had beaten his kind were long gone to dust by now, and their descendants gone again, and *their* descendants. The knowledge did not exist anymore, Tyrr was certain of it, just as the ability to return to the world of man barely existed anymore in the realm of the demons—or those who would dare to try.

But none like Tyrr had been born in many ages. Since the time of his early youth, Tyrr had known this, had seen those around him give up altogether, or try only to give in to their natural desires—nearly absolute power making fools of them absolutely—time and again. Tyrr, meanwhile, had perceived the value of restraint, the concept of acquired assets such as allies, like Kaafk, distasteful though the idea continued to be.

Among those few demons who had grown powerful enough to attempt entry into the human world since the banishment, none had been wise enough to see the value of such a plan. And none had learned to hide themselves so well. Deceit was such a wonderful and simple thing with humans, usually a trifle compared with the constant efforts required to retain the human construct Tyrr had built around himself. Yet this, especially, had been worth the effort. Something Tyrr had planned for, having seen the value of such extremes.

Since arriving in this world, nothing had arisen, not one detail, which he had not been prepared for in some way—except King Andarys' most unreasonable refusal to die.

Tyrr tried once again to add to the death spells, speaking yet another phrasing, this one slightly different than the rest. The old king moaned in his sleep and rolled slightly to one side, then the other. His face grew tight from the pain within his body, but in a moment the torment faded from his features, and peace returned to his slumber. So Tyrr tried a quick, angry spell, one that would have caused any ordinary mortal to burst instantly into raging flames. There was no effect, other than a slight warming of the king's skin as Tyrr reached out to touch it.

But just then a thought came to mind! *Of course!* he thought. *What an idea!* His plan was, thankfully, adaptable. Minor changes could be made. He would need more humans, he decided, to aid him. . . .

Deceit could also be all the more wonderful when it began to breed of its own volition!

Tyrr basked in his sudden revelation, his adroitness at turning failure around, or at least limiting its effects. *Who among the rogues of darkness could compare with me? Who among them might dream of such solutions?*

None, Tyrr concluded. He was utterly unequalled, immune to the foolishness and weakness that plagued those who had gone before him, and those who remained behind.

Tybree was wrong. All of them were wrong!

Turning away, forcing any trace of trepidation from his mind, Tyrr made the body leave the room, but only for now.

Chapter V

"Demon's work!" the old man Urid cried out, clutching the front of his coat tightly closed, though the evening was not cold. This had been his house, after all, home to the son who stood beside him. And inside, still hopefully alive and in one piece, was his daughter as well.

The spell was a good one, Frost thought, but it was not without its shortcomings. He watched intently as Urid's son Aul crept forward. Immediately the front wall of the house began to ooze a darkly glowing liquid fire from every pore and crack of its mortar. Not the whole of the wall, rather a section of it that spread up from the ground on either side of the front door like a broken horseshoe and threatened to mend above it. Smoke rose from the site in thin gray and black clouds, and the smell of sulfur spoiled the air. Soon glowing pools of lumpy fire began to form along the sides of the path before the entrance.

"Enough, Aul!" the old man shouted to his son. "Stop where you are!"

Young Aul turned and glanced over his shoulder, his gaze passing over his father, finding Frost. He waited. Frost nodded. "I have seen enough," he said. "Now back away."

While the young man returned to his father's side, Frost raised one hand and motioned to the three Subartan warriors standing just behind him. They came forward in a single fluid movement, taking up their positions, forming the defensive triangle about their master so that he might work freely. Urid and Aul stepped cautiously back and away from the towering, blade-wielding figures.

Frost closed his eyes and began focusing his efforts, drawing from the energies within himself, burning up no small amount of his considerable body's surpluses even with this small endeavor. No matter, he thought. The long weeks of late summer in Camrak had been quiet and bountiful ones, and he had quickly gained back the weight lost at Highthorn Pass. Indeed, tall and big-boned as he was, he could scarcely recall having ever been quite so fat! He had been forced to pilfer an entirely new wardrobe for himself, in fact, though of course the tailor had had it coming. Prices so high! And workmanship so low! And no sense of humor whatever.

He reached out, clearing his mind, opening himself to the nuances of the little glen, the forces within the house itself, and the ground below. The young daughter was there inside, still alive, possibly unharmed. And *he* was there, the vagabond journeyman sorcerer that had seized what must have seemed a reasonable opportunity at the time. Though certainly, that time had passed.

Frost left the fool alone and spoke instead to the earth, concentrating on the source, and at once the fires began to change, cooling and shrinking back into the walls, turning to sludge not unlike glowing molasses as the flames congealed. Already the hissing had quieted, and the hanging veils of blackened smoke and steam had begun to disperse.

He turned his attentions back to the fool, to a mind he found to be suddenly, acutely troubled. A mind no longer seeking to force its disagreeable desires on others, nor interested, for that matter, in anything but making new and distant plans, then hastily attending to them. Plum was the man's name, it seemed, or something very close to that. He was no one familiar.

Frost introduced himself by pushing a narrow wave of his powerful will directly at the fellow, forming it into an icy chill he knew would strike straight through the other man—fair warning of the frigid torrent that was about to rush in.

Enough, Frost thought, relaxing again without waiting to verify the effect, for he was certain there was no need.

"The life fires that fill the earth run close to the surface here," he said, his voice somewhat faint as he opened his eyes again. "Your intruder's spell has drawn them out. I have sent them back, though I cannot be sure they will never return of their own accord." Frost took one slow, deep breath, then another, a deliberate action. He looked at the old man. "I recommend that you move."

The man's son drew his sword and turned his full attention to the front door of their home. "First we will rid the earth of the bastard conjurer who has dared to claim my sister and my father's home!"

"For luck against fools, be sure to enter with your right foot first," Frost called after him. Then he paused a moment, considering. "Or is it the left? In any case, he has no doubt fled, boy. Out the back, into the woods. No stomach for a fight, that one. Nor talent. Nor brains, either!" Frost began chuckling quietly.

Young Jaffic was suddenly there. "Shall I pursue him my liege?"

"Wait," Frost said, and as he did, the door of the house came slowly open. A girl of no more than fifteen stepped gingerly out onto the walk, carefully eyeing the dying glow of fresh molten rock to either side. The old man and his son rushed forward and swept her into their arms.

"Is she unharmed?" Frost asked, moving to join them. The girl nodded. The old man began to weep.

Frost turned. "Now," he ordered, and then Jaffic was gone, a memory of movement at the corner of the little house. "You said you would pay any price to be rid of this nuisance and have your daughter back," Frost reminded Urid. "What do you offer?"

Urid's face lost its luster of a sudden. He lowered his eyes and began looking about his feet, as if searching the ground for a particular pebble. "I have my home," he said. "And my lands, though I have only a few acres. They are all I have, but yours if you wish."

"Doubtful," Frost replied. "I have no wish to live in this province, and if I chose to do so, I have no doubt that in a few weeks some helpful, insistent stranger would find me and require that I come to assist the poor, starving, homeless family of Urid seen daily by the road."

Urid looked stricken. Frost smiled at Urid's two teenage children. The old man's face suddenly turned rigid, and he clutched his daughter to him, then his son. "You would save one only to take two away!"

"Oh, no, no," Frost declared, shaking his head. "I do not want your progeny, either. I am certain children are bad luck! No, they are yours to feed and clothe, not mine." He looked out toward the man's planted fields, at the hens in the side yard, the small herd of goats and a pair of milking cows just visible behind the fence rails. "But I would take certain provisions," Frost said. "Cheeses and bacon, bean-loaf, and bread sticks, water and wine. Perhaps a goose. Whatever you can provide. And a few gold coins, if you have them."

"Yes, of course!" Urid said, obviously relieved. "There is little money to give you, but you may have it, and please take all that you need of the rest, anything I have!"

Frost fastened a baleful eye on the old man. "Let me ask you, friend. First you offer me all your possessions, then all your money, now all your livestock and stores. But what, truly, would you do if my needs were to come to *all* that you have?"

Urid hesitated, eyes darting, his face tightening to reveal a man grown taut as a sail in a tempest. "I—I suppose that, if you thought you must take it all, you would take it all, and I would find some way to live after that."

Frost shook his head again, then fixed Urid with a long and sour frown. "Not necessary. But it is remarkable that you cannot see how foolish that answer is. Tell me another thing: How did you come to have that awful little fellow in your home?"

Urid shrugged. "He came off the road seeking hospitality. A pilgrim, I thought. So I—"

"So you give this stranger your home. It is a lucky thing that I was able to get it back before you offered it to me. Really, Urid, you must learn to be more sensible in such matters! Never, *never* give away everything, my friend. *Never* risk all that you have on a single chance! Even if all the omens and signs are with you. Such kindness is naught but weakness, and such a man is a fool, like the fool I chased away."

Frost looked away, his eyes finding Rosivok. "Only what we will need," he said. Rosivok turned to Sharryl and muttered a few words; she seemed quick to understand.

With that, both Subartans went and collected their mule, a hearty young animal Frost had only just purchased, and which so far had gone unnamed. They led it from the road, then followed behind as Urid and his two children walked toward the side of the house and the fence beyond.

Frost stood alone, looking slowly about himself, glancing up to the clear sky and the gray, already nearly leafless branches of the trees, then away to the dusty little manor road. He listened to the quiet of early evening, breathed the rich scent of the autumn woods that came on the cooling breeze. There was an omen, something about wind at your back, or a changing wind, or wind before the rain, he wasn't sure—but there wasn't much wind, and he was fairly sure that all had to do with sailing anyway, which was something he would likely never do!

He felt no alarm here, only a growing sense of peace and comfort. Surely a good sign in itself. Despite the best traveling and warding spells a wizard of his considerable means could conjure, omens, Frost held, were never to be ignored. They were, in fact—despite all good reason—the only things he dared not challenge.

His belly rumbled, a most common occurrence, particularly after the exertion of expelling that vulgar little rogue from the house. It would no doubt be some time before Jaffic returned, late enough to warrant their stay for the night. Time enough to consider this place a while, and to learn whether there was anything to the daughter's reputation as a cook!

"We were most fortunate that you were passing near the village," Urid said. His daughter brought deep bowls of steaming meat and cabbage soup to the table, then headed back toward the hearth for more.

"I know," Frost said,

"Have you other business here, then?"

"Oh, no, not *here*," Frost said, chuckling. He paused

to sip the broth and vegetables. "*Here* is really not any-where."

"Then perhaps you could tell us of the reason for your travels," his son Aul said, putting a deep tone in his voice—as much as he could manage.

"Very well," Frost said. "Word has reached me of late, an offer to go to Neleva, something to do with the sea, a beast in the shipping lanes, I'd imagine, though unfortunately the messenger carried very few details. It seems ships bound for Glister are finding trouble at sea, several lost and so forth, which is why I suspect a creature of some sort. Something needs to be done about it and a *huge* profit is promised."

"You seem no sailor," Urid said, looking up.

"No, that I am not."

"You would go all that way on foot?" Urid's daughter asked, returning again with a basket of warm bread.

"And so late in the year," Aul remarked. "You'll be hard into winter long before you arrive."

"A good point," Frost told the boy. "Luckily, whatever task awaits me does not seem an urgent one. There is no shipping through the winter months, and any other purposes will keep as well. I agree, I should wait until spring."

"And what other purpose would you have?" asked Aul.

Urid glared distastefully at the boy's lack of deference to their guest. Frost relieved the old man of any blame with a wave of his hand.

"More good words from a bright, inquiring lad," Frost said. "In fact, the answer is partly a personal one. The city of Glister has become one of the largest seaports in the world in recent years. Traders come on ships from lands most have never heard of, bringing endless rare goods and cultural wonders, and strange knowledge. All these things I find quite valuable. It is an adventure I wish to have while I am still young enough to appreciate it. A place I wish to visit again. As well, I am sure there are many in Glister who would pay for the multitude of services I can provide."

"He is growing bored," Sharryl said, speaking for the first time in the presence of Urid and his family, startling them as she did. "Mostly, he is just bored." They each looked at her, speechless themselves. Sharryl did not look at Frost directly, her face expressionless. She wore the face of a warrior well, giving nothing away, except, of course, when she wanted to.

"And always he is in need of wealth and good fortune," Frost added, chuckling again.

"And what else?" Urid asked, glancing at his daughter, a look of worry returning to his face.

Frost grinned at the other man. "Your daughter is lovely, my friend, but she is safe. I have no need of that."

"A lie?" Sharryl said, thin black eyebrows going up.

Frost knew it was. Sharryl was no man's mate, though she had beckoned Rosivok more than once—and he had gone to her as any man with eyes and needs and common sense would have. But Frost had known her in that way as well, after the battle in Rinouer, and after his long, unfortunate duel to the death—*its* death—with the mage-serpent of the black waters in Holitoel.

Both times he had used up enormous amounts of energy, until finally he had burned away nearly all of the extra bulk he tended to carry, until all that remained was the sturdy frame and great, hardened muscles that lay beneath, a man who could have easily bested an ox in a pulling contest, or lifted the ox off the ground, given the desire and the energy.

In such times as those, though, left without reserves, Frost considered himself vulnerable; muscle was not so easily replaced once it was used for fuel. But this lighter condition had other, strange effects on him. He found himself easily aroused. And the condition seemed to have a similar effect on Sharryl, who was profoundly adept at both war, and its near opposite.

He filled his mouth with a spoonful of soup again, swallowed with a grin. "Not a lie, for now," Frost said. "But in truth, life has been a bit quiet lately. No wars to speak of, other than skirmishes between fiefs, most of which tend to get so messy they're impossible to sort out and seldom show worthwhile stakes. The dragons are all but extinct, and there have been no demons of note since the forging of the Demon Blade, or shortly thereafter, to be correct."

"Still," Rosivok said, also speaking for the first time in the family's presence, "we somehow manage to keep quite busy." Rosivok had finished his soup and started on a second hunk of the bread.

"There are many rumors about the Demon Blade of late," young Aul remarked, gnawing on his own bread.

"There are always rumors," Frost muttered.

"These," Aul went on, "say that the Blade is somewhere here about, near Bouren or Jasnok. And the rumors are enough to bring strangers and soldiers alike into the area from many lands. Travelers all speak of this."

"A very old wizard known as Ramins has possession of the Blade, and has for many decades now," Frost said. "This is common knowledge among those who practice my profession. And no one, perhaps not even Ramins himself, is certain where he is these days."

"They say that now he is dead."

Frost looked up from his soup, then he grinned wryly. "They always say that he is dead."

"The spring may be worse for travel through Ariman than the dead of winter," Urid said after a pause. He seemed to wait for someone to ask why.

"Why is that?" Sharryl obliged. She kept one muscular forearm on the table as she ate; the other, still bearing the forearm straps and edged steel blade of her subarta, she kept politely out of sight.

"With the illness of King Andarys, Ariman is a troubled land," Urid said.

Frost's eyes widened. "The king is ill?"

"So we have heard, and so anyone will tell you."

"We must make mention of this to Jaffic," Frost said, eyes narrowing again. "He asks after the Andarys family now and then."

"Though he will never say why," Sharryl noted simply.

"What sorts of trouble?" Rosivok asked.

Urid took a breath. "The way grows more treacherous every day. Grand Chamberlain Ferris sits on the throne with King Andarys' blessings, and he has already imposed new tolls and taxes. And new laws every week, so the travelers tell."

"He builds a much larger army, by conscription and with money for mercenaries," Aul added, a twitch at the edge of his mouth, a restlessness in his eyes as he spoke. "There is talk of war with Bouren and the other great fiefs in the north, though I've heard Lord Ivran is quick to deny that."

"Yet his son, Prince Jaran has been out in the fields enlisting young men, and maybe looking for the Demon Blade himself," the father added.

Aul leaned over the table and lowered his voice to a conspiratorial whisper: "It is said that Lord Ivran may have had a hand in King Andarys' illness. Sorcery, perhaps."

"We have heard of this," Rosivok said, looking at Frost, eyebrows raised. "*Much* trouble."

"And we think little of it," Frost remarked. The Subartans were charged with his protection, so they tended to worry too much. A bother, now and then. Still, it was a condition Frost gladly accepted as it allowed him to occupy his mind with other, more intriguing things. "We will find the way in whatever condition we find it in and consider it then."

"Enough to say," Urid added, "that a wise man would do well to mind his own business along the river next spring, and his back."

"We are grateful for your candor, sir," Frost replied.

Sharryl rose quietly and went to stand beside the room's only window, a view that looked out on the walk and the road.

"Your friend does not return," Aul said, which earned him a strong "shhhhh" from his father.

Sharryl looked at them, then turned back to the window. "He will come," she said softly. "As always."

"He knows what to do," Frost explained. "He will pursue our little fool until he captures him, or kills him, or until it no longer seems a worthwhile endeavor. Jaffic would be the fool to do more in such a situation as this—that is, one in which my life is in no way threatened. And he seems no fool to me."

Aul looked at him a moment, then nodded.

"What do you plan to do until spring, then?" Urid asked after a time, passing the empty bread basket to his daughter and motioning to her to pass the flagon of ale toward the center of the table.

"I would speak with you of that," Frost said. He sipped the last of his soup—a very satisfying soup, he thought, as hearty as a soup would allow, and seasoned just so. "Of course, I had heard of your predicament here." Frost grinned as he chewed a final bit of meat. "And of your daughter's very fine cooking. Might I have the ale?"

The young girl averted her eyes as she passed the ale, a gentle blush touching her cheeks. Urid seemed to consider her, then he looked at Frost and tipped his head. Frost looked straight at the other man. "And we heard that you have an extra room."

Aul looked up from his meal. Urid's face formed the slightest of grins. "You are awfully sure of yourself, aren't you?"

"Indeed," Frost replied, settling back. "I am."

Rosivok woke him, as usual. "Urid's daughter is preparing breakfast," he said.

"That," Frost replied, rubbing his eyes, "is very good news!"

Rosivok waited while Frost got to his feet and searched for his tunic and his cloak.

"Jaffic has returned," the Subartan said. "He did not find the one he sought. That one has taken to another house along the road, no doubt, but which house it is hard to say."

Subartans were not well known as trackers, but that was not why Frost kept them. "Annoying someone else, no doubt," he said. "He could provide me a good regular income for a time."

"I told Jaffic of the rumors of King Andarys' illness. He was shaken by it. He is concerned, though he hides it well. Perhaps that is where he came from; he is eager now to continue our journey."

"A safe guess," Frost agreed. "But he will tell us when he is ready, and that is when I will be ready to listen. And spring is when we will leave."

Rosivok only nodded.

"Come, we will eat."

The warrior made no reply, but waited quietly while Frost dressed. As they left the tiny room where all four of them had slept the night, Rosivok paused. "You truly believe there is nothing to the rumors these people repeat?" he said.

"So many rumors, my friend. And all of them like raindrops in the air; if you go out, some will fall upon you, but most will not. I will keep us as dry as possible.

Meanwhile, we are fortunate to have such a gracious host for the winter, and only good omens, so far as I can tell."

Frost straightened the full-length satin cloak he had worn the day before and pulled it on. "For now, I smell porridge at a boil!"

"Yes, my liege," Rosivok replied, and followed close behind.

Chapter VI

The village was small, only a dozen mud-and-stone huts with thatch roofs. Madia had never gotten quite this close to such a place, had never been in the house of a serf. One of the huts was much larger than the rest. She could see a few sheep and cows inside its wide open door, and more sheep wandering nearby in a fenced-in field.

Small fenced gardens were in back of most of the huts, and chickens seemed to be everywhere. Two women carrying pails and followed by three young children came out of the largest hut and headed toward one of the others. They dumped the dark lumpy contents onto a big mounded pile at the near edge of the village, then stayed to throw dirt onto the pile. Another woman carrying a large earthenware pot and dogged by a handful of small children came wandering out from between a pair of cows near another hut. *Milk*, Madia thought, and her insides ached from hunger.

For three days since the attack she had stayed in the woods or crept through fallow fields, afraid to show herself to anyone, anywhere. No goblins or leshy had accosted her, no spirits had haunted her path, and she had seen no more robbers or soldiers about, but all her fears, both real and imagined, were beginning to pale in comparison to the physical punishment she had endured. She had found water in the small streams that trickled through the countryside, but she hadn't had nourishment of any kind, and she didn't think she could go another night or walk another step with her stomach so empty.

She hid among the trees of the standing wood several hundred feet from the tiny village. As the cool of evening settled upon her skin, her hands shook. The sun began to set and she watched other villagers returning from the fields, a few more women and children, and twice as many men. Not long afterward, what seemed like the whole population of the village gathered on the little main road and headed for the manor house—a small arrangement of walls and a keep barely visible on a rise to the south. They would take dinner there, Madia thought, and then they would return.

She watched them go, then watched the huts for a time after that, looking for movement, thinking of cow's milk. When she thought it was safe, she began to crawl out of her hiding place.

The fields around the huts had already seen a harvest; only torn and trampled leaves and the withered remains of once growing produce were left. Cabbage, Madia realized, crawling past a few discarded, rotting heads. She checked them carefully, then began crawling in a more serpentine pattern, checking for heads that might have been missed. She found none. Finally she reached the little garden behind the nearest hut.

Most of what grew here had been dug up, but there were small green beans still on some of the shortest bushes, and a row of carrots, still fresh and growing. She dug up a carrot and ate ravenously. The carrots were sweet and absolutely wonderful. When the food was gone, she crawled round to the side of the hut.

The nearest window, shutters open, faced away from the manor house. She waited for her dizzy head to clear, for her heart to slow its pounding. She peered inside and saw no one, then pulled herself over the sill and let herself down inside.

Coals glowed dark red in the small open hearth. The scent of the smoke filled the room, nearly covering many others—soured milk or cheese, unlaundered bedding, wooden tables and dirt floors soaked in ancient food spills. Across the room, through the open doorway, fading daylight sketched a table and chairs, a butter churn, a pair of short barrels, and a pair of beds from the shadows as she strained her eyes. One candle burned near the hearth, kept to light others, the one thing that reminded her of life at Kamrit Castle.

She worked her way around the little room, looking for anything that might be considered food. Inside one of the barrels, wrapped in burlap, she found a fair-sized piece of oatcake. It lacked sweetness and was already getting old and dry, but she was careful not to lose a single crumb as she ate it.

Then she spotted an earthenware pot near the door. She picked it up and shook it and heard a faint splash, then she tipped it to her lips. There was barely any milk left, but she was not displeased. She stood up again, the room in darkness now but for the glow of the fire and the one candle's flame. Outside the sun was setting, leaving a clear moonlit sky behind. Madia stayed still; the shaking hadn't stopped.

She tenderly crossed her arms, tucking her hands beneath them, and hugged them against her. *Better*, she thought. Then renewed fatigue seemed to fill her mind and body, rising like the moon outside, replacing one pallid reality with another. The shaking moved to her knees and she sank to her haunches beside the door.

Better, again, she decided after a moment. She just needed a moment's rest without the cold night dew settling on her hair, without the frightening unknown sounds of the night in the forest all around her, without the running. . . .

She closed her eyes briefly, huddled on the floor, leaning against the doorway. She opened them again to the sound and sight of shoes on the floor beside her.

Man, wife and child, Madia gathered, looking at them. They stood around her in a loose semicircle, staring at her in silence. The woman and the boy held one lit candle each up in front of them. Madia realized they could see her much better than she could see them. She got slowly to her feet, straining to gather detail. They were dressed in the simplest of clothes, nearly the same dresses, shirts and pants worn by beggars in Kamrit. The man had an ax in his hands, held at the ready.

"Had enough of our bread?" the woman said in a strong voice with a cold, even tone.

"Who are you?" the man asked in a deep, rough voice that was less taciturn. He looked to be in his thirties, and he still had several teeth. His breath smelled heavily of ale.

Madia opened her mouth, but the answer caught in her throat. Her instinct was to inform them of their place, tell them she was the royal princess of Ariman and was owed the service and allegiance of every soul in these lands, then tell them her bidding after that. But she still did not know who in Kamrit had sent the lone knight to attack her, or what he had wanted, or why Lord Ivran's men had killed the girl who wore her clothing—she didn't know who might have good reason to help her enemies by turning her over to them. How would these people react to the truth, she wondered, if they chose to believe her at all? . . .

The man looked at his wife and shook his head. "She's a thief, that's all! A stinkin' thief. We can take her up to the manor and let the lord deal with her."

"No!" Madia said, nearly startling herself with the outburst. "No, you can't do that."

"You see?" the man said. "She *is* a thief, wanted by the king's men, sure. Out with you, to the manor! I'll not have your likes in my house."

"Please," Madia said, finding the word somewhere. She tried to think of something appropriate—not the truth, certainly, but a lie, which was something she had a good deal more experience with.

"I am wanted for something I did not do. You must believe me."

"Where are you from?" he asked.

"Kamrit," she said, having no idea what else to say.

"What are you charged with?" the woman asked.

Madia searched her tired mind for lucid thoughts. These were ignorant folk, of course, so anything simple would do, and she had concocted the most elaborate stories at the castle dozens of times, often with no more notice than this. . . .

"The Princess Madia thinks I enticed a nobleman who was courting her," she said. "She ordered me thrown in prison. But I swear I did no such thing! I have no idea what drew the good fellow's attention, as I never so much as looked at him, and I only spoke to him when he spoke to me. Yet I am blamed! I barely escaped the city and have been alone on the road since then—four days now, without food or proper shelter."

"Aye, the good princess is a graceless, vexing little imp!" said the woman. "The whole kingdom knows it! Be the king's ruin yet, and everyone knows that, too."

"You have met the princess?" Madia asked, trying not to flinch, straining to hold her tongue.

"Oh, no," the woman said, shaking her head from side

to side. "But it is common notice. The king's threatened to put her out in the cold, you know, is the latest word about. Same justice she did you! Sure serve her right, too."

"I hear the stories myself," her husband said. He frowned, the candlelit shadow of his ax growing longer across his rough, unshaven face. "But what of this one?"

"Could just put her out, on her way," the woman said. "It was the full moon that brought her, so we could just give her back."

"She is sort of pretty." The boy's voice. Madia could not imagine how he might see such virtues in her as she appeared just now—filthy, ragged, putrid—although she had already noticed that the smell was something these people were well enough accustomed to. She looked the boy over more closely. Quite young, really, perhaps thirteen. Nervous boy-eyes of a kind she had seen times before. Madia very nearly smiled.

"Thank you," she said.

"No need to steal a man's bread," the boy's father told Madia, looking her over much more carefully now himself. "You can ask."

"I really am sorry. I was not sure who to trust," she added, thinking this, at least, was quite true. *I can't trust anyone!*

"Could be there's a nice bounty on her head?" the man added, looking to his wife. Even the boy seemed to perk up noticeably at the idea. Madia thought of the gold coins she had carried, a pittance to her then, a fortune to her now, more than enough to buy the loyalties of these people. But she was poorer than they just now.

"I doubt there is any bounty," she said. "But your lord may wish to gain favor with the royal house by turning me in. I do not want to go to jail."

"She talks so fine," the man said, rubbing his chin, thoughtful. "High breed, or a servant to a high house."

"A servant, truly," Madia responded, "to many a fine lord and great baron who has visited the king." *True also, in a very special way*, she thought. "So you see, I know something of hospitality."

"Never mind that!" the woman snapped. She stepped forward once and stood toe-to-toe with Madia, breathing ale-soaked breath at her. Her face fell into shadow, but Madia could gather much from the ire in the other's tone. "There'll be no hospitality for outlaws here, believe that."

"Alright, Faith," her husband said, taking her by the arm, pulling her gently back. "Just a bit." He walked to one side of Madia and paused, puzzling, then went around to the other side near the boy. "I'll bet she knows something about work, bein' a servant to the king so long and all." He found Madia's eyes. "We got behind on cuttin' the lord's grain, enough so we'll have to work long and Sundays to get the last of our own garden done and stored for winter." He turned again to the others.

"What I mean is, we might let her stay about for a few weeks, or so, till we're done with harvest and stores, and we might feed her a little now and then. As well my brother could use some help." He made a gesture behind him, toward some other part of the village, then looked at Madia. "You can sleep with our cow, if you want." He stopped to look at his wife and chuckled. Madia saw her grin and shake her head. "And who is going to watch her?" she said.

"I can watch her," the boy said.

"Aye, and sure there is more than one young man about who will help with that," his father said, grinning.

"I guess that's right," the woman said, apparently relenting. "She is not so large. Might not eat that much anyway."

Madia did manage a meager smile now, a genuine smile. She didn't know if staying here was safe, and she had no idea what they would want from her, but peasant work had never seemed that difficult, and it had to be better than shivering and starving, or being set upon by more outlaws. "Thank you," she said, adding, "and you, Faith."

"Rous," her husband said, introducing himself. "And this is young Aust, my son. Now, tell us who you are."

Madia went to speak, saw the error in doing so and nearly choked on a hasty swallow. The three of them were waiting. *Faith*, she thought, seeing it now. . . . "Hope," she said.

"Same as my cousin's daughter," Rous said, nodding in apparent wonder. "Easy to remember! Come then, we'll show her where to sleep. And best sleep well," he added, then he nodded to his wife.

Faith gathered a blanket off the end of one of the beds and led Madia through the heavy burlap drapery that hung at the back of the room. They stepped through the opening into another, smaller room, no more than three or four yards across, then Faith held her candle up. The roof pitched down from the wall of the main house, too low to stand under at the far end. The floor was covered with hay. The room's single other feature was a sleeping cow. Opening its eyes, the animal looked dreamily at the two women; it stirred slightly, then shut its eyes again.

"See you come sunup," Faith said, handing Madia the blanket. She turned to go.

"Wait!" Madia said. "What will I sleep on? And—what of the cow?"

Faith stared at her for a moment, then something other than the candlelight flickered in her eyes, and she burst into a hearty laugh. "Aye," she said, "at least you still have a sense of humor, and after all you been through. You might do well after all, girl. Now, good night."

The woman slipped out and was gone. Madia turned

in the darkness and made her way to the near wall, then she inched along, stopping as far from the cow as she could get—but the smell of dung grew heavy there, and she realized she was in the wrong corner. She slid back, then up the other side until she was in front of the animal, as far as she knew. She could hear it breathing. Leaning closer, she could feel the warmth from its large body. She lay down and wrapped herself in the blanket, listening to the cow's loud breathing, wondering if she would ever sleep a single moment like this.

A couple of days here, she thought, was all she would be able to stand. She thought of nothing after that until she woke.

Faith returned just after sunup. She told Madia to fold the blanket, then she brought her out to the table. Breakfast consisted of a barely edible gruel and wonderfully fresh milk, though Rous drank ale with his meal. Following that, Rous gathered scythes and rakes from the cow-shed and handed them to his wife and son. "A friend, Empil, lost his wife this past month," he told Madia, "so he will have an extra scythe you can use." Then he turned and went outside.

The air was brisk, but there was no wind and the sun shone clearly above the horizon. Warmth on the way. Rous introduced Madia to the other villagers as they gathered on the village street. She met nearly three dozen people whose names she forgot almost as soon as they were told her. Too many to remember, she thought, and she didn't see that it mattered in any case. Not for the few days she would know any of them.

They showed her the midden, an open heap of manure and dirt, the same one she had seen the women dump the buckets on the day before, then they told her now was the time to use it if she had to. She didn't. Rous told the others that "Hope" was from the town of Rill, which apparently lay somewhere east of the manor, and he explained the terms he had given her. No one seemed to object. Then everyone set out for the fields.

Most wandered to different sections of the manor fields, where they began to cut the tall browning grasses; some others set about raking and piling what had been cut and laid out a previous day. The hayward came by, overseeing the day's start. He wore a dark coat and brimmed hat and rode a well-groomed horse, the kind of man Madia might have teased at the castle more than once but never actually spoke to, except to give the most despotic decree. Here, he was master. She did not recognize this man, but she tried to glimpse his face as he road near, hoping he would not know her and would pass her by. She saw no recognition in his eyes.

Madia took up her scythe, watching the others work, and began to swing. The grasses fell, progress being made. She thought this would almost be fun, the novelty alone providing an entertainment of sorts. But after an hour, her hands and back were sore. By the time the hayward's horn sounded lunch, the day had warmed considerably. Sweat had soaked into her clothing and her hands had begun to blister.

Women came bringing bread and cheese and watered ale from the manor house. Madia followed everyone into the shade of the trees along the pasture's edge and ate as much as she could. She showed Rous her hands.

"What did you do in Kamrit?" he asked, shaking his head. Faith took a look and began to chuckle. "Hide from her duties, I'll wager," she said.

"Here," Rous told her, handing her a pot of ale. "Drink as much of this down as you can, and you will feel better about it."

Madia enjoyed the wine her father imported from the ports in Neleva, but she had never liked ale, even good ale, which her first swallow told her this was not.

But she drank, then drank some more, until she was nearly too dizzy to get up. When the horn sounded a second time, though, she did get up, ignoring the stiffness in her back, and took her scythe to the wheel for sharpening before going back to the fields. By the end of the day, her hands were bleeding and her back hurt so that she could hardly walk. The ale had worn off and left her with a throbbing head as well. But the field was nearly all cut and raked.

She watched the hayward come around and talk to some of the men, including Rous, then he sounded the horn and everyone headed for the road. She went along, limping from the misery in her back and holding her hands against her ribs, palms up, arms crossed at the wrists. The evening meal lay ahead. Strangely, she wasn't awfully hungry.

"Will you go to the lord's house for supper?" Madia asked as they walked, trying to think ahead.

"Aye, every night. We get meat and fish twice a week," Rous said as the walked. "But you can stay behind if you want." He made a wicked face, not a kind sort of look, then he seemed to soften. "Maybe we can bring you something back, if you are afraid to go up."

Afraid, she thought, repeating the word in her mind. She had never been afraid of anything in her life. She was terrified of everything now—of just getting through another day.

"We will have two more boons this week," Rous said after Madia didn't answer. "Two more fields, and next week we take bundles on the wagons to go up to the manor yard. Week after, we got our own fields to finish, and what's left of the garden. Then we make ready for the coldest months, which is when you'll be on your way. You best figure what you plan to do for the winter."

Madia heard all his words, felt her head pound and spin. Her hands burned and her body ached. She didn't have a plan. Other than going to the trading city of Kopeth upriver. She numbly tried to tell them about this.

Rous looked at his wife and son, and all three of them frowned.

"What is it?" Madia asked. She stumbled, then got her footing before she fell. No one slowed or even seemed to notice. She forced her legs to propel her forward.

"You claim to worry about being caught and taken back to Kamrit, but soldiers and traders from all lands can be found in Kopeth. And freemen and mercenaries of every sort. You'd best hope you told the truth about the lack of a ransom on your head."

"It is a big and busy place, though," young Aust said, eyes distant and bright as Madia looked at him. "Travelers tell of Kopeth at every chance! I have always wanted to go there, just to see. I hear—"

"One tale too many, for a fact," Faith said, cutting the boy off. "It is a dangerous place for the unwary, and this girl is as unwary as any I know."

"Plenty of other towns in the north," Rous said. "Places where a soul could stay years and not be of notice to the rest of Ariman. Places only the tax collectors know."

"Then that is what I'll do," Madia said, thinking she could not work another hour in the fields, let alone many days. Any city would do. She knew dressmaking, and she had been taught to cook a little bit, and how to care for the sick and wounded; she knew something of the use of plants and herbs—sage and lavender, fennel and horehound and wormwood. And she could read, something no one of these people and not many in even the largest towns could do well. She would find less painful work and better food and real architecture, and perhaps a real bed that was not to be shared with livestock. *A few days*, she recited again in her mind. *Maybe only two. Then I will go.*

* * *

The following morning, Faith gave Madia two strips of soft cloth and showed her how to wrap her blistered hands. Then she cooked eggs and milk together in the kettle on the hearth, a meal that filled Madia's stomach with a warm and heavy glow, each mouthful tasting better than the last.

Rous watched Madia eat, fumbling the chunks of egg with fingertips that protruded from the wrappings. "You will stay here today," he told her as he rose, preparing to go. "Give those hands a chance to heal some. Stay in the house, if you know what's good for you. Others here about dislike anybody around their things, and the lord himself might ride out for a regular look. 'Course, were that to happen, we three would know nothing about any crimes at Kamrit. You heard what I told the others about you."

"Yes," Madia said, thankful, more truly thankful than she had ever been to anyone in her life before. They were good people, but she couldn't expect them to lie for her at risk to themselves, and she didn't think less of them for it. They were not so ignorant, either, not quite, anyway; they knew of an entire life that she did not.

"I understand," she added. "I will not bring harm to you or your family. I swear it. And as soon as my hands get a little better—"

"He knows, girl," Faith said, smiling a bit. "We would not have kept you if we felt you was no good."

Which was an odd thing to hear; she had only just barely begun to think of them in that way, yet apparently they had decided many things about her a full day ago.

She wanted to say something, but she didn't have any words just at the moment. It didn't seem to matter. Faith had already turned with her husband and son and headed out. Then she paused at the door, glancing back.

"See what you can do to clean the place," Faith said, gesturing broadly. "Tomorrow is only half a day of work. In the afternoon, we can see about making you an extra set of clothes."

Just a week, then, Madia thought. *Maybe two. Then I will go.*

November's first winds blew whispering half-bare tree limbs against each other and swirled leaves through the air, piling them against fences and doorways about the village. Madia finished her bread and bacon breakfast and sighed; she stared out the window, thinking about staying in the hut again most of the day, doing little else. There was no more work to do on the big fields or anywhere on the manor, even on Rous' own acreage. Rous and the other villagers had lately begun slaughtering many of the animals, thereby making room in their sheds, and were keeping busy putting dried meat up for the winter.

In two months' time Madia had put on a few pounds weight, though most all of that was muscle. She felt strong, fairly healthy, and . . . restless. She thought of the months ahead as she got up from the table, and decided that perhaps it was time.

Not that staying in the village was *all* bad—even though that meant getting used to smelling and looking and feeling like one of Kamrit's street beggars, but she had grown fond of these people, especially Faith, who had shown her the unusual art of cooking with almost no ingredients, and who seemed to possess an inner strength and endurance that left Madia in constant awe. In fact, Madia had grown rather fond of her own new personality, too, of "Hope" the servant girl, the peasant girl—though it was a role she would not cherish forever.

She had never guessed how hard such a life could be, nor how simple; too simple, at times. And too cruel. She had seen a newborn girl die of fever her second week here, and men and women whose bodies were so old and worn that they were like walking dead, yet they were no older than her own father. Rous was becoming such a man, and Faith, worn and weary, old ahead of her time. And the boy would follow them, accepting who and what he was. Something Madia had never given much thought to—in the past.

She did not want to spend the winter here, or the spring after that, or all those to come. She had already talked with the others about everything she dared talk about, and though there was no doubt much more they could teach her, she was only just so willing to learn the ways of such a place; she didn't want to die here.

And this village was still much too close to Kamrit for comfort, yet too far from the life for which she had been bred.

She started to bring up the subject of going, then decided to wait until after the meal that evening. She spent the day making clothes with Faith, then waited as usual as the villagers went up to the manor for the evening meal, but when they returned, Rous came to Madia and stood silently, looking at her, his expression strangely unreadable.

"There is news," he said. "You may be able to return to Kamrit, or eat at the manor with the rest of us if it suits you better. They say she is dead."

"Who is dead?" Madia asked.

"The princess, Madia, daughter of King Andarys," Rous replied, turning out a thin smile. "The very bitch what caused you your grief!"

"He put her out of the castle, he did," Faith said, wrinkling her nose. "The king warned her once and for all, before she brought the kingdom down around his ears, and she crossed him still! So by the gods he put her out on her own, and that was the death of her."

"How do they know she is dead?"

"No one has seen her in weeks," Rous replied. "And the pendant she was wearin' turned up in a merchant's stall in the market square. Fell victim to outlaws on the river road, they say. So you see, she won't likely be back."

"Yes, I see," Madia said, trying to sort everything out. But it had only been a few weeks! To give up hope so quickly meant that someone in the castle, perhaps even her father, truly must have wanted her dead and gone and must know of the attacks on her—one of them, at least. More, it meant that no one cared for her life; not her own father, certainly, and not anyone else! Her only value had come in death.

She still didn't want to believe that.

"How could a father do such a thing to his own daughter?" Madia asked, not looking at anyone.

"That would depend, I guess," Rous said, shrugging his shoulders, "on the girl."

You wanted to leave here, she told herself. *Now you'll get your wish.* Though of course, she could not leave to go back as the ghost of Madia Andarys. Obviously, there were those who would test her mortality.

"Well and good," Madia said, trying to smile. "I will go in the morning."

"And we will miss you," young Aust said, grinning at her, gazing at her with eyes that spoke of friendship now.

"All of us," Faith said, and Rous nodded, smiling too, just like the boy.

"I—" Madia said, telling the truth, seeing it as she spoke, "—I will miss you, too."

With the morning, Madia put the extra clothes Faith had made for her into a homemade shoulder bag and wrapped a thick cape around herself. Rous gave her dried pork and a hearty loaf of barley and rye bread. Finally she headed south, waving good-bye, watching them watch her go. When she was well out of sight, she slipped off the road and doubled back, heading northwest again, walking away from Kamrit, away from home.

Madia had never been one to overlook a good resource, and a patently effective piece of fiction had always been just that. She modified some of the details, foremost her approach; she walked straight into a most likely looking little peasant village *before* the onset of darkness. Wearing a lost-cow look, she began hunting for the most likely looking faces, then told her story as convincingly as any bard or minstrel at her father's castle ever had. The villagers listened intently, clinging spellbound to every word as she explained her crimes of insinuated passion, then pleaded the case for her innocence.

"The king thought I was in part responsible for his daughter's misbehavior," she finished, adding this newly concocted bit. "The princess tried to lay blame on me in order to satisfy her own misplaced jealously!"

The villagers, having little access to insider royal gossip so far afield, found Madia to be an innocent yet scandalous fountain of it. And they had yet to hear of the princess' supposed demise.

She asked for only a few days' food and shelter in return for her tales, and found that several families were willing to argue over the privilege. But before she grew to dislike the accommodation, and before she ran out of real or embellished tales to tell, she quietly moved on, traveling only by day now, wary of the bite the winds of November had begun to carry.

The third village she stayed in was larger than the others and was visited frequently by the manor's lord, a sour, rumpled man who seemed to look that way even in fresh clothing. There were no meat and fish meals at the manor house, but Madia learned that he paid wages high enough to allow some of the serfs to buy their freedom, or more land of their own on which to grow cash crops to be sold in the markets at Kopeth. There were even a few travelers about, relatives and peddlers from other villages, for the fief itself was a very large one.

Madia began to feel almost comfortable here. She came to stay with a mother who truly needed help with many things, a widow named Arie and her two daughters, girls half Madia's age. With no sons and no husband, Arie and her girls had learned to do a man's work each day, and bore a look in their eyes and posture that testified to this. She said her husband had died during the winter past, something wrong in his gut, a painful passing. The other villagers had helped with whatever they had, and still did, more generously than any people Madia had ever known at Kamrit Castle.

So Madia offered to help Arie with putting up the last of her winter stores, then she helped make ale and noticed, tasting older brews, that she had begun to develop a taste for the stuff herself.

She met other girls her own age here, most of them married, though a few that were not, and there were many young men, though she only flirted with them; she had known too many men of learning and power, men of adventure who were greater adversaries in games of romantic lure and chance. Already she had almost forgotten what that was like, though not completely. Food and shelter were one thing, but a princess' fancy was quite another.

She stayed nearly three weeks until, come a Saturday afternoon, Arie returned from taking a wagonload of the last of the season's apples to the market. When the wagon drew near, Arie was off the back and hurrying toward the hut before the wheels had stopped.

"Hope!" she said, a terribly serious look on her face. "I have news of Kamrit, of the king!" She said it all in one breath, then drew another. "We should go inside."

Madia nodded, went in and waited while the girl composed herself, waited for her to say that the princess was presumed dead, and so it might be safe for the servant girl Hope to return to the city of Kamrit.

"The long illness that plagues King Andarys has taken a turn, they say, and has worsened. The grand chamberlain, Lord Ferris, is carrying out the king's wishes for him."

Madia felt her gut tighten. *My father, ill! And that cretin Ferris running the kingdom. . . .*

"They say Lord Ferris is hunting enlistments, and his soldiers are said to be everywhere lately, especially in Kopeth, looking for young men to join their legions."

"Perhaps they will stay in Kopeth," Madia muttered, her mind going in two directions.

"But don't you see, they will come here soon, searching for freemen, or any man willing to serve the king. Did you not say you were still wanted by every soldier in Ariman? Or do you think, with the king's illness, your crimes might have been forgotten?"

"Perhaps," Madia said, paying strict attention now. "Though . . . I would doubt that."

Of course, she still had no idea who else was involved, which made trying to understand the possibilities just as frustrating as it had been the day she was attacked.

"Then I fear for you. You said that your service in the castle made you known to all."

"That is true," Madia replied. "When might they come?"

"A few days, I think. Perhaps a day."

She had heard of a town beyond Kopeth, known as Kern, nearer the northern border of Ariman—though not too close, as anywhere close to Bouren was nowhere she wanted to find herself just now. Still, there might be nowhere else to go. Except home. "Then I must leave tonight."

"You must let me help you."

"You say the king's illness is an old one. Do you know anything more?"

"No, only what they say."

Madia had never known of any such illness, so she thought it might well be a lie. Her father wouldn't do her the favor of getting sick and passing on. Rumors could start, though, and spread. . . .

"Where will you go?" Arie asked.

"I have a place to hide," Madia said, because Arie didn't need to know any differently.

"Will you be back?"

Arie stood looking at her the way Lady Anna used to, nights when Madia would leave her chambers; like Rous and Faith and Aust had looked at her the day she had said good-bye to them. She had said good-bye too often of late.

"Yes," she said, knowing it wasn't true.

"Then I would have you borrow something of mine." Arie went to the corner of the room, reached behind the pine storage chest there, and retrieved a sword. She handed it to Madia. A crude weapon, the blade was short and blunt and made of poor steel, most of it rusting and pitted at the edges. The hilt was homemade, carved from oak, and there was no scabbard.

"It was found in the fields, leftover from the wars," she said. "It might afford you some protection against the hungry beasts, or men. My husband taught me how to hold it, to protect myself when he was away. It is not hard to learn."

She went to show Madia what little she had learned. Madia let her, not letting on to her own abilities with a weapon.

"Thank you," Madia said when they were finished. She wrapped the sword in rags and tied it to her back. "I will return it, I promise." And she realized as she said it that, in fact, she hoped she might keep her word.

She dressed as warmly as time and the villager's generosity would allow. She took food for a week, hoping it would not take that long, uncertain she would survive longer in the cold that had gripped the land in recent days.

For a moment, she began to wonder if it might be better to just go home, or go to Kopeth, better to face her enemies and risk being killed or hauled away by her father—or by his enemies. At least that way, she thought, she might die running toward her life, instead of away from it—*because that is what you are doing!* It was an idea she still felt uncomfortable with, one she could examine only indirectly. Yet there were other concerns.

What if my father really is ill. . . .

But if she were ever to go back with the intent to survive she would need to know more, to understand many things that eluded her now. The decision could wait, a few days at least, until she'd had time to think things over a little more, time to decide what she was afraid of, no matter where she was; or perhaps, with luck, she would be able to learn something new in a real town. One way or another.

With the first light of the last day of November, she set out again, feet crunching on the morning frost covering the grasses in the fields along the road to Kern.

Chapter VII

Silently Anna stood over him, watching him breathe, ignoring the ache in the bones of her tired feet. She knelt and took her thin leather shoes off. The cool stone floor felt good against the soles of her feet.

The king stirred, one hand twitching slightly; Anna held the hand in hers, squeezing gently. She liked to come here as often as she could, then stay by Kelren Andarys' side until she could no longer stand. The king had deteriorated slowly before her eyes, fading away physically and mentally until he could barely move or speak, or recognize anyone. Still, Anna spent time at his side, fussing over his appearance, his clothing and his hair.

Lord Kelren reminded her of all that had been, of the times when her husband was still alive, when the castle was filled with visitors and host to countless gatherings, when all Kamrit was as bright and alive as he was. Sir Renall and Kelren had been great friends, and Kelren had been a good friend to her when her husband was taken. The king had trusted her with the care of his only daughter.

A trust she felt she had betrayed, at least in some ways. Like her husband, Madia was also gone, and Kelren was all that remained of her, too. . . .

Every time she looked at him, she remembered all this. When he died and all that had been the best parts of her life died with him, she would have nothing at all.

She stood back as her feet ached again in protest, then she sighed, considering giving in to the hour, to the inevitable. Her thoughts drifted again, only to be interrupted by the click of the latch on the door behind her. She turned to find Lord Ferris entering the room. He was accompanied by the seneschal, Tristan, two squires, and behind them a pair of serfs and Lamarat, the court physician. Ferris greeted her; Tristan only gave her a nod. They approached the bed, but only Lamarat did not stop short. He edged in front of Anna, and she quickly retreated.

"We must tend to him now," Lord Ferris said, taking Anna well aside. "You may come again tomorrow, if you wish."

Anna barely looked up. Ferris had the most unsettling eyes she had ever encountered, and a certain way about him: agitated at times, frightening, like an animal gone mad. "Yes, my lord," she said, bowing to him. "Tomorrow."

"Good night," Ferris said.

She faded back and quietly let herself out.

When Lamarat was finished, he stepped back. "Forgive me, my lord," he said, "but there seems to be nothing left to do. His fate lies in the hands of the Greater Gods."

"It is enough that you have tried," Tyrr told him— made the mouth tell him. "More, no one can ask."

"Perhaps a priest or a wizard," Lamarat said. "I fear there may be sorcery at work here, though I cannot be sure."

"A priest will be called if one is needed," Tyrr assured him, working to form an appropriate expression on the construct's face. "But I fear Kelren's suffering is nothing more than nature's own cruelty." He paused momentarily, just long enough, then he turned to the others. "Please, leave me now, all of you, so that I may pray with my king in silence."

He waited while the physician left, taking the seneschal and the squires with him. The two serfs, however, remained. These were the men Tyrr had picked out, along with several others, to become more of his special allies, a rare dimension added to his perfectly evolving plan. He had given them special training and guidance, then set about working new spells with old; they were his now, completely. Soon, there would be many like them.

He nodded to one of the serfs, who turned and latched the door. Tyrr positioned himself, held the construct still, then focused the rest of his energies on the feeble, failing body of King Andarys. Even this newest incantation was similar to others he had tried, made to cause a specific human suffering; it was especially designed to draw much greater energy from both the natural world, and from the great reserves inherent in the power differentials between the human world and Tyrr's. This night Tyrr labored carefully, tirelessly, fighting his natural urge to rush in and finish up, to substitute raw energy for a sustained methodology. This was as much a test of his own resolve as it was a means to accomplish his goal—the death of the king.

He had reasoned that perhaps his failures so far were due to a lack of attention to detail and not to errors in his spells or their intensity. A problem, Tyrr believed, that had plagued his kind throughout the ages.

Until now.

The king was gravely ill. He looked terribly thin and pale, skin dry and limp, eyes nearly always closed, glazed when they were open. There was no doubt that Tyrr's efforts so far had had their effects, and the entire kingdom was convinced of the apparent sad outcome of Kelren's strange, worsening affliction—but somehow the man still lived! And clearly, that had gone on long enough.

Magic was at work, certainly, since no amount of mortal fortitude could have kept any man alive under Tyrr's repeated assaults. But even magic, no matter how layered or perfected, had its limits, its weaknesses, its gaps. Tyrr simply had to construct a spell that worked.

He made the mouth speak the spell's final words as he placed the construct's hands over the bed, palms open and facedown, letting the power of the spell flow to the king. Tyrr bore down, concentrating with all his faculties, letting the incantation do its work.

When the spell was finally spent, he looked down with his own vision, as well as through the eyes of the human construct, and examined the body of Andarys. He saw an utter lack of movement, sensed nothing there at all. A faint excitement began to build inside him, the hope of final victory! Then the king's chest rose, and fell, and rose again.

"No!" Tyrr said out loud, realizing in the same instant that he had done so unconsciously, that he was losing definition—slipping! "Don't let it control you," he said, again out loud, this time on purpose. Rage and frustration could force the quick unraveling of all his carefully adopted constraints and resolutions, could make the construct too real or destroy it altogether.

He saw the door to failure again creeping open before him—a trap, the same trap that had swallowed so many of his kind in ages past, and one he had sworn to outwit! Mild panic swelled within him. He sought to suppress it, to replace it with any sort of calm and confidence. But already he noticed that the body construct he had labored so long to complete was beginning to dematerialize. . . .

"Think," he made the mouth say. *Control*, he told himself. *More thinking is needed, and more control!*

He turned away from the body, then paced the room for a time, diverting the energy of the storm of emotion within him to the walking motion as he had seen humans do. Like shouting, this seemed to help, though he was not quite certain why.

Think!

Finally Tyrr returned to the bedside and looked down.

And there it was! The answer nearly struck him like a blow: try as he might he could not make the king die—this, sadly, was *truth*. The solution, then, was to simply *lie!*

Anna was halfway up the east stairs when a slab of rough stone scuffed her toes, and she realized she'd forgotten her shoes. She hesitated to go back—Lord Ferris would hardly be pleased, no doubt. *Perhaps he and the others will not stay long*, she thought. *I could go and wait near the door for a bit*. And if they didn't come out directly, it could wait until tomorrow.

She went back down the stairs, along one quiet corridor, then turned into the next, nearing the king's chambers. Here she passed by the doors to other chambers unoccupied for a generation, where Hual Andarys had kept family and friends, and finally Madia's room, now empty as well. When she reached Kelren's chamber door, she paused, listening. She heard nothing, so she pressed her ear against the door.

Mumbling drifted through the thick oak, but nothing she could understand. Then she heard something that sounded like grunting. Suddenly she was aware of footsteps echoing faintly, somewhere behind her. She spun about, hurried up the hall, and ducked through the door to Madia's chambers, then pressed the door carefully shut behind her.

She could hear the footsteps clearly as she huddled near the floor: someone passing by the door, stopping at Kelren's chambers. Then a knock, a voice begging entrance, the voice of Ceanlon, the new prelate of Kamrit's Church of the Greater Gods, a priest that had become a close spiritual advisor to Lord Ferris since Kelren had taken so ill.

They have given up hope, Anna thought, feeling the loss in her own heart as the implications forced themselves upon her. Then she heard the chamber door open and close. She waited a moment to be sure no one else was outside the door. When she was satisfied, she slowly pulled the door back a crack. Voices grew suddenly loud as the king's chamber door pulled open. Anna quickly retreated. She could hear Ferris talking to the prelate Ceanlon, and to other men, who made brief, mumbled replies. She couldn't be sure what any of them were saying, though she was certain she did hear the word "body" mentioned twice.

So he is gone, she thought.

As the group moved down the hall, Anna took a breath, then held it, and inched the door back just far enough to get her nose into the opening. She could see Lord Ferris and the prelate moving away. Between them, two serfs carried the body of the king. Anna's heart sank still further. She had wished to be near when death finally came to him, to say her own good-bye. She waited for the party to reach the adjoining corridor at the end of the hall—to turn left toward the west wing of the castle, the way that led to the underground catacombs and vaults, where Kelren's father had been laid to rest. The place where Kelren's body would be prepared.

They reached the intersection and paused, speaking momentarily, then Ferris and the prelate turned west as expected and disappeared around the corner. The serfs and Kelren's body, however, turned the other way, and headed east.

Still in bare feet, Anna padded down the hall, staying well back and out of sight, but close enough to follow the faint echo of scuffling feet ahead. She trailed the serfs through numerous corridors and down two main levels, then down another. She finally stopped when she reached a turn no citizen of Kamrit wished to take. Beyond lay a large open stairway leading down to the castle's oldest, darkest dungeons.

She poked her head around the corner. Only one torch lit the top of the stairwell; the second was missing, taken down the stairs by the serfs. A small table and two chairs stood next to the stairs, a place for the guards—though, as far as Anna knew, only the new dungeons had guards these days. A single soldier stood by the table now.

What for? she wondered. *Here to guard the king's dead body?* But from what? From whom?

Only darkness filled the stairwell beyond. Then she heard footsteps again and saw the helmet of a second guard rising out of the black hole that surrounded the light from his torch. The two serfs followed, empty-handed. Anna felt a chill rake her spine, felt her feet ache, her head beginning to throb. She turned and hurried away.

Chapter VIII

From the knoll, Madia could see most of the town of Kern, a huddle of houses and larger buildings around a single town square, all set in a natural hollow that rose beyond to the horizon's low wooded hills. In the flattest fields on either side of the town, between small wooded lots and rocky mounds, water stood in pools and furrows, the result of three days' near constant cold rain. The weather had turned bad enough to threaten Madia's survival, and she suspected, soaked, weak and shaking as she was, it might yet do the job.

She had slept the first rainy night under a stand of pines, but the water had dripped down and soaked through the ragged tapestries she had brought to cover herself. The next night was better, spent in a tumbled down lean-to; she shared the space with a pair of goats, both female, no doubt from a nearby manor, and their warm milk had been something to savor.

But she had begun to shake sometime late yesterday, a condition that got no better even after walking all day, or after finishing the last of her provisions, trying to gain strength enough to recover. She could not remember ever being so cold; a cold she thought would never leave her bones. The shaking had grown worse this past little while. Her teeth had begun to rattle.

She had no idea what to expect in Kern, whether soldiers from Kamrit or Lencia might be there, whether anyone would recognize her, or help her even if they did. But there was no choice now.

She took a deep breath, waited for the worst of a fresh wave of shuddering to subside, then headed down into town.

The square was open and empty, its booths packed away for the winter months, merchants and peddlers gone to warmer climes or huddled in their houses. But as she examined the signs and markings outside some of the shop doors, she saw some remained yet open: clothier, cartwright, cobbler, smith, candlemaker and a few more. It was better than anything she'd seen in months.

A large inn made mostly of stone stood at the far end of the square, the only inn, so far as Madia could tell. She wiped rain from her face and made her way forward.

As she approached the door, it swung open and two men appeared. Involved in their conversation, they stepped out onto the wooden walk and closed the door behind them, not quite steady on their feet. They looked up and fell silent as they fixed their eyes on Madia. Next they looked to each other, expressions unreadable. Madia's mind whirled; she searched for the knowledge of the other life she had lived, her long experience manipulating men.

They were poorly dressed and groomed and clearly uncaring of the fact, with skin made rough by the elements, the way her own hands had already become. Theirs were large hands, though as one of the men pointed at Madia, she saw that he was missing several fingers. The other man, the heavier of the two, wiped his mouth on his sleeve and squinted in Madia's direction.

They were both tall, both bearded, and hatless. The rain began to wet their balding heads, beading and running off the oil in their dark hair and whiskers. Thieves or unemployed laborers, Madia thought, the two of them drinking the winter months into oblivion. And no women, she guessed, or none that would have them, though such men were quick to feed each of their hungers all the same, when they could.

"I think you are right," the heavier one said, taking one step in Madia's direction, nodding. "She be a woman at that!"

Madia felt herself shake violently as a sudden wave of anxiety—of fatigue wrapped in fear—swept her. Then came a round of fresh chills. She knew she should be gathering words to say, thinking of something to do in case this situation got out of hand, but her mind would not operate and her spirit seemed too drained.

"Not good, but she don't look real bad, either," the one with the missing fingers replied. Madia knew that wasn't true—*not now.*

The bigger one stepped off the wooden walk. "Where you from?" he asked, grinning, displaying a lack of teeth.

"The south," she said, finding speech uncommonly hard. "A village."

"All alone?" Fingers asked, scratching the whiskers on his cheek with just his thumb. "And in such a rain?"

Lies, Madia told herself. *Think of something—*

"I was traveling with my husband, but we were set upon by outlaws and he was killed, three days ago."

"Traveling where?" the large one asked.

"Ahh—here, of course. I—rather, he was a, a—" She tried to recall all the trades she had just counted on her way into town. "A baker," she said. "Do you have one?"

The question gave them pause, then Fingers made a negative shrug. "Well, anyway, we got lots of folk who bake, so it don't matter. Where'd you learn to talk like that?"

Madia felt another shiver, the strength leaving her body; her speech still retained much of what her appearance did not. "Some years ago, I was a servant at Kamrit castle," she said, picking up the same old line.

"Aye, I'll bet, and I was the king's mistress!" Fingers chortled, slapping his friend backhanded. "Now, what else is it you aren't sayin'?"

Madia only stared at them, wishing they would vanish. Wishing she could call the guard and have these two sent to the dungeons or executed.

"Got any coin?" Fingers asked her suddenly.

"No," Madia said. "The robbers took that."

"Lessee just what you got in that sack," the large one said, grinning now, nearly toothless as well. "You don't mind, do you?"

Not again, Madia thought. She could understand the lure of the rich-looking bag she had worn from Kamrit, but the wet sack she carried now was not the least bit appetizing, unless they were just that curious, or bored, or stupid—or all those things.

"Please, let me pass," she said.

The heavier man reached into his coat and drew out a blackened stiletto, then pointed it toward Madia. "When we come to it, dear," he said. His nose began to run; he sniffed fluids back, then swallowed.

Madia remembered the sword on her back. She stepped back, heart pounding as the possibilities settled in her consciousness. She shrugged off her bag and pulled the cord free, then wrestled the blade from its wrappings. The two men faded back just a step, then Fingers began to laugh, and his friend did, too.

"Maybe we oughta get us some help, 'fore she runs us through!" the fat man roared, spreading his arms, holding the stiletto with just his fingertips as if preparing to drop it; Madia didn't think he would. Fingers started moving right, working his way around so as to get behind her while the other man slipped the knife back into his fist and came straight ahead.

Madia swung the blade at the man on her right, forcing him to back away. The bigger man jumped at her, lashing out with the stiletto, apparently aiming for her arm. She reacted just in time, countering with a short and unexpected thrust that found the front of the big man's thigh. He stood back, gaping down as blood soaked his knee and spread down the gray-brown trouser leg. Then he looked at Madia again with a strange, contorted face, and he began to howl.

Madia checked on Fingers, found him standing too close, no smile on his face now. She put two paces between them, but already the big man's stiletto was lashing out again. He was swinging wild, too fast for Madia's battered mind and body to defend against. She fell back, stumbling, parrying his moves by rote, but he began to catch on, anticipating what she might do next. He lunged twice, and the second strike caught her sleeve and tore it nearly off. She thought there was blood, but she couldn't pause to look. When she glanced sideways, she realized she couldn't see Fingers anymore.

A second later he found her, hands grabbing her from behind. The other man straightened, a rain-soaked look of satisfaction spreading over his chunky features. Madia felt exhaustion take her, felt the chills overwhelm her. She slumped back into the smaller man's arms and let him take her weight.

"Have to hurt you for this," Chunky said, pointing to his leg.

"Earned wages," Madia tried to say, the only thing she could throw at him, but she didn't think the words came out.

She heard the door on the inn burst open behind them and looked up to see another man stepping out. Both the men with her turned and looked. He was tall and broad-chested, if a bit round at the middle, and dressed much better than these other two. He wore a sleeveless fur tunic, his face was shaven, the hair coiffed out of his eyes. A handsome man, in fact, despite being early in his fifties if he was a day.

She noticed now that he had a full broadsword sheathed in decorated leather and lashed to his side. She hadn't seen the like since leaving Kamrit Castle.

"Go on back inside, Hoke!" the man holding the stiletto said. "This be none of your affair."

The man they called Hoke simply stood there, silent, arms folded in front of him. Madia suddenly realized he wasn't looking at the two men at all, but was staring straight at her. Then a part of her mind tried to tell her she had heard that name before, sometime long ago, or heard mention of it, though nothing would come clearly to mind.

"Yours, either, I would wager," Hoke replied, looking at them.

"Well, she is goin' with us, you hear!" Fingers said, shouting in Madia's ear. "Just simple fact!"

"Leave her," Hoke said. "You don't need her. She looks half-dead anyway."

"Gonna be all the way dead the way she's actin'," the fat man said, shifting his weight, his leg bleeding worse now. "Just go back to your business."

"You are keeping me from it," Hoke replied. "I say she was headed inside, in need of a meal and a room."

"Never do you no good," Fingers said. "She's a beggar. Got robbed on the road, and her husband killed."

"That so?" Hoke said, surprise in his eyes. "A husband, was it?"

Madia barely realized he was talking to her. She

nodded, then felt the man behind her jerk her once for her efforts.

"Just bring her," the big man said, waving his slender knife toward the near side of the square. The sound of Hoke's sword leaving its scabbard drew everyone's attention. He stepped down and approached Madia and the two men. She noticed he seemed to limp on one leg just as the fat man did, though he was apparently much more used to it.

"Leave her!" he said again, his voice both louder and lower this time. He stood at arm's length from the fat man and brought the tip of his sword into gentle contact with the stiletto, then slowly forced it downward. "Or I will lose at least one customer."

The other man seemed to struggle against the pressure, then he gave up and withdrew. "You are not makin' any friends, Hoke," he said, still holding the knife defensively, though the killing mood had left his eyes.

"Never needed many," Hoke said, then he took another step forward. The man behind Madia let go quickly enough and slid sideways to join his friend, leaving Madia to find her legs again. The two of them stood watching Hoke and Madia, already putting distance between themselves and Hoke as they walked slowly backward. They began mumbling, though not loud enough to hear the words.

"Speak up!" Hoke said, shouting. He stepped toward them at the same time. Both men jumped involuntarily, then turned and hurried off, mumbling all the more.

Madia watched Hoke put his sword away. She felt her legs giving out.

"Thank you," she said, making certain he heard.

Hoke smiled quietly then, as though he'd come to some agreement with himself. "It is my sworn duty," he replied, looking at her.

She swallowed, took a breath. "Your duty?" She felt herself going to her knees. Hoke stepped toward her and slipped his arm around her waist. "I could hardly let them kill the king's own daughter!"

She woke in a soft bed—*a room at the inn*, she thought, in part because Hoke was standing over her bed.

"Is it morning?" she asked. She remembered going inside the inn, and eating soup, and being wrapped in something warm. . . .

"Afternoon," he said. "You missed breakfast and lunch, but you are in plenty of time for dinner. I'll wait for you outside." And with that, he disappeared through the doorway.

She felt like staying in bed a while longer, snug under the warm blankets, but her stomach would not let her, any more than her curiosity. She dressed in the simple, blousey dress she found laid out beside the bed, then found a comb and used it on her hair. When she joined Hoke outside, he led her downstairs to a quiet table at one end of the big room, where the meal was served.

She learned that the clothes had been provided by a woman Hoke introduced as Keara—a woman nearly twice Madia's age, tall and thin, with long dark hair and calm, set features. Keara stuffed Madia full of cooked pork and carrots in a brown gravy, and fresh oat bread, and the best ale Madia had ever tasted. There were two very large stone hearths complete with chimneys at either end of the room, one of them just behind her. Inside a great fire burned, warming her back.

Hoke ate quickly, then went about the room, still limping, speaking to a few of the other guests. He returned just as Madia was finishing. He took to his chair across the table from her, getting the bad leg out from under him first. Keara excused herself and went to fetch more bread and ale, half of which she gave to two younger couples on her way back.

"How would you say she is faring?" Hoke asked Keara after she joined them, nodding at Madia.

"Well enough, considering," Keara said, holding a folded cloth, shaking her head. "One more day out there and nobody could have done her any harm."

"How long were you on the road?" Hoke asked.

Madia felt the remnant of a chill pass up her spine as she thought of that journey. There was much she wanted to put out of her mind, and more she needed to know. She wanted to ask questions, not answer them. "Seven nights, and eight days," she said.

"Keara is right, you know, a lot of folk would never have lasted so long. A traveler's got to have the know-how to pack in weather like this. And strength—plenty of that, certainly. And fortitude. And, I think, sensibility!" Hoke leaned over the table, eyeing Madia as though she might disappear at any moment. "So," he said, "you are a puzzle, because as the Greater Gods are my witness, Princess Madia was never a woman of any such qualities!"

Madia swallowed back a gulp of ale and nearly choked on it. "Oh," she said, nose down. "You knew her?"

"I knew *you*," Hoke replied. "When you were much younger.

"I . . . see." Madia looked up and sat still a moment, trying to read the man's dark eyes. "Who are you?" she asked directly.

"Hoke."

"I know that, but why does your name sound familiar?"

"I was captain in your father's royal guard and fought beside him in the Voller uprisings before you were born. I used to tickle your sides when you were just a small girl." Madia found vague memories stirring, becoming clearer. As she recalled her history lessons, the Voller wars arose when a small number of Ariman's eastern coastal fiefs, led by Baron Voller, had challenged the rights of the crown. In the final battle, King Andarys had been captured by a raiding party led by the baron himself, then held for ransom. But a small, outnumbered band of Andarys' finest knights from the royal guard overran and defeated the kidnappers almost at once, and the king had escaped unharmed. Baron Voller, however, had not survived, along with most of his men.

"I have been told of this," Madia said. "You are the captain who led the rescue attempt?"

"The same."

"But he was badly wounded," Keara said, glancing back at the handful of others seated about the room, then sitting herself down as well. "Nearly lost his leg."

"That was twenty years ago," Madia said. Her eyes strayed toward the leg, but the table blocked her view. "It never mended?"

Hoke shrugged. "Well enough. But I'm not much good in a fight."

"I would never say that," Keara disagreed, scowling at Hoke. He shrugged again.

"I lack agility," he said.

Keara made a face. "Yes, but there is something to be said for skill. He was the finest swordsman in all Ariman in his day, mentor to all the great knights."

"It is true," Madia said, more of her lessons coming back to her now. "That is just how it was told to me. You became a great hero."

"I became a burden, kept on because of your father's charity."

"It was gratitude," Keara corrected, looking at Madia, ignoring Hoke now. "And *need*. Your father put Hoke to work training the best of the many young men-at-arms that came to his service. And every man was grateful."

"Why aren't you still there?" Madia asked. "I can assure you that there is lately a great need for competent instructors."

"My own decision. I was not . . . comfortable. Your father offered me a small fief near Haven, but I never fancied myself a baron."

"So he offered money instead, and Hoke bought the inn and settled here," Keara finished for him. "Which most of Kern has long been pleased about, especially me, though I should never let him hear as much." She rolled her eyes at Hoke. He rolled his eyes back at her, and Madia could see something of the strength and spirit between them.

"You are husband and wife?" Madia asked, certain of the answer. But both of them began to laugh.

"No," Hoke said, still chuckling. "Though we nearly were, quite some years ago, when we still both lived in Kamrit. Her husband was my dear friend, as was she. He was with me when we rode to rescue our king. He did not survive."

"Hoke has looked after me," Keara said. She reached toward him and put her hand on his. "We were something like lovers for a time."

Hoke looked at her, a brief expression Keara seemed to recognize. "He still looks after me," she added.

"It is the other way around," Hoke said, pulling free of her. "My own mother did not watch me so well."

"Stop your lies," Keara scolded. "Or I'll have you limping on both legs!"

Hoke laughed again. Madia suspected that it was not the first time Keara had made that threat. They were like the people she had met in the villages, Madia thought, working together whenever they had to, finding humor at the edges of pain, but they were a little like her, too, as no one she had met since leaving Kamrit had been.

"I am grateful to both of you," Madia said.

"Gratitude is also not a quality of the little princess I knew," Hoke said. "The girl I've heard much about in recent years. 'Please and thank you,' and all—I don't know. In fact, the girl I recall had almost no good qualities at all. I would have let those men outside do what they would with that girl—if she were not her father's daughter. No, I'd say getting killed has had a profound effect on you."

"I was *almost* killed," Madia said, then she told him about the knight on foot from Kamrit, the others on mounts from Bouren, even about the villages she had lived in. Both Hoke and Keara listened intently, their eyes fast upon her, until she told them of the last village she had visited, and the news of her father's illness.

"You do not know, do you child?" Keara said, looking at Hoke as she did.

"Know what?"

Hoke leaned over and reached one large hand across the table, beckoning, then waited until Madia gave him hers.

"Your father is dead."

"I swear," Hoke said, when Madia had recovered enough to call him a liar, then to tell him that it was impossible.

"It is true," Keara said.

"I am certain of it," Hoke continued. "I still have many friends in Kamrit, many inside the castle itself. Word comes to me, and the same story is told by everyone. It was the illness, as you say, though some of my friends believe his illness was not natural. They have no proof of treachery, nor any clear motives. But in all the years I served him, Kelren Andarys was never ill. And now we know someone tried to kill you, though the murder of the king, like your own, is a difficult thing to understand and a harder thing to prove.

"I do not believe for a moment that your father sent one of his own men to kill or kidnap you on the road, and I am not alone. He loved you, Madia. No matter how badly you hurt him, he would never have hurt you."

"Yet he did!" Madia said, though she felt sure of nothing just now. She remembered Anna's last words to her outside the gate—remembered, too, her own words to Anna, and she wondered if anything had been the way it had seemed that day.

"You must know it's true," Hoke went on. "I'll wager your father intended to have you collected and returned after a time. More than likely, the foot soldier was someone sent to protect you, or simply to keep watch and send back word about you."

"Then he failed," Madia muttered.

"Apparently," Hoke granted her. "Poor bastard."

"Perhaps," Madia said, thinking of the soldier as protector for the first time, remembering his rush toward her—and her attackers.

"Truly, I find it at least as hard to believe that Lord Ivran would send Bouren soldiers into southern Ariman to kill Andarys' daughter," Hoke added. "Those two men have been allies for many years, and good friends."

"Someone did," Madia answered, still trying to cope with too much grim information. "They may have been renegades. Does Lencia often hire mercenaries?"

"Not many, if at all. They have never needed to."

"But it is a safe guess that if someone did have a hand in your father's death, they may also have tried to do away with you," Keara said. "To keep you from claiming any right to the throne."

"For the time being, it seems, Grand Chamberlain Ferris has taken control of the kingdom," Hoke explained.

"So I have heard," Madia said. "I was never fond of him, though he did not seem especially dangerous."

"Some obviously suspect him. Many at court have mistrusted him for a very long time. He speaks constantly of war and building Ariman's armies, and since the king's death he is going about it, calling for homage and raising taxes and tolls, in part to pay for his mercenaries. He insists there is a threat from the great northern fiefs, yet I see none.

"There is vague talk of unrest among the desert tribes far south of Neleva as well, but it is only talk, I think."

Hoke paused, eyeing Madia from a fresh angle. "Did you ever hear from Jaffic?" he asked.

"No," Madia answered. "Not in a year."

"Men have been sent to find him, then. They came through here a week past, men-at-arms, none I knew well. They were headed upland, but none would say for certain what they were about."

"They think he is dead," Madia said, finding the words difficult, her mouth growing stiff. "My father must have thought I was dead, too, didn't he?"

Hoke looked at her with eyes too dark to fathom. "Yes," he said. "He must have, as everyone does."

"He never knew," she said, feeling something intangible slip from under her, feeling her spirit slip with it. "He thought he sent me to my death. He would have blamed himself, I am sure of it. I never wanted to believe he would abandon me, not completely, not even after all that I did to him. But he died never knowing that, either."

"What you did," Hoke corrected her, his voice resolute, "was completely abandon him. You humiliated him. You cast doubt among his people over his ability to rule. It is hard to bear such an insult from one's own daughter. Both of you became a joke that was laughed at in every corner of Ariman."

"I know," Madia said, dropping all rhetoric, seeing no point. She had learned enough, talking to villagers and travelers, to make her believe that her father would have been justified if he truly had wanted her dead or taken away, simply to be rid of the stench of her. She simply hadn't bothered to realize what she had done!

"It's all right to cry," Keara said, and Madia realized her cheeks had grown wet.

"I—I did love him, you know, I just—"

"The young are prone to error," Keara said. "It is good you can see that you have made a few."

"A few?" Hoke said, and Madia felt renewed guilt welling up inside her. Hoke fixed her with a cold stare. "Kelren died never knowing you truly felt anything for him, and you allowed it. If you had been the daughter your father deserved you would have been there to help him in his time of need, instead of adding to his afflictions. He would not have died believing that you had betrayed him, or that he had betrayed you. And if there was a conspiracy, you might have been able to save him from it. Or perhaps he died of remorse!"

Madia dropped her head onto her forearms and began to weep out loud, the tears of many weeks, of many years, suddenly coming out all at once. She had no strength to stop it.

"Easy on the girl," Keara told Hoke. "She has suffered, or are you too blind to notice?"

"No, it is true," Madia sobbed, lifting her face. "I would have watched him, seen his illness progress. I might have suspected, if something were wrong. Everyone at court would have been suspect!"

"You cannot say what might have been," Keara told her. "She is right," Hoke said. "She might have saved him. But think of this, girl. If someone is indeed behind these things, and if you had stayed, they would have had you killed as well. You'd be no good to anyone! Perhaps it's someone plotting with one of Lord Ivran's disenchanted vassals, who in turn may have sent men to find you. There are many possibilities. The banishment might simply have provided them an unexpected opportunity, although—"

He paused for a moment, scratching his chin. "Although, they must already have been in Ariman. Bouren soldiers in Bouren could not have learned of your banishment and then made such a journey in so short a time." He paused again, still considering. "No, that doesn't quite fit. On the other hand, your father—"

"Hoke!" Madia shouted, feeling the grief welling up inside her—too much emotion crushing down on her all at once. "Don't you see? I might have saved us both. And even if someone had killed me, too, I would have been there for him—*with* him. We would have faced death together. If I had listened and never forced his hand, I would have been there. He would have known I cared. *I* would have known. My father would not have died blaming himself!"

She realized she was shaking again, the way she had been yesterday outside in the cold and drizzle. She saw her father more clearly now than she ever had, and for the first time in many years she missed him—terribly. She felt she had finally found something of him, of herself, and then lost it again all in the space of minutes. Or a lifetime.

It felt awful, like nothing she could ever recall. She needed to do something soon, because she couldn't bear to just sit there. Wiping her face on her sleeve, taking a breath, Madia tried to compose herself. She could do nothing about the past, but the future was a different matter.

"I have to find out," she said. "I still want to know who tried to kill me and why. And I need to know more of my father's death. I must have justice, Hoke; what else is left to me? I must return," she finished, "to Kamrit, to my home."

"You'll go nowhere till spring," Keara corrected. "You must know that."

"She is right," Hoke said. "I'll just have to keep you here, let you help out a little around the place, maybe even teach you a little more humility, if I can."

"I *am* learning," Madia grumbled, making a face, though fatigue was entering her voice, the heat of the past few minutes cooling quickly now.

"Then you'd best give consent to the idea," Keara remarked. "And you may take time to consider your plans. Don't forget you are an heir to your father's throne, even if you are a ghost. Kelren's murderers will yet become yours, and they will doubtless try to do more permanent work next time."

"Whatever your plans, you'll need to know much more than you do now," Hoke added. "And you will need friends, *my* friends, to help if you are going to do any good. Only a miracle of the Greater Gods could get you anywhere near the throne again, I think, and I doubt even miracles could keep you there. I know you want revenge, Madia, but it may not be possible. And I fear you could never be queen, even if you desire it. Your name does not inspire loyalty."

Madia stared at him, unable to respond. She had never wanted to be queen, and she had not realized that this was what her own words had just implied, not until Hoke put it that way. *You could have been queen,* she thought. Jaffic had never been her father's first choice; he was just the only choice they could both agree on. But like her father's love, she had thrown her inheritance away as well.

She felt her muscles grow hard. She made a fist on the table, a vague attempt to redirect the tension and the anger building within her. She did not want to believe it was all so hopeless. She could not. And yet. . . .

"I don't know what I can do, but I will try," she said." I can think for myself, and I can fight."

"Not from what I have seen," Hoke declared, sitting back in his chair. Madia found him grinning.

"I was rather tired when I arrived here," she said evenly.

"As you wish," Hoke said.

Madia nearly spit. "I have taken lessons from some of the best swordsman in all Ariman. I have learned—"

"Very little, I would say." Hoke chuckled.

"Perhaps she has not had the *right* teacher," Keara said, looking at Hoke with big round eyes. His grin began to fade.

Madia eyed them both. "The finest my father could find," she said.

"Some are finer than others," Keara replied.

"Then," Madia said, growing somewhat annoyed, "perhaps you might know of someone . . . qualified?"

Keara stared at Hoke. "I don't do that anymore," Hoke said, beginning to fidget in his seat.

"For her, you will," Keara told him. "You know it."

"I don't need him," said Madia. "I truly can fight."

"Not as he can teach you, girl."

Keara held Madia with her gaze; this was something she knew, Madia saw, the way the peasants in the villages knew when to plant their gardens, or when a new calf was due—something to be believed.

"Perhaps—I need you to make me even better," Madia told Hoke.

"If anyone can," Keara said, "he can."

Hoke scowled deeply at them both. "She'll still only get herself killed. You're not the leader your father or his father was. You will need to gather both the truth and the men to listen to you tell it, men who will get behind you, and neither will come easily. Not by a long way! It takes more than a little of the king's blood and some battle skills to lead an army, to lead Ariman, dear princess." Hoke shook his head. "Much more."

"The whole kingdom cannot be against me," Madia

said. "There must be a way to reach them—your friends and others like them."

"First, there must be something to convince them *with*."

"I will find it."

"And some means to make them accept you."

"I will find that, too."

"Forgive me if I harbor a bit of doubt."

"Well, then, I must begin with you, Hoke. You said I was not the same girl you remembered," Madia offered. "Truly, I am not."

"We have until spring," Keara said then, shrugging her shoulders. "To learn of warriors, of leaders, and much more."

Hoke drummed his fingers, scowled.

"Please," Madia said, adding a faint sniffle as she did. "Help me."

Hoke made a groaning sound somewhere deep in his throat.

Keara turned to Madia and smiled, just barely, and Madia knew that it would be so.

Chapter IX

Warm sun shone on the muddy seas that were Urid's pastures. Ripe buds hung fat and heavy on the tips of tree limbs and shrubbery. The road was already drying up. In another week, maybe two, the land would be ready, and Urid would begin to clear and plow and sow. All very hard work, Frost rather imagined. It was time to go.

The little manor house had been a fine enough home, and Urid and his children had served as good hosts, but they were people of minimal inspiration and endeavor, and their best efforts to entertain Frost and his Subartans had only bridged a small part of the long winter's seasonal gap. Frost had largely resisted the urge to toy with these folk, though there had been a slip or two.

Nothing serious, no more than a bit of mayhem with items set down here, only to turn up there, or a dab of illusion, allowing Urid to get up one morning and find wolves asleep in his children's beds—but if he stayed much longer, temptation might finally overcome him. And he liked these people too much for that. Urid, for all his limitations, was a man quick to humor and slow to judgment, as were his children; traits Frost could not discount.

Frost waited as his three Subartans came out of the house and joined him, standing just behind him, basking in the bright sun and sniffing at the sweet spring air. Then Rosivok leaned to Frost's ear. "This day?" he asked.

"Yes," Frost told him. "A clear sky, a clear road, a clear mind! And I have checked what must be a mulberry tree, there, across the road, and there are plenty of small sprigs on its branches—a sign that another freeze will not come. I think . . . Go, and gather what we will need." He reached inside the heavy, full tunic he wore, fishing about, then pulled out his hand and gave Rosivok a few gold coins. "And give these to Urid. His long hospitality is payment enough for my services."

Rosivok nodded, then turned to Jaffic and Sharryl, and the three of them headed toward the storage sheds at the back of the house. Urid came out next, just as Frost was heading back inside. He watched the Subartans disappear around the corner, then he looked at Frost; a question was in his eyes.

"Yes," Frost said. "We are leaving."

"Be careful on your way, then," Urid said. "Watch for signs of changes. It has been a long winter."

"The omens appear favorable," *so far as I can tell,* Frost thought.

"There is already a bad omen," Urid said.

"You mean King Andarys' death," Frost replied.

"No, another."

"Very well," Frost said grimly, "though it does not seem fitting that any small darkness should tarnish such a bright day." He hated to ask: "What omen, my friend?"

"I burned the bay leaves this morning," Urid explained, referring to the bay branch he had cut and placed over the hearth in the fall, to ward off disease.

"And the leaves crackle?" Frost asked; this was an ancient practice he knew.

"Yes, loudly," Urid said. "A very bad omen, indeed!"

"I thought that no crackle was bad, and crackling was good." He *thought* he knew the practice.

"I do not think so," Urid replied, though he seemed to quickly lose himself in careful reflection of this. Then he looked up, and shrugged. "My wife knew such things," he said, "but alas, she is gone."

"A pity," Frost replied, shrugging in kind. There were more rumors, of course, from Urid's neighbors and a traveler that had stopped in need of shelter for a night. All spoke of the changes already occurring everywhere in Ariman, especially since the rumors of Kelren Andarys' passing: new laws and tariffs, new taxes, new tolls, and soldiers, a growing number of them showing up almost everywhere, and people growing uneasy.

Nearly cause for worry, whatever the leaves might mean. . . . Still, he had no more patience for this place, and since the news about Andarys, Jaffic had begun asking after their departure nearly every day. He seemed different, moody, in his way, and quite preoccupied. Unfortunate qualities for a Subartan in Frost's service, whatever the cause.

"I must go," Frost said. "The trip to Neleva should prove extremely profitable, and the only way I know to get there is through Ariman. And while I knew his father, I didn't know *this* Andarys very well, so I will personally miss him very little. Ariman, I trust, will suffer more. I have an interest in the well being and prosperity of the realm, of course. Perhaps I will pay a call to this Ferris fellow just to introduce myself. So rich a sovereign should be aware of services I might be persuaded to render."

Urid smiled, used to this by now. Frost smiled back.

"Come in when you are done," Urid said, "and we will have a good breakfast to start you on your way."

Frost paused and glanced downward, assessing his considerable girth. He had kept to his exercises, lifting every available object he could find in Urid's house, and walking in the nearby hills whenever weather allowed. He had retained the power and endurance such a big frame demanded. But he'd eaten well enough through the winter months, *very well,* he thought, patting his belly with one wide-spread hand.

No matter, he thought—*it is bad luck to take up a long journey on an empty stomach—or it should be.* He grinned and nodded to his host.

"I'll have Aul go tell the others," Urid said, and started back inside. Frost lingered, thinking of the opportunities that awaited him in the lands to the south, of how lackadaisical he and his Subartans had become, staying in this place these past many months. The idea felt complete in his mind. He was eager for the road.

After two days travel, following the twists and turns of the upper Saris River, they reached the edge of the Ikaydin Plateau. Below, at the bottom of a tumbled-down wall of earth and rock that rose more than four thousand feet and stretched to both horizons, lay Bouren. Here the Saris cut a deep gash in the escarpment and broke into great waterfalls, then dark pools. Frost stood looking out into the distance, and saw the first green traces of spring spreading across the rich forests and pastures that ran to meet the horizon. This sight had not changed over the years; he did not expect it ever would.

The weather was holding warm, even during a light rain the day before. A good omen, Frost thought, ascribing that much less to chance. He followed the worn, easy trails that wandered down along with the river and joined the main trade road, then took the road for another day, until finally they arrived in Lencia.

He had not seen the city in more than a decade, but it too had not changed notably. A fine city, in fact, large enough to accommodate most of the major trade and merchant guilds and a healthy central marketplace, even a winery, though imported goods were often few and dear.

The market was open as they strolled through the main square, so Frost took time to browse a few of the stalls along the way, while his Subartans kept a careful watch on the crowd. Frost purchased a finely tailored silk shirt, then encouraged his Subartans to each get one of the same.

"Very well," Sharryl said, the only one to do so, and chose a rose blouse with white lace trim at the sleeve openings and collar. She used the serrated edge of her subarta to cut the threads and free the lace, and gave it back to the merchant. "It is fine this way," she told the vendor, and tucked the blouse away.

Frost nodded approval. Subartans were seldom vain; in fact, Frost was amused to see her purchase anything so feminine at all.

They continued to the south of the city, toward the only high ground the region had to offer, until they arrived at the massive walls of the castle of Lord Jurdef Ivran, King of Bouren at Lencia. A fine and gregarious man, Frost recalled, strong of mind and principles, a man who had seen to the well-being of Bouren in every detail, and one who believed he would not live long enough to repay the debt his father before him owed to the wizard Frost. In truth, Frost saw no debt outstanding; those times had been too long ago and he had been compensated in kind even then. Nevertheless, the young king's enduring hospitality was not to be refused.

They arrived inside the walls late in the afternoon. The castle seneschal was eventually brought to greet the new visitors, then he went off again to formally announce their presence. He returned directly, and led them to a great dining hall, just in time for the evening meal.

"A proper feast!" Frost proclaimed, famished from his journey, eyeing the roast fowl and breads and bean dishes being set about the massive table.

"I would serve no less to such honorable guests," Lord Ivran said, entering at the other end of the room. He was a dark-bearded, prosperous looking man of proportions similar to Frost's, though not quite so tall, and without so much of the hard muscle Frost maintained beneath his own extra padding.

He sat at the head of the table, directing Frost and his three Subartans to come and sit with him. There were nearly a dozen others present: noblemen and ladies, members of the royal court. Squires scrambled to bring a few extra chairs to accommodate their displaced lords—who in turn seemed to find little humor in the arrangement.

One young lord in particular, a fair-sized, well-groomed man dressed in the finest velour and silks was forced to sit at the table's farthest end. He stood beside his chair, staring at the king and his guests. "Tell me," he asked the king after a time, loudly and clearly. "If those at the head of the table deserve the greatest honor, what manner of dishonor is it to be placed at the other end?"

Ivran looked up, sized up the situation and burst out with a rolling laugh, as did the others at the head of the table. The young lord barely smiled, then sobered, as did the king. Frost, however, could not stop so quickly. The lord at the far end began to frown, then frowned still harder as Frost abruptly found this new expression quite humorous as well and made mention of the fact.

"I take offense, sir!" the Lord replied, his face grown suddenly stern, his lips pursed. He moved as if to draw his sword—purely theatrics, Frost knew, but the three Subartans rose in a single motion, gleaming blades all poised. The young lord quickly stayed his hand and then stood still, no doubt reviewing the situation.

"His threats are as empty as my stomach," Frost told the three warriors. "We cannot kill the king's only son over poor humor, after all."

"At least not during dinner!," Lord Ivran said, exchanging glances with the younger man. Now the Subartans seemed to ease just slightly.

"The prince?" Rosivok asked.

"He is," Jurdef Ivran replied, "my son, Prince Jaran."

Frost leaned toward the king. "You must understand, I haven't had such simple fun in months," he confided. "I trust the prince will recover."

Jurdef nodded, then shook his head and smiled.

Two women brought wine and ale to the table. Jurdef sipped at each, chose the wine, choosing for all, and then began filling his plate. Everyone else immediately followed.

"You look much larger than I remember you," Frost said, when the meal had progressed to a more leisurely pace.

"I was a young man, hardly older than Jaran," Jurdef replied. "And you are every bit as robust as I remember you."

"I spent this past season well," Frost said. He finished his meal and took extra bread, then began eyeing the milk pudding being set about. "It appears Bouren is prosperous these days," he went on. "From all that I see and hear, you have done well."

"It is easy. Bouren is the kind of land that does well on its own when its king has the sense to let it. And I have the sense! Bouren and I take excellent care of each other."

Frost smiled, raised his wine in a salute.

"I know you travel for profit," Jurdef said after that, swishing a bit of wine in his own mouth, swallowing. "So it interests me to know who in Bouren would require the aid of such a talented and expensive sorcerer."

Frost briefly chuckled. "No one. I go to Neleva." Frost told Ivran of the messenger, the offer he'd received. "Glister is still the richest city in this part of the world," he added, "and one of the most interesting."

"You have heard of the changes in Ariman?"

"Some. Not much since rumors of King Andarys' death and apparent succession by the grand chamberlain. Some new tolls, I've been warned, and more soldiers."

"Many more of both, my friend. And the king's death is no rumor, it is so."

"You are sure?" Jaffic asked, a look of darkness on his face that Frost found almost profound.

"I am," Jurdef said. "As I am sure of the problems Lord Ferris creates. He has increased each tax and added new ones, all to build his armies, as far as I can say. Armies to march against me, perhaps, though I have no idea why."

"It is strange," Rosivok said, finishing his own meal. "If Ferris seeks to conquer, Neleva is the prize in the region. There is no wealth here that Ariman does not already possess, and to war with allies serves no purpose."

"All things I have considered," Jurdef said.

"Unless Ferris fears the great lords of the north might march against him if he attacks Neleva." The voice was that of Prince Jaran. He got up and moved around to stand just behind Jaffic. His father motioned him forward, and he continued to the head of the table.

"That is my son's idea on the matter, and one I endorse. Kelren Andarys kept fair trade flowing to and from the southern seas, just as his father did before him, but with someone else sitting on the throne, this trade is threatened. Ferris could use his new armies to conquer Neleva, then strangle Vardale, Jasnok, Thorun, and

Bouren. Even Ikaydin relies on the southern routes for many things. If Ferris believes we might oppose such a plan, he is right."

"He can raise prices in the meantime, until we cannot afford what we need," Jaran said. "All while he prepares for a move against us. He would get richer, we poorer."

"There are rumors that you are already plotting against him," Frost said. "That in fact the great lords of the north were plotting against King Andarys before, and will now be all the more eager."

"Lies!" Jaran snapped. "Spread by those who would see Bouren diminished. They try to fill the heads of all the nobles of Ariman with fears and distrust, with ideas of war. We have no designs on Ariman, nor have the other three great lords. We've each kept our loyalties to that crown—within reason."

"But we are not dealing with reasonable men," Jurdef said. "The meeting of the Grand Council in June has already been postponed. New troops are training daily. And we hear tell of dark rituals in the city of Kamrit itself."

"Rituals?" Jaffic asked.

The young prince looked at him carefully before he went on.

"Yes," he said, "the work of a new fellowship, one that is gaining power there, feared by most, yet some say they are sanctioned by the crown."

"My men report that the roads and towns of Ariman are already busy with soldiers this spring, and the prisons are near full with anyone who would raise objections," Lord Ivran said, frowning, the darkest expression he had yet made. "They have even dared to ride on Bouren soil."

"An army?" Rosivok asked.

"A few squads," Prince Jaran replied. "People have seen them along our southern border, riding the western edge of Golemesk Swamp, entering it from time to time. We have no garrison in the region, and there have been no incidents, at least none that we know of, so we have not yet tried to oppose them."

"I have never known an army to take such interest in another lord's swamp," Sharryl said, again entering the dialogue. "Golemesk has no strategic value."

"It is centrally located," Jaffic said, apparently quite familiar with the subject. "Parts of the swamp lie in all five lands."

"But so much of the area is impassable," Jaran explained. "And much of it is unexplored. And there are dangers there from bandits and leshys and worse. Few men enter far, and fewer return."

"They ride the swamp in search of the Demon Blade," Lord Ivran said, taking a spoonful of pudding as Frost passed it to him, filling his bowl. He passed the pot to the others. "Rumors abound. They say the Blade rests there."

"So I have heard," Frost said. "But Ramins, an old wizard, still has the Blade, and even I don't know where he lives these days."

"He has died," Jurdef said. "Or so they say. Hunters claim they found a man's body on the edge of the swamp, carefully laid out—a very old man in strange robes, his hands folded over a staff carved of white birch. The villagers gave him a proper burial. Some there claimed that the body was that of the wizard who kept the Blade, and that the leshys must have left him there to be found."

"Where is this staff now?" Frost asked.

The king shrugged. "Sold, or buried with him, perhaps."

"There are many old men in the swamps and forests, my friends, and villagers are known for their love of embellishment," Frost replied, shaking his head slowly, wrinkling his nose just a bit. "Every tale becomes legend on their lips. But you can be sure that if it *was* Ramins, and he died in the swamps, then the leshys have the Blade. They've always had a fascination with weapons, especially with blades, as well as a keen sense of magical properties.

"But I must insist that Ramins would have sensed his time approaching, come out of hiding, and given the blade into another wizard's keeping, the one chosen, picked by Ramins and the council ages ago, when the Blade was given to him. And news of that would have reached me. I say the body was not his."

"Still," Jaran said, at ease now, "even the chance that the Blade is there, and that it might fall into the hands of our enemies—"

"That chance has existed for centuries," Frost said, shaking his head again. "As have rumors of the Blade's whereabouts and the health of the wizard who holds it. Any army would welcome the chance to possess the Demon Blade, but none know of its secrets, even I do not, and great care and sacrifice has been given to insure that none will. If I were you, I would worry more about the soldiers themselves than what they might find in the depths of Golemesk—those that return, of course."

Frost finished his pudding and decided he was growing tired of the banter already. He loved to visit with most acquaintances, and especially to dine with them, but when the meal was through, he very much liked to go about his own business and be done with theirs. Usually they understood, and if they did not, there were many ways to encourage a more sympathetic attitude in the future. He grinned quietly at the thought.

"Tell me, Frost," Jaran said, "why we should place any value on your advice? These are not your lands, your people. You have no stake in any of this and every reason to want the Demon Blade for yourself."

All three Subartans tensed just noticeably.

"It is all right, Jaffic," Frost said, smiling at the young sovereign, who stood so straight and bold. "This is a question, not an insult, if I read him right."

"You do," said the prince.

"Quarrels between barons are not really his concern," Lord Ivran told his son, putting a hand up to a ask for pause. "Unless he is directly requisitioned by one side or another. And even then, only if he likes the paying side. I know of a time decades ago, a story your grandfather told, of the mountain wars far to the north of the Spartooths. Frost had been offered a fortune to engage in a battle between armies, until he found that the emperor who had called him was mad, a man who took pleasure in torturing to death the young women of those villages he conquered while the children and old ones watched; the emperor's armies were slaughtering mostly peasants defending their homes. Frost turned against the emperor and took no payment from anyone. I've never told the boy the old stories, I'm afraid," Ivran added, turning to Frost, smiling. "He has grown up so fast."

"Well, it is never too late!" Frost said, then he leaned back and belched. "Go on and tell him more!" He looked to the king, and the both of them broke into laughter.

"Tell me, how are you planing to continue?" the king asked in a moment, a look of concern growing on his face, mild yet unmistakable.

"How would you recommend?" Frost asked.

"By road along the Saris to Kopeth, of course. Most take a barge the rest of the way to Kamrit, then the coastal road through Neleva to Glister. But you can turn west at the little town of Chelle, where the river forks just north of Kamrit. There is a road to the coast there, and passage by boat from Lina or Riale. I can send a few men with you, if you need them. They'll know the way, and know their swords."

Frost nodded in deference to the king, then shook his head. He disliked travel by sea almost as much as he disliked famines, and there were good omens for the journey he had begun: an aura had been seen around the setting sun these past two nights, and the pattern cast by the handful of tiny stones given to him by a magic man from the deserts, many years ago—although, he had largely forgotten how to read the stones, and had even lost a few, and it was possible that an aura at sunset had something to do with rain, after all. . . .

Then again, omens, as far as Frost was concerned, could mean different things to different people.

"We *must* go to Kamrit," Jaffic said, leaning toward Frost, wearing a face so serious the wizard thought the young warrior might never smile again. Frost smiled for him.

"A generous offer, dear Jurdef, but I have protection enough," he said. "The road will be kind to us. And I rather like the idea of a visit to Kamrit!" He looked again at Jaffic. "With so much mystery in the air, so much going on, I'd never forgive myself if I didn't go by for a look."

"Will you hire a rider and send word back of goings-on?" Prince Jaran asked, stepping back as Frost got up.

"No doubt," Frost replied.

"There will be those who know you in that city," the Lord Ivran cautioned. "Some who still may wish they never had."

"It has been a very long time," Frost said. "But few men are without enemies, my friend." Frost grinned, glancing first at Jaran, then his father. They only stared back.

"Dear lords," he added, "if any man chooses to battle me, even the grand chamberlain himself, I will send his head to you along with my messenger. That should put you both at ease."

"You will need supplies, perhaps a pack animal," Lord

Ivran said, hatching a warm, hearty smile. "I'll see to it. And may the Greater Gods go with you!"

"In their way," Frost replied, "they no doubt will."

The seneschal showed them to their rooms. Each had fine beds covered in silks and sequestered by thick draperies. In the morning they ate heartily and bid their farewells, then took to the river road again. By the end of the day they had crossed the border into Ariman.

Chapter X

Madia came through the door shaking the brisk chill of the late April afternoon from between her shoulders. She spotted Hoke halfway across the room doing his fast hobble, getting to one of the tables. He stood and began pouring from a tall earthenware flagon, filling tankards with ale. Three young men, flashy travelers apparently just off the road, took up the mugs and drank deeply.

Hoke seemed to linger a moment, considering them more closely now, as Madia then did. She saw the clouded, brooding look of a November day in their nervous eyes, and too many lines on their young faces. Highborn, one might think, taking them at a glance, since they were dressed as noblemen: fine boots, white shirts, short tunics of leather and fur, and unusually fine swords and scabbards dangling to their heels, with hilts carved in rare detail, imported workmanship from the ports of Neleva. But there was nothing so noble in their deportment or their faces, or their speech—which was clearly audible above the subtle voices of the inn's other patrons.

They had not been men of such means for long, Madia decided, though they may well have come upon such men quite recently, from behind. . . .

The spring market fair was to begin the day after tomorrow, and already Kern had begun to fill with all manner of folk. Soldiers were on hand in unusual numbers, along with a few visiting men-at-arms, and merchants and pilgrims from Vardale and Thorun, Jasnok and Bouren, and even parts of Ikaydin were growing plentiful. But no amount of troops could guarantee a traveler's safety.

The roads were filled with hazards these days, with so many citizens—lords and freemen, peasants and beggars alike—falling on hard times under the weight of new taxes and the conscription of sons and husbands. The number of bandits had increased dramatically. Perilous times for all, Madia knew—and even the most perilous of folk were known to take ale like everybody else.

Madia saw the look in Hoke's eye—acute, restless. He stepped back cautiously, still watching the three, with no awareness of the rest of the room; Madia didn't think he'd seen her enter. *Though he may have,* she thought after that. *If he was concerned there might be trouble, he would purposely avoid drawing attention to me. . . .*

One of the travelers, the tallest one, wearing long hair and a painted leather hat, stood up suddenly and took off the hat, then used it in a motion directed at Keara, who had the misfortune to be passing nearby at that moment. When she didn't slow, the man tossed his hat at her. When this finally caught her attention, he stepped forward and reached out, grabbing Keara's arm.

"Surely you have a moment to talk," the man said. His two companions grinned as they looked on, both of them examining his catch. Then one of them, the shorter, stockier man, stood up in support of his friend. He seemed to eye the coins on Keara's tray.

"No, thank you," Keara said, bowing her head, forcing a smile. She tried to move away, but the hand held firm. The shorter man moved around to block her intended path, chuckling to the others. Madia recalled the two men who had greeted her outside the inn half a year ago; the same sort of men or worse, she thought, though now some things had changed. She touched her palm to the hilt of the long sword Hoke had given her, felt the now familiar shape as she slowly wrapped her hand around it. She watched Hoke step forward.

"Right!" Hoke shouted. "That'll be enough of that. Let the lady be. You go on to your tasks," he told Keara. The third man, stout in a brutelike manner, wearing a full beard and grayish cloak, abruptly rose and pulled out his sword, and pointed the tip in Hoke's direction.

"She's your daughter, then?" he asked, grinning with a mouthful of darkened teeth. Hoke made no sound. "Or maybe your wife?" the man prodded. He sidled away from the table, extending the sword to within an easy thrust of Hoke's chest. After a moment he drew back slightly, grinned again. He leaned over without looking and picked his tankard up off the table with his free hand.

"If she's not, then she's not worth dyin' for, is she? So you'd be wise just to keep your say and be about your own tasks. We'll give 'er back." He drank back briefly then set the tankard down, but he kept his eyes on Hoke.

"Let me be," Keara said, neither fear nor daring in her tone. "Do as the innkeeper says."

"She works for me," Hoke explained, controlling his voice, at least temporarily, Madia thought. Patience had long been one of Hoke's hallmark qualities, though he did not possess it in endless abundance. During the long winter months, Hoke had shown her many things, how to fight, and when, but also he had helped her to hone her knowledge of the hearts of men, and to read more in the messages people constantly delivered in a hundred different ways. Such men as these saw only something for themselves in the lives of others. Madia held no hope of a peaceful end to this.

The short one glanced about, surveying the inn, people standing still or sitting motionless at their tables. He seemed to find nothing to cause him worry. He turned back to the others. "Sure she works for you, when she's done workin' for us," he said, cackling in self-amusement.

"No, that won't do," Hoke said.

One of the men mumbled something, then all of them laughed. The man pointing his blade at Hoke and bore forward again. "You don't feel like livin', do you inn-keeper?" he said. "Maybe another bad leg could change your tone?" He waved the blade toward Hoke's feet, then pressed it into the white linen of Hoke's blouse.

"That threat doesn't work on him," Keara said. "I've tried it."

Madia began to move slowly, quietly, just a bit at a time. No one else in the room was moving at all, and she knew how conspicuous that made her. The three strangers hadn't been here long, hadn't had much to drink yet, so they were as sharp as such types could get at the moment.

She slid around one table and between two others as all three men concentrated on Hoke, who was making dark faces, switching his attention between the three. Keara found Madia with her eyes and stared at her in silent earnest. Madia gently nodded to her, exchanging messages. Keara took a breath, then turned to the man still holding her and giggled just audibly.

All four men looked at her.

"Well, maybe I would not mind a day off," she said, leaning toward the ringleader, putting her free hand gently on the arm that held her captive. She turned then,

moving around so that her back was to Hoke. She leaned
her head to one side and favored the shorter man with a
remarkably wanton look—a look Madia had a sudden,
deep respect for.

"Maybe these bold young men are . . . rather *welcome*." Keara kept smiling.

The Greater Gods bless you, Keara, Madia thought,
inching forward again. She looked to Hoke and watched
until his eyes flashed toward hers for a brief instant. He
cleared his throat loudly, then slowly put up his hands,
palms face out.

"Wonderful," Hoke said. "You see, there is no need for
argument after all. Perhaps we have solved this simply.
In fact, I have good reason to wish that no blood be
spilled here this night."

"And what reason is that?" the bearded man asked.

Madia, close as she was likely to get, drew her sword
and leaped. She swung the blade high, then brought it
down and across, following her momentum, cutting deep
into the short man's side and belly. The bearded man
turned just slightly at the commotion. Hoke took the
opportunity to step back and kick with his stiff leg, more
club than leg anyway. His boot caught the man's
extended arm and the sword came loose, hitting the wall,
then clanging on the inn's floor. Hoke fell to his knees
and snatched it up.

The bearded man pulled a dagger from his waist and
held it out as he began to back away from Hoke. Keara
let her legs fail, and sank to the floor.

Rather than be dragged down with her, the taller man
let go. Madia jumped over Keara's limp body and met his
sword with hers as he tried to defend himself. She could
see the sudden fear in his eyes, the awkward way he handled the weapon. She parried twice, then drove her
blade into his upper ribs, forcing him backward. She let
go, letting him take her sword with him. His eyes lost

focus as he fell to his side on the floor, gasping, blood foaming at his chest as air escaped from the wound.

Madia stood back from the body and looked up—in time to see the bearded man's head snapping back and forth, panic in his eyes as he faced off against Hoke. Abruptly Hoke picked up the flagon of ale beside him and threw it at the man, then he followed with a swift cut to one upper thigh as his opponent raised his arms to fend the tankard off. The man howled and went down in a jumble of flailing arms and ale and spurting blood.

Hoke jerked forward and thrust the sword into the downed man's back as he tried to roll away, then he withdrew the sword. Madia leaned and pulled her blade free as well. The bearded man, wheezing, bleeding heavily, flopped over and curled up on his side.

"The reason is," Hoke said, answering the man's question, "I hate to have to clean it up." The other man's eyes rolled up and he was still.

Hoke walked around the table and helped Madia get Keara up and sitting in a chair. He comforted her as he did, congratulating her at the same time, and she thanked him.

"You are welcome," Madia said to the both of them, just loud enough.

"Oh, and thank you," Keara said to her. Hoke looked at Madia, saying nothing. Then he glanced about the room. People were gathered in clumps, looking on from the corners. He looked down again, eyeing the bodies. Blood seemed to ooze everywhere. "We'll need a mop," he muttered.

Keara turned to the table and dragged all three flagons near, then lifted one and downed the better part of its contents. She looked up, wide-eyed. "And another flagon of ale," she said. She bent down and picked up a second flagon, then started to drink it. Madia smiled at her, then at Hoke. "I'll get it," she said. Hoke shrugged, then sat down to join them.

"There'll be more trouble before the fair is through," Hoke remarked, taking a seat at an empty table, one of many. "Pity. Dead customers have a way of spoiling the appetite. We will need to stay close to the inn for the next few days."

Madia sat down with a sigh across from him. "We've been cooped up inside for months," she complained. "The weather grows warmer by the day. I was looking forward to meeting travelers, listening to their tales, hearing more news of Kamrit."

"And buying the merchant's wares," Hoke added, smiling.

"Perhaps a thing or two."

"You will find that most travelers and news come to us at day's end, and after enough ale, they will tell you or sell you anything you like."

"They bring mostly trouble," Madia said, making a face, holding up one foot, and on it a shoe still wet from mopping the bloodied floors.

"Don't worry about any of it," Hoke chuckled. "I've made arrangements with some friends in the town, good with a sword. We'll have help on hand the next few days, enough so you and I can enjoy an afternoon or two of freedom."

Madia nodded, felt her heart buoyed somewhat; she missed the stories and songs and tricks the many minstrels and jongleurs had brought to her father's castle. She missed a great many things, in fact. More all the time. . . .

"Tomorrow?" she asked, the way she always asked Hoke for permission, even though, by right of her heritage, his first duty should have required him to do her slightest bidding. There was a time Madia would have sought only a way to conquer a man like Hoke, a conquest of the spirit, of position, but in truth she had never known any man quite like him—or she had never realized that she had.

"Tomorrow, I think. I'll send Keara home shortly, and we'll close up a little early tonight. Start fresh in the morning. I may even go out with you."

"Good!" Madia said. "I have the feeling tomorrow is going to be a most wonderful day."

"You just hope it's better than tonight," Hoke grumbled.

"Yes," Madia sang, "I will."

They strolled the square, picking out trinkets and clothing, wares for the inn, metal tools, a blown glass statue, and spices and fragrances that tinged the air, blending with the blooming fragrance of spring fields and the rich aroma of too many horses in town. Hoke nearly bought a strange sword made by the desert tribes far to the south, a large gleaming weapon, its blade curved like a quarter moon. But the price was too high, and he said it felt wrong, the weight too great on the end. Madia tested it herself, wielding it conservatively in the air.

Just then two figures came up behind Hoke, men-at-arms from Kamrit Castle dressed in light armor and leather and mail. They each slapped Hoke on the back, then called him by a number of titles that were neither kind nor true, though their faces held no anger.

"Still living, the both of you!" Hoke exclaimed, grinning as he did. "By the Greater Gods!" He shook hands with each, former comrades-in-arms, Madia thought, then she realized that they might know her as well. She stepped away, fading to the edge of the booth, and kept her face turned away. Hoke took each soldier by an arm and began hauling them off toward the inn, away from Madia. He never looked back. She decided he had thought the same as she.

Madia waited until they had gone, then tried the great curved sword once more before handing it back to the merchant with a shake of her head.

"Perhaps a gift for someone," the merchant suggested.

"No, no," she told him.

"It is nearly as big as you are," another voice said just behind her. She turned and found a very tall, very fat man standing before her wrapped in two brightly colored tunics and carrying an intricately carved walking staff, roughly half his height, made of a dark wood. He wore a soft silk hat that covered the top of one ear, and a most arrogant smile. His eyes were dark and unreadable, but full of energy.

"Though she handles it well," said someone else, a more feminine voice. Now Madia saw the three figures behind the first, a man and a woman, both very tall and muscular, both with straight black hair and clean faces, and skin the color of tea; they wore thick cloth tunics under reinforced leather armor, and each one was armed with strange bladed weapons that were lashed to one arm from just below the elbow.

The third was another man, younger and somewhat shorter than the first two, and certainly of less sturdy stock, though equally well armed. He had lighter skin, long wavy hair and a bushy beard light in color, and there was something about him that Madia found . . . familiar. She looked at him more closely, but the answer didn't come.

Then she noticed the way he was looking at her, as if she had something horrible on the end of her nose, as if he were looking at a ghost. . . .

He knows me, she thought, *or we know each other, perhaps.* Though anyone who had visited Kamrit in recent years would likely recognize her face, and she had met so many young men. He seemed to change moods then, and he looked away.

The three stood calmly, quietly, surveying the booths and the crowds, not one of the three ever looking in the same direction at the same time. Madia had never seen their like before. She couldn't take her eyes off of them.

"Thank you," she said. "But I prefer my own." She put her palm on the hilt of the long sword Hoke had given her, then looked sidelong at the plump giant before her. "You know much of swordsmanship?"

"Ah, well," the first man said, nodding to her, "only what I see. I leave matters of weapons to my Subartans." He indicated his companions. "When I am pressed to fight, I usually prefer to turn my opponents into something less threatening—cowards, for instance, or cowards with no swords!" He chuckled at that, for just an instant.

Madia shook her head, deliberating. A sorcerer of some sort, of course, and a brazen one at that, up to promoting himself at the first chance. Her father had kept a wizard or two through the years, most of them better at boasting and gimmickry than they were at spelling a man's courage or sword away. Still, some wizards were men were to be reckoned with. And certainly the three warriors with this one were.

"What sort of weapons are those?" Madia asked, still eyeing the blades each of the warriors wore. She noticed now that each of the blades were serrated on one side and gleamingly honed on the other, a weapon that could no doubt be used to rip anything from silk to saplings. She looked at the wizard again and realized that he was still watching her.

"Subarta, of course," the largest Subartan replied.

"You seem to like my friends," Frost said.

Madia realized she was staring and tried to compose herself. "Where did you find them?" she asked.

"Here and there. Do you have a name, girl?"

"Do you?" Madia countered, raising an eyebrow.

"Frost," the wizard said. "Now, you will tell me yours."

He reached out suddenly, put both his hands on the sides of Madia's head, and closed his eyes. Madia raised her hands to stop him, but found the three Subartans gathering closely around her, looking at her with cold, steady eyes. She froze exactly as she was, hands open and raised halfway. She looked at Frost, at his eyes, still closed, then jerked as he opened them suddenly wide. Madia felt a slight tingle run across her scalp as he let go.

"Madia? Named after the princess of Kamrit, I see. A questionable honor, I would say."

"She looks rather a little like her, too," the youngest Subartan said now, grimacing quite strangely. "Though, what in the name of Hual would the Princess Madia be doing here?" He leaned towards her, eyes growing narrow. "One might think the daughter of Kelren Andarys would be at Kamrit, mourning her father's passing and seeing to the affairs of Ariman. Though, from what is known of her, she well might be hiding instead in just such a place as this."

Madia winced, then shook her head, trying to cover up. He was a devil, this fellow, and he was making her extremely nervous, and a little ill. But the voice, like the eyes, was indeed familiar. She almost had him placed, almost. . . .

"Have you nothing to say to that?" Frost asked, breaking her thoughts. Frost was quick to act and to gather information, and he had some talent, certainly. Madia smiled at him, then at all three warriors now standing at ease around her. These were quite possibly the most interesting people she had met since leaving Kamrit Castle, though she wasn't at all sure whether that was a good thing.

Before anything else was said, a small troll of a man wandered up, drawing everyone's attention. He was unkempt and unbathed, with a full winter's hair and whiskers grown all about his head, and he wore layered tunics instead of a coat. He nearly passed between Madia and Frost, but just as he reached them, he glanced up, then down again, and went round, past the booth, eyeing the weapons displayed on the wide boards that ran across the front. He lingered there, apparently interested in a stunning cinquedea dagger.

Madia had seen too many men of this sort—large and small alike—traipse in and out of Kern these past few weeks. They reminded her of the peasant villagers she had stayed with, of a life she had nearly been sentenced to. The merchant came over and spoke to the little man, who in turn shook his head and waved him off. No money, and no prospects to acquire any, Madia thought. Only big eyes.

"You have not told me where you come from," she said to the sorcerer, growing curious about it.

"Neither have you," the youngest Subartan said to her. "I would be most interested in hearing that."

"Many lands, many times," Frost said in answer. "Recently, Ikaydin, and before that the Lagareth province beyond the Spartooth mountains. But many years ago, I walked these very hills."

"How far have you traveled?" Madia said, feeling her pulse quicken, letting her mind fill with images of exotic places described to her by minstrels and bards since childhood.

"There is a country to the south," Frost said, "beyond the Kaya deserts, called Breshta, where I—"

"I have heard of it!" Madia said, enamored of the chance to talk of such places again, their people and their ways, to imagine visiting them one day when she was . . . older.

"You have heard of Breshta?" Jaffic asked now, much too craftily for her tastes. *I do know him,* she thought, certain now, *from Kamrit.* He reminds me of—

No, she thought, *that could not be.* She found Frost eyeing her with a puzzled look, an ill-fitting look for him, somehow. The wizard intrigued her at least as much as the young Subartan bothered her, but she wasn't willing to trade one for the other.

"Well, yes, a tale or two, as told to me," she answered the Subartan, though the teller of the stories she remembered had in fact been a diviner of some sort in her father's court, and much of what he had said remained in doubt; he had described it all admittedly secondhand.

"And where would a young lady of Kern hear such things?" Frost inquired.

"From a wizard, like yourself, passing through the inn."

Frost glanced up the street at the big inn and nodded. "I see. And would you know if there might be a room there? We will need quarters for tonight. We can pay any price."

"There may be," Madia said, smiling coyly. "For a *fair* price, and a promise of stories from your travels."

"Good enough," Frost said, then he looked about, considering other nearby booths. "For now, I wish to do a bit more browsing. Can you go and tell the innkeeper?"

"I'll tell him when we get there. I would like to browse along with you, if you don't mind."

She didn't really make it a question. Frost found her with one discerning eye. "I see. I am being held captive."

"Something like that."

"Very well," Frost said, hiking a large leather pouch off the ground and over his shoulder, turning to go on. "You can tell me what other places passing wizards have told you of, so that I do not bore you with old news."

"Bore me," Madia said, and started after him. "Please."

She glanced at the youngest Subartan as they walked.

He looked away as she did. *No*, she thought again, *it couldn't be....*

They paused three booths away and Frost, setting his pouch back down, began sniffing at the table's many jars, asking the spice merchant about the contents of some, in particular a cluster of painted white pots. Madia noticed the little troll-like man again, at first standing almost beside her, then moving around between herself and Frost, eyes twitching in his head. A sudden commotion stole her attention.

She looked behind her to find a half dozen soldiers coming toward them at a jog. She didn't recognize any of them, but that didn't mean they might not recognize her. Mercenaries, certainly, as many in Lord Ferris' new army seemed to be, at least the men that had passed through Kern. Still, that didn't mean they hadn't been informed of her presence here by someone who knew her—possibly by the men with Hoke, in fact.

It was too late to go anywhere. She stood tense but still, casting about for possible escape routes.

"Stop, thief!" one of the soldiers began yelling, the sergeant. Madia realized they were not looking at her but past her. She turned and saw the little man glancing hastily over his shoulder, his body dancing erratically in place. The soldiers pushed Madia out of the way, then went around Frost's much larger bulk, eyeing the Subartans as they passed. They grabbed the little man by the arm and held him. Then a merchant arrived just behind them, the armorer, red faced and pointing a finger accusingly—at the little man, and at Frost as well.

"It's one of them!" he shouted, panting through gritted teeth. "Search them both!"

The Subartans came quickly forward, forming a shallow triangle with the large male Subartan directly in front of Frost, the young one to the right, the woman left, a defensive posture, Madia noted. Frost stood back against the spice booth, barely managing a thin smile.

"I am sure you'll want to search this other fellow first," Frost said. "He likely has what you seek."

"Dead men are easily searched," the sergeant snarled, placing his hand on the hilt of his sword. He seemed to size the situation up, then nodded toward their short, shaking prisoner. Two of the men searched him perfunctorily but found nothing.

"Now, you, step away from the booth," the sergeant asked of Frost. The Subartans closed ranks. All six soldiers drew their swords.

"You'll join the dead, then," the sergeant said, "but to what end? What have you to hide?"

"Nothing," Frost said. "But I will not be searched, nor will I let you plunder my things." He bent down and picked up his sack. The cinquedea dagger lay on the ground just behind it.

"Get him!" the sergeant shouted. The soldiers moved in quickly. The Subartans suddenly exploded forward. Madia jumped back, trying to get out of the way. She glanced at Frost, who had put his things back down and closed his eyes, apparently lost in concentration, and apparently certain he had little to fear. She turned to the Subartans again and watched them cut three of the soldiers to pieces almost immediately, leaving torn and bloodied bodies, mortal wounds all. They parried with the rest, but already another group of soldiers, nine or ten in all, was approaching from the east end of the square. They joined in the fight and drove the Subartans back.

Madia fell back again as well. Four more men lay on the ground by the time she came to rest. Then the bearded young Subartan lurched to one side. He dropped low and came up again, one blade caught in the ribs of a soldier who had been trying to get around behind him. Three of the other men saw their chance and lunged.

The Subartan tore his weapon free and struck as the first sword slashed his leg. He cut off the attacker's hand with a single pass, but another blade had already found his left side exposed. He feinted to his right and pulled himself free. Blood ran from both his wounds as he repositioned himself, crouched nearly on his knees, parrying more blows from the two remaining soldiers. They moved too quickly, forcing their way closer, trying to finish their downed opponent from two sides. Madia took her long sword in her hand and ran into the fray.

She cut the nearest soldier down, striking through one side of his back, then pulling away. She moved forward again and saw the third man turn. Finding his eyes with hers, she looked high, then swung low, a simple deceptive move Hoke had taught her. An effective move, she found, as the soldier screamed and collapsed on his half-severed leg. She swung again unopposed.

When she looked around, she found the other two Subartans still engaged, standing on the bodies of dead men now as they fought the last five able soldiers. She took the man nearest to her. He noticed her approach and turned to face her, his look one of mild surprise. Madia had seen such looks before, the first reaction of a man finding himself opposed by a young girl. Then he swung almost absently, raking the air with his sword, apparently intending a quick, easy solution to the problem. She used his moment of misjudgment to dodge and thrust, and found a solid target. She withdrew and moved toward the next man.

There were only three soldiers left now, but even as she took stock of them, she could see that they were changing, their bodies beginning to glow with a satiny white corona. Their skin began to wrinkle as their eyes glazed over, their postures shrank slightly and arched forward, their hair turned a pure white, then fell to their shoulders. Rosivok and Sharryl stood back, watching as the three men dropped their swords and lowered themselves voluntarily to the ground, breath heaving in and out of their chests, fear and exhaustion on their faces. Their arms lay at their sides as if there remained no strength to lift them anymore.

Madia looked at Frost, whose eyes were open again. The young Subartan lay a few feet from him, unmoving.

She started toward him, but Frost was there first, bending and putting his hands on the young man's head, much as he had done to her. In a moment he stood again and turned to the remaining two Subartans. He shook his head slowly, side to side.

Madia looked at the other two, saw them each nod, no apparent emotion on their faces, though their eyes barely moved from the still body. Frost had lost the smirk Madia had believed was engraved on his features. In its place was a languid, empty look, an apology of sorts, Madia thought, meant for the others.

"We should get off the streets," the male Subartan said after a moment. "Before more of them come." He waved his blades at the bodies strewn all around them.

Madia looked across the square. There were but two other men about in any form of armor, but their surcoats bore the crest of Jasnok; no one was moving in their direction.

"I think we've killed every soldier in Kern," she said.

"There will be more," Frost said, turning to her, a subtle, yet surely unfavorable look.

"Yes, but perhaps not for a day or two," Madia replied. "I will have your friend's body taken from the square."

"You were a fine warrior, Jaffic," the male Subartan said, and Madia knew that it was true: Jaffic had been her cousin's name, Jaffic Andarys, Duke of Kamrit. He had changed so much in the years since he had left the castle, but behind the tanned and hardened skin, the remarkably improved body, the thick beard and long hair, behind all that, she could see it was him. They had never been close, and it had been so long, but the loss still gripped her now, a solid thing that lay in her belly and squeezed at her chest.

Jaffic had finally come home.

The street was growing busy now, people beginning to crowd in again, gawking, talking among themselves. Madia looked at their faces, found them looking back at hers. And it occurred to her just how public this whole unfortunate event had been.

"You must think of yourselves," she said, swallowing dryly. "You'll still need a room for tonight. You must come with me."

She went a few steps, then turned, waiting, looking sternly at Frost. In a moment he nodded. He picked up his bag again, then the dagger beside it. He handed the dagger to the armorer, scowling deeply. The little man who had taken it was nowhere in sight.

"I would sell this quickly," Frost told the merchant. He waved a hand at the lifeless soldiers. "As you can see, it is very bad luck!"

Madia stepped through the door and found Hoke seated at a table just inside, still joined by the two knights he had met in the square. The three of them looked up, staring at Madia as she stared back. They eyed Hoke briefly, then stood and bowed at the waist. "Princess," the one on the left, the older of the two, said. "We are at your service."

"It is all right," Hoke said. He looked at Madia's three companions, then glanced quickly around. There were fewer than a dozen other patrons in the room, a mix of townspeople and travelers, but some were beginning to take notice. "Come," he said. He got up, indicating a table near the back wall. "We'll talk over there."

As they made their way to the table Madia noticed

Frost looking at her as if she had stolen his purse. She let it wait until they wre in the back of the room, then Hoke asked loudly, "Who are they?"

"A wizard from beyond the Spartooth mountains, and what remains of his guard. His name is Frost."

"My Subartans," Frost said. "Rosivok and Sharryl."

"One of them was killed," Madia said. "There was a fight. I—I became involved."

"Of course," Hoke remarked, frowning at her.

"There is more," she said. "The Subartan who died was someone I knew, and you as well, I think. Jaffic Andarys, my cousin."

"The long lost nephew?" Hoke asked her, obviously surprised, though not apparently devastated.

"The same."

"I knew him," Hoke went on. "A wild boy, when I saw him last, though he played your father like a lute when he desired. No more comfortable than you were with the prospect of royal responsibility. He left without blessings, to find adventure, though it seems he may have found too much. And left Ariman with one less heir, as well." He looked straight at Madia with this last remark, a look of accusation.

"I had no idea," Frost remarked. "He came to me when news of my need for a third Subartan reached him. And he was working out very well. It seems his loss is a loss to many."

"Who's employ are you under?" Hoke asked Frost.

"No one's," Frost replied. But he was still looking at Madia, another look that seemed to hold an air of accusation as Madia studied it. And then it made sense to her. But she hadn't lied to him, simply allowed him to assume she was named after the princess, and wisely, she thought. There had been no need for him to know the truth, and no reason for her to trust him or his Subartans in the least. And her own cousin had kept a truth from her, after all. Frost could have been in league with the Lord Ferris, or worse—though, if he was, the bodies outside would likely strain their relationship.

She looked about and noticed no one was talking.

"Perhaps we should start over," Frost advised.

They pulled seven chairs about and sat down, and Hoke finished the introductions, including the two knights, Sirs Olan and Delyav, then Madia told the others what had happened outside. Silence fell once more.

"I have heard of your death," Frost told Madia, after a moment. "You fight well for a ghost."

"And I have heard of you," Hoke said to Frost. "They say a man can never know whether to trust you or fear you."

"What more can I ask?" Frost said, chuckling. "Other than to hope he might smile while he opens his purse!"

Hoke frowned. "I see."

"Your troubles outside were most unfortunate," Delyav said, looking at his hands. "Olan and I may have to explain why we were not killed along with those others."

"You knew nothing of it," Hoke replied. "You were here with me!"

"Drinking at an inn might not be reason enough. We should be about arresting all of you right now."

"Unless of course Lord Ferris never learns we were here," Olan said. "Though it is unlikely."

"There are few in Kern, or elsewhere in Ariman, who feel a bond with Andarys' apparent successor," Hoke replied. "Word will be slow to travel, and details can be missed, at my urging."

"And then what of you two?" Madia asked, still watching the two soldiers.

"They knew Kelren well," Hoke said. "Olan fought at my side many times, and Delyav a few as well. Unlike that lot rotting outside, they can be trusted. They believe, as I do, that the king's death, like your own, was planned, and that the grand chamberlain cannot be trusted. They have news of Kamrit, and I think you should hear it."

"First, Frost and his friends need a room," Madia told Hoke. "And the body of Jaffic needs to be taken care of. Quickly. Perhaps we could see to it."

"Of course," Hoke said.

"Thank you," Rosivok said in a low voice. Hoke gave him quiet acknowledgment. Then he excused himself, rose and went to the other side of the room where a boy was bent over an empty table, scraping at dried food with a dull knife. He spoke to the boy, who then nodded and disappeared out the door.

"I am traveling to Neleva," Frost said as Hoke rejoined them. "But of course I must pass through Kamrit. I too would like to hear what these men have to say."

"Lord Ferris is consolidating his control," Delyav began. "He will proclaim himself king before long; no one doubts this. All Ariman believes you are dead, and they have all but forgotten poor Jaffic."

"Lord Ferris is not the man your father was," Olan said. "He is strange, especially lately, and troubling to be around. He seems taken with himself and easily agitated. He metes out justice without mercy, with no compassion for any man, an insult to your grandfather's legacy, and your father's. He finds favor only with the rich merchants who frequent his chambers, men eager to help him finance his new army in return for trading preferences in the new order Lord Ferris seeks to forge."

"And what order is that?" Madia asked.

"Most of us, those still loyal to your father's ideals, believe he intends to expand Ariman's control over the entire region, from the Ikaydin Plateau to Glister, by force if necessary," Olan answered. "An army such as the one he is building can only be used for conquest. He may have plans for Ikaydin, too."

"He is too ambitious," Delyav said. "He seems to have no conscience for the hardships his tolls and taxes have already caused."

"No one protests?" Frost asked. "Are there no land barons willing to see Andarys' vision through, no men of justice?"

"There were," Olan replied, "but some of those most opposed to Ferris' conduct have been accused of crimes and put in prison, or blocked from trade with the merchant cartel that Ferris has assembled. It has all happened so quickly!"

"And two of Andarys' greatest compatriots have recently been attacked by bandits on the road and killed," Delyav added. "Much like Madia was—or nearly so," he corrected. "Both men traveled on good mounts and with good men, no easy target for peasant robbers on foot. Rumors and speculation abound. I have even heard tell a squad of Bouren troops, led by Prince Jaran himself, was seen near abouts after both attacks, and that he is behind them."

"This too has helped Lord Ferris," Olan said, "who insists Lord Ivran and the other northern vassals are plotting against Ariman, and plan to—"

"Nonsense!" Frost snapped. "I've come from Lencia just three days past. I know Lord Jurdef Ivran, and his son, and knew Jurdef's father before him. Trust that they are as concerned as you over goings-on in Ariman. They have done nothing to foster these rumors, and do not understand them. But I can tell you they don't trust Lord Ferris any more than you."

"In that you are wrong!" Madia argued. "It was Bouren troops that tried to kill me. The same lot, no doubt, and Prince Jaran with them. I don't know why, but I know what I saw."

"Jurdef Ivran claims no plots exist, and no troops have been sent, and I believe him," Frost said, then he looked around the table. "Although, troops from Kamrit have been seen riding the western edge of Golemesk Swamp inside Bouren."

"Lord Ferris sends troops to Golemesk to search for the Demon Blade," Olan said. "There are many new rumors that it now rests there."

"There are *always* many rumors!" Frost said, obviously irritated by the subject. He paused, rested his hands on the table in front of him, and linked his fingers. "And even if they are true," he added, more calmly, "the Blade is of little use to any who do not know its secrets, and none do; probably not even the one entrusted to keep it. It has been too long, and the secrets were kept too well, I think."

"I would worry less about the Blade and more about Lord Ferris. The fellow intrigues me. He creates trouble and events out of nothing with an almost magical talent. A jongleur of the fates. Has he a wizard in his circle?"

Olan and Delyav looked at each other, then shrugged. "No," Olan said. "King Andarys had only a few magicians, entertainers for the most part, but Ferris sent them away."

"Indeed?" Frost said, fingers beginning to rub and curl.

"Indeed what?" Madia asked.

"Ferris has enjoyed such a remarkable fortune of events, yet he has had no wizard or mage of any sort to help ensure it."

"That troubles you?" Hoke asked. "Not everything that happens owes tribute to your trade."

Frost smiled at him, remarkably serene. "Of course," he said. "But you miss my point. I dislike puzzles that seem so complete, yet have so many pieces left over."

"There is now a mage's guild in Kamrit," Delyav said. "Dark mages, they say. And those who want to be such. Dark magic and secret ways. Witches, that's a better name. None of them seem to have any real talents, mind you, but every soul in the city has a story to tell of them."

"Lord Ferris is known to take council from them," Olan added. "And their members have been seen to visit his chambers as the merchants do."

"Perhaps they aid him with black magic," Hoke advised.

"I find this interesting as well," Frost said. "Another extra piece of the puzzle, you see, and one that does not bode well for the future of Ariman, not as you men must envision it."

"Nor I," Madia said.

"If the Demon Blade was found," Delyav offered, "and Ferris and his mages should actually acquire it and learn its secrets, there might be no way of opposing them."

"He would need more than a few witches to make use of such a tool," Frost declared. "Worry not."

"I want to go back, and soon," Madia said, abruptly leaning forward, gathering everyone's attention. "To take Ariman back, to rebuild the prosperity my grandfather won and my father preserved. Jaffic is gone. I am all that remains. I owe this to my father, to my cousin, to myself. And I want what is mine."

She paused, looking solely at Hoke. He was eyeing her cautiously, though no longer as if she were a child just learning to walk, the way he had looked at her when she had spoken of this in times past. She leaned on the strength that a winter spent with Hoke and Keara had given her, and an autumn spent with peasants, and time spent with just herself. She almost didn't know the girl that had been exiled from Kamrit those months ago; the girl who let everyone down—including herself—let her father suffer and die full of guilt and doubt and pain at the hands of assassins, lacking the company of his only child. Lacking the knowledge that she loved him. Though this last was something she hadn't realized until it was much too late.

She couldn't change what she had done, but she could do justice to her father's memory, to herself, to Jaffic and the rest of Ariman, and to the lands Lord Ferris sought to exploit. She could do what must be done. . . .

"Still," Hoke cautioned her, "you cannot go alone."

"Hoke is right," Madia said, addressing the two knights.

"But men such as you can help me find a way to take control of Ariman back from Ferris and his merchants and his dark mages. You know his allies, and those who oppose him."

Olan and Delyav were looking at each other again, deep concern on their faces.

"What is wrong?" Madia asked.

The two soldiers looked expectantly at Hoke, who only shrugged.

"Well, of course," Olan began, shuffling his feet under the table, "most everyone thinks you are dead. They may not believe you are indeed Madia. And those who do . . . "

Delyav cleared his throat. "You must understand that you have . . . that is, that you are remembered . . . what I mean is, in the past, the name Madia has been . . ."

"He means to say you were a trollop, a coward, a fool, and an embarrassment to the crown, and the only thing you may command in Kamrit is sour humor," Hoke finished for them.

"Yet the woman I saw fight outside was not one to laugh at," Frost said, sitting back in his chair. "And no coward of any sort."

"She has the blood in her," Rosivok said. "Watch her. Only a fool would think otherwise."

Madia sat looking at Frost and the Subartans, warming in the glow of their unexpected praise; in truth, even the most lavish compliments of young courting nobles did not compare.

"Hoke speaks only the truth," she said. "But I am learning. And I will learn even more. I wish to change what has happened, to atone, but I must start with you, Olan, and you, Delyav. I must ask for your help as well," she told Frost. "I have seen your magic, and I've seen these Subartans fight."

Frost began to chuckle. "I am inclined toward straightforward and profitable tasks, dear girl. I am not much interested in political troubles, nor in lending my Subartans to such, though you are welcome to my advice."

"Ariman is quite rich," Madia said. "As are the lands that stand to profit from a return to a more gentle and just rule. You would be paid *very* well for your troubles."

"If you are successful," Frost qualified.

Madia only looked at him.

"Go more slowly," Hoke suggested, leaning toward Madia with a knowing smile. "You can't ask men to forgive your past and risk their lives all at your sudden whim."

"But Frost and his Subartans are already wanted men," Madia said, addressing them. "There were many witnesses to what just happened outside, freemen and merchants from all over the province. Word of what has happened will spread no matter what Hoke or anyone else does. And I will doubtless be wanted once it is learned that I am still alive. We might act to help each other!"

"A valid point," Frost said, nodding to her. "I dislike being unwelcome in large countries. A nuisance, truly."

Madia smiled. "You would always be welcome in *my* country."

"I am sure. Still, I will have to think it over. You

intrigue me, but there is much to consider. Whatever his past, I have lost one of my Subartans, a man not easily replaced. This trip has already proven quite expensive. And taxing. You mentioned a room?"

Madia nodded slowly, letting it go; the only tactic she could follow for now. "A room. Of course, later we must talk more of this."

"Oh, of course," Frost replied, adding a tenuous grin. Madia turned to find Hoke watching her, shaking his head, a much larger grin on his face.

"What is it?" Madia demanded.

"Just that the Madia I used to know would have thrown a royal fit just then," Hoke replied.

"My thoughts exactly," Olan said, smiling too; he was nearly as old as Hoke, and the lines at the corners of his eyes grew deep and black as the grin broadened his face.

"I hear tell soldiers killed that girl, last fall," Madia said.

"So Hoke insists," said Delyav.

"A great fortune that I never knew you until now," Frost exclaimed, looking smug.

Madia turned to him. "And that now, you do," she said. "My lady, if it serves Ariman, I pledge my sword to you, whoever you are," Olan announced, standing up, bowing from the waist.

"And I mine," Delyav added, rising as well, bowing with his friend. "On the word of Hoke, and on your own."

"And I mine, in spirit," Hoke said. "I am too old and damaged for such a mission."

"You serve well enough," Madia said. "My well-being is proof of that. No more is asked of you." She turned her attention again to Frost. "Sleep on it if you like," she told him, "but I am going with you to Kamrit. And Olan and Delyav with me, if they will. You are in need of a third

Subartan, someone to complete the triangle. I will take my cousin's place."

"You are no Subartan, my dear," Frost said.

"I can learn," she said. "As I'm sure Jaffic did."

"Perhaps," Frost said, puckering his lower lip. "Perhaps you can at that."

"Then you're agreeing to help her?" Hoke prodded.

"I make no contract with anyone," Frost explained, "so that I am free to change my mind about anything, at any time. But, as I said, I will consider the situation."

"Your ways could make a man a little nervous," Olan remarked.

"That cannot be helped," Frost told him. He looked at Madia again, took a breath and let it go with a sigh. "You would trade in hearsay, whims and speculations, dear girl, and they are not enough. You may travel with me, and perhaps I will help you, in some manner or other, but it is best to make one decision at a time, for the making of too many plans can bring bad luck."

"As can too few," Hoke responded.

"You are a most arrogant man, Frost," Madia ventured, watching his reply.

The big wizard winked at her. "As I insist," he said, and with that they both began to chuckle.

Keara came through the door just then and headed straight to their table. Hoke introduced her to the others.

"Should be stew in the pot," she said. "Can I bring some to anyone?"

"And plenty of bread and ale," Hoke added, getting up himself to go and help her. In a moment they returned, setting wooden bowls and spoons and clay tankards and hard loaves all about, and talk gave way to the sounds of hungry mouths.

Chapter XI

Tyrr looked up as the door came open, assessing what the eyes told him. Across the table, Kaafk pushed his ledger aside, then wrinkled his nose.

The soldier Ingram stank of horse sweat and swamp decay, all made damp and pungent again by his own rank perspiration. A beard of several days darkened his face, and nearly every bit of mail, leather and armor plate that he wore seemed to have acquired some blemish or other. He had removed his helmet as he entered Tyrr's chambers, revealing the stiff, matted mass his hair had become underneath it. He now stood still and waited, chest heaving; he was apparently still out of breath from his arrival and subsequent efforts to report at once upstairs, as he had been ordered.

A reliable, enduring commander, Tyrr thought, and one who put duty ahead of all else—including hygiene.

"You were successful?" Tyrr made the Ferris resemblance ask a question already couched in doubt; Ingram had been away to Golemesk three weeks longer than planned, and no messengers had been sent with news, indicating there was little of it.

Ingram looked stricken. "We were not, Lord Ferris."

Calmly, Tyrr absorbed the knowledge. "Explain."

"We worked the edges of Golemesk, talking to people everywhere in the region, but no one seemed to know anything, even when offered gold coins, even when tortured. So we began a search of the more habitable parts of the swamp, working our way inward, checking each trail and dwelling we uncovered. Then incidents began to occur."

"Incidents?" Kaafk asked.

Tyrr silently awaited the captain's answer.

"At first only noises, a sudden splashing, or the snapping of branches nearby, a faint growling noise around dusk, but never within sight—and whistling, though it was an animal sound, not like any I have heard. Then my men began to vanish."

"Vanish?" Tyrr made the mouth ask.

Kaafk silently awaited the captain's answer.

"Squads returned short a man or two, saying they had been riding a path, nothing strange about it, and the next look around, there was one of the horses with an empty saddle and no trace of the soldier, no sound or scuffle."

"Ah," Kaafk said. "Good! This tells us that someone there has reason to chase you off."

"I began to suspect these areas, of course," Ingram continued. "So I mounted a force of thirty men and began a thorough search in the region where the last man was lost. We found nothing, but as dusk approached, *they* found us."

He looked off momentarily, growing distant, his mind apparently distracted.

"Who?" Tyrr insisted.

"Leshys."

Tyrr absorbed this, too. Something he had vaguely considered in his plan, of course, though only so much was known of such creatures, the knowledge passed on by those that had gone before. "Creatures of nuisance," he affirmed. "What of them?"

"A most deadly nuisance," Ingram replied. His breathing had slowed to normal now, but his posture was beginning to sag, blending with the general air of physical and personal defeat that shone in his face, despite his efforts to hide it.

"They came from the shadows of dusk as we tried to leave," he said. "We didn't know what we were fighting at first. You cannot see them until they are upon you, until their horrible animal faces fill your eyes. My men have many teeth marks, those that survived." Ingram turned and displayed the wound on the back of his own neck: twin half ovals made of pointed red punctures that had begun to scab over. "They hang on with their teeth, then hack or beat a man to death with knives and stones and thick branches.

"I lost eleven men in the first encounter before the creatures suddenly vanished as if by magic. There was nothing, not a sound nor a trace anywhere, by the time we rallied. We waited in the area awhile, searching nearby, but nothing else happened.

"Finally we gathered our dead and began to ride out. The second attack came only moments later, just like the first, though in near darkness. I split the men into pairs and ordered them to cut the beasts off each other. We killed a few, but I lost seven more men before the attack ended. We looked for the bodies of the creatures we'd killed, but the others must have dragged them all off. Or—"

Ingram stood there a moment, mouth half-open, as if some thought or other was stuck there and would not allow it to close. "Or they do not die," he said finally.

Tyrr watched a chill rake Ingram briefly.

"A very *great* nuisance, apparently," Kaafk said, looking at Tyrr, raising his eyebrows. "Soldier's work, certainly."

He smiled, looking across the table, then dropped the smile and rubbed his rather large nose. "Well, they must be hiding something."

Tyrr absorbed the knowledge. "Perhaps not," he said. "This is the way with leshys. Annoying, fascinating, rather delectable creatures, really," he added, recalling stories of what good sport they had been when demons had last walked on this world, how tasty they were supposed to be once you caught enough of them to make a good meal. "They need no reason to kill those who enter their domain, I think. Still, there may be more to it.

"I have many advocates throughout the land, from the southern seas to the Spartooths, all gathering information. I grow ever more convinced that the Demon Blade has come to reside in that region, and I want it found. There must be additional searches made. If it is in Golemesk, then that is where we must go to retrieve it. If all the leshys must die, then die they must. I can arrange some help for your leshy problem if you need it, Captain. Go and clean yourself up. And report to me tomorrow. We will discuss your new orders then."

"I am sorry, my liege. I have failed in my mission. I will accept whatever action—"

"If I were truly disappointed, Captain, you would know it," Tyrr said. *Control*, he reminded himself, denying his first thoughts with practiced efficiency. It would be inappropriate for the grand chamberlain to show disfavor by consuming the good captain. And, of course, quite wasteful! It would have been too easy to let himself slip again, to let his essence show, more signs that his carefully forged construct and controlling spells were beginning to erode. They required constant attention, as did his demeanor. But he knew that too well. *That is how the many who came before me failed,* he thought.

The longer he remained in this world, the more difficult it would become to contain himself within his
human form. The longer things took . . .

But there was no reason to get—excited. There
would be time enough, or he would think of ways to
ensure that there would. There was no cause for worry.
No need!

"Go," he told Ingram. "I'll have no need of you until
tomorrow." The captain bowed, turned and hurried out,
closing the door behind him. Kaafk slid the ledger back
in front of him but did not look at the figures.

"You don't strike me as a merciful, forgiving man, my
liege," Kaafk said, gazing through the room's only window, then finding Tyrr with the corner of one eye. "Yet
sometimes your lenience surprises me. You don't intend
to discipline Ingram at all."

Tyrr saw that it was more statement than question.
And perhaps part of a calculation. Kaafk was like most
men of power, lacking discipline yet expecting it from
others, enjoying his own ideas of success while
berating men of lesser stature at every turn, preying
upon them, even those he relied on. In this they were
like demonkind—a deficiency, Tyrr thought, no matter
how intrinsic it seemed, that ultimately divided men
and wasted resources and opportunities in ridiculous
proportions. And like his own kind, men seemed slow
to learn from their mistakes and those of others. Tyrr
would shine against their dimness as he outshined the
old demons, would soar above them as he soared
above Tybree.

"He does his best," Tyrr said, certain of that. "He is,
after all, only human." Another slip, Tyrr realized, but an
affordable one.

Kaafk looked at him in silence, considering the
remark, then he seemed to let it go. He went back to
his ledgers, to completing his account of the already

remarkable profits enjoyed by his guild and the others that had aligned themselves with him, with the "new" order. Though this was nothing, Tyrr insisted, compared to what would be theirs once Neleva and the great northern fiefs were finally conquered. Then Tyrr could shed the human construct he wore like a prison, and reclaim the glory that had once belonged to demonkind—the world that had been taken from them.

He watched a familiar smile of contentment spread across Kaafk's heavy face.

"I am pleased that you are pleased," Tyrr made the mouth say.

"Here," Kaafk said, chuckling. He lifted his pen and slid the ledger across the table. "As you can see, by the end of the month—"

"Your figures do not concern me, Kaafk. I need only what I need, and you seem well able to provide it."

"How will you know if I cheat you?" Kaafk asked, looking up just enough to fix Tyrr with a measured gaze.

Tyrr made the lips smile. He could force the merchant to tell every truth the man had ever known, if he thought it necessary. But Kaafk seemed to have a refreshing and useful lack of tolerance for hypocrisy in any form, and a limited desire to see his throat slit. He would cheat Tyrr sooner or later, of course, but as yet, he had not.

"I will know," Tyrr made the mouth say.

Kaafk seemed to ponder this a moment, then he pulled the ledger back and, without looking down, broke into laughter.

"You do not fear me, do you Kaafk?" Tyrr asked, curious as to what the man's answer might be.

Kaafk paused, finally glanced back down at his writings, then let another chuckle slip. "As much as I think I have to, my liege," he said.

"Beware your estimates," Tyrr replied.

Kaafk, for just an instant, displayed a clear flicker of dread. Then he shook his head and grinned, and returned to his figures.

Tyrr absorbed the notion, and felt a twinge of pleasure.

Chapter XII

The walls surrounding much of Kopeth had been laid open in the last great war and never restored. No garrison had been maintained there in decades, so Madia was surprised as they arrived, then quietly entered the city through a pathway on the western edge, to see soldiers walking the remaining gantries. She followed Frost, who claimed to know the place. He stayed in the narrow streets, moving through an old section of the city made up of the houses of laborers and beggars, thieves and whores. Western Kopeth lacked markets and tradesmen, places where the grand chamberlain's soldiers would be found.

Only once did Frost stop, gathering everyone into the shadows, including the two royal mounts and the mule, while he sent Olan and Delyav towards the city's center to reconnoiter. Upon their return they reported that Ferris' troops were present in great numbers, and the city's citizens seemed filled with unrest and fear.

"I expected this," Olan said. "Ferris has begun making Kopeth a northern stronghold. Since the first thaws,

175

many men have been sent here, and more will come. He has claimed there is a need for a strong presence nearer the Jasnok–Bouren borders, to insure against possible raids and to discourage an outright invasion."

"This army's plan is not one of defense," Rosivok said. "They have no fortifications anywhere on the roads or around the city, and we saw no patrols as we approached."

"It seems our friends in Lencia have much to worry about," Frost said. "As I feared."

"Then my journey is all the more urgent," Madia said. "And its end. And this will help."

"Why is that?" Frost inquired, in a voice better suited for use with a child.

"People are unsure and unhappy," she said, ignoring his tone. "So they will likely be more willing to listen to another. Even . . . myself."

"Have you yet thought about a plan?" Frost asked her.

"Several," she said, surprised he had not asked the question already during the past two days on their journey from Kern. She assumed he might simply have no intention of sticking around long enough for it to matter, or that he had a plan of his own. Now she imagined he may have been waiting for her to offer the information all this time. Only she didn't exactly *have* a plan, beyond gathering information and allies, all she could of both, then choosing the best course of action after that.

"I would like to hear them all," Frost said.

"Now? Here in the streets? With soldiers only a stone's throw away? Surely it can wait."

"Now is just fine."

"My plans take into account all my knowledge of the castle's inner workings, and the many lessons learned at—"

"You are going to make it up as you go, aren't you?"

Madia glared at the wizard, unable to see his eyes in

the shadows, hopeful he could see the fire in hers. She said nothing at first, then, too late, she realized that this was a mistake.

"I suspected as much," Frost remarked. "Very well, you will each do as I say." He turned to the others. "Rosivok, Sharryl, go with Olan and Delyav. As soon as you find a proper stable, sell the horses. Then go and gather what additional supplies we will need to carry us through. We will meet back here, before dusk, and go to buy our passage on the Saris River to Kamrit."

"No one appointed you lord," Madia said.

"Nor you," Frost replied, a tinge of ire in his voice.

"Passage should be easy," Delyav said. "There are many barges, for a price."

"But we must find just the right one," said Frost. He turned to Madia. "And you must come with me for now. I have a friend I would visit, and I want you to attend."

"We will stay with you," Rosivok insisted.

"Not in this. Madia will provide me with protection enough, and we are almost there, in any case. Now, each of you, abide my wishes!"

Rosivok and Sharryl nodded, silent, and turned to go. Olan and Delyav looked at Madia, seeking approval. She didn't know what else to do. She nodded, and they set off behind the two Subartans.

"Who are we going to see?" Madia asked.

Frost started off down the street without a reply. He went by only two houses, then stopped and knocked on a door. "One of the great living sorcerers," he said. "If indeed he is still alive."

The voice was not audible to Madia, but Frost seemed to hear it all right. He pushed the door open and let Madia in, then pulled it shut behind them.

Inside was the oldest human being Madia had ever seen. He wore robes that hung loosely from his round, hunched shoulders and covered all but his hands and head completely—a bald head of countless wrinkles, skin spotted and dark with age. And he was so thin, Madia thought, for a sorcerer! He sat in a chair by a hearth that held no flame just now, only the dim glow of old, dying embers. He was writing in a very large, page-worn book, and painstakingly completed a word before looking up.

Madia saw his eyes then, barely visible in the dim wavering light from a cluster of candles on the table nearby. Eyes that might be older still, Madia thought; eyes she could not easily focus on, like shadows near dusk—though, from all Madia could tell, the old man was nearly blind. She followed Frost to the table and sat with him. The other man turned toward them, a complex effort, it seemed, which took a long moment.

"To answer you," the old wizard said, a low, hushed voice that rasped and growled and barely functioned, "I am still alive, but I am nothing so great anymore."

"While *I* am getting better all the time," Frost replied. "As you always do."

"No one troubles you here?" Frost asked.

"Not to speak of. The neighbors value me. I am the wise old man of this place, and these people are forever desperate for advice and healing potions. They care for me well enough, and I for them."

"Are you *well*?"

Madia thought this an odd question, since, at such an age, simply to be among the living at all was extraordinary. But then she saw the look in Frost's eye, and the way the other man looked back. The question went beyond health—a question of spirit, a question of wizards.

"I could use a hundred or so of your pounds," the old man said, tipping his head and squinting at Frost from several angles. "I cannot eat quite as I used to."

"Pity," Frost said, and shook his head. "I cannot imagine."

"How should I know?" Frost replied.

Madia shook her head some more.

"You too were in the flames," the old man said.

"Yes," Frost remarked. "As I believed she would be. Which is only sensible, and one reason, after all, that I accompany her."

"Because you think I am supposed to go to Kamrit, and Lord Ferris is not supposed to be there?" Madia asked, trying harder.

"Of course."

Madia sat considering a moment. She had never expected destiny, luck, or the Greater Gods to be on her side before, and she rather liked the idea.

"Does this mean you are definitely going to help me?"

The old man raised one trembling hand and placed it on Frost's arm, then waited until Frost looked at him. "She has no chance alone," he said. "You saw as I did."

"I know." Frost took a deep breath, then slowly let it out. "But while they are likely not substantial, the risks involved are unknown, and I—" He stopped himself, a different look on his face, worry, perhaps, or frustration, though Madia couldn't be sure. "We are between a full moon and a new moon," he said, clearing his throat, forging ahead. "Not the time to—"

"You are not still enamored of superstitions, are you?" the other man asked, glaring at Frost and raising his voice much more than Madia had thought possible. "Still throwing salt over your shoulder and carrying a bent coin? Or those damned stones you keep? I thought I'd cured you of all that nonsense ages ago!"

"A bent coin?" Frost asked with interest. "What of them?"

"By the Greater Gods!"

Frost glanced at Madia and she saw a look of embarrassment, though she could hardly believe it.

"In truth," Frost said, "I merely take into consideration the timeworn lessons and observances of the many cultures I have encountered in my—"

"And you still aren't willing to take chances, either, are you? Always a character flaw with you, Frost. 'Never risk everything,' you used to say, even though to get up in the morning is to do so! The great and pompous Frost, judge and jury and diviner of all men in all lands, especially if the price is right, but let your personal cost estimates grow too great, or let some unfortunate peasant's black kitten cross you once, and you are as hard to find as bread among beggars!"

"This is a side of you I've not seen yet," Madia declared, considering him carefully now. He seemed to mind the scrutiny.

"I see no fault in applying common sense to any situation," Frost insisted. "I can do no one any good if I fall prey to harm!"

"You are doing no one any good now. How have you pledged yourself to this young woman?"

"I am here. And if, in the course of events, I see that there is a fair need for—"

"If!" the old man barked. "Always you say 'if'! You are still in your prime, Frost, strong and fat as an autumn bear, and you saw what was in the flames, yet you cannot say what you intend? Are you waiting for a rabbit's foot to find you, perhaps? From a rabbit more courageous than you, preferably?"

"He intends to help me," Madia said, finding Frost looking at her again with an unreadable expression. "I have felt it ever since we met on the streets of Kern."

The old wizard nodded slowly to her, a half-smile. "And how is that?" he asked.

"I—that is—I just know a little something about men, I guess," she replied. "I can just tell."

The old man only hummed.

"I did not come to engage in arguments," Frost said.

"Perhaps not, my friend," the other said. "Then again, perhaps you did just that?"

Frost sat quietly a while, looking into the old wizard's eyes. Both men seemed wrapped in some deepening spiritual embrace that Madia could not fathom.

"Perhaps," Frost said at last. "But . . . there is more."

Then the older man slowly closed his eyes and slumped down slightly in his chair, motionless, looking for all the world as if he had died. Barely, Madia could see his chest rise and fall.

"Does he have a name?" Madia asked after a time, a whisper in Frost's ear.

"Yes."

Madia waited. There was nothing more. "What is it?" she asked.

"I don't know, but these days he is called Aphan."

"What?" the old man said suddenly, eyes slightly open again.

"There is talk of the Demon Blade," Frost said, as though their conversation had gone uninterrupted. "They say it rests in Golemesk."

"Yes," Aphan replied. "And so it does."

Aphan drifted. Frost waited until his focus returned, then asked, "Ramins still holds the Blade?"

"This came to me a few weeks ago." Aphan turned and slowly pointed a finger to a place not far to one side of the hearth. Frost rose and walked to the spot, and collected a short wooden staff made of white birch. He then examined the engravings on it. "It bears the feel of Ramins," he said.

"He has died," Aphan declared. "I am sure of it. And before he could fulfill his vow, I believe. The peasants who came to me with that said they found the body in the fields in Bouren, at the edge of Golemesk. He must have been carried there so that he would be found. The leshys, I think. But some of what they say is strange."

Frost came back and set the staff on top of the table. "How so?" he asked.

"I am also told that Ramins was even thinner than I, nothing but bones, as if his magic alone was all that had kept him alive. But how he could have summoned the power to utilize the Blade, or withstood its force if need be, I cannot imagine. One assumes he never did. Perhaps that is how he died—although, so close by, I would have sensed the use of the Blade's unique magic. I'm sure of it. But those secrets, like many others, must have died with him."

"Then the leshys must have the Blade. They have a keen sense for such things."

Aphan nodded. "They will have taken it deep into their realm."

Frost made a face, like someone tasting spoiled meat. "The barrows," he remarked.

"Most certainly."

"It is safe enough, then. The leshys can make little use of it, and not even an army of fools would be fool enough to enter the barrows after it."

"What barrows?" Madia asked. "What place is that?"

"Tell her," Aphan said, slumping again, though trying to keep his eyes open.

"A great battle took place there, long ago," Frost began, sitting back. "An army led by a Holan conqueror mage known as Tiesh was cornered and destroyed there in the time before your grandfather, the time of the Holan Empire. By then the empire had control in name only, and Tiesh took advantage of this to further his own holdings. Those who resisted his rule were killed. Hundreds died, until a small army of men and mages found Tiesh and his army camped along a shallow bog inside Golemesk. They surprised Tiesh and destroyed them all, then they bound

Tiesh's spirit and those of his men to the bog, and buried the dead in barrow mounds, as was the custom.

"But over time, the spirit of Tiesh freed itself, then gradually set about conjuring the spirits of the other dead back into their remains, and the barrow-wights have since each fashioned their own doors, so that they can come and go as they please."

"They leave the swamp?"

"No," Aphan said. "They cannot leave the bog and cannot leave their barrows in strong daylight."

Madia considered a moment. "Then couldn't someone ride in during the day, try to find this Blade, and get back out again before dark?"

"The bog rests near the center of the swamp now," old Aphan explained. "Golemesk is nearly double the size it was in those days. It would take several days journey through leshy lands to reach the central bogs, even on horseback, and the Holan barrows lie mostly submerged, so they are difficult to find. There are no paths that the leshy have not dismantled, and no one who ventures there has ever returned."

"Truly a bad omen, dear Aphan, as even you must agree," Frost said. He turned to Madia before the old man could reply. "Little daylight reaches that part of Golemesk, in any case," he said, "except where the water lies deep enough to drown the ancient trees. Even if the barrow-wights were not a threat, there are shadows enough so that the leshy can attack at any time, and do."

Madia leaned toward Aphan, lowering her voice to a conspiratorial whisper. "Could a sorcerer, like Frost, say, get to the barrows, and back out again?"

"Doubtful," Frost said. Madia ignored him and kept to Aphan, who looked up, eyeing both of them. Finally Aphan shrugged. "Very hard to say," he said.

"Aphan can call a council of wizards," Frost remarked.

"They will reveal the name of the Blade's next intended guardian and seek him out. That one will in turn lead a party of sufficiently talented sorcerers and assistants to retrieve the Demon Blade."

"What if they can't find that person?" Madia wondered.

"Then a new council will be held, and another will be chosen."

"I would have gone alone, into the swamp, in my prime," Aphan said, working his face into a dim smile.

"On such a dangerous mission?" Frost asked him, winking. "How ever did you live so long?"

Aphan worked his face into a tight grin. "Luck!" he said.

Silence fell about the table. Madia sat thinking over all she had heard and all she still wanted to say. "Who else knows the secrets of the Blade?" she asked, mostly of Aphan.

"Only Ramins did," Aphan said solemnly. "And no one is quite sure of that."

"But he's dead."

Both men nodded.

"We will be leaving now," Frost said, rising again. "We must join our companions. Is there anything that you need?"

"No," Aphan said. "But tell me, as a favor to these old ears, where is it you intend to go?"

"He is going to help win Ariman back, of course," Madia said, then grinned as Frost looked at her.

Frost shrugged. "I am going south, toward Neleva," he said. Then he shrugged again. "Through Kamrit."

Aphan closed his eyes again. Frost turned to go, and Madia slowly followed him out. She said good-bye at the door, but Aphan was sound asleep.

"We are very different, you know," she told Frost as they entered the street, squinting at the harsh light of day. She walked up the street beside him. "Aphan said you never like to take risks."

"A fool's approach."

"You may be right, for I have never lived any other way," Madia said.

"We would both do well to consider where that has gotten you, I think," he said.

Madia started a hot reply, then realized she could not. Not yet, anyway. She followed him in silence.

"We have a boat," Rosivok announced, standing alone and greeting them as they neared the river. "Sharryl and the soldiers are aboard."

"Do you trust the boatman?" Frost asked.

"Well enough. He is a simple man, young and poor and with a wife and children. Loyalty to Lord Ferris does not run deep among the boatman, and wages are few. Some have been to Kamrit already this spring. They talk, and others listen. The river tolls are great, and penalties severe. The stories are mostly bad. He took our coins quickly enough, and will not want to give them back."

"Well, then," Frost answered, "take us there."

Madia went with them, past the last houses at the edge of town, then past a stable and a small inn. A group of men, five in all, stood about in front of the stables, their conversation kept low. Soldiers, Madia thought at first, though she wasn't certain why, since they wore no colors or armor. Then she noticed the battle swords they each wore, and their dress, much alike, styled linens and leathers—free men all.

The other four grew silent as one of them spoke, the way the peasants had been silent when the lord's hayward brought a message. The speaker seemed much too lean to be wearing the only two-handed sword in the lot. He stopped talking and looked up as Madia and the others passed, watching them, squinting to see in the fading light of early evening. *Watching me*, Madia thought, though she could not be sure.

But then the stables were out of sight and the river was just ahead. She kept checking as they walked, looking back over her shoulder, but no one followed. In a moment they reached the river's edge and headed aboard the boat.

The girl was not familiar, but Grear knew the man and the two strange warriors that walked with him; it had been years ago, somewhere in Achien or Lagoreth, he thought, beyond the Spartooths, but he remembered the fat wizard's arrogant face quite well—and his name, Frost, owing to his supposed prowess with a deadly kind of aging spell. The wizard had been known in the region for stopping a plague of locusts by making a heavy rain turn to ice as it touched the fields where the swarms had landed. The locusts had not only died, but had been used as meal and compost.

But he was known to be unpredictable, apparently depending on whatever framed his mood, even after an agreement had been made and fees met. Grear had thought to hire the wizard himself at the time, a precaution in the killing of a local noble who himself had hired a formidable mage—alas, a noble whose lady seemed to place great value on a swift, unconditional end to the man's life. Finally Grear had done the job with just his own men, and had lost most of them, he recalled, to a dizziness spell that forced them to keep their backs against the castle walls to prevent them from falling to the floor.

He watched the group wander out of sight, kept staring at the empty street after that.

"What's wrong?" one of the others asked after a time.

"Those merchants in the square yesterday," Grear said. "Do you recall the story they told?"

"The fight in Kern?" the other asked.

Grear nodded. "Fifteen of the king's soldiers killed,"

he added, thinking out loud. "And three of them turned old and white where they stood by a very fat mage."

Several of Grear's men nodded. Grear rubbed at the stubble on his chin, then he pointed to two of his men. "Follow them that went by just now; see if they go to hire a boat downriver."

Both men acknowledged him and set out at a brisk pace, disappearing around the corner.

"What are we up to?" one of the remaining men asked.

If Frost was headed toward Kamrit, Grear reasoned, he had either been hired by Kaafk, or by Kaafk's ene-mies—though if the stories from Kern were true, Frost was no ally of the crown. Which was valuable informa-tion, Grear decided, either way.

"We're trying to get a bit richer," Grear explained, then he told them what he knew. He found the others eager to listen.

"He is one of Grear's men," Kaafk said, standing as near to Lord Ferris as the great arms of the throne—made larger of late at the grand chamberlain's direction—would allow. He spoke as quietly as possible, so that the others assembled in the court would not hear. The soldier in question stood ten paces behind.

"And what is the trouble?" Lord Ferris asked.

"He says Grear recognized a man, one in a group of travelers buying downriver passage from Kopeth. A rogue mage who is known in other lands by the name of Frost. He makes the journey with two of your own men-at-arms, and three more unknown warriors. Grear believes the soldiers may be traitors, and may have hired the mage to aid them in some way."

"In what way?"

"How should I know?" Kaafk put both hands out, palms up. "A plot of some kind, perhaps, against you!"

"Do you believe this is possible?" Ferris asked, apparently unshaken.

Kaafk looked carefully at the soldier standing behind him, the crude armor he wore, the fine battle sword. Grear and his men had been a wise purchase, Kaafk thought, an investment that was already paying off. *The good Lord Ferris would do well to take lessons from Kaafk.*

"Many things are possible, lord. But I have met with Grear enough to know that he would not pass on such information unless, in his own mind, he thought there was good cause. Unless he thought it was . . . valuable."

"You," Lord Ferris said, speaking to the soldier. "Tell Grear I want these people followed and closely watched. If he learns more, I'll want to hear. It is possible the northern vassals have hired someone to help cause mischief, and some of our guard as well. And they may have friends in Kamrit itself, people we will want to know about. I have tried to leave alone as many of Andarys' knights as possible, but I may have been too lenient with them."

"There is more," Kaafk began, waiting to bring it up, recalling how thoroughly aggravated Ferris had become upon first hearing the news of that embarrassing, unfortunate defeat in the square at Kern. The grand chamberlain was not entirely sane, Kaafk was convinced of that, but he was almost entirely reliable in certain other respects.

There was something especially disquieting, now and again, about the man, however, in his manner, his answers at times, his questions—but it hadn't seemed to matter in the course of larger events. Probably, Kaafk thought, it never would. "Grear has found people from Kopeth who say this Frost and the others came on the north road from Kern just two days after the battle there. Frost, it seems, has a reputation for his aging spells. Three of your dead guardsmen in Kern were found—"

"I remember."

Ferris sat silently awhile, and Kaafk noticed it again, the strange look, the eyes. Perhaps a spell that this Frost had created was having some effect. Or Ferris might be some sort of wizard himself and had simply never shown his hand. Kaafk sighed quietly and put these thoughts aside. The possibilities were nearly endless, enough to make worrying over them too great a task, especially when it didn't seem important.

"Also inform Grear," Lord Ferris said suddenly, jogging Kaafk from his thoughts, "that I would like Frost and the others intercepted and questioned before they arrive at Kamrit. If they are the ones who killed the guards in Kern, I'll want Grear to kill them. If they object to the questioning, he may kill them anyway. I would prefer to have the men-at-arms brought in alive if possible, for trial, but Grear may use his best judgment. We will pay him for each head, in any case."

"Very well," the soldier said.

"You may go as well," Ferris told Kaafk, using a satisfied tone. Kaafk felt reasonably good himself. He turned and motioned the soldier to one side and out, then he bowed to the lord and swept himself away.

Chapter XIII

The river ran wide and slow from Kopeth south into Chelle Lake, then split, one small arm flowing inland while its main arm continued south and west to its mouth at Kamrit and the sea. The journey took three to four days most of the year, but the waters north of Chelle were high and muddy from the spring rains, and unusually swift. The boat arrived at the lake's northern tip by the end of the second day, and with morning, they set out again across the wide waters.

Frost sat back near the boatman and watched the others, all gathered nearer the open bow, and tried not to think about the situation. The river was not wide and no deeper than a man was tall in most places.

But the lake was more menacing; water was a barrier to most magic, a thing not easily controlled or understood, a void that could swallow even a great wizard in a single, unremorseful gulp. There were far too many omens and practices for good and bad luck to do with the sea, most of which he was not familiar with.

Such voyages were a thing Frost had always sought to avoid. Yet at times, there was no reasonable choice.

He watched the shore pass by as the long, deep lake gathered all around them. Then he noticed Madia turned around, staring at him as he looked back. She got up and made her way toward him, climbing over piles of raw wool covered with burlap, the boatman's bonus cargo. She crouched beside him in silence at first, watching the shore with him now. A group of villagers were gathered on their knees at the water's edge, sinking pails to gather water.

"I have done that with buckets," she said, "and worse, living in the villages just west of here, before I found Hoke."

"Few nobility ever know what life is like for most of their people," Frost told her. "You are fortunate."

"It didn't seem that way at the time."

"Yet you survived."

"Hoke helped me, and so did Keara. They expected me to act like 'Princess Madia,' just like everybody else, but with them, I began to *want* to."

"So many things make us what we are, like the many things that affect a realm."

"I never wanted to be queen."

Frost could not help a smile. "Nor do I."

Madia smiled back, then her expression grew more serious.

"So tell me," she said, "what does Frost want?"

He said, "That has a tendency to change from one day to another."

Madia leaned closer, her eyes fixed on his. "I know. So just today, then?"

"Soon enough, I will let you know."

"But it *is* soon enough. I keep insisting you will help me, and you don't argue, but that does not mean you will. I stand little chance against Ferris without your magic and experience, but I can't make plans when all I know for sure is that you may not always be counted on."

Frost considered his reply. He was still too busy eyeing the waters and reading the signs and thinking over all that Aphan had said to him, but a number of possibly unpleasant decisions were growing ever more imminent. He was impressed with Madia, more so all the time, and he held no doubt that she was the true heir to the throne at Kamrit—and that if she were somehow successful in displacing the grand chamberlain, she would pay him well enough. Money was not a concern. But the issue was more complex.

He had helped her grandfather create this realm, and Madia's blood alone did not entitle her to control its destiny. He had already learned enough about the grand chamberlain to convince him that Lord Ferris must ultimately be removed, and that he might well need to lend a hand to the task, but that did not require that Madia be made queen. She held great promise, but she had not proven herself as yet.

We will find ourselves opposed by very powerful enemies indeed, he thought, looking at her. *But she needn't know that now.*

"I have kept away from feudal squabbles these many years," he said in answer, "because they tend to grow much too messy, just as this entire affair seems to be. Politics do not suit me. Now, an evil curse, natural catastrophes, rogue creatures conjured or natural, out wreaking havoc: these are far more palatable challenges."

"You know," Madia said, "even among the most pitiful villages, a man with a well cow will share milk with a poorer man's children; the strongest men will help a weakened neighbor with the gardens; the best weavers loan their hands to the worst."

"So we have a responsibility to others, because of the blood we were born with, is that what you're saying?"

Madia looked away. "Yes."

"How completely charming," Frost replied, "to hear these sentiments coming from your own lips. You have made your point, but my abilities are of consequence to no one, and my first duty is to myself. You felt as I do until quite lately, I understand, or have you forgotten already?"

"What if I was but a fool?"

"Suit yourself."

She was quiet for a moment, pursing her lips, eyes darting with the energy of her thoughts as Frost considered her, readying a parry for her next counter-thrust. She was not easily shaken, nor easily refused, this girl. And not easily fooled, either. An impressive combination, in fact.

"Most men of magic align themselves with a crown," she said.

"In order to surround themselves with the protection afforded by the crown's armies. But I have never felt the need." Frost glanced toward Rosivok and Sharryl. "I have always kept my own personal guard. I consider them more trustworthy than noblemen and mercenaries retained by others, men who truly owe me nothing." Though there was something to be said for nameless castle regulars, he thought; in return for their pledge to him he had always pledged his protection to his Subartans, and Jaffic had died.

Madia let the matter rest. The day passed slowly, and silently, while both pondered the deep waters the barge passed through. As early evening arrived, Madia was watching the village of Chelle pass by as the boat reached the far end of the lake, and again entered river waters. A relief, Frost thought.

"Do you see them?" Madia asked him, breaking her long silence, pointing toward the shore. The boat was just rounding a small pine-covered isle set in the middle of the stream. The boatman stayed to the right side, avoiding the rocks that seemed to be everywhere on the left. A small group of men and horses stood on the river's right-hand shore, waiting just at the water's edge.

"Better sit down," the boatman said, guiding the boat steadily right of the island, directly toward the men. "River's shallow on this side, too. We'll likely hit bottom a time or two."

"What of them?" Frost asked, waving toward shore. The boat drew close to them now, six men in all, unfamiliar, wearing light, mostly leather armor and carrying swords and crossbows. Soldiers from some distant land, Frost decided. Mercenaries, perhaps.

"I think I saw them in Kopeth, at a stables near the river," Madia said, pointing to a man who seemed to stand at the head of the bunch.

"You're certain?" Frost asked.

Madia nodded. "That one, the short one wearing the double-handed sword, he watched us go by, like he knew us . . . or knew me."

"Rosivok!" Frost shouted. The boat jounced once off the river bottom, rocking its passengers. Rosivok waited an instant then got up, followed by Sharryl, and tried to step to the back of the boat. They hit bottom again, and the boat rolled hard to one side as the two Subartans stumbled over wool and burlap.

"Stay still, the lot of you!" the boatman shouted, fighting the rudder to keep the boat straight in the mixing currents. Frost held his hand up to Rosivok, staying him. He pointed toward shore. Rosivok and Sharryl turned toward the men.

"They seek us out," Frost told the two. The Subartans nodded, then slowly settled into ready positions.

"They have a rope across," Sharryl called back, pointing just beyond the bow into the water. Frost saw it then, one end of the line tied to an island pine, the other to the saddle of one of the horses just behind the waiting men.

"When the boat stops, talk to them," Frost told Madia, his voice near a whisper. "See what they want."

Madia looked a question at him.

"I will need a moment," he said.

Madia nodded, then turned and got forward just a bit, putting herself between Frost and the shoreline as the bow contacted the rising rope. Olan and Delyav were both on their feet, knees bent for balance, swords drawn, following the lead of the two Subartans. Frost breathed deeply and closed his eyes, drawing on his ample reserves, then set about assembling the two spells he thought would do the most good. When he looked again, he saw the lead fellow on shore, his boots just touching water, press the heel of one hand to the hilt of his two-handed sword. Another man, taller, just as lean, held the line of horses while their four remaining companions drew crossbows from behind their backs.

"We'll have a word with you!" the leader shouted. Frost glanced up and examined the look in the other man's eyes—tense but focused, cold. The face was older and more keen than Frost had thought.

"Who are you?" Madia asked, leaving her own blade in its scabbard, planting her hands on her hips. Frost couldn't help but notice the defiance her manner implied, the courage, warranted or not.

"Name's Grear," the man answered, grinning now precisely like a trapper observing his catch. "Now who are you?"

"We are citizens of Kamrit, on our way home until a bandit's rope stopped us."

Grear didn't smile. "Those all citizens behind you there?"

"They are."

"What's the big, fat fellow's name?"

"My name would mean little to you," Frost said in a quiet voice, remaining seated. He glanced at the boatman, who had a most troubled look on his face and who seemed to be squatting as low as possible. With the current, the stern was drifting around to the right away from the men on shore; nothing to be done about it. Frost reached back with one hand and touched the boatman's leg, trying to comfort him, then he turned again toward shore.

"Just answer," Grear replied. "I'll be the judge."

"This boat and its cargo mean nothing as well," Frost said, louder now. "We have little money and only some spring wool. Hardly worth the wear on your rope. Let us pass."

"Your name is Frost!" Grear came back, shouting it, obviously aggravated now, the grin suddenly gone. "You hailed from Achien once, some years ago. You were a well-known sorcerer there, and all for hire."

"Do you wish to hire me, then?"

"I would know who has."

Frost saw him repeatedly glancing from Olan and Delyav to the Subartans and back. The four bowmen behind Grear kept their weapons up, held at ready. Frost concentrated on the wood, completing the first spell he had begun, speaking under his breath.

"We have simple business in Neleva," Madia said. "Nothing so exciting as you would imagine."

"All of you have yet to introduce yourselves!" Grear insisted.

"The Subartans are my personal companions," Frost said, ready now. "These others are simply fortunate enough to share a part of my journey with me. Where they go is not my concern. And none of yours."

"You're lying!" Grear snapped. "I say you're the ones who did in two full squads in Kern. You and the girl. And Lord Ferris wants to know why you did it. If you won't tell me, he wants your heads! You'll fetch a fine price, either way. *All* of you," he added, slowly drawing the big sword out, wrapping his other hand around it. Frost saw the Subartans turn the straight-edge of their blades to face the shore. He had seen them deflect arrows in the past, moving faster than conscious thought. But at such close range, and with no way to get to the bowmen quickly enough to prevent them from reloading . . .

He didn't want to be hauled into Kamrit under guard and thrown in a dungeon, forced to strain his wits and palate under the those awful conditions, any more than he wanted to lose another Subartan.

"Lord Ferris has already cost myself and others far too much, my friend," Frost told the soldier. "Far more than I am likely to forgive, though now, there is at least a chance. Unless you insist on doing everyone a disservice."

"You are a bigger fool than I imagined," Grear replied.

"Very well," Frost said, bowing from the neck to Grear and his men, then he turned one hand palm-out, concentrating again on the wood in the bandit's hands. All four crossbows turned black, then burst into flames.

The men tossed the bows from hand to hand for an instant, then let them drop to the ground, wringing their scorched fingers. Madia was the last one out of the boat, close behind Olan and Delyav and the two Subartans. Frost turned to the boatman, who was crouched, clutching the rudder, his face paralyzed in a wide-eyed gape. "Prepare to continue," he said, then he seated himself again and looked back to the soldiers.

Grear was dead already, struck down before he could swing the big sword twice, padded leather armor torn apart by the Subarta's serrated blade where Sharryl had laid his breast open. Now another man lay dead and bleeding just beyond Grear's body. Frost watched as Olan and Delyav picked one man each, showing the prowess of their years of service, dodging then striking, forcing their opponents back until they could take advantage of their momentum in a brief flurry of successful thrusts.

Rosivok toyed with another man momentarily, advancing with erratic motions while Sharryl went after the soldier who had been keeping the rope taut. But as she approached him, circling the horses to get at him, he made the animal bolt, then clung to it somehow as it disappeared into the bright green trees and shrubs. Far too fast for anyone on foot to follow.

Rosivok seemed to suddenly tire of the fight. He sprang, a direct attack to his opponent, followed by a thrust that left the man nearly torn in half. Only one stood against them now, locking swords with Delyav. Madia joined that fight, and in a moment it was ended.

Sharryl had already collected one of the other horses to pursue the escaped bandit. Frost shouted ashore: "Leave him!" They might wait half the day for her to return, he thought, and he had no desire to do that.

Those on shore set about dragging bodies into the brush.

The boatman, shaking noticeably, wrestled his craft ashore thirty yards upriver, where the others pulled it up far enough to allow Frost to get ashore without wading. "I have no wish to be wanted by the crown," the boatman said, apparently expanding on something he and Frost had already begun to discuss. "My family—"

"We will part company here," Frost said to the others, by way of explanation. "I cannot ask this man to throw his life away. He will say that we forced him to carry us, and that he let us off at the head of the lake. We will go ahead on foot. I am sure we would find the river ports of Kamrit much too crowded with waiting soldiers, in any case."

He turned to the boatman, then reached into his bag

and produced a few gold coins. As he handed them over, he placed his other hand on the man's shoulder. "Keep our full payment," he said, "and something extra."

"Thank you," the boatman began. "I—"

Frost cut him off. "Go," he said. "And the Greater Gods be with you."

They waited until he got back aboard, then everyone helped push the heavy craft off the soft muddy bottom. Dark clouds drifted away in the waters around their feet.

"Your reputation is more widespread than I was aware," Madia said, approaching Frost.

"I seldom mention it," Frost replied. "It is a burden I must carry."

"*We* must carry," Madia corrected.

"Perhaps."

"No matter," Delyav noted. "Lord Ferris seems to be expecting us and is seeking compensation for the loss of his men in Kern."

"*I* expect compensation for the loss of my father and my cousin, for the dishonor he has brought to the throne of Kamrit," Madia corrected.

"Interesting," Frost said, "that you should speak so of dishonoring your father's throne."

"Or that you should speak of honor at all, since you say you honor only yourself," Madia snapped back.

"As you wish," Frost taunted, grinning at her, savoring the sour expression he drew in return.

"They were but killers," Rosivok said, looking upstream, ignoring the conversation. "They would have taken us nowhere."

"I agree," Frost said. "Mercenaries. And expected to succeed, I'm sure, so we might hope to meet with very few others like them for a time."

"You sound so intent. So . . . committed, perhaps?" Madia said, looking at him.

Astute, Frost thought again. She was a worthy ally;

the time had come to seek a common ground. "These men were hired to learn what they could, then kill us all," he told Madia. "I take a dim view of such behavior in a monarch—and I already had a dim view of Lord Ferris, I assure you. Come, and we will talk as we travel the road. By the time we reach Kamrit, we must be ready.

"Rosivok," he instructed, "gather one of their horses to serve as pack." Then he turned back to Madia and wondered when she would see fit to ease that foolish grin of hers.

Tyrr lent an ear to Kaafk as the other man leaned close. One of Grear's soldiers stood below, several paces behind Kaafk, the same man who had come before, Tyrr thought. He listened as Kaafk explained what the man had to say about the incident at Chelle, especially the flaming bows. Tyrr found the account most intriguing.

"And do they know that you lived?" Tyrr asked the soldier, who seemed reluctant to look at Tyrr directly.

"They must," Kaafk replied. The soldier nodded.

"I wish to take them prisoner, at least the wizard. They will leave the boat, since they must assume we are expecting them and since a boat is a poorly defensible place to be. We will put patrols on all the roads until they are located, then reduce the guard on all the main gates to the city, so we do not scare them off. We'll let them come. I still want to know their plans, and who their friends in Kamrit might be.

"Once they have been found, I can follow their progress, then destroy them as I choose." And Frost, Tyrr mused, if he was truly as talented as he appeared, would provide a rare amusement, a chance to exercise his true prowess, which was something Tyrr had lately developed a dire craving for. *One of many things. . . .*

"I will help in any way I can, my liege," Kaafk said, though of course, Tyrr observed, reading the expression on the merchant's face, there was obviously nothing for him to do.

"Very well," Tyrr made the mouth say summarily. He dismissed Kaafk and the entire court for the day, thinking of his needs, his plans. . . .

He left the hall and made his way through the castle to the kitchens. He chose a small piglet, only four hands tall, from the kitchen yard and instructed one of the cooks to slaughter the animal. Then he sent the cook away and drew a black velvet sack from beneath his cloak. He put the piglet in the sack and tied it shut, then carefully worked the spell he had constructed. The bag lay suddenly flat and empty. Tyrr put it back under his cloak and left.

He descended two levels, past the guards—men chosen and prepared especially for the job—and continued down into the subterranean chambers that were part of the old dungeons, rooms that had not been used since the time of the first kin. In the largest of the ancient cells, the imps waited for him, still in their demon forms, held there where he had bound them. They were each identical, each perfect, the only two lesser demons Tyrr had been able to summon out of the dark realm before the gate he had fashioned collapsed.

Already, though, they had grown weak, kept here away from all sources of energy, from even a meal of animal flesh, since none could be trusted to feed them and Tyrr had not taken the time. He fed them now, siphoning power from the friction between the worlds of darkness and light, then giving it to the creatures using a spell he had taken great care to perfect. The imps grew more substantial, more energetic, then they began to drool as Tyrr drew the velvet sack from under his cloak and concentrated on his spells again. The sack grew suddenly full, and he reached inside to withdraw the piglet.

When the imps had devoured the animal fully, Tyrr told them exactly what he wanted them to do, then set them free.

Chapter XIV

They circled around to the south, following a small and barely passable rocky road through the apple orchards, then approached the gate in the city's walls nearest the inner bailey, where Madia's carriage had always entered. One of the most secluded, this was also the gate Madia was most familiar with. The only drawback was that the guards were quite familiar with her, but Frost insisted she should not concern herself with that. As they neared the wall, the wizard stopped, planted his staff and turned to her, reciting twice over four words not meant for her to understand. Then he closed his eyes and slowly opened them again.

She felt no different, and the Subartans showed no reaction at all, but Olan and Delyav looked quite surprised.

"What is it?" she asked. "What has he done?"

"You have a different face," Olan explained.

"And a different figure," Delyav chuckled. "Quite plump. You could be the wizard's daughter!"

She glanced at herself and saw only the body she was

used to, a body grown leaner and harder than when last she had passed this way. She shrugged and looked at Frost.

"You see nothing because you of all people cannot be fooled as to who you are," Frost said. "Something you would do well to remember." Then he turned again and continued toward the city. Madia frowned and followed him.

The gate sentries asked after their business, and Delyav and Olan vouched for everyone—friends they had made while touring northern Ariman, they said. All were allowed to pass. The castle, Madia thought, would prove more difficult.

She felt a strange sensation as she passed unnoticed among the people on the streets, the very same laborers and tradesman, beggars and squires who had lined the streets when her carriage had passed not so long ago. But they did not look quite themselves to her, either. Each face stood out, especially the poorest of them, lines and expressions that told their sad stories. She felt almost as if she truly were a ghost, and only these people were real.

Frost asked her to lead the way now. She did so, taking the shortest routes until they reached the end of a narrow street and emerged onto a wide crossroad. Smooth, flat stones spanned the distance from the shops and houses to the castle walls, some fifty paces across the way. Madia began to notice the quiet—the usual clutter of citizens and carts was not there.

"It's as if everyone is hiding," she told Frost. "This way is normally a popular one."

Frost nodded, then motioned to the two Subartans. They took up defensive positions on either side of him while Frost pulled Madia close. "Whatever your plans, you are pledged to be my Subartan, for now," he said, reminding her of it.

She nodded, then did as he asked and stood by while

the wizard put himself in another focussed trance. A faint greenish sheen shimmered briefly about him. She watched it spread to her, surrounding her as well. The green seemed to brighten momentarily, and then it was gone, leaving no visible trace at all.

Frost came to again, then paused to gather himself. "A warding spell," he said, "quite useful," then gave the signal.

"We will go first," Delyav announced, looking at Madia, Olan nodding along with him. "We cannot allow you."

She smiled at them, letting it slip. They were very good men, she thought, in just the right ways. The Subartans found new positions, one behind and one ahead of Frost, and they all started off again. Madia went just in front of the trio, following Olan and Delyav.

"There is an entrance to the lower levels," Madia said. "One that leads into the storage rooms."

"That will lead us to the kitchens and the lower banquet hall," Delyav said, nodding at her plan. "From there we will have many choices."

"If we get in," Olan cautioned. "We're bound to meet someone there."

"We will get in," said Madia. "If there are guards when we reach the entrance, you two will say you caught me hiding from duties in the kitchens. We can dispose of the guards as they let us pass, if they are not too many, and they should not be." She turned around to face Frost and the others. "You three will have to wait out of sight."

"Suppose these guards are friends of these men?" Rosivok asked, talking to Madia, but watching Olan and Delyav carefully.

"That is possible," Olan said. "But if they are truly our friends, then they will *help* us pass." Delyav seemed to agree. Rosivok quietly nodded, and again the two knights led off.

Madia followed along as they entered Kamrit Castle through a small oak-and-iron doorway, then turned to the left. The storerooms were well stocked but deserted.

In a moment Frost and the Subartans came out to join them. Cautiously, silently, they approached the kitchen and found it empty, too. Madia couldn't recall this ever being the case.

"They know," Frost said.

"They must," Madia agreed. "I had hoped to make surprise an ally."

"If we are met by many troops, be wary of my lead," Frost advised. "I have prepared one or two surprises."

"We must go further," Madia said. "I've not come all this way to leave with nothing."

"I know," Frost said, leaving it at that. They made their way across the kitchen to the dining hall door. Madia tested the door, pushing it partway open with little effort. She couldn't see anything in the huge dim hall beyond.

"Wait out of sight again," she told Frost, and he moved slightly back. She turned and pushed the door fully open with her foot and stepped through. At once the doorway filled with a burst of thick orange flames that rushed in from all sides, enveloping Madia, turning instantly red then changing again, violet, saffron, and finally yellow-white as she held out her arms and looked at herself. The heat forced the others back with hands over their faces, though she felt nothing at all. Then she was through the arch, and as quickly as they arose the colored fires died back to a dim glow that traced the doorway opening for an instant, and was gone.

"You are yourself again," Delyav said, staring at her as everyone was.

"The warding spell as well as the false glamour I provided you has been neutralized by the spell that protected the entrance," Frost said in a somber tone.

"A fine defensive effort," Rosivok remarked, looking the doorframe over.

"The equal of Vasip, or even Montiby," Frost replied, stoking his chin.

"What does that mean?" Olan asked.

"That we are off to a poor beginning," Frost responded.

"Good, I feel much better," Madia moaned, still a little dazed, her heart pounding. The image of the quick inferno still blazed in her eyes.

"The magic is spent," Frost said. "We may continue safely."

Delyav led the way again, though he seemed to use great caution. They started across the dining hall, a huge open room hung with ample tapestries and set about from wall to wall with four long, wide tables. Only a few of the room's many torches burned, making details hard to see. But again, there seemed to be no one about. Olan lit an extra torch from the wall nearest the door and held it up, then went on. When they were nearly halfway across the room, the tapestries came to life, bustling with movement as men wielding crossbows came from behind them and opened fire.

Madia felt hands upon her back, felt herself being thrown to the floor, and realized it was Sharryl. Rosivok was rolling away on the floor just to the other side of her. She looked up to find Olan and Delyav faring far worse, arrows bristling from both of them, blood running from too many places as they stumbled forward and fell to the floor. She turned as she heard Frost shout from behind, repeating a short exotic phrase. Arrows impacted on the greenish air all around the wizard, but none seemed to reach him. Then the image blurred as the wall torches gurgled and puffed and filled the room with thick, gray smoke. Madia smelled a faint whiff of sulfur, nothing more; her eyes did not water, but everything had disappeared.

"I can't see," she whispered to Sharryl, feeling the other woman's hand still on her back.

"We don't have to," Sharryl said. "Listen."

She heard bows firing, arrows flying, bouncing off the stone walls above her head, then men screaming and cursing and dying all around her.

"They're killing each other," she said.

"Yes, a few anyway. Now, crawl!" Sharryl told her.

She heard Frost moving behind her again as they started off and decided he was on the floor as well, crawling as she was. The warding spell had protected the wizard from the initial barrage, but such things had limits; by now he too was probably vulnerable—and enormously unhappy about it.

"We're near the room's north wall," Sharryl said, after navigating a stout table leg, then pulling Madia after her. "Where would you like to go?"

"There should be a stairwell just ahead of us."

They crawled a few more yards until they encountered the wall, then Sharryl followed Madia, tracing the stone, until their hands found the raised stone of the steps. Sharryl paused then, waiting for Rosivok. She rose and stumbled up, then out, through the doorway at the top of the stairs into a wide, empty corridor. The others quickly followed, pulling the door shut behind them.

Rosivok and Sharryl stood guard while Frost renewed the warding spells on both Madia and himself, though he left her appearance alone; there was at least a possibility that she might find herself among friends, he explained, and she was inclined to agree, though she was by no means certain.

"We will not be caught unawares again," Frost said after that. He held his staff close to his breast and whispered to it, moving his hands over it as he did. When he finished, he turned and held the staff toward the door just behind them. The thick end in his hand began to quiver. As he moved the staff away again, the motion subsided. Without another word, he turned and set off down the hall, leading with the staff.

"Which way?" Frost asked, slowing as they neared a junction. "The shortest route to Lord Ferris' chambers?"

"Through the courtyard, this way," Madia said, taking the lead again. Another two hallways and the group found themselves in a private courtyard filled with flowering shrubberies and stone benches. "There," Madia said, pointing to the balconies above the far side of the yard.

They paused, watching Frost's staff, then continued when all seemed well. Halfway across the yard, Frost's staff nearly leaped from his hand.

Across the yard a cluster of swordsmen burst through a row of arches, trampling shrubs and low hedgerows as they came. Frost stood pat, already engrossed with his spells. Madia followed Rosivok and Sharryl as they moved forward to meet the attackers.

She took on the first man she came to, fending off a clumsy thrust and countering with a messy but deadly blow to the throat. She looked left and saw Rosivok already standing over three dead men, saw Sharryl cutting the middle out of her third kill. *Impossible to keep up with,* Madia thought. Then she found three soldiers confronting her, and a fourth joining in, and she began backing off, deflecting a flurry of blades as the soldiers closed in.

Suddenly they each stood back and froze in place, wearing looks of surprise and anguish. As they tried to move, Madia saw them wince, and heard their muffled moans. She chanced another glance sideways and saw that all of the attackers were so afflicted, all standing as still as possible.

Rosivok and Sharryl advanced on them, scything them

like an unwanted thicket. Madia followed, cutting first one man down, then going after a second. Most went hobbling away, backward at first, getting themselves turned around as they went, groaning through gritted teeth with each step they took. She looked back and saw Frost leaning easily on his staff, just watching.

"Enough!" he called out. "We will go and have our visit with the grand chamberlain without further delay." He looked at Madia and she nodded. Then a voice, loud and echoing among the courtyard's stone walls, called out from somewhere above them: "He awaits you now!"

Madia looked up to see a figure high on a balcony, staring down at them: Lord Ferris.

"You appear to be a formidable mage," Ferris said. "Able to embarrass my guard, and conjure the image of our dead princess upon this poor girl, so to fool the court, no doubt. And such a large, strong fellow, capable of great endurance, surely. You will be remembered well . . . by some."

"And known to many!" Frost replied.

"Your legacy ends here," Ferris said. "You are also a formidable nuisance. I would ask of one so wise in years and magic, such as yourself: what is it you hoped to gain by these incredible actions?"

"Justice, perhaps," Frost replied, holding himself erect by clutching his staff in both hands.

"You feel your death will represent some sort of justice? Then tell me, who have you wronged?"

"Madia has been wronged, my lord, and her father, and the memory of her grandfather, as have the people of this realm. It is that legacy I champion, and your right to it which I contest."

"This made-up girl you bring makes no difference to anyone. And my legacy is my own. As for you, I had thought to make you perform for my court, payment for sparing your life, but I can already see that you are far too confused to honor such a bargain."

Madia noticed both Subartans moving at the right edge of her vision, keeping low, ready stances. They faced a creature no more than a yard or so tall, a thing with black eyes and dirty crimson flesh, a naked, knobby, pointy-faced imp that seemed almost humorous at first glance, though much less so as it came closer, growing more distinct, baring deadly black teeth as it grinned and opened its generous mouth. It leaped abruptly and landed exactly between Rosivok and Sharryl.

"No!" Frost shouted, and the Subartans stepped back and stood still, each still facing the thing. It glared at them, features twisting, then it turned to Frost and its expression changed. The wizard pointed his staff and shouted a single sound, and the creature shrieked, then leaped again, howling and screaming as it went. It landed halfway across the courtyard and began rolling about, still howling: a high-pitched shredded sound, like a wild dog being horribly maimed.

Madia glanced back up at Ferris and saw that his expression had changed as well, had become one of agitation. He raised his arms and moved his lips, and the air within the courtyard seemed to ignite. The flash was blinding, the sound deafening. An invisible wave of air rushed against Madia like the slap of some great hand, knocking her hard to the ground, stunned. Her body ached everywhere as she tried to move, but she raised her head enough to see that her companions were laid out as she was, including Frost.

Fresh movement called her attention. Soldiers were edging back toward them, their paralysis apparently receding, their temerity restored. Rosivok seemed to notice, too, and began pulling himself up; Sharryl was slower, but in a moment both Subartans were largely on their feet again.

They helped Frost up, and Madia saw the look in his eyes: a ferocious, blazing indignation, all traces of balance and reason vanished now. He reached up toward Ferris and spoke a series of rapid commands. The balcony itself began to shake, threatening to give way as bits of stone and mortar crumbled and fell.

Then Ferris shouted back strange words of his own, and the shaking and crumbling stopped.

Frost was already adding new phrases, waving his arms and staff about, a wild man now, as Madia had never dreamed he could become. He took his eyes off the balcony and looked about, then pointed his staff. With a shout he raised one of the yard's many stone benches off the ground and sent it hurtling at Ferris. But before it arrived, Ferris somehow managed to blast the object into dust and gravel, all of which fell to the ground below, sending soldiers scurrying to get out of the way.

"Madia!" Rosivok shouted. She turned to find the two Subartans engaging the approaching soldiers. He was calling for her help.

As she gathered herself and started forward, she heard Frost scream like a man being brutally tortured. Madia looked to see him staggering backward, shaking, clutching his staff tightly in both hands as he held it out horizontally before him. Ferris had his own hands held out and up over his head, his eyes closed, his mouth open. She could hear a sound coming from him, too: a long, low tone that hardly seemed possible for a human voice, a steady note that carried on without a single breath of interruption.

The smaller demon-creature was up again, recovering now; it circled Frost, getting closer and apparently getting excited about it. Rosivok broke off suddenly and lunged at the thing, which made it leap as it had before. But to his credit, Rosivok, seeming to anticipate the move, bounded up to intercept the imp's trajectory. He sliced through one of the creature's knobby legs as it passed over his head and the demon screamed again. It fell in a misshapen heap a few yards away and began flopping about, its head thrashing as it continued to scream, black blood running from the stub of the severed limb.

But already the soldiers were closing, working their way toward Frost, bold, as though he were no longer a threat. Madia looked at him again and saw that this was true—saw Frost's arms drop suddenly. He turned and fell to the ground where he lay breathing but motionless, beaten. On the balcony above, Ferris had opened his eyes again and lowered his hands. The terrible intensity on his face was already softening, being replaced by a growing calm.

"They come!" Rosivok shouted. Madia turned her attention back to the soldiers as they rushed in. She dropped further back, nearer Frost, joining the two Subartans as they moved in close to where the wizard lay. The attackers were not great fighters, but there were at least two dozen of them now, and no amount of prowess was a match for so many. Some of them held back, still cautious, but most found courage enough. Madia heard Sharryl shout out to the Greater Gods and glanced left to see blood running from her right arm. She moved still closer, and the three of them found themselves nearly standing on top of Frost.

Run, Madia thought, seeing this as their only choice, but she knew the two Subartans would not; they would stand and fight over his body until they were dead.

Then the light of day was gone.

Madia looked about frantically, blinking her eyes. *The sun!* She could see nothing at all in the total blackness. But it was not just the absence of sunlight, she guessed, for even a moonless night was filled with stars. *I am blind,* she realized. Completely. And then, just as suddenly, she was not.

She saw the courtyard exactly as it had been, the soldiers pressing in all around her, but they did not attack. She thought they might still be blind as she had been, then noticed that their eyes seemed to work well enough. Several of the soldiers looked directly at her, but then they looked away as if she were not there. She looked at Sharryl and Rosivok and saw that they had changed, that they were not exactly themselves. Their own images remained, barely visible in a jumble of images, but what she saw for the most part were two of Ferris' own soldiers. More illusions of some sort, she decided. False glamors, like the one she had worn into the city.

Frost!

She looked down and saw a very large soldier lying behind her, rolling over and struggling to get to his feet. . . .

"The knaves must have run while we could not see," Rosivok said abruptly, playing out his new role, apparently aware of the implications.

"Which way?" one of the "real" soldiers asked.

"Up, to the lord's chambers!" Rosivok shouted.

"Aye!" another man said. "Assassins, and they are up to it still!"

"Aye!" half the other men chimed, most of them making their way back toward the arches through which they had come, the way to the king's chambers—*Lord Ferris' chambers,* Madia corrected herself, a knot growing in her stomach as she weighed the thought.

"Now," the man that was Frost said from behind her, in a voice almost too soft to hear, "we will go *that* way." He nodded to indicate a retreat. "Rosivok," Frost added, "tell them a good lie."

"We will go down the way the intruders came!" the Subartan shouted, indicating Sharryl and Madia, and Frost. "To be sure they did not run out instead."

"Very well," one of the men, a sergeant, agreed. But then he indicated two other men to go along as well. Rosivok nodded, and the six of them made their way back out of the yard. Madia kept watch on Frost, who was clearly having trouble keeping up. He seemed devoid of energy, barely able to navigate the courtyard's walkways. She could see just enough of his true image to notice that his clothing hung on him now, as though he had lost a great deal of weight—as though it wasn't Frost at all.

The instant he passed through the archway, Frost stumbled and fell against the stone wall of the corridor beyond. Rosivok and Sharryl quickly turned their blades on the two soldiers. In an instant, both men lay dead.

The Subartans took one of Frost's arms each and continued down the hall, back toward the lower banquet hall and the storage rooms beyond.

When they finally reached the stairwell that led to the street, Madia made the others pause.

"We can't leave," she said. Then, "I can't leave."

"I know," Frost mumbled, hoarse and fading, but rallying himself somewhat. "I know how you feel, but we *must* leave. All of us. The creature we faced is not the grand chamberlain as he pretends, nor a man of any kind. I have never encountered anything . . . to compare." He closed his eyes, breathing heavily, then looked at her again. "Ferris, the thing that he is, commands great powers, more than the greatest of sorcerers, more than any creature of this world.

"I did not believe, not until I saw the imp he set upon us." Another pause. Madia waited.

"None but a demon prince could command such lesser demons," Frost went on. "I know what I felt, the power he brought to bear against me." He faded yet again, hanging like a dead man in the arms of his two

Subartans. Then the eyes slowly opened once more. "Trickery saved us once," he said, "but do not count on it again."

Madia was swept by a wave of implications, both future and past. What Frost was saying could mean many things. "Then my father," she said, feeling a chill as she realized it, "never stood any chance at all."

"None," Frost replied, eyes closed.

"And neither do we," Rosivok said, his voice edged with the first real sense of doubt, perhaps even fear, that Madia had ever felt from the Subartans. More than the soldiers and the imp, more than Ferris himself, this frightened her. Their confidence, and Frost's, had been an inspiration, a foundation on which to build. She felt something within her coming completely apart, and knew of nothing to stop it.

"Come!" Rosivok said, moving again. "Come now!" Madia complied.

The false glamors on each of them had already begun to fade as they hurried up and out into the city's streets, into the waiting shadows across the stone way—helping Frost along at first, carrying him entirely after that.

"Who do you know here?" Rosivok asked. "Who can we go to for help?"

Madia looked about her at the many houses, the peasants and beggars and freemen and others, their numbers scarce as night approached. She felt something immensely heavy inside of her now, a burden, terribly old and awkward and consummate, which the truth had forced upon her. She stared at her feet, fighting the sway. "There is . . . no one," she confessed.

The Subartans looked at each other silently. "Of course," Sharryl said. Madia had no response.

Then they turned and set off again, carrying Frost, who was now clearly a hundred pounds lighter than he had been when he'd first arrived at Kamrit. In a few minutes, they entered a small square ringed with shops and a scattering of guild halls. There was still a fair sized crowd here, apparently on hand for a public execution. A platform had been erected in the center of the square, and an axman's block stood at its center. Guards waited there with a man in irons, all standing to one side.

Madia followed Sharryl and Rosivok as they hastened along the back edges of the crowd, largely unnoticed. In the streets beyond the square, they finally found a place to hide—a small stable, filthy for lack of attention and empty but for a single horse. They settled in a stall and waited for nightfall. In the stable's utter darkness, they let Frost rest, and began to discuss how they might get out of the city without his help—whether, with the guards alerted now, it was reasonable even to try.

"Perhaps I can help," a new voice said, a faint silhouette that spoke from just inside the half-open stable door; a woman, though her form grew invisible as she entered further. Madia did not need to see the woman's face. She knew the voice, and this time it took her only a moment to place it.

"Anna?" she asked.

"Yes, my lady. Yes."

"I saw you in the square," Anna said, her form barely visible where she sat on the stable's floor close to Madia. "I followed you here."

"Others may have recognized you as well," Rosivok said. "We must get away from Kamrit. The master must heal. No more battles for now."

"I know," Madia said.

"I have never before spoken to the dead," Anna whispered. "Tell me you are real."

"I live," Madia said, "though it nearly wasn't so. I was set upon by robbers, then by a knight from this castle, then by soldiers from Lencia, perhaps lead by

Prince Jaran himself, and all because—because *someone* betrayed me to my father, dear Anna. But how much of this do you already know?"

"I've told you Madia, I did *not* betray you! Someone else must have told your father of your plans that evening. Lord Ferris, no doubt."

"Perhaps," Madia said, seeing it now, how simple it was.

"He has taken over the throne with such zeal, I can't believe he didn't plan it all along," Anna continued. "I think he somehow made your father ill. He tried to kill him, and may have done it, but—but I think he did not."

"What do you mean by that?" Madia asked.

"I saw Ferris' own serfs carry your father's body out of his chambers, but they did not go to the vaults. They took him to the old dungeons. I think the body that went to the vaults belonged to someone else, and your father is still alive, or at least he was when they carried him away."

"Please, don't tell me my father lives, for if he does not and I believe you . . . "

"I swear, my lady, what I say is true!"

"But why?" Madia asked. "Why feign his death? If Ferris was intent on taking the kingdom from him, why not simply kill him and be done with it?"

"I don't know, but I know that Lord Ferris is an evil man, Madia. I *know* it. You have not seen the change in him since you and your father were declared dead."

"Oh, yes, I have! We met—briefly—in the castle just this afternoon."

"The master says he is a force from the nether regions, a demon prince," Rosivok explained. "One that commands powers not seen in this world for ages."

"Many have said he is not mortal," Anna told Madia. "Most fear him. He has had so many people killed these past months. Those who would speak against him. And many more have suffered. I made the mistake of questioning him about the imprisonment of a squire, one of my young nephews, and I was put out into the streets for it!"

Anna's voice cracked, then the sound of sobbing followed, and Madia thought of the things she had accused Anna of, the doubts she'd already had—another on the list of mistakes you have made. "I am sorry," Madia said, "for many things. It has been so hard to know what to do and what to think. And now you tell me my father may still be alive." She fell silent, waiting for the thoughts in her head to slow their terrible spin. Even as they did, the weight already gathered in her stomach seemed to grow heavier.

"I must avenge my father, Anna—and all the people of Ariman," she said. "I will learn the truth of what has happened. Ferris will not go unchallenged."

"He will for now," Rosivok said, moving in the darkness, a shuffling sound. "We stand no chance against him."

"What's happened to you?" Madia asked, finding Anna's sobs affecting her, fighting the urge to join in. "You were all so sure of yourselves before, so extraordinary! The great Frost and his Subartans! Masters of all, servants to none! How can it be that there is nothing to be done, no hope at all?" She stopped herself, realizing how it sounded, knowing that it was not that simple.

"We face not a man but a *thing*," Frost said, whispering from somewhere deep in his throat. "I know of nothing that can be done against him."

"How do you feel?" Madia asked.

"He nearly died," Sharryl said. "He may *yet*. Leave him alone." She moved near him, stroking his head, Madia guessed, listening more than seeing. His breathing seemed to soften.

"We must leave this place," Rosivok said. "There will be time to talk of this later."

"He is right," Sharryl said. "For now."

"I know," Madia muttered. "I know. I just find all this so hard to accept. I've never felt so awful about everything, not even when I was starving in the countryside. I want to find my father, dead or alive, and . . ."

"Do not dwell on that, my lady," Anna said.

"I came here to try and do something right, for once, and everything is going so wrong!"

No sound touched the darkness for a time. Madia felt an aching in her head, the weight in her gut turning solid. Nothing made sense anymore.

"You must come with me," Anna said, a very quiet voice. "There are dung wagons that leave the city each night. One of the drivers is a close enough friend. No one will look for fugitives in his cargo."

"With good reason," Madia replied.

"It is better than being found within the city by Ferris' mercenaries," Rosivok corrected.

"Much better," Sharryl agreed.

"Then you will let me help you?" Anna asked.

"Of course," Madia said, still more softly. "Yes."

"I will prove to you, Madia," Anna went on, "that I am worthy of—"

"Anna, I was wrong about many things, especially you, I think. It is I who must prove myself. I am in your hands."

"Yes, my lady. Please, all of you, come."

She led the way out into the darkened streets, using no torches, staying well out of sight. Not far from the stables, they came upon the wagons. Anna disappeared for a time, then returned with an armful of clothing and rolled burlap.

"Use these to wrap yourselves," she said, then helped them with the job. Madia joined the others, wrapping herself up first, then struggling to get into the back of the wagon.

"I will come back, no matter what," Madia mumbled, trying to talk through the material. "I swear it."

"I know," Anna said. "Now shut up."

Madia held still while Anna and the driver wrapped her face and shoveled extra straw and manure over her. She felt the wagon being covered, then felt motion as the driver urged the horses on. There was a brief pause, then the wagon was moving again. *The gates*, Madia thought—they aren't even going to check.

She kept silent, fighting the urge to vomit as the heavy odor in the wagon caught in her throat with each breath. After a time, the smell didn't bother her. Finally the wagon stopped again, and the driver called everyone out.

As the cloth was removed and she looked about, Madia saw that the moon was high in the night sky, but barely a quarter full. Still, its light revealed a small dirt road that wound through grassy fields and disappeared into a vast stand of woods ahead. The driver was alone. He was back in the wagon even before the Subartans had finished getting Frost unwrapped.

"Thank you, and tell Lady Anna again how grateful we are," Madia told the man. The driver looked at her, eyes hidden in the shadow of his hat, an old man, she saw, and a kind man, certainly. He nodded without a word, as if he were afraid to speak, and Madia realized that many in Kamrit must be that way, in the habit of being afraid to say anything at all. He swung the wagon around and drove away north, back up the road toward home.

Madia turned and followed the others south—walking away from home again.

Chapter XV

"The roads in northern Ariman are no place to be these days," Mauro said. He glanced at his younger brother, Umblic, who was standing just behind him. "Especially for a lady like yourself," Umblic added, with a nod.

"All of Ariman is no safe place for anyone not loyal to the Lord Grand Chamberlain," Anna replied. Mauro's house was small and his dinner fire had been a hot one. Anna used the sleeve of her dress to dab sweat from her brow. "Should we stay in our beds, then? Or hide beneath them?"

"We should wait, Anna, for the right time. For things to change so that others will offer their—"

"Things have changed enough for me already."

"I think," Umblic offered, choosing a softened tone, "that what my brother is trying to say is—"

"That he is of no use to the good people of Kamrit any longer, and that he is as fearful of Ferris' power as everyone else!" Anna glared at both of them, then felt some of the fire within her cool as she fathomed the look in their eyes. They were good men, but like so many in Kamrit, they had lost something of themselves in recent months—their notions of self-worth, the foundations upon which had stood their convictions, their chivalry, their loyalty. Both saw little good to come from Ferris' reign, Anna was certain of that; but they were sworn to a duty that required them to defend a leader who was no longer theirs, and to aid him in turning Ariman into something not theirs as well. They had no immediate solution. In all Kamrit, no one did. Anna, regardless, could no longer live with that.

"I'm going with or without you," Anna said, getting up from the little table, moving away from the hearth. "We need help, and there is no one else."

"You waste your time," Mauro said, which prompted another nod from Umblic.

"You two may find it easier just to lay about, counting woes, but I do not," Anna said, looking at Mauro, a man of great strength and experience, though age was beginning to take its toll. Lately he was spending most of his time training younger men, and Umblic, like so many others, had been doing his best simply to stay out of sight. There were fewer citizens every day willing to speak openly against Ferris. And for good reason.

"Counting woes and going on a wild goose chase are two different things," Umblic replied. "My brother is right."

"*I* am right!" Anna persisted. "Hoke is one of the few men I know we can trust who can rally the others."

"But what can he do?" Mauro asked, shaking his head. "What can anyone do against Ferris? Hoke is an old man, much older than me, and a cripple. He commands no one anymore. The army follows Ferris' captains now. Even the greatest knights of Kamrit follow him, or they pretend to, and that will likely continue. Pity Hoke, my lady. You would ask a minnow to save a drowning man."

"Those with enough courage would be inspired. You are not the only knights who disapprove of Lord Ferris," Anna reminded him.

"Yes, like this, among ourselves, but public dissent is a different matter. How many men have been found guilty of crimes and executed, how many have been banished? My friends and yours."

"Your friends suffered less because they stood up for themselves, for what they believed, and more because they did not stand together." Anna held his gaze for an instant, then turned her head away.

"Or they were simply foolish," Mauro told her. "What difference if Ferris destroys ten good men or one hundred? Those that have fallen can little help you or anyone else now. And what of the lord's powers? What if he is truly a demon as you say? All the knights in Ariman might stand no chance against him."

"So you would rather sit and ponder," Anna snapped. "And let your fears betray your honor. Very well, but I must do something. Have you not heard a thing I have said? Can you simply forgive the demon his nature, accept that he has poisoned your true king, or forget that Kelren Andarys may yet live, imprisoned in his own dungeons?"

"All things you have said might be true," Mauro told her, "but we have been to the dungeons and he is not there."

"The old dungeons," Anna corrected.

"They are long abandoned."

"Not anymore."

"There is an order that no one is to go there," Umblic said. "It might make one wonder."

Mauro set his jaw. "Then we will go."

"There are guards posted, loyal to Ferris," Anna said. "You will not get past them alone. We would need many men, and someone to lead them. If not Hoke, then perhaps Madia."

Both men made a sour face. "Hard to imagine," Umblic said. "And no one else has seen the princess, either. Perhaps in the darkness your eyes and ears fooled you. Or you saw a ghost after all. And the story about the lost young Duke Jaffic, that is just too much to endure."

"But true!" Anna glared at them, feeling as though she might scream loud enough for Ferris himself to hear if she spent another second in the presence of such men. Yet they were still her best hope.

"There are only a handful of knights and squires I can turn to," she went on, controlling her tone, "and fewer women, and none of you are willing to take any chances. I do not mean to say that yours is not a sensible approach, but if you had been witness to the pain in Madia's eyes, the defeat on the faces of those who had been with her, if you had heard them tell of Ferris—things that a part of everyone in Kamrit already knows—" Anna stopped herself. She drew a long, troubled breath.

"I cannot content myself with observations and secret discussions, not any longer," she said. "Believe what you want to believe." She pulled her cloak around her shoulders and started toward the door. "I will go alone." She paused and looked back as the two men rose and stood beside the table. "I believe Kelren deserves better," she added, her voice growing faint. "As does his daughter."

"Too bad she didn't feel as you do," Umblic mumbled.

Anna felt her features tremble. "She does now."

The brothers looked at each other, expressions Anna could not read. She pulled at the door, and realized her cheeks were wet.

Mauro spoke: "Wait, my lady."

They were looking at each other again, then both at her.

"Yes?"

Umblic cleared his throat. "We . . . we will be going with you."

*   *   *

Ingram and Kaafk stood gazing out the window of the
tower at the streets of Kamrit below. Tyrr enjoyed receiv-
ing men up here. The tower seemed to lend them a
sense of power and importance, the view seemed to inspire. He stood just behind these two, encouraging their
reverie. He made the mouth talk, easy conversation, as
he had heard so many men do, then he gradually turned
their talk to his own agenda. The construct was not holding up nearly as well as he had hoped; it would not last as
long as the pace of events seemed to dictate it must,
therefore events, for this and other reasons, must be
speeded up.

But there was a second urgency as well. The threat
remained small, but real enough. And any threat to his
true being must be removed without delay.

"I want the Demon Blade," Tyrr said, "and yet I do
not have it. This must change."

"My men are still searching for it," Ingram said. "They
follow every clue."

"It lies in Golemesk Swamp, I am certain," Tyrr
replied. "That is where you must continue your search."
He was not, in fact, completely certain, but nearly so.

"We have searched as we could, my liege, but the
northern lords object to our presence more strongly
every day. My men have been run off of some lands altogether. And in the swamp itself we still encounter leshys
who—"

"I have no patience for this anymore. If Lord Jurdef
Ivran or any of the other great lords dares to object, then
you will mount a force and attack them, Captain. I sug-
gest you start by sending men enough to keep their
armies occupied. Wear them down, for it is only a matter
of time before we march against them. As for the swamp
itself, take as many men as you need to complete the

search, and this time, I will send my advocate with you as well."

Tyrr paused in concentration, and summoned the remaining imp to the tower from the small, darkened room where it waited below. It scurried in and obediently stood beside him. The two men turned and grimaced slightly as they looked upon the thing, then controlled their expressions. They had yet to question Ferris about his true nature, about the source of the powers he had let them see, though surely by now they must wonder. But they didn't seem to mind the idea enough to chance losing their authority, or cutting themselves out of the increasingly lucrative situation Tyrr had created. Men had always been like this, Tyrr knew; their weaknesses were legendary.

"The imp is sensitive to the aura of the Blade, and to the approach of a leshy," Tyrr said. "He will supply much of what you lack."

"Why is the Blade so important?" Kaafk asked, watching the face of Chamberlain Ferris closely as he waited for a reply. "Why do you . . . fear it so?"

Forethought, Tyrr told himself, *and control.* He was already losing sight of both. "I do not fear it, but in the wrong hands, the Blade could be an unfortunate obstacle. I am not so sure of its value as I am of yours, my merchant friend. But in my hands, it could be the key to this world. I need to learn its secrets before anyone else does. There is no alternative. Do you understand?"

The old stories spoke clearly of the time when the demons of the world had been driven out by men possessing the Blade, but the nature and limits of the Blade's magic, and the methods used, were not at all clear—to man, or to demon, so far as Tyrr knew.

Kaafk grinned tightly, nodded slowly. "Of course," he said. "Certainly."

"What happened to the other creature like that one?" Ingram asked, indicating the imp. "My men say it was wounded in the battle against the intruders."

"I had to . . . dispose of it," Tyrr made the mouth say. A considerable loss of resource—a thought that brought with it another small surge of outrage to add to those still smoldering within. He sought to control this, too, renewing his resolve yet again. Yesterday's incident had not gone as he had planned. Frost and his companions had surprised him by coming directly to the castle and had proven far more resourceful than expected, which gave rise to questions of how many others there might be, just like them, or more powerful still. . . .

Control, he reminded. His plans were intact otherwise; almost nothing had gone wrong. And he was not truly angry with Kaafk, after all, or Ingram, really—so following his plan still made sense. He had vowed not to give in to that part of his nature, vowed not to kill humans indiscriminately simply because at times it made him feel better.

"Tell me, my liege, were the intruders ever found?" Kaafk asked.

Tasked yet again, Tyrr thought grimly. He disliked the look on the merchant's face, a poorly hidden glimmer of amusement. Kaafk remained the best man for the job, of course, but Tyrr took pleasure in reminding himself that he was not the *only* one.

"No," he admitted. "My commanders insist they are still within the city, but I have searched for them as well, in my own way, and believe this is not so. I have ordered a thorough search of the countryside."

"Begun yesterday," Captain Ingram said, nodding respectfully.

"Good luck," Kaafk said. "I have heard of this Frost. He is said to be a formidable enemy when he wants to be."

"The question is, why would he want to be?" Tyrr replied. "Why risk death by coming here to confront me? He is not of this land."

"Well paid by the lords of Bouren and Jasnok, Thorun and Vardale," Kaafk suggested. "Some of them have their own court wizards, but none such as Frost. I am more curious about the girl that travels with them, the one who resembles the princess. Reports have come to me from the road, from others who have seen her before she arrived here. They say it truly is Madia."

"It is a spell the mage has put on some wretched swordswoman," Tyrr said. "A false image."

"Then she has worn it for some time, I'd say." Kaafk looked to Ingram and rolled his eyes.

Tyrr despised the implications.

"My men have told of similar stories," Ingram said, taking it up. "There are rumors throughout the city today that Madia is alive, that only the princess herself—" The captain stopped himself, averting his own eyes.

"That only she would dare to attempt a confrontation with you," Kaafk finished for him. He rubbed the knuckles of one hand across the bottom of his rounded chin. "My lord, what if it *was* her?"

"When the girl is found, and before she is killed, I will ask her many things," Tyrr said, slipping, letting the mouth tighten, the teeth meet. "She will tell me whatever I would know."

"Oh, well, of course," Kaafk said evenly.

"Perhaps I should join in the search," Ingram said.

"You will be going with more troops to the north, as I said. Do what you must, but deliver the Blade to me. With or without the heads of the northern lords. You will search every leaf and bog and cup of water in Golemesk until it is found!"

Tyrr realized he had raised his voice, that he was slipping much further. He felt the body reel inwardly, weakening as his anger surfaced, stressing the spell that held the body in corporeal form. Once again he fought the urges and turned the tide, imposed a calm within himself.

"I go at once, my liege," Ingram was saying, bowing low, heading for the door. Tyrr waved, and the imp scurried after the captain—who glanced nervously over his shoulder at it. *He may get over that,* Tyrr thought, *or he may not.*

"The great lords themselves will find fault with such plans," Kaafk commented, standing close to Tyrr now, closer than the demon prince preferred. "They will strongly object."

Tyrr made the lips smile. "Only while they live."

Chapter XVI

"We must get out of Ariman as soon as possible," Rosivok insisted. "There are too many of Ferris' soldiers looking for us."

Madia nodded agreement. They had been forced to hide off the road twice since climbing out of the dung wagon the day before. "So what about him?" she asked, indicating Frost. The wizard lay dozing beneath the trees at the edge of the road—as he had been for hours.

"He cannot make such a journey in his weakened condition," Sharryl insisted. "We will need to find some place nearby, with food and shelter, where he can recover. Then we can go on."

"Sounds simple enough," Madia grumbled.

"The master has always seen to such things," Rosivok said. He sighed, a disheartening sound to Madia's ears. Again she felt helplessness, hopelessness, like a sickness that spread though her, a relapse. Not even the peasant villages to the north would provide safe haven now.

Though, perhaps, those further to the south . . .

Why would the peasants here be any different? Why wouldn't such people help her again? She needed no story to tell now other than the truth. *Help your princess,* she would ask, in a way that would make them understand, and they would, she was almost certain of it. She told the others.

"Some may wish to turn us in, in hopes of getting favors or rewards," Sharryl cautioned, when Madia had finished.

"Then we will pay them first," Madia replied. "Frost has more than deeds with which to pay for aid. There are plenty enough gold coins in his bag to ensure the peasants' loyalties. For a few days, at least, which may be enough to get him back on his feet."

"If he is fed well and left to rest, yes," Rosivok agreed. "A few days, perhaps a week, will do."

"Good." Madia sighed. "I will choose the village, then go in alone and talk to them. I know what to say."

The Subartan nodded, then went to collect Frost. By dusk, Madia had found just the place. A village much like the one she had first stayed in after being sent from Kamrit, with people much like Faith and Rous and Aust. There had been no soldiers by in several days, they said, and they seemed truly glad to find their princess both alive and here among them, bringing gold.

Madia fetched the others and gave each man and woman in the village a few gold coins, then bid them bring the best foods they could find. Within hours, Frost had been sheltered in a hut, where he was given milk and porridge and berries and ale. With prodding, the wizard woke, ate all he could hold, then slept again till dark.

When he finally woke again, both Subartans and Madia were there, ready to feed him once more by candlelight—an idea which seemed to suit him well. By the end of the third day, Frost had gained back a few pounds and a good deal of cognizance. And a physique. In laundered slacks and a short-sleeved tunic, he looked rather comfortable, in fact, and rather . . . *impressive.*

Madia had never thought of him as a "man" before, though now, seeing him thinned down like this, the way he moved, the way he looked as he pulled in a stretch, she could not help but feel a twinge of attraction. She realized that she was the second woman to do so, though. Sharryl had been remarkably attentive to Frost's needs these past two days, and Madia was not about to fight her for him.

"We are grateful for our stay," he said, finishing his evening meal, seated at a small table just outside the hut were he'd been sleeping. He sat back and belched—a huge sound that carried for yards—to the amusement of a number of villagers just returned from the fields. Frost and the others were a great entertainment for them, and Madia had encouraged this.

Though Frost, so far, had been very little help. He was still drained from his ordeal, more so than anyone, but the damage was more than simply physical, Madia was certain of it. Frost had changed, like a turtle pulling into its shell, a bear changed somehow into a rabbit.

"We are grateful," Rosivok agreed, "though we have already stayed too long."

"I am better now," Frost insisted. "And glad to be away from Kamrit."

"Soldiers are looking for us," Madia said. "But they have yet to come here."

"Then we will leave before they do."

"To Neleva?" Rosivok asked, though he, like Madia, seemed already to have the answer. They needed a good safe haven now, and Frost, after all, had been summoned to Glister by the council itself. That was the obvious choice.

"Neleva, tomorrow," Frost replied to unanimous nods,

though he sounded as if the acknowledgment was somehow painful.

More coins were given around at Frost's encouragement, and again the villagers were only too glad to accept them.

"Now, leave me," Frost asked, rising from dinner, turning toward the hut behind him. Everyone began to wander off, except Sharryl. She and Frost stood quietly a moment, just looking at each other, then a strange smile found her lips, finally mirrored on his, and she followed him inside.

Early the following dawn, the four of them gathered their supplies and slipped away.

I was a fool, Frost thought, again reliving the encounter in his mind, then he tried not to think about it at all, and found it impossible.

The pace was slow in deference to him; he was still a bit weak, still too thin, but he admitted to no other choice and kept going. There was not much talk among the others, not even the usual lessons of battle that Rosivok and Sharryl had taught Madia in the idle time before reaching Kamrit. Frost said almost nothing, preferring the silence. There was much to think about, much to decide.

Nothing, he thought, *is the same.*

On the eleventh day of travel, they arrived in the mainland half of the twin city of Glister, capital of Neleva, and Frost, getting his bearings, pointed the way toward one of the better inns the city had to offer. *Once settled*, he thought, *once I am ready, perhaps I will send Rosivok to contact the ruling council.* For now he was in no condition to fight any sort of mystical beast or indeed to do any magic at all. And in no mood to face anyone, even Madia, much more than necessary.

His powers were there, returning slowly along with his

physical strength; they would continue to grow, like his fortitude, along with his waist, but he had not tried even the slightest spell since the battle against the demon prince. Sometimes, thinking about it, he began to feel cold inside, as if he might freeze to death if he touched the magic again. Sometimes, he was not sure he ever would. Ever could.

He had never lost before.

Never. . . .

Nothing is the same.

The city's streets called his attention, bustling with people from many corners of the world, people of color and unusual dress, and as often speaking in different tongues. They came from beyond the Spartooth Mountains and beyond the Kaya Desert, from the Teshcta tribes Rosivok and Sharryl called their own, and from distant shores across the southern seas—the merchants of Kresa and Iquar and Boulisti. Frost had not been in this city for many years, and he was impressed by the way it had grown bigger and richer, and even more diverse. He had long preferred such cities, where the possibilities for interesting employment were multiplied. Where exotic folk and ideas were as common as peasants. A place where a wizard and three companions could pass largely unnoticed. Soon enough, they found the inn.

"Go and buy the best foods and drink you can find," he told Rosivok and Sharryl, once he had taken a room and settled into it. "You will stay here," he told Madia, "for my protection, and yours."

"When will you go to visit the council?" Madia asked, a question Frost knew he must answer soon.

"In a few days, a week, perhaps. You may come if you wish, to introduce yourself as the rightful heir to the throne of Ariman."

"Are you so sure that is a good idea?" Madia asked

then. "The councils of Neleva had agreements with my father, but I have no idea what state those affairs are in right now."

"We have heard that there is ongoing trade," Frost said. "But there is as much unrest, perhaps more than in Ariman. You may need this county's goodwill and its arms, Madia. We will see what sort of diplomat you are."

"What would you have me tell them?"

"The truth, I think, and see what that brings us. I need to learn what small task they would ask of me, of course, and you need to make friends. Perhaps, if events favor us, we will soon both know better how to proceed."

He watched the look on her face sour somewhat. Hospitality or protection, there was little difference, and Madia was as aware of this as he. But without open hostility between the two lands, the council would be foolish to do more. *Yet she will have to try,* he thought. There was no hope of facing the demon again by themselves, especially when he still was not certain why things had gone so wrong the first time. Perhaps this was what he saw in Madia's eyes now.

"What is it?" he asked after a moment. "What is wrong?"

"I—I am no idiot, Frost. I was there. I saw what happened. I too am opposed to getting beaten again, or killed, all without any gain. I don't know what can be done, what anyone can do, even an army. But I do not want to hide, either. I have done too much of that already. I want my father's legacy. I still must bring honor to his name, and to mine."

"Ferris is no mortal man, Madia. You are right to think that none can stand against him. You cannot understand the dimensions of his powers. Armies will be needed, yes, but also the help of wizards from the Kaya to the Spartooths and beyond, to battle him again. Anything less would be the greatest fool's wager, a leap into almost certain oblivion. We have already made . . . fools of ourselves. Learn from this, as I have, so that some small purpose is served."

"Is there no hope that once you restore yourself, you will find the right spell to use against him?"

"You are not listening! Your heart leads your mind, Madia. Not a quality one desires in a prospective monarch."

"Neither is cowardice!"

Frost felt the word buffet him, felt its force combine with something sharp already twisting deep inside him. He was not a coward, he thought, not anything of the sort. He simply wasn't going to be made a fool again! That was the way of looking at it. He had not weighed all the odds, had not properly considered the omens, had not remained sensible! *Never give everything,* he reminded himself. *Never risk all that you have on a single chance!* He had ignored his own best advice.

He had never lost before.

Never. . . .

"Prudence, not cowardice, Madia. The lack of failure is itself a success."

"It is death," Madia snapped, teeth held together.

"I must rest," Frost said. "You must stand guard."

"It is true, is it not?" Madia said evenly. "You *are* terrified of Ferris, scared out of your wits."

Frost weighed his reply. "You do not fear him?"

"I do, but not as you. You could go back and face him, but you are afraid to try, afraid even to think about it. He did not beat you, Frost, he destroyed you!"

Not true! Frost thought again. *She doesn't understand. She has no idea. . . .*

"Say something!" Madia demanded. "Tell me the truth!"

"You have a great deal to learn," Frost said, lying back on the bed, closing his eyes.

244 Mark A. Garland & Charles G. McGraw

"I have learned I was a fool to rely on you."

"That you are a fool, I will not argue with." Frost took a deep breath, then held still, allowing no movement, calming his mind. This was a conversation he no longer wished to continue. He listened to Madia move about the room, heard her find a chair and sit on it. His thoughts soon found their way back to the battle at Kamrit—thoughts that had not left him in days, and followed him into his dreams.

They fought furiously in the little street, blades clanging and pinging, two well-healed bodies leaping, spinning and dodging, displaying reflexes to be admired even by the uninitiated. Frost watched the street, guarding against interruption. Then Sharryl showed her prowess in a sudden combination of movements, flashing steel high and close to Madia's face, then a leg thrusting out at Madia's feet, and the princess found herself sprawled on her buttocks with Sharryl standing over her, grinning. It was not an expression a Subartan wore lightly.

"I know," Madia said wearily. "I am too easy."

"Untrue," Sharryl told her. "You become more adept each time we practice. You had a great natural talent, and good training, but now you have more—a level of skill that can truly serve you."

"You and Rosivok always win," Madia said.

"We are born to it," she said. "We are one with the subarta."

Madia got up and looked at Sharryl. "You will always be better," she said.

"Yes." Sharryl grinned again.

"But she will never be more than she is," Frost said, speaking to her now, though he did not look at her. Madia put her sword away, then all of them grew distracted as two women came up the street, glancing over their shoulders at the tall dark-skinned warrior figure looming just behind them. They looked ahead again and busied themselves with minding the rough stone and errant sewage, obviously nervous. Frost greeted the ladies as they passed. They hurried on. Rosivok came to rest at Frost's side.

"The council awaits you," Rosivok said. "They are eager to talk."

"Was there any word of their . . . problem?" Frost asked.

"They made no mention of it."

Frost examined the other man's look: subtle but troubled. "You believe that something may be wrong?"

"No, only that they seem to have much on their minds."

Frost had a number of things on his mind as well, which he wished to talk over with Neleva's powerful ruling council: what was the precise nature of their needs; how much were they were willing to pay; and how indefinite, should he choose, were they willing to make his stay? But he was also aware that the council members would know much about goings-on in Ariman, perhaps more than anyone—and he needed to learn what they knew, especially about Ferris.

The more he learned, he thought, the better he might be able to deal with what had happened, with fear—his, and others'.

Fear was something Frost had almost no experience with; a gruesome garment that fit poorly and pulled at the seams with every movement, dragging him down like rain-soaked wool; he wanted to shrug it off, but all his knowledge and prowess seemed useless against it now—strength without leverage.

He was getting better in other ways, nearly forty pounds heavier than when he had entered Glister four weeks earlier, and many dreams removed from the fitful nights that had followed his visit to Kamrit. But he was not "well." The world did not seem the same place anymore, and he still had no stomach for magic. There seemed to be no need, really, as he saw it now. What good did it do? *Or you are afraid of that, too?*

He had lately begun to look for signs, for omens; at the moment he was quite content to stay out of harm's way.

He looked closely at the others: the street clothes and leather protection they wore, the weathering their apparel had taken. "We will stop at the market square on the way back to the inn and buy new clothes, so that we do not go before the council clothed like beggars!" Everyone else glanced self-consciously at themselves, except Madia, whom Frost found staring at him. They had barely spoken since arguing on the day they arrived in the city. More often than not, he was grateful for it. He owed her nothing by any rational assessment, and it was obvious that she blamed him, at least in part, for their failures at Kamrit. She wanted more from him, much more than he could possibly think about giving to her. To anyone, now.

"What is it?" he asked her.

"I wasn't sure you would even go," she said.

His fears were something Madia had tried to use against him like a weapon, but he had also seen the trepidation in her, different than his own but very real, no matter how she sought to suppress it. This last was not meant as a barb, he decided; she was simply asking.

Neither was I, he wanted to say. "I know," he said.

He set off toward the palace.

The Kresaians, olive-skinned people who had arrived in ships and settled, establishing trade long ago, made up the bulk of the ruling council of Glister. They had brought with them many rare and wonderful items and skills which the lands to the north had seldom or never seen. They excelled at ornamentation, weavings, and pottery, their artists created the most exquisitely detailed paintings, their metal-smiths crafted the finest swords and tools that were known, and they built structures the like of which no nobleman of Ariman had ever imagined—similar to the cities of the desert tribes but on a far grander scale.

Here stood high walls and towers detailed with engravings and set with sculptures, and domes covered with shining metals that topped every dwelling of importance, including the homes of the rich—and in Glister, there were many rich. The palace itself was tall and grand, glittering and ornate, as were the members of the ruling council.

Frost allowed himself an inward smile as he and his three companions, dressed now in the finest boots and tunics the market and Frost's dwindling supply of gold coins would offer, entered the council's chambers. *They would do*, he mused; *just*. The memory of recent days of struggle on the road was fading rapidly.

The reception hall was warm with the soft colors of richly textured tapestries. A table filled the center of the hall, surrounded by high-backed chairs, each covered in soft leather. Bowls of fresh fruit decorated the center of the table, and flagons of water and wine stood beside them. The six council members were dressed mostly in Curien linens and silks trimmed in gold lace. They sat at the far end of the table, four Kresaians, another man who was obviously a desert tribesman. The sixth, who was a very dark-skinned, large-boned fellow, greeted everyone as they entered and seemed inclined to speak for the rest.

"We have waited a very long time for your arrival," he said, extending a hand to indicate the table's empty chairs. Frost sat between Rosivok and Sharryl at the table's near end, while Madia sat along the right side, between the two groups. Frost watched her as she acknowledged each council member, calm and respectful yet completely alert, even accomplished, and he decided her choice of seats had been intentional.

Madia, after all, was here because none of her own plans had worked out, more than anything else, and because tagging along after a bag-of-wind mage was all that was left her, for now.

Of course, he had no plans beyond Glister, either. He had thought at first to simply go to a land where they had never heard of him, there to stay until he felt . . . *differently*. But if he did, he might never be able to show his face in this realm again. Still, he reflected, such an exile was a price he might yet be willing to pay.

"I am Andala, First Counselor," the big, dark man said. He introduced the others, Tienken, Basmur, Basonj, Ghastan, and Javal. Frost introduced himself, the two Subartans, then Madia. A distinct flicker of surprise touched each of the councilmen's eyes.

"You have raised her spirit?" Andala asked, eyes wide.

"She has not yet died," Frost explained. "There are many lies about in these lands today. Now, we begin with truths."

He watched Madia weather their stares. They asked no immediate questions, and Frost decided this was probably all for the best. He decided to proceed.

"Why have you requested my presence?" he began, but the man nearest Madia, Javal, ignored Frost completely. "If what you say of her is true," he asked, "why do you bring her to this council?"

"Madia expressed a desire to replace the Subartan guard I recently lost. Her cousin, in fact; the young Duke Jaffic Andarys. She is presently in my employ."

"Jaffic is dead?" Javal asked in surprise.

"He is," Frost replied.

"Another reason to ask why she is not in Kamrit, assuming her duties," Andala said, leaning forward, more intense. "Here with you she may as *well* be dead, for all the good she does Ariman or Neleva."

"You speak of telling truths," Ghastan said, staring at Madia from the table's other corner. "Do you know all that has happened since your strange, temporary death?"

"In Neleva, or Ariman?" Frost asked.

Andala frowned. "Both."

"We were going to ask what you knew," Frost added quickly. "But yes, we have been to Kamrit quite recently. Perhaps we can share our thoughts on these matters."

He had no idea what their thoughts were, in fact. Neleva might be partially allied with Ferris, even though Frost doubted this. Or the council might be indifferent, which Frost had largely assumed . . . until just now.

"Let me ask," Basmur said, "how was your visit to that city? What were your impressions? And you will let the girl answer, so that we will know she is more than spirit."

"I was not pleased," Madia said rather tersely; Frost did not see this as perhaps the best response. He waited for Madia to add something, realized she was letting him lead again—trusting him again, he thought, *or beginning to*. . . .

"Yes, most unfavorable," he replied.

"You met with Grand Chamberlain Ferris?"

"You . . . you could say that," Madia answered.

"And he did not welcome you?" Andala asked, and Frost noticed that all six council members attended closely to the answer.

"We disapproved of each other," she replied clearly, apparently unwilling to give Ferris even the slightest endorsement.

"And do you also feel this way?" Andala asked, addressing Frost, who found Madia turning now, watching him, eyes set. There was no going back.

"Yes," Frost said.

The council members glanced at one another. Most of them nodded.

"May we speak in confidence?" Andala asked.

Frost nodded. "Please!"

"The rise to power of Lord Ferris and his subsequent activities present a great danger," Andala said. "We believe he intends to control all lands from the southern seas north to the Spartooths. His troops haunt our borders and abuse our hospitality when they visit our lands. They grow more provocative each day, and our officers fear a confrontation is inevitable."

"They also see little chance of a victory against the forces Lord Ferris has amassed," Basonj added grimly.

"Continues to amass," Basmur corrected. "And the new tariffs he has imposed now affect all goods that leave or enter Ariman. Trade has suffered, and the profits of our merchants and tradesman have suffered as well."

"He uses the money not only to sweeten his treasury but to pay for the killers he hires," Basonj said, speaking to Madia. "We have enjoyed a prosperous peace for many decades. Lord Ferris now threatens to destroy all that, to bring bloodshed to our people and an end to the progress made by your father and your grandfather, and this council."

"The great lords of Bouren and Jasnok, Vardale and Thorun are also concerned," Frost said. "They have problems with Ferris' troops similar to your own."

"We have recent reports from the northern fiefs," Andala disclosed. "It seems their problems have already grown worse than our own."

"We believe that soon, Ferris will attempt to bring those lands completely under his control," Basonj added, now to Frost. "This may occupy his considerable energies for a time, but eventually he will concentrate on us. That is why we called upon you. Ferris has made diplomatic gestures to indicate that such troubles are strictly an internal affair and nothing for Neleva to worry about, but his actions say otherwise."

Frost sat back, carefully examining each council member. "There is no sea monster," he said, as much to himself as to them. "Is there?"

"Sea?" Andala asked. "No, but there is a human monster in Kamrit, a far greater threat."

"He is a poison," Javal said, a vital look on his face. "A man unlike you or me. He is without compassion or reason, it seems, and without limits to his ambitions. You, Frost, must help us stop him. And you," he said, looking to Madia now, "do you intend to take your place as ruler of Ariman?"

"Yes, I do," Madia answered, then she turned to Frost, waiting.

"He is not a man," Frost said, sighing, ignoring the knot in his gut. "Ferris is not human at all."

Silence fell about the table for a moment. Frost took a breath, folded his hands on the table in front of himself. "I confronted him in Kamrit and I felt his powers. He is a creature of the darkness, a demon more powerful than any of you can imagine—or I, had I not encountered him myself."

"There have been many stories," Tienken said. "Dark mages in the city, dark magic at the castle, it is said; we have heard that misfortune befalls those who—"

"We also have heard," Madia said. "It seems the stories are true."

"Then why does Ferris seek the Demon Blade?" Andala asked. "Such a creature should fear the Blade above all else, yet even now his men search for it in Golemesk Swamp."

"He may fear that others might find it," Frost explained. "As long as he has the Blade, it cannot be used against him. And he may simply be curious, as demons often are. If he were to discover the Blade's secrets, he might also find a way to use its powers for his own ends."

"All the more reason to stop him now, before something like that can happen," Andala insisted. "Skirmishes have broken out already in the northern fiefs, most near the swamp, and there have been losses. We hear that Ferris' men have enjoyed a number of recent victories."

"Many believe the Blade is there," Javal added. "The body of a wizard known as Ramins has been found, and—"

"We know," Madia said. Frost found her looking at him again, no reservations at all, a look that made him feel even more uneasy than he had before. *There were always rumors of Ramins death, of the Blade.*

Always. . . .

"You say you encountered Lord Ferris," Basonj said. "Can you tell us what happened?"

Frost stared at the other man, intensely aware that, despite all his rationalizing, he could not bring himself to admit fully to his errors, to the defeat he had suffered. He tried to find other words, but they were not at hand.

"We lost," Madia said for him, her voice low and heavy. "The creature Ferris nearly destroyed all of us."

Again, silence.

"We had heard," Andala said to Frost, slowly, "that you were a mage of . . . considerable talents."

"I was not prepared," Frost said, unwilling to let things stand as they were. "It became clear that to make another attempt under more advantageous circumstances might be wise. So we retreated."

"We certainly did," Madia said, briefly rolling her eyes. "And it seems there will be no other attempt."

"You've given up?" Basmur asked, voicing the question that was obvious on the faces of the others.

Frost found all six councilmen staring at him, found Rosivok and Sharryl doing the same—and Madia bearing the harshest eyes among them. The omens, those he had been able to read, were bad, all of them. And logic spoke even less kindly of trying again. His best magic, after all, had not been enough. What was there to prepare? How could any single mage, perhaps even an army of them, face the powers the demon Ferris possessed?

"The Blade must be found," Rosivok said. "By allies." Everyone turned and looked at him.

"Yes," Madia addel coldly. "If we can find the Demon Blade before Ferris, and then learn its secrets, Frost can use it to destroy him. Is that right, Frost?"

"Of course he can!" Andala said. "And we will help!"

"Thank you so much," Frost muttered, placing one hand flat over one closed eye, half-hiding his expression. *They do not understand,* he thought. *Or they choose not to.*

"But how can we find this weapon when an army has so far been unable to?" Madia asked.

"Frost can sense such things," Sharryl said. "He has a spell that can bring him to it."

"And thank you, as well, Sharryl, so very much." Frost furnished her with a dire glare. Sharryl nodded graciously.

My Subartans are attacking, kidnapping me, he thought. *They have already loaded me onto a boat and set sail for the swamps!*

"We will supply you with anything you need," Andala said. "Men, horses, ships, weapons, gold. You will require a large enough force to—"

"Not a large force," Frost corrected, looking at his hands now. His head felt as if it had grown much too large and might well fall off if nothing was done about it. Still, a part of him seemed to want to go, seemed to hope that—foolish and complex though the idea truly was— there might be some hope, some way to turn the odds.

"A ship, then, and gold to buy men along the way if we need them," Madia suggested.

"Must there be a ship?" Frost moaned.

"It would be unsafe for you to travel by land, of course," Andala replied.

"Yes," Basmur said. "This is a *marvelous* plan. Let us see to it at once!"

Frost eyed his Subartans, then Madia, and found all three of them looking at him as if he were about to change colors, each one wearing an unmistakable smile.

Chapter XVII

He looked more like a highwayman than a ship's captain, Madia thought as they boarded, with his thick brown hair and short knotty beard, durable linen shirt and trousers accented by fine leather boots and vest. He wore an ornate sword and a sheath of the sort fashioned by the desert tribes. He was not a young man, perhaps as old as forty, but seemed quick enough as he strode the deck, and quicker at barking orders to his crewmen—a motley lot Madia thought looked more worthy of a jailor's keeping. Kinade, the captain called himself. Madia was certain he had been called much worse.

"I see the name of this vessel has been painted over," Frost remarked as they stood about, waiting for Kinade to acknowledge them.

"Aye," Kinade said, pausing as he passed, then adding nothing more.

"It is bad luck to change a vessel's name."

Kinade closed one eye. "So I hear, but we never changed it, we just took it off." He turned and listened as one of his men borrowed his ear.

"What is the wisdom of a ship with *no* name?" Madia asked Frost, scrutinizing his reaction.

"I will have to think about it," he said curtly.

"Never worry, she's a good, fast ship," Kinade told them, turning back, grinning now, slapping Frost on the shoulder. "Not large enough for a heavy cargo, but built wide and low, a shape that stays down out of the wind and high up on the water. The bow is strong, double-beamed, unstoppable! And you see the masts?" He pointed. Madia looked up, following the mast skyward. "Lots of sail, and oars if we need them." Kinade indicated the rowing stations along the side rails, amidships. "We'll have you to Kurtek quick enough."

"The quicker the better," Frost replied. "I have no wish to spend much time at sea."

"Not a seaman, then, aye?" Kinade asked.

"A voyage at sea means trusting your life to a ship," Madia said, "and Frost is not so trusting."

"I simply prefer solid ground," Frost corrected. "Much more reliable."

"Of course," Madia said, letting it go. She saw Frost's face continue to frown. A strange look, on him, though one she was getting used to, since he had worn it for most of several weeks now. She knew well enough the thoughts behind it, and she felt a similar pang of uneasiness at the thought of where their journey would finally lead, at the memories of what had already happened there.

She had always acted on her desires, no matter the consequences, while Frost had always considered the outcome first. Now, when pressed to talk about the future—the voyage, Golemesk, the Demon Blade—he seemed not to look ahead at all. She and the others had largely forced him to go on this journey, but even now, it was as though he wasn't here. She more or less understood: Frost had been humiliated for the first time in his life; for her, the experience was not so new.

All the pushing and shaming she or anyone else could bring to bear would do nothing to assure Frost that everything would not go wrong again—or convince him to use his talents again. He had done no magic at all since leaving Kamrit. Madia hadn't noticed, but Sharryl had pointed it out. No one had yet asked him, and he hadn't said.

"There is bedding and stowage below," Kinade said, his rough voice pulling her from her thoughts. "Best get there. We are ready to leave port."

"We can stow our things, then come back up on deck for a while," Frost said to Madia.

"You might like it better below, where you will not see the land run away," Kinade remarked, overhearing.

"No," Frost said, looking at the other man. "There are many unknowns in the sea, but I am told there is also great strength, boundless and soothing, and that is what I wish to explore."

Good, Madia thought. *Good for you!*

"Very well, but if anyone goes over the side and don't come up, I make no promises, and I keep my fee," the captain said. "I can tell you what *is* bad luck—havin' two women on board, as any man here can say." He made a dark face, then he turned to Madia and smiled. "Though, how bad can it be, in your particular case?" he added. Madia looked away, suppressing a grin of her own. He was a swine, of course, but she had something of a soft spot for rogues, and he seemed able to influence it.

Frost turned to Rosivok and Sharryl, who were waiting silently behind him, watching the crew rig the sails. "Agreed, of course," Frost said rather snidely. "But if anything should happen to you, or this ship, we will get our gold back."

There was a changing look in the captain's eyes, a touch of surprise, then a good deal of calculation. Finally he grinned with most of his teeth. "Fair enough!" he said. "We have a contract."

Madia watched the wizard shrink again as Kinade walked away—a moment of bravado inspired by the captain, gone now. But there was hope for Frost, she decided, in his simply being here, in this attempt to protect the ship in some way. The ship would be within sight of land for nearly the entire journey around the cape at Brintel and up the bay, north to Kurtek. Which was twice fortunate, since she had never been to sea herself, and already that thought combined with the thick smell of dead fish and salt water and green, tide-washed rocks had affected her.

"He could be a danger," Rosivok said, meaning Kinade.

"I know," Frost said, "but I think he is not, at least to us. And if we run into trouble, he should be an asset. Which is why the council chose him, I am sure. I have no desire to sail with timid men."

"But you are not a woman," Madia said. Frost looked at her, and she grinned.

"Of course," he said.

The crew were taking up positions at the oars. The bow began to swing out, and they faced the open sea, leaving Neleva behind.

The first two days passed without incident. By the end of the third day, the ship had rounded the cape and the city of domes and towers that was Brintel. Dozens of other ships were seen entering and leaving the busy port, and many more were moored beyond Brintel's northern shores, in the shelter of the cove. Madia watched the vessels and their crews pass, and she could not help making comparisons. There were none just exactly like the boat she was on, nor the crew she was with. And all the other ships had names. She wondered whose fleet

Kinade and his men belonged to, what nation they had originally sailed from. But the question had an uncomfortable feel to it. Even Rosivok and Sharryl seemed reluctant to talk about who these people were, though they, and Frost, seemed to have a fair idea.

By nightfall, watching Kinade and his crew navigate in the dark, treacherous waters of the bay with near perfect adeptness, she had the unmistakable sense of being in the company of a band of seagoing mercenaries.

Though they were not exactly that, she decided.

She finally cornered Kinade strolling near the stern on the second evening and asked him: "You are pirates, aren't you?"

Kinade chuckled. "Yes," he said simply, then he continued on his walk.

Madia fell asleep that night imagining what pirates did with captives, but she dreamed of what they did with friends.

"Kinade expects we will make port at Kurtek by dark," Frost said, standing on the aft deck platform just ahead of the wheel. The late afternoon sun had warmed the air and the deck to the point of discomfort. Sweat glistened on Frost's brow, and Madia used her sleeve to wipe her own. Sharryl and Rosivok stood just below, leaned against the portside rail of the main deck, idly watching the sea roll past. Like herself, Madia had the impression that the two Subartans had seldom known this experience; they kept their moods well hidden even now, but with each large swell of the sea, each subsequent fall of the deck, a look of pale affliction crossed their faces. Frost, remarkably, was holding up well.

"Have you decided what we will do once we arrive?" Madia asked.

"No," Frost answered. Nothing else.

"Why not?"

"You had no plan when you insisted everyone follow you to Kamrit, not even when we arrived!"

"I was foolish."

"I know."

"Very well, but have you at least thought about it?"

Frost was silent a moment. "Perhaps," he said finally.

You will, she thought, *because I will force you; there has been enough foolishness.* "I hated leaving Kamrit again," she said. "I hate having to wait even one day to do something about Ferris, something that will erase the awful things that have happened. I need to know your plan. I can't just do nothing!"

"So it would seem," Frost said, careworn.

Enough, she thought. *Make your point.* "When we boarded this ship, and the idea of going back to Kamrit became real, I felt—I felt badly. I know that wanting to do something and actually doing it are two different things. But I keep thinking it over."

"Thinking what over?"

"Everything, I guess. I don't want to go back to Kamrit, and yet I do, and I want you to go with me. I think maybe we both have to go back, even if it is hopeless. But then I wonder, is our course so hopeless? If we find the Demon Blade, that is?"

Frost looked at her and she thought how strange his expression was. He had almost begun to look himself again during the past week: brash, curious, even wearing that impudent smile of his once or twice while talking with Kinade. But all of that was suddenly gone again now.

"I don't know any of the answers," he said. "The Blade has been kept secret for centuries, and even if we manage to find it, then live to tell about it, we will not know what powers it has without Ramins to tell us, if even he knew. How can I say whether it might be used against Ferris?"

"Nothing at all is known, no hint?"

"No. You see, we have only an ancient legend, whimsical intentions, and no good reason to think one might speak to the other. And I see a bad omen or two, which everyone else seems content to ignore."

"Never mind the omens. Tell me what you do know about the legend," Madia pressed.

Frost simply looked at her for a moment, then slowly began, "The Blade was used by the ancient wizards to defeat the demons when their numbers threatened to overwhelm the world, but the knowledge of how this was accomplished, all specific knowledge of the Blade, was purposely guarded—perhaps too well—and for centuries has rested solely with the wizard appointed keeper."

"Ramins."

Frost nodded.

"Yet Aphan believes he is dead."

"That may be true."

"Then there is no hope. Yet you must have a plan of some kind, or you would not have come at all."

"We may find allies among the court wizards of the northern kings, Grish, perhaps, or Marrn—both competent men, in their right. If we find the Blade, they and others like them might help me learn its powers. But even then, I doubt they will move with us against such a power as Ferris without a great army to back them, and that army may not exist."

"But we don't know that we can trust any of them," Madia said. "Bouren soldiers tried to kill me, after all, and distrust has spread throughout the realm, according to the council at Glister."

"The northern kings are under attack in their own lands by marauding forces from Ariman even now."

"I still hold that Lord Ivran and some of the other great lords may have been in league with Ferris, at least until Kamrit's soldiers came looking for the Blade, or perhaps until Ferris decided he did not need their loyalty any longer. Either way, I can't count on them. They must still believe Ferris is only doing my father's bidding. They will not wish to trust the daughter of a king who betrayed them in life and in death. Especially . . . me."

"All quite true," Frost said. "Still, we have begun, and we should continue. We will . . . take our chances."

I will be taking most of them, Madia thought, looking out to sea. Then she decided that Frost meant it as a joke; she would not have realized the humor only a few weeks ago. She felt the deck move gently beneath her, rising, falling, and noticed that her stomach wanted to churn. Though this was just an excuse.

"I pushed myself, and you, all the way to Kamrit, and then out of Glister as well. And yet I don't really know what the hell I am doing at all. 'Never give everything, never risk everything on a single chance.' You told me that once. Yet that is all I keep doing. Maybe you're right, Frost, but neither way seems to work all the same."

Frost nodded. "I have long preferred that the odds be firmly on my side, and they have not been."

"Exactly." She looked at Frost, a long look. "But they still aren't. So if you can't go through with any of this, if you want to leave these lands and forget about the trouble I've caused you, I will understand. Sometimes I think I was better off not caring about anything, just looking out for myself, and maybe you were, too. I'm trying to become someone new, someone who can atone for all the wrong that she has done, but maybe I can't do that. Maybe I never will be that person."

"I think almost no one ever is."

He looked away, far away, eyes going blank as he turned inside and lost himself there; he seemed to leave her, to leave the world, for a moment.

"So, why are you here?" she asked.

Frost turned suddenly darker, more fixed. "One's

image can be a consideration. To others, and to one's self. 'The wizard that runs away,' you see. 'The worthless wizard.' Even you think me a coward. I have purposely never dwelled on *self*, as it is too demanding. Who am I? What am I? After all, who needs to know? Though now, thanks to you, I find myself forced to take a proper good look."

"I am sorry," Madia said.

"No, it may be a good thing . . . eventually."

"What do you see?"

"I am still looking."

"Well, so am I."

She looked up as the sounds of a fresh commotion reached her ears. Men were suddenly running in all directions. Captain Kinade emerged from below, then came around and mounted the aft deck, joining Frost and Madia and the young man who stood behind them at the wheel.

Kinade lifted a small telescope to his eye, then extended it to focus. The ship was clearly visible to any eye now, off the port side, sailing due south. "Man the oars!" Kinade shouted. "Prepare to ram and board!"

"You two might want to get out of sight," Kinade said, acknowledging Frost and Madia briefly. He looked below then, to the main deck. Sharryl and Rosivok were headed up toward him. "Those two, though, they might want a part of this."

"Part of what?" Madia demanded, feeling her pulse quicken as the pilot spun his wheel and the bow came around, bearing straight on toward the passing vessel.

"She'll be a merchantman from the fleet of Lord Ferris," Kinade explained, raising the telescope to his eye once more. "Out of Kamrit, like as not, then Brintel, then Haven, now on to Kurtek, same as you. She'll still have a cargo, along with whatever they collected in gold to pay the good Lord Ferris' heavy taxes. We've managed to take a couple like her, and been well pleased we did!"

"But the council made no mention of this!" Madia blurted out, feeling her voice nearly break into a squeak. "What of your duty? You are at our service now!"

"And ours, my lady," Kinade responded, briefly grinning at her. "And it is my duty I'm about! We have our principles, after all, like any men."

"What do you know of principles?" Madia demanded.

"We know who we are. You look for a magical blade, but I am content with the one I have." With that Kinade drew his scimitar from its scabbard and held it up. "The Lord Ferris just about begs to have his purse stripped. He is too rich, and getting richer, and draws sympathy from no one. When a man's wool grows thicker than that on the fattest sheep in Ikaydin, I say he needs a bit of shearing."

"So you just sail around sinking Kamrit's merchant fleet? And I suppose you keep the booty for yourselves?" Madia pressed, watching the other ship draw closer, sensing the increase in their own speed as the sails filled again and Kinade's oarsman got their rhythm.

"Ferris cares not whose money and goods he takes, or how many men are ruined by it," Kinade answered. "What that says to the likes of us is that I can do the same to him. And I won't wait, my lady, no matter what. Ferris has already started putting armed men aboard some of his fleet. Soon enough, the takin' won't be so easy. That ship, by my notice, is manned by an ordinary lot. They don't fight much, not when they can swim to shore."

"But what about us?" she demanded again. "You were paid to deliver us safely to Kurtek, not to take us into a pirate's battle!" She looked to Frost, silently pleading support. He cleared his throat.

"I too object, Captain, since this action will put us at risk. If something should go wrong, if your ship sinks or you and your crew get yourselves killed, we might not get to Kurtek at all. We may be the ones swimming to shore. I would expect you to restrain yourself, under the circumstances, no matter how inviting a target that ship is."

"Of course," Madia insisted, "you must use proper judgment!"

"I am doing exactly that, my lady," Kinade said, grinning now like a boy in a bordello. "We are pirates, after all. That is who we are, and this is what we do. And we are very good at it, I assure you. No harm will come to you. Now, go below, both of you, and try not to worry yourselves sick. What of your Subartan friends?"

"They are retained to guard me and will have no place in this adventure," Frost told him.

"Too bad," Kinade said, and he went to join his men. Both ships were drawing close together now.

"What about a warding spell of some kind to protect us?" Madia asked Frost. "Like those you used at the castle."

"No," Frost replied, looking past her. "Come with me. I fear that if we go below we may never come up." He took hold of Madia's arm and led her to the rail just behind the wheelman. She held on, and looked back to see the other ship now dead ahead, just a strong stone's throw away. She steadied herself as the oars pulled back once more, united as the heavy bow rose cleanly on a swell, then crashed amidships like a god's own thunder into the side of the merchantman.

Most of Kinade's crew leaped to the deck of the other ship as soon as lines had been tossed. True to Kinade's predictions, many of the merchantman's crew in turn leaped over the starboard side into the sea and began swimming toward the coast of Ariman. The few men who stayed and fought died quickly, no match for the proficient pirate swordsman.

Without prodding, Kinade's men hurried to all corners of the captured vessel, and soon began emerging with sacks and boxes and armfuls of rolled materials. The merchantman was already listing badly, taking on water through the split in her hull. The other men quickly followed, bringing what they could aboard, then casting free their lines. Kinade came just behind them. He shouted fresh commands and the oarsmen went to work again, backing the ship away from the sinking merchantman. As soon as they were free, the pilot turned the bow north once more, toward Kurtek.

Madia watched the whole thing with the sort of awe usually reserved for the most violent late summer thunderstorms—so many elements all coming so quickly together, then the flash and fury of the event itself, and the intense tranquility that seemed to drift cool and wet and pungent through air and the mind afterward. *How extraordinary,* she thought.

How exciting. . . .

Kinade had been right, she knew. This was who he was, what he did, what he *had* to do. They were pirates, after all. No excuses, no choice.

"Frost," she said, leaning close to his ear, "whether we find the Blade or not, I have to go back to Kamrit, I have to try, even if there is no chance at all. There isn't any other choice for me." *For the daughter of the king,* she told herself.

"I know," Frost replied.

She looked at him, and she knew that he saw this too, that he had somehow come upon almost the very same thought.

"It is a painful truth, but undeniable," he said. "Much as I think I would like to, I find it difficult to consider walking away from Ferris, or from you, forever. But you were right, Madia, Ferris did not just beat me, he did more than that. The injuries inflicted upon me were . . . many. Ferris has made me less than what I was, less than what I would be."

"So," Madia said, trying a weak grin, "neither one of us is sure about you."

"I have come this far."

"I know." She stood close to him, very close. "You are going back with me, Frost, aren't you, no matter what?"

"I would rather not think of it in quite those terms."

"Think of it however you like, but it all seems rather simple now. We go to do what we must."

"I see," Frost said, barely glancing at her, but she saw the light in his eye, the *magic*. He walked a few paces along the deck rail, looking out over the sea to the curved horizon beyond. "Perhaps," he said, nodding, "you are right."

They spoke little the rest of the day, but Madia thought she could sense something different about Frost every time they were near each other, a different look, or something in the way he carried himself. But he would not talk to her, not about anything, and she wasn't sure what that meant.

The sun had nearly set when Kinade weighed anchor a hundred yards from the shore at Kurtek. Orange colors washed the sky among the long straight clouds on the western horizon, fading quickly, revealing a rising full moon.

"My men will row you in," Kinade explained. "We are not entirely welcome in this port. We sail again before first light, and you are on your own."

"That will have to do," Frost told him, checking the supplies Rosivok and Sharryl had gathered.

"I think we are ready," Madia added, looking at Frost, his round face half-lit by the moon. He nodded to her, though she could not read his look.

They followed Kinade to a rope ladder, then climbed down into a wooden boat manned by four oarsmen. Shoulder bags filled with supplies were handed down after them. In minutes the boat was slipping between the dark, silent hulls of other ships in the harbor, then bumping gently against docking planks that hovered barely above the level of the high tide. Distant voices and the smell of fish and water-soaked timbers rose to greet them, mixed with the foul smell of the city's harbor district just beyond. As soon as the four of them were ashore the boat was gone.

"We too must leave the city before morning," Rosivok said. "Ferris' soldiers may look for us even here, and there is plenty of trouble to be had even if they do not."

"I agree," Frost said. "The best road to Golemesk passes through much open country, and much of that in Ariman. We will travel due west instead, then climb the wall into Ikaydin. We can follow the edge of the plateau then, until we reach the Thorun River. The river will lead us into Golemesk from the north."

"A good plan," Madia remarked. "There may be very few others in that part of the swamp."

Frost nodded. "It is our best chance."

"Though a very long journey," Rosivok said. "Are you up to it, master?"

Frost shrugged. "I will let you know as I find out."

"Then let us get started," Madia said, picking up her pack, turning toward the torches of the city beyond.

"Wait," Frost said, putting a hand on Madia's shoulder. "As Rosivok said, these streets can be filled with dangers. A small warding spell is in order." He closed his eyes and spoke briefly under his breath. Then he let go and set off along the wharf, giving the others no choice other than to catch up.

Madia brought up the rear carrying a smile inside that warmed her slightly. *Magic,* she thought, *and none too soon.* She had traveled into unfamiliar lands before; this time, though, was nothing like the others.

A storm was brewing, elements all coming together; the flash and fury were yet to come.

Chapter XVIII

"Three travelers have come asking for you," Keara said, standing in the doorway. "Friends from Kamrit, they say. They wait at the corner table, near the window."

Hoke looked up from his ledgers. "Would they not say who they were?"

"No, but they are two men, both knights, and a woman. A lady, I'd say."

"Really." Hoke put the ledger away, then paused as he stood up. Whoever they were, a woman among them likely meant they were not here to start trouble. Still . . .

There had been few friendly visitors from Kamrit in recent weeks, which itself was not a good sign, and the news an occasional sympathizer did manage to bring kept getting worse. He gathered his sword, then followed Keara out.

Hoke recognized all three visitors the moment he set eyes on them. All slightly older than he remembered, but a welcome sight nonetheless.

Lady Anna leapt up the instant she saw Hoke. He had been friends with her husband, Lord Grand

Chamberlain Renall, and he had returned to Kamrit for a short time to comfort Lord Renall's widow after his death. He and Anna had come to know each other well enough.

She was no adventurer, Hoke knew, and not at all the type to keep company with soldiers, though in the brothers Mauro and Umblic she had chosen her company well. Fine men, both of them, and two names he had heard other visitors make mention of when talk turned to old loyalties, and to disaffection with the new.

Anna came around the table and they threw arms around each other.

"Where are you headed?" Hoke asked, sitting with them, calling to Keara for ale.

"Here," Anna said.

"To Kern?"

"No," Mauro replied. "We have come for you."

"I had not heard how Madia and the others were fairing," Hoke said, as Anna and the brothers finished their long explanations. He gazed past those at the table, out through the window beyond. He had been worried Madia would never reach Kamrit, that her cause would abandon her and she would give up along the way—or worse. Her crusade had been lacking in design and assurances, though now it seemed that did not matter; it seemed that she, like himself, had not realized what they were up against.

Now Hoke took solace from the fact that the princess had kept her new allies and taken her cause all the way to Kamrit Castle, though he winced as Anna told him of their defeat and narrow escape, of their new exile, and the demon prince they believed Ferris to be.

"No wonder the changes have come so fast and have gone so unopposed," he said.

"That is what weighs on our minds," Anna said.

"I see," Hoke replied, "but if even a powerful wizard is helpless against him, what hope has anyone?"

They looked to each other first. Hoke studied the expression on Lady Anna's face, an ironic half-grin. Then he noticed this same look on the faces of both brothers, and he began to feel uneasy.

Hoke pressed her. "What is it you want?"

"We need help, of course. Where a few have failed, many may not," Anna said, her eyes suddenly dour, staring into his. "But no one in Kamrit seems able to rally the people, or even the old loyalists in the army, against Lord Ferris." She paused long enough to scowl a bit at Mauro and Umblic. "That is why we need you. All Ariman will be lost, perhaps the great fiefs and Neleva as well, if something is not done. War will destroy all that both Andarys kings have built, all that men like my husband fought to preserve. But there is more."

Hoke looked at her, waiting.

"If I am right, the king himself is not dead, but being held captive in his own dungeons."

"Now you go too far!" Hoke told her, but then he listened while she tried to explain. The more he listened, the more persuasive her story became, but in the end he still could not accept that Andarys lived.

"Enough," Hoke said. "Even if I am to believe all that you say, and even if I did as you ask, I see little promise in the effort. If there are none in Kamrit who would stand against Lord Ferris, then I cannot create them. In order to begin, there must be a beginning. Can I preach righteousness to men who fight only for wages, or teach courage to those who fight for their enemies out of cowardice? In any case, I am old and damaged. I have served my king and country, and well, and there is little more I can do."

"That is what I told her," Mauro said, and Umblic nodded sympathetically.

Anna made a fist and thumped Mauro's chest, causing him to wheeze. "Your king still needs you, all of you!" she said. "And you are both wrong. There are men who would act, but they have nothing to bind them together, no one to lead them. You can lead, Hoke, as perhaps no other man in all of Ariman. You can inspire men to follow you."

"But still there will be too few of us," Umblic quietly argued. "And so many who do Lord Ferris' bidding. What could Hoke do but lead us to doom?"

"An honorable doom, then," Hoke said, looking at the brothers.

"A great comfort," Mauro said.

Hoke picked up his ale and drank deeply. When he had finished, he let a thick, airy burp boil out. "Of course, the arguments are good ones," he told Anna. "But Madia went with a great wizard and good fighters, and from what you say they failed completely, and my friends died. I am afraid old Hoke and a few dozen heros would fare no better."

"I don't have enough answers, but you were my greatest hope," Anna said, pain welling up in her eyes, tears barely held back. "My last hope. Surely there must be something, some way. . . ."

Hoke shook his head, then reached across the table and took one of Anna's hands in his. "You have not heard me out," he said. "There may be a way, but we must find it first. Surely something must be done. Much has happened in these lands these past few months. Ferris' men have spread throughout all of Ariman and into the great northern fiefs. Every day I hear of more troops in the north. I hear reports of attacks and men dying. An undeclared war has begun. Borders are being ignored, trade is being strangled by robbers and tolls, and there are fewer merchants.

"Most nobles dare not show their heads for fear they

will be singled out. No, I did not mean that I would not help—this is still my country, whether Kelren lives or not." Hoke squeezed Anna's hand. "I am proud of Madia, truly, and I fear for her now, for all the sons and daughters of the realm. I simply don't know how to help. Not yet."

He looked past her again, out the window into the narrow street beside the inn. Two of Lord Ferris' soldiers, passing through on their way from Kamrit to the great fiefs, were walking by, trailing their horses, as they did so often lately. Several local citizens hurried to give them room and let them pass unimpeded, smiling as they did. Hoke watched as the soldiers continued across the square, and the people in the street turned and spat on the ground where the two men had stepped.

"Ferris inspires much bitterness," Anna said, and Hoke realized she had been watching, too.

"Which could be used against him," Hoke added. "Yet most people seem willing only to show their feelings among themselves."

"So you have said, but perhaps—"

"They are not strong enough to risk anything else," Mauro said.

"True," Hoke agreed. "Though one can only imagine how troubled and angry the rather powerful great lords of Bouren, Jasnok, Vardale, and Thorun must be."

"Their anger remains their own, as do their loyalties," Umblic said, shaking his head.

"They each quarrel with raiders from Ariman that ride onto their lands," Hoke went on, "but they believe the rumors they hear of the other great lords, each half-suspecting the rest of collusion with Lord Ferris. Or expecting the next lord to start a war with Kamrit that they in turn will be drawn into, like it or not. They have never worked together before, not since their fathers did in the time of Haul Andarys. But there has not been a need, nor anyone to point one out."

"If Ferris has called them to homage, they have not complied," Umblic said.

"But does anyone truly know which rumors are true, or which lords can be trusted, or even how troubled they are?" Mauro asked, squinting, concentrating on the thought. "These things we would need to know. And Ferris is prepared for the great fiefs to move against him in any case."

"Perhaps, but certain troops and their commanders are more formidable than others," Hoke stated with authority. "While it might be impossible to unite the folk of Ariman under Ferris' nose, it might be possible to bring together a force outside Ariman's borders. I propose that in the morning we should begin a journey north to the four great fiefs. Perhaps they only need someone to lead the way. To make them see. Even Neleva might eventually join a proper effort."

"I do not think so, but I will go," Umblic said.

"As will I," chimed Mauro.

Anna was smiling at Hoke. He let go of her hand, then leaned closer. "Let us hope we are right about me," he whispered. "And that the time has not already passed."

"I sense concern," Tyrr said, gesturing toward the largest chair in his chambers.

"These military maneuvers of yours are ruining trade north of Kopeth," Kaafk grumbled, sitting down to dinner: a large roasted fowl, split unevenly between the two plates, with Kaafk's portion by far the larger of the two. "Everyone fears the battles will spill over into Ariman, and all four great lords are in a mood to kill anyone so much as near their borders. Merchants—*my* merchants—have been detained, robbed, even killed!"

"A temporary condition," Tyrr said, embracing calm, forgiving the other's tone. "Begin, now," he added, nodding. Kaafk paused a moment, contemplating, then he cut into the tender chestnut-colored meat and tasted a piece. He seemed quite pleased. Tyrr cut off a tiny bit, made the jaw chew slowly—let it continue, absently. "Perhaps you should be on hand there to minimize the effects."

Kaafk looked up suddenly at this, his expression even more intent. "I can't be everywhere! There are many things that require my attention. Problems abound. Worst of all, Neleva has slowed its exports to almost nothing. They do not trust you, my lord, and they've begun to make trade difficult for anyone associated with me."

"There *is* no trade without you, without Kamrit."

"This is obvious to all, and yet . . ."

"Yet what?"

"Yet they seem willing to injure themselves in order to protest the control we have gained. Many of my associates have returned from the ports of Neleva, as well as from the north, with stories. You should listen to them sometime, so that you might know how the Nelevans, and others, see you."

"Of course you will tell me."

Kaafk pushed another large piece of bird into his mouth, lips smacking, a sincere effort, then chased the swallow with wine. He barely looked up.

"Many have heard of the ceremonies you attend, the sorcerer's tricks that some have seen you perform these past few months. They worry over the many citizens and soldiers you hold in the dungeons, the many more who have been executed. They fear your powers and your wrath, perhaps beyond the point of reason. Many, especially in Neleva, are not certain what most of the jailed and beheaded have done to reap such penalties."

"They must be told that the prisoners and the dead were my enemies, and that I intend to treat my friends very well. Surely you can attest to that."

Kaafk looked up again, chewing and grinning. Tyrr met his eyes and felt what meaning there was within them. Kaafk must have his own reservations, certainly, and he had seen Tyrr do more magic than most, but wealth was a more powerful force than any kind of fear for this man, an answer to the most impossible questions, or at least a means of denying the need to ask. "Already," Kaafk said, "I am rich beyond even my own dreams."

Tyrr swallowed his tiny bit of meat and contemplated another. "And that satisfies you?" Tyrr asked, testing.

"For now." Chuckling.

Tyrr allowed the banter. "They will come around," he elaborated. "Not all have openly opposed me. Many, I think, might have opposed your control of the markets, but fear has prevented that."

Kaafk nodded. "Of course."

The sentiment was genuine. Tyrr made the mouth grin. Despite his attitude, or because of it, Tyrr mused, Kaafk remained one of his better decisions.

"One by one, the northern fiefs will ultimately declare their wars against Ariman, or each other, whether they mean to or not," Tyrr went on. "I have a report only this morning that our troops have met with resistance in Bouren, and some of Ingram's forces have taken the fight to Lencia itself."

"Your forces remain thin in those regions, as I understand, my liege, and much of the rest are scattered all over Ariman. They hardly seem prepared to invade the north, or even defend our northern borders."

"For now, a great army is not needed in the fiefs. And gathering my forces would send too large a message to *all* our neighbors. As you say, they are already nervous."

"Then, at some time, before it is too late, Ingram and his men will have their battle joined?"

Tyrr reflected on the thought. "Perhaps," he said. "On the other hand, I grow somewhat dissatisfied with him.

Despite every opportunity, he still has not found the Demon Blade for me."

Kaafk nodded and stuffed the last of the bird into his mouth, then he began looking over the carcass for anything he'd missed. "The search continues, then?" he asked as he reached over and started on the bowl of fruit.

Tyrr pulled a second, very small bit from his own portion, put it into the mouth. "I have already engaged the services of another, a wizard known as Gray, and his compliment of men. He is known to many as a very powerful mage, and he insists he is capable of obtaining the Blade from Golemesk, if it is still there. His price was ridiculous, but if it buys the results I need, I may even pay it."

Kaafk was slowing down, filling up. He worked his face into a half twist, then let a great belch escape his lips and smiled briefly. "I am curious as to the Blade's powers. What makes it such a prize?"

How could he tell this fellow that he didn't know the answer? How could he go on not knowing it himself? Yet there was no choice!

Tyrr felt a tremor move through the body, the semblance beginning to loosen around the edges. He paused again to reinforce the spell and reminded himself once more that the increasingly annoying task would not be his forever. Soon enough, the world would know him for what he was and would be too vulnerable to object. Unless, of course, something went wrong—unlike Tybree and the others like him, Tyrr had learned that at least: something could always go wrong.

"The Blade is a mystery," he finished, "and one I must discover. *I* must be the one to learn its secrets, no one else." Secrets that could be put to good use, he thought, if possible, or kept from the rest of the world, if need be, forever.

The fruit was gone. Kaafk sat back, draining his mug.

"If you wish, I will go to the northern borders, but not until it is safe, my liege," he said. "I will do what can be done to restore whatever is lost, and replace whoever has died, but I must live long enough to do so."

The chuckle was back, grating at some part of Tyrr's construct—or Tyrr's self. He pressed on:

"Safe trade will resume, I can assure you. Trade by my law is preferable to no trade at all. Eventually, all the people of the realm will become accustomed. The needs and desires of so many never go unserved for long."

Kaafk belched once more, then nodded.

"Perhaps," Tyrr said, thinking about it, "when the time comes, I will go with you. I have never been to the northern fiefs, and those lands will be mine before Neleva."

"We will save Neleva's warm southern beaches for last, aye, my friend?" Kaafk grinned privately.

Tyrr attempted control, refused his urge to strike out, and allowed the insolent address. "Neleva and her rich harbors must be taken slowly and carefully. I want a gentle surrender, in order to insure as little damage as possible. Patience, Kaafk, as well as tolerance, are virtues—no matter how difficult the process tends to be."

"Of course." Kaafk seemed to grow uneasy as Tyrr looked at him, and Tyrr savored the thought of this slight intimidation, but then the big man shrugged his shoulders and excused himself for the evening. Tyrr let him go.

When the other was gone, Tyrr summoned his servants. His own two pages entered the room, both moving slowly, somewhat awkwardly, as if re-thinking every step—a side effect of the controlling spells Tyrr had fixed upon them. They cleared the table, including the largely untouched meal on Tyrr's plate. In a moment, one of the men returned with a whole goose, still alive.

He placed it on the table before Tyrr. The bird honked at the construct, then began strutting nervously. Tyrr placed a holding spell upon the creature and it grew still, moving only its eyes. Then he picked the bird up and pulled feathers out, several handfuls, and bit into its throat.

The blood ran down the chin and arms of the construct, warm and fresh, feeding the body, feeding Tyrr.

The pages stood and waited until he was finished, then cleared the carcass away.

Chapter XIX

Prince Jaran watched from the woods as the soldiers from Ariman grew visible, appearing with the dawn in the clearing below the hills, preparing for war. Two hundred at least, he guessed. The young prince had only a handful of men with him, down to seven now, three having died just yesterday from wounds received in a skirmish on the edges of Golemesk. There had been twelve men in the squad of encroaching troops they'd caught emerging from the swamp. Jaran had intended only to warn them back to Arimanian soil, but they had attacked before a word was spoken, and fought nearly to the last man.

The news had come just an hour after that, a rider from home sent to inform the Prince that Lencia was under attack. "The offenders have been repelled, and all goes well," the message said, "but beware their presence upon your return." The rider explained that the king had been ready, that the Arimanian forces had broken off quickly and fallen back. From what Jaran could determine now, though, they had not given up all together.

"There are a few more men scattered to the North, and still more nearer Lencia to the South, all from Ariman," Purcell, Jaran's first man-at-arms, whispered to him. Jaran turned and looked back into the woods. All of his remaining men were assembled there, including the two he had sent on reconnaissance.

"Are they up to moving?"

Purcell shook his head. "No, they are staying for now. This force must be the one that attacked Lencia. The others may have arrived since then."

"And what is their strength?"

"Before you," Purcell said, indicating the encampment below. "The others are not many."

"Hardly sufficient to defeat my father," Jaran said with a tenuous sigh of relief. "He could defend Lencia against three times as many. The best they can hope is to eventually starve the city."

"There may be more on the way, we cannot know. Surely a report of their failed engagements has been sent back to Lord Ferris."

"If there are more troops on the way they would be waiting to attack again, just as they are. Still, I would not think the Arimanian commander too eager to admit his failures to Lord Ferris. They may be reassessing their plans, hoping to invent a better strategy. A good time to strike back at them, if true. I must tell my father."

"But how do we get to him?" Purcell replied. "Ferris' troops roam the roads and fields and forests, blocking our way."

"We will circle far to the south, then north, up the wall to the Ikaydin plateau."

"Then follow the Saris River into Lencia."

"Yes. My father would not let the invaders gain control of the river, I am certain of it."

"We will be two days at least getting there, maybe three," Purcell said, apparently just pointing it out.

"I know," Jaran said, placing a hand on the hilt of his sword. "Which is why we must begin at once." He turned and faced his men. "Bring the horses!"

Purcell stood back, then lowered his head. "Yes, my Lord."

The great wall of the Ikaydin plateau stood as an imposing barrier before them, though here, where it met the borders of both Bouren and Ariman, where the wall came to a westward point before sweeping back again, the land had been worn away to make the grade passable. Jaran led his men up the southern side of the point as the afternoon waned, and by dark they reached the top.

They slept the night on Ikaydin soil along the trail that followed the edge of the plateau, continuing for hundreds of miles. They took what shelter they could beneath a small stand of trees alongside the trail. Up on the plateau the winds never died, but tonight they were warm and light, and smelled of distant grasses and the heavy blossoms of nearby flowering bushes. Sleep came easily. Just after dawn, the last sentry woke the camp in a sudden hurry. He scurried from man to man, whispering, "Someone comes!"

"Where?" Purcell asked him, and the soldier led the way to the edge of the trail. Purcell glanced briefly into the distance, looking south, then nodded and made his way back. "A small group, all on foot," he told Jaran. "Trailing a mule."

"Behind the trees then," Jaran commanded. "And get the horses down."

The men moved quickly, coaxing their mounts to lay in the tall grasses between the trees, then lying down themselves. Jaran knelt low behind one of the larger tree trunks and waited until the travelers appeared. There was a very fat man cloaked in a flamboyant robe, a peddler, Jaran thought, or a man of magic, and two large, lethal looking warriors with him, one of them a female; finally there came a much smaller figure, dressed more plainly than the others, a female as well, though even she was well-armed. Then, as they passed nearer, he suddenly realized who they were. He stood up as the travelers passed and shouted: "Frost!"

The huge wizard stopped and turned, just looking, while all three of his companions instantly spread out and made ready to fight. Jaran nodded to himself, impressed with their prowess. His own men were good, but they were not Subartans. Though neither, he thought, was the smaller female. He walked out from among the trees and approached the trail.

"I am Prince Jaran Ivran, of Lencia," he said, taking it slow.

"So you are!" Frost shouted, grinning now. "And have you your father with you?"

"He is at Lencia, defending the city, in fact, against barbarians from Ariman."

"Not truly Ariman," the small female warrior said, stepping forward—a girl not at all like the female Subartan, Jaran noticed. Then he noted that she had drawn her sword and not put it away, that she was in fact still moving towards him, leading with it. "They are the hired fools of Lord Ferris, not patriots," she continued. "And as for barbarians, what say you of men who would ride into Ariman to kill the daughter of the king? Of lords who spit on the bonds of generations, and who pay homage by treachery? What of murderers? What of traitors? Bastards!"

She stood only at arm's length from him now. The sword suddenly bridged the distance between them. She kept the point in check while Jaran's own men drew their weapons, making troubled faces, surrounding her.

Prince Jaran stood fast. He looked Madia over. "This is

someone new, is it not?" he asked Frost. "Someone not
with you on your last visit. I would have remembered a
woman such as this. Though, if she does not mind her
behavior, I may be forced to mind it for her."

Madia just snarled.

"That is correct," Frost replied, nodding to the prince.
"We met in Kopeth. She is Madia Andarys, daughter of
Kelren Andarys."

Jaran paused in surprise. "A ghost, then? They say
Madia was killed on the road, after, ahh . . . "

"I'm never going to live that down, am I," the girl
snarled, apparently to everyone.

"She is real enough," Frost replied.

"But such accusations," Jaran said, feeling the need to
defend himself, though against what, exactly, he wasn't
sure. "My Lady, had I come to kill you, I would have
done so. Obviously you are not dead. I am no murderer,
and no traitor to Kelren, God rest the King. And neither
is my father." He leaned forward a little and glared at the
Princess Madia. "You are the one threatening murder
here."

"He may be an arrogant fool," Frost said, looking
toward Madia, "but I agree, he is an honorable one."

"It was Bouren soldiers killed a girl on the road outside of Kamrit last autumn, a girl they thought was me,"
Madia explained. "You must have sent them. You may
even have lead them. Assassins hold no honor with me."

"Impossible!" Jaran said. "We did no such thing!"

"For months, all of Ariman has known of the discon-
tent among the northern fiefs. And I know what I saw."

"Ferris himself must have spread those rumors," Jaran
insisted. "None of them are true. Even now, my father
defends Lencia against an army sent by Lord Ferris."

"The wolves devour each other," Madia said.

Jaran stepped back. "I will not stand for your lies!"

"I say he speaks the truth, Madia," Frost interjected.

"I visited with Jaran and his father on my way to Kern, and found only great concern for the well-being of all these lands, and for your father. I knew Jaran's grandfather, as I knew yours."

Madia stood firm. "I know what I saw."

"Perhaps not," Purcell said. "There were reports of mercenaries masquerading as Bouren soldiers, though they were only hear-say, and we have heard nothing since. We assumed they were not true."

"I was nearly *killed*! By men such as you! And you want me to believe that they were imposters?"

"You could consider it," Jaran replied, grinning at her insidiously. "From what I gather you have been mistaken about many things, and for many years now. That is the true reason for any misfortune that may have found you along the way. Tell me, how is it you came to be alone on the road in the first place? I have heard it is a story worth telling."

"Now you say it was my own fault!"

Jaran folded his arms. "You might consider that, too."

Madia leaned forward again and raised her sword to his throat, which caused Purcell to step up and touch his blade to hers, which caused both Subartans to take a step, subartas at ready, while Jaran's remaining troops did the same. Jaran watched Madia, who was standing absolutely still, gripping the hilt of her sword with ferocious tightness, knuckles going white. For a moment he thought she might try to cut off his head—but then she let the blade down, scowling at Jaran before she turned away.

"As spirited as I've been led to believe," Jaran commented, speaking generally.

Madia turned again and looked at the Prince. "Do not speak of what you do not know."

Jaran paused, feigning a pout, then bowed his head.

"Tell me," Madia said then, "why do you leave your

land and your father in such a time of need?" Her voice was soft, mocking. "War breaks out, and the young Prince Jaran runs away. Not as easy as preying on defenseless travelers?"

Jaran concentrated on his own temper and on the look in the girl's eye. She would not quit, he saw, yet if they kept at this he might be forced to run her through, or she him, which he didn't really want. *Walk away*, he thought.

"You have no idea what you are saying," he said. Then he turned to Purcell. "Make ready to leave," he commanded. Purcell started shouting his own commands. Men began gathering their horses from the trees behind them.

"Leave for where?" Frost inquired.

Jaran spoke to Frost. "Home."

"We could not reach Lencia because of Arimanian troop encampments," Purcell explained. "We had been returning from Golemesk."

"The swamp is being searched by soldiers from Ariman, as well as men from other lands," Jaran added, "interlopers from the Spartooths to the southern Kaya deserts, all looking for the Demon Blade."

"That, I'm afraid, is where we are going," Frost admitted. "Though I occasionally question the reasoning."

"Don't tell me you also search for the Blade?" Jaran inquired.

Frost smiled. "All right, I won't."

"We do!" Madia snapped. "And you will not stop us."

Jaran shook his head, then looked up the road. "Of course, and good luck to you. But I have begun to think it is not even there. With so many looking, it would have been found by now, I think, or it already has been. And good luck to he who has it! I have never been certain what the Demon Blade was supposed to be capable of, but I'd wager no good will come of it. And like as not it is just a sword after so many ages—no magic is timeless. Whatever its powers once were, there must be nothing left. The metal itself may have rusted away to nothing."

"Continuous magic is short-lived," Frost agreed. "But the Demon Blade has always been a simple blade to most, like any other, possessed only of a slight aura to give it away to those who have the sense. And so it remains, until it is used by one who knows its secrets. Otherwise, it is a key that fits no door."

"And then what?" Jaran asked. "What are its secrets?"

"If Ramins is dead, then perhaps no one knows, for he was the keeper of that knowledge."

"The old wizard they found near the swamp," Purcell stated.

"So it seems," Frost replied.

"Then," Jaran said, "the Blade is no good to anyone."

"Frost can find the door," Madia said, the ire still plain in her tone. "Once we have the Blade in our possession."

"And how will you among so many discover the Blade's whereabouts?" Jaran asked.

"Frost will sense it," Madia replied.

"Oh?"

"The others may not know where to look," Frost explained. "If the Blade was in the swamp, and Ramins died there, then the leshy have it by now and are keeping it in an especially safe place."

"What place is that?" Purcell asked him.

"A bog in the swamp's darkest depths, near the Bouren—Jasnok border."

"I know of the general area, though I've never been there," Jaran said. "There are only marshes and bogs, and no roads, and a legacy of death to those who enter. A place known only to leshys and apparitions."

"The Holan barrows lie somewhere within," Purcell noted.

Frost sighed, a draining sound. "That they do."

"You will find no Demon Blade there," Jaran insisted. "You go only to join the dead."

"We go to save Ariman from the wicked thing that rules it, and to save Bouren as well. If you and your people are truly enemies of Lord Ferris," Madia insisted, "you should offer your assistance!"

Jaran tipped his head. "I see. Just the four of you and the mythical Demon Blade, and victory is certain?"

"Ferris is some sort of demon himself," Madia said. "And very powerful. The Blade is our only hope of defeating him, and yours."

Jaran looked to Frost, his mood suddenly staid. Frost met his gaze. "Yes," Frost said. "It is true. He is much too powerful. No mortal man can hope to defeat him, nor any mortal army, I fear. He will eventually rule all the lands he desires, and his desires, I think, are many."

Jaran stood silently thinking over the wizard's words. His father took great stock in Frost; he wondered what his father would do now, faced with this news, what his father would expect *him* to do? Faced with so many uncertainties, and all of them bearing such consequence. Not the least of which was the question of Madia herself. He wondered how she was supposed to fit into all of this, and whether he could accept whatever the answer was; he only knew of her what he had heard. . . .

But saving the future of the realm outweighed many a misgiving, surely—outweighed everything. "I do offer my service," he said, "and that of my men."

"Of course," Madia said, "but we don't want you!"

"I will favor Frost's opinion," Jaran replied.

"One day," Frost began, speaking to Madia, "you may rule Ariman, as Jaran may rule Bouren, unless Lord Ferris is allowed to succeed. You might need Bouren or the other northern fiefs as Allies in the future, as well as now, if you hope to oppose Ferris, just as I may need the help of their mages. Jaran and his father may be the key to any such alliance. Perhaps cooperation between you two would be an important step, and you should see it as such. We had no idea so many others were searching Golemesk. I have confidence in my Subartans, and in you, but I very much like the odds that Jaran and his men will lend."

"When did you become such a diplomat?" Madia asked.

"I seem to have no choice," Frost told her.

"Nor do I," Jaran said.

"Nor I," Madia conceded. She looked at Jaran. "But let me ask you something."

Jaran nodded.

"You would throw in with us, perhaps to die at the hands of soldiers or leshy or barrow-wights, and leave your father to defend your home alone?"

"If the Blade is our only hope, and Frost our only hope of finding it and discovering its secrets, then I serve my father and my people best by helping him. And truly, my father can take care of himself."

"I thought much the same thing, once," Madia said. "But each set of choices is different."

"Yet there is a chance that something might happen to your father in your absence, don't you see? And that you might end up feeling . . . responsible, because you weren't there for him when he needed you."

"Perhaps," Jaran said, looking at her. He raised his thumb and finger and gently rubbed his chin. He was beginning to understand. He had only one answer, the truth.

"No," he said. "No, I think, because I have *always* been there for him, and that he knows."

Madia slowly nodded, then she looked away in silence.

Men and horses had gathered around them. Nervous hooves and scuffling feet stirred the dry soil. Frost turned and motioned to Sharryl and Rosivok, and then Madia, and they started up the trail once more, followed directly by Jaran and his soldiers.

Chapter XX

Beyond the high falls that fell from Ikaydin, the Thorun River pooled, then ran wide and predictable through the low, forested hills. Here the population was sparse, tiny villages and small, often isolated manors close to the riverbanks. Frost followed the river as much as possible, though he and the others were careful not to encounter any of the local folk.

Frost and Madia chatted from time to time as they went, occasionally joined by Sharryl or Rosivok, but the Bouren prince talked only to his soldiers, and they only to him, until the trail along the river split.

"We will take the right fork into the swamp, then turn west," Frost said. "And luck will be with us."

Jaran frowned at this last. "And how do you know that?" "There are many good omens," Frost explained, noting the warm, sunny weather that had marked the last two days, the wind that never came at their backs, the pattern his augur pebbles made when he took them from their little bag and scattered them on the ground. The pebbles, he claimed, had helped him choose the way ahead.

"I put no faith in these," Jaran said.

"Nor do I," Madia said, "but I have noticed that Frost does, and I won't enter Golemesk on my own, so I am for staying along the water."

"A wise choice," Frost recommended. "Only a fool would risk all that he hoped for on his own knowledge alone."

"I wouldn't expect you to disagree with him," Jaran told Madia.

She fixed her eye on him, glowering. "What do you mean by that?"

"Nothing, of course," Jaran said, glancing at his men, grinning as they each did.

"You mind yourself, Jaran Ivran!" Madia snapped. "I will not be made a fool by any man!"

"One cannot do that which is already done, my lady."

Madia took a breath and started toward Jaran.

"All jests aside," Frost said, stepping calmly between them, "I think I can ensure our safe passage. And truly," he added, glancing toward Madia, "I would enjoy whatever confidence any of you might place in me."

Jaran studied the wizard a moment. "How can you be so sure?" he asked. "I don't say that I doubt you, but even you cannot know all that we may face in the swamps."

"I will put your mind at ease," Frost said. "Ask your men to form a line, just for a moment."

Jaran turned to face his soldiers and was startled. "Where are they, what have you done to them?" he demanded. He stood gaping at first, then glanced nervously in several directions.

"Go ahead," Frost insisted. "Tell them to form a line."

"What have you done with them!"

"If you will just give the order to your captain . . . "

Jaran stood fuming, still casting about, knuckles white on the hand that gripped the hilt of his sword. "Very well!" he said finally. He faced the empty road. "Purcell, have the men form a line!" He turned back to Frost, lips pursed, eyes drawn narrow. "Done."

Frost looked to Madia, grinning for himself now, and watched a similar smile appear on her face. "They seem well trained," he said. Jaran turned again—and nearly jumped. The men were there, of course, all of them, and in a very neat row. Frost's grin widened.

"But how did you make them disappear?" Jaran asked, obviously a little unnerved.

"I did not," Frost explained. "You were the only one affected. It is much easier that way." He turned and continued walking slowly along the riverbank. Jaran stayed put with his men for a while, and they drifted out of sight. Not long after that they appeared again on the trail, catching up.

No troops of Ariman crossed their path, nor anyone from the Thorun palace at Ginns, though the trail proved more difficult than expected. They had not yet reached the edges of the swamp as the day waned, and they were forced to make camp for the night.

Sleep came easily and lasted long with so many to take turns standing guard, and with the added comfort of the warding spell Frost carefully conjured all around the camp site. In the morning, full of breakfast and walking again, they found the river growing wider until it embraced lush groves and thickets and muddy islands, and was a river no more. The hard trail gave way to mud and undergrowth, and an uncertain path thick with moss and fallen trees.

On the border between Thorun and Vardale, with Frost and his Subartans leading the way, the small party entered into Golemesk.

Camp this night was a small hollow formed by a hillock and a massive fallen tree. A tiny fire glowed with warmth and light against the damp, pungent cold and thick darkness of the night swamp. The trail had become lost in the marshes, the heavens lost to cloud cover and huge ancient trees. The air was heavy with the scent of green water and decaying vegetation, laced with the fragrance of water-plant blossoms. Sharryl and Rosivok made dinner, a soup of dried beans and some leaves they had picked along the way, and Purcell passed flat bread around.

"We're already lost, aren't we?" Purcell asked generally into the silence that hung over the camp when the meal ended.

"I'd wager," Jaran said. "A consequence of following, rather than leading, I think."

"You would have us following you?" Madia asked.

"Perhaps," Jaran replied.

"Frost leads the way," Rosivok declared, again breaking his almost regular silence, turning all heads.

"Of course," Jaran replied, turning to the wizard. "But might you share with us what you know?"

"As I said, the Blade has a faint aura," Frost explained. "I believe I have begun to sense something."

"And is it where you thought?" Madia asked.

"And have you a plan to deal with the lords of these swamps?" Jaran asked further. "Or whatever else finds us?"

"Something of a plan," Frost said. "Most men see the world through narrow eyes. Many creatures, even the most terrible, are often greatly misunderstood, or tragically mishandled."

"Most men that run afoul of leshys and barrow-wights in this swamp never see another day," Purcell said, causing a stir of quiet voices to rise among the other men. "I understand that fine. And the boorish rabble that's crawlin' about everywhere in Golemesk. We already lost three good men, not far from here."

"The swamp is full of men from every land," Jaran added, nodding. "We came to chase some of them off, but we did not expect so many. I have seen dark men from beyond the southern seas, and men from the mountains, and soldiers from half the fiefs in Ariman and beyond, not to mention robbers and scum, diviners and freemen. We were surprised by the troops from—"

"Then you and your men will be a great aid to my Subartans in any future encounters," Frost said.

"Although, they have not fared well so far," Madia noted. "By their own admission."

"A valid point," Frost replied. "Still . . ."

"I will not stay in this camp another moment!" Jaran announced. He stood up, motioning to his men. "None of us will. We will not be insulted by the likes of *her*!"

"Are you always so easily bested?" Frost chided him.

"First you ran from these swamps and then from your father's war," Madia scoffed. "You even run from mere words. Such a man! Such a prince! Such a *coward*." She sneered maliciously.

Jaran held his tongue somehow, though he was shaking visibly with the effort. He turned and moved through his men, then beyond the camp, taking stiff, deliberate steps. Purcell and the others started after him.

"They may yet be of use to us," Rosivok remarked. "As you said."

Frost nodded. "Yes, if Jaran has the will. Meanwhile, he will follow, no doubt. If what they tell us of the others in the swamp is true, we cannot know what will be in front of us, but we will at least know what is behind us."

"If they stay near, we can count on them if need be," Rosivok agreed.

"And if they do not stay, better to know of it now," Sharryl said.

They watched the men silently mount their horses, ghostly shapes at the edges of the flickering light from the fire. They spoke among themselves, a mumble Frost could not discern.

"I wonder whether they have that kind of courage?" Madia asked, staring after them. "*Any* of them."

Frost looked again and his eyes counted too many shapes in the darkness, too many horses—suddenly accompanied by the sounds of clashing iron and the howl of a man meeting death.

Two of Jaran's men fell almost instantly, their horses trotting nervously in circles, saddles empty. Another fell a moment after that, then the muddle of shapes became too confused to sort out. Madia drew steel and started toward the fray, but paused as Frost called to her. Rosivok and Sharryl stood at his sides.

"Stay," Frost said. "Here!" He pointed to a spot just in front of him, the third corner of a defensive triangle. "There may be others. I must work quickly."

Even as she moved to comply, the forest around them rustled to life. At least two figures lunged and were met at mid-stride by Rosivok, then Sharryl faced an attack. Madia spun about as another man fell upon her. She stepped to one side and drove her blade deep, then pulled back and swung out as still another man took the fallen soldier's place. This next was more wary than the first, unwilling to follow in his companion's footsteps. Madia traded blows, waiting her turn. A voice screamed somewhere behind her and she saw her opponent glance briefly toward the sound. She kicked, caught one of the man's legs, then thrust her sword into him as he stumbled.

Now two others took his place, pressing in. They stood on the bodies of the first two men and used the added height to their advantage. Madia swung and blocked furiously, holding them off at first, then losing ground as her strength began to falter. She stepped back once, twice, then sensing herself very near to Frost with her back almost against him, though she dared not turn around.

Suddenly one of her opponents arched at the waist, mouth open, and stumbled back. The second turned his head frantically as he witnessed the event, checking all sides. Madia found the tip of a broadsword emerging from the first man's midsection even as she plunged the end of hers into the second. She pulled back to let the nearest man fall with his friend, and stood facing Jaran.

They stared briefly at each other, left alone somehow by the battle around them, if only for an instant. A very long instant.

"Thank you," Madia said, and saw Jaran nod to her graciously. Then both of them seemed to notice that the sudden calm was not imagined but was apparently quite real. All around them the attacking soldiers stood in place, gaping at the darkness or each other. Rosivok waved to gain everyone's attention, then pointed to the soldiers in earnest, indicating the attack.

"The same spell Frost used on me, on the road," Jaran said, grinning suddenly. "They cannot see us!"

"But they hear!" Madia yelped, stepping sideways as a pair of soldiers turned toward Jaran's voice. Jaran spun about, signaling his men as they came out of their collective trance, then he struck as a soldier's blade slashed wildly in the air. The second man went down and Madia stood over him. Within minutes every remaining assassin lay dead or dying.

"They attacked as soon as you and your men stepped beyond my warding spell," Frost said to Jaran.

"Why didn't the spell protect you?" Jaran asked.

"Once they were within its bounds, once they knew, it did no good."

Jaran nodded. "You handle yourselves well," he said to

the two Subartans and Madia. She favored him with a very tight grin. "As do you, my lord."

"How have your men fared?" Rosivok asked. Jaran turned and called them round, counting heads, looking them over. One of the men was bleeding from the arm, another from the face, though neither wound seemed serious. Four men and Purcell. Just the two dead.

"Well enough," he said.

"I will build a new spell to warn us of another approach," Frost said. "And yet another warding spell. One guard should be enough. These are some of Ferris' men. I doubt there would be more than one squad in the same area at the same time. The rest of the night should go more quietly."

"But Ferris' men are not the only ones we have to worry about," Purcell reminded.

"I know," Frost replied. "I do what I can."

Purcell turned and showed the other men to the bodies of their attackers, and they began hauling them into the trees. Rosivok and Sharryl remained with Frost.

"When will we reach the barrows?" Jaran asked.

"Perhaps tomorrow."

"Then this may be only the beginning."

"Beginnings," Frost said, "are better than ends."

"Perhaps, but I have just lost two good men. You and I may yet join them."

"Unlikely," Frost replied. "You and your men have a propensity for foolishness, while I do not. There is cause for worry, my young prince, about a great many things— for all my powers I cannot foretell the future, and some of the signs, as best I can read them, now seem to point to doom. But we must stay to our plans."

"Which are?"

"Get some sleep tonight, then wake up in the morning," Madia contributed.

"You never told me you were such a philosopher," Jaran remarked.

"A good answer, nonetheless," Frost said.

"And goodnight," Madia added, making a face.

"Oh, a wonderful night," Jaran said. "The two of you deserve each other."

"And more," Madia replied. For a long, silent moment Jaran stood facing her, and Madia felt herself being wrapped in a dark anticipation that seemed to fill the air where they stood. He would not look away, and neither did she, until at last Purcell came over and addressed the prince.

"Should we bury them?" he asked.

"Not tonight," Jaran replied. "Tonight, it seems, we sleep."

"We will all help with that task come morning," Frost declared. Madia and Jaran each went to make ready to bed down, on opposite sides of the fire.

The bogs that lay along the border between Jasnok and Bouren were all but impassable under the best conditions, and this day, with dark clouds filling the sky and light rain drizzling through the thick canopy of green and brown above them, navigation was nearly impossible. The land frequently lied, a conspiracy of thick foliage and mists covered everything, and what seemed solid ground beneath thick green cover was often revealed to be water or peat or mud when tested with the weight of a man.

Several times Frost called everyone to a halt while he tossed his bag of stones and worked a perambulation spell, all to enlighten him as to the value of one path or another. In most cases, Frost thought, this seemed to work.

Until at midday when he broke from a brief meditation to Rosivok's yelp and found the Subartan hanging from the branch of a tree, his feet kicking air over the edge of a steep, previously hidden, bank. Below lay a small green pond.

"The way was level!" Jaran said, rushing up behind the others, then helping Sharryl and Madia pull Rosivok back.

"An illusion," Frost said, looking into the wet gloom. "And a good one. Not even I sensed it."

"A trap," Rosivok said, examining the pond below.

"Perhaps, but not made for us," Frost replied. "For the leshys, I think. There is an aura. I am not the first mage to pass this way. The one who did this is clearly talented, and probably not alone, and probably at least as intent on recovering the Demon Blade as we."

"Then where is this mage?" Jaran asked.

"Not far. This type of illusion will not stand for long without renewal. Less than a day. We may find them below."

"This way," Rosivok said, pointing left to a dark ravine that cut through the hill to the water below. "We will walk around, then down."

They went slowly, minding their footing on the damp, mossy rocks and rotting fallen trees. When they reached the bottom, they followed the soft ground to the water's edge. Mist gathered across the little pond and nearly obscured the far shore, though it was not far. There was no sound at all. Not even the chatter of birds.

"If this was a trap set for leshys," Jaran said, "it does not seem to have worked."

"The trap is fatally flawed," Frost explained. "Leshys associate themselves with natural objects: a certain tree, a bend in the river, a small pond. A leshy of this place would already have been here when the spells were cast. The mage, whoever he is, does not understand his subject. He asks a question that has no answer."

Rosivok led the way further along the shore. As the

other side of the pond emerged from the mist, a small clearing came into view, a place where several trees lay felled, their stumps cut to jagged points. Closer, among the fallen trees, lay the bodies of four men, three of them soldiers, another dressed in more ornate robes and a hat embroidered in gold lace—a much fatter, much older fellow. This one clutched a dark wooden staff in one white, stiffened hand. The Subartans stayed with Frost. Madia went with Jaran as he took his men forward to look the bodies over.

"All dead," Jaran announced directly. "Strangled, I think." He looked to Purcell, who had hold of the head of one of the soldiers and was tugging it to one side. Purcell nodded agreement. "And what of these small wounds, here and here, lots of them?" he added.

"Bite marks," Frost said as he came forward and looked for himself. "At least a dozen leshys, I'd say. I know this one—a formidable sorcerer. Gray, his name was."

"That is encouraging," Jaran muttered.

"Where are the leshys now?" Purcell asked, standing up and peering into the swamp.

"They are here, somewhere," Frost said.

"Should we leave them?" Rosivok asked, nodding toward the dead.

"Yes," Frost answered. "I am sure the leshys have plans for the bodies. We will not deprive them."

"Deprive them?" Jaran stood fast. "What talk is that? I care little what plans they have. Leaving them to lie here like this is not decent."

"Here, in Golemesk," Frost said, "what *you* think is decent behavior is not what matters. Propriety is a relative thing, Lord Jaran, and here the rules are made by the lords of Golemesk. Unless you plan to join Gray and his foolish friends."

"You must do as he says," Rosivok urged.

"Yes," Madia chided, "you must. Is that not right, Purcell?"

Purcell, of course, said nothing. Jaran closed his eyes, keeping something inside, then he opened them and nodded at Frost. For Madia, he had a less affable expression. Rosivok set off, leading the way again.

By late afternoon, the living canopy above them had grown so thick as to bring an early dusk to the land. But Frost had already found the place he was looking for. The very depths of the bog spread out before them. The smell of stagnant, rotting waters hung so thickly that the air was nearly unbreathable. The dusk grew almost tangible, a cloak that moved just ahead of one's vision, obscuring anything distant that the eyes tried to focus on.

Another pond lay just ahead, visible now through the breaking tangle. The wide shallow waters were pierced and crisscrossed with standing dead tree trunks and fallen trees, their branches reaching, crooked and bare, like the rigid arms of drowning creatures toward the still living canopy of green above. All around, in the shadows and crowded undergrowth, a quiet motion could be heard.

Rosivok turned to the others. "Look," he said, pointing just ahead. "More dead."

Frost and the others followed cautiously. These were all soldiers, twenty when counted, two low ranking officers among them and no captain, so far as anyone could determine from the uniforms and weapons. All of them had died from loss of blood. Gaping wounds marked their flesh wherever it was exposed. But not all the dead were human.

"That creature is an imp," Frost explained. "A lesser demon like the one we faced in Kamrit. These are Lord Ferris' men. Imps have the sense, of course. It was sent to sniff out the Demon Blade, certainly, and may have done just that. I am sure it is here, very close."

"Horrible little thing," Jaran said, speaking mostly to Purcell, poking at the knotty, ruddy body lying near his feet. Everyone nodded.

"Hold now!" Frost whispered, raising his hands, palms out.

"I hear it," Madia said.

Jaran stood next to her. "So do I."

All eyes were fixed on Frost as he gazed into the mists. "Leshys," he said.

Jaran's men reached slowly to their swords.

"Draw no weapons yet," Frost told them. "This contest will not be won by brawn or steel. I will speak with them."

"You cannot talk to leshys," Jaran insisted, "as many a dead man can attest."

"Perhaps," Frost said, "that is why they are dead."

Jaran motioned his men to stand still. In the brush, all stirrings abruptly stopped.

Chapter XXI

"Who leads?" Frost said, raising his voice, calling into the near reeds. No answer came. Frost stepped over a dead soldier's body then kept walking, slowly, motioning to the others to stay close to him. Another few paces and he reached the edge of the wet bog. Out on the thick brown and green waters, among the mists and shadows and floating plants, the rounded tops of the Holan burial mounds were visible, at least two dozen at a glance, though certainly there were more. Frost signaled for calm. He raised his hands and closed his eyes while Rosivok, Sharryl, and Madia took up their defensive positions.

"Feel my presence," Frost told the air, the trees, the bog itself, in the language of life. "Feel my touch!" A gentle breeze, warm and moist, began to drift through the trees and plants, carrying a scent so sweet that it could almost be tasted on the tongue. The plants swayed gently, then began a movement separate from the touch of the wind, a shivering. Colors grew deeper before the eye, leaves grew full; from a fallen trunk just to Frost's left, tiny leaves sprouted up, here, then there, and began to fatten.

"I come without tricks, without malice, without deception!" Frost shouted to the world.

Fresh green life swam up from the bogs. Vines twisted and clung to everything as they sprang up and headed in all directions. The forest air grew thicker as it filled with a wet mist, cool and fresh and organic.

"I bring truth, and the power of the ages. I take nothing but that which I must, that which I need."

Flowers bloomed on small plants and large bushes, even on some of the trees. The moss beneath Frost's feet grew thicker and darker, a carpet that raised everyone up two fingers. The canopy above grew more dense, and on the dead limbs out on the bog itself, new growth sprang forth.

"I will do no harm unless harmed."

Everywhere the swamp lived, thrived, *sang*. . . .

"But what I do for you, I can do against you."

The breeze died away as Frost brought his arms back down. The mist slowly cleared, taking with it the sweet, herbal scents.

Frost turned and glared into the reeds again. "That one!" he snapped. Rosivok spun half around and leaped into the brush. Something howled, a thin and jolting sound not possible from any man, then the Subartan emerged with one arm carefully wrapped around the chest of a kicking, growling beast. It wore a garment of sorts, a shirt made of a dark, limp cloth, half-sleeves and open at the front to expose the thin fur on its round belly—thicker on its narrow chest. The face, pointed and nearly as furry as its arms, seemed wracked with agony. Long, sharp nails clawed at the air.

"Your king," Frost demanded, bending to the creature, while keeping well out of range of both claw and spit. The leshy's small black eyes burned with rage. Frost pointed his staff at the creature's dangling genitals. "I will not ask more than twice!"

The creature screamed as though emasculation had already commenced, when in fact, Frost had done nothing—yet. Still the leshy held its tongue. Then motion began again all around them, movement in the water, the reeds, behind the trees.

"Why don't they attack?" Jaran asked in a loud whisper close to Frost's ear.

"They are wary of me," Frost said. "Of what I might do to their swamp, or to them, and so they wait. But they may overlook their fears in a moment. You will also remember that the leshys are not the only ones we must contend with here, something the leshys know only too well. The worst is yet to be, unless *this* one can be made to talk."

Frost raised his staff up and touched the captive leshy's forehead with it, and the creature went completely stiff. "The name of your king," Frost asked again, leaning much closer now. Narrow leshy lips trembled and began to move. Then the green waters of the bog exploded.

Rosivok let the leshy fall boardlike to the ground as the dead rose up and came toward shore. The barrowwights seemed to wade at first, but it was quickly apparent that they moved by forces much stranger than legs—their limbs and torsos were naught but bone draped in the ragged remains of hair and flesh, cloth and leather. Some wore bits of bronze armor, others seemed to go without, but all of them wielded swords or daggers of one kind or another. Empty eye sockets gaped at those onshore as the water rolled out of them, and from their dead open mouths came a hissing chorus like wet rocks thrown into a fire.

The first of the spirits to reach Rosivok seemed to fling itself straight upon him as though its momentum gave it no other choice. Rosivok twitched the subarta blade, standing his ground. Rotted wet bone flew about in bits and chunks. Rosivok brushed pieces of the thing off himself, then dodged the blade of the next barrow-wight—only to be spattered again as Sharryl joined the fight and dismantled the second creature, just above Rosivok's head.

Jaran and his men joined the Subartans then, followed by Madia. They formed a line along the shore just in front of Frost, all of them hacking furiously at the flying, hissing dead soldiers. Frost began to concentrate, finishing a carefully planned warding spell meant solely to muddle the dead's perception—a quick variation on the spell of "sight" he had been using, which was really all a barrow-wight had to go by. As the greater part of their numbers reached the shore he released the spell, and the creatures seemed to grow disoriented. They wheeled and spun about, swinging their weapons wildly at thin air and trees as much as their intended targets.

Seizing the advantage, the living spread out and worked quickly, using their swords two-handed to chop and cleave in all directions until the air was finally silent, and the ground was littered with sodden chunks of darkened bone and cloth and twisted metal.

Frost turned back to the captured leshy and spoke to it through the trance that still immobilized it. "Your king," he said again. "What is his name?"

Once more the leshy's mouth began to work, and a whisper came forth: "Ergris."

Frost released the spell and the leshy came quickly around. It shook briefly, head jerking side to side, eyes wild as it tried to look in all directions at once. It turned, glanced once over its narrow shoulder, then ran into the cover of brush and trees. Frost watched it go, then turned his back to the others to face the surrounding bog.

"I come on behalf of Ramins," Frost said, enhancing his voice, making his words unnaturally loud in the silence of the swamp. "I come to speak to Ergris!"

He stood quietly for a moment—until the brush began to stir, and the leshy king emerged.

He came surrounded by a dozen of his kind, distinguished from them only by the ornamental dyes that had been applied to the smoothed-back fur on his head and the dark, nearly hairless skin of his face. Ergris paused a few paces from Frost, ears twitching, eyes quick as he examined each of the human intruders.

"What know you of Ramins?" the leshy king asked, speaking in the human tongue.

"I am as he was," Frost replied. "Know me as you knew him, and we may share what was shared."

Ergris stood staring at Frost, his round belly expanding and contracting as he breathed. "You make the forest grow," he said.

Frost nodded, almost a bow.

"Only Ramins did this."

"True."

"Ramins and Ergris shared many things," the king affirmed. "Time and thoughts, food and drink. Many things."

Frost stood eye to eye with Ergris, saying nothing.

"You seek the Demon Blade?" Ergris asked.

"Yes."

The king's expression soured—a severe condition on a leshy face. He looked about at the small army of leshys in the reeds and gathered knee-deep in the nearby waters and poking out between the trees and undergrowth elsewhere. Barrow-wight bones and garments had already begun to move—slowly, indirectly, but certainly toward each other—had already begun to reassemble themselves. *Like the wolves at Highthorn, these dead refuse to die,* Frost thought.

"Then you will go," Ergris muttered. "Alive, if you go quick. Dead if you do not."

"I, too, am good at making threats," Frost replied. "We can threaten each other at length and destroy what we each value, but in the end this would not be sensible. I can hold your forest hostage while you hold the Demon Blade, but the Blade does not belong to you, any more than Golemesk belongs to me."

Ergris seemed moved by Frost's logic. He wore a strange, perhaps embarrassed look for an instant, though it was hard to tell, then he seemed to come to some conclusion. He shook his snout as if it annoyed him, then he turned and began a rapid, grumbly, snarling conversation with the leshys directly behind him.

"There is more to consider," Frost said, beginning again the instant their voices left a silence. "There is a new ruler in Kamrit."

"The leshys know of this. Lord Ferris sends men into Golemesk. They too seek the Demon Blade, like the other unwanteds who have plagued us since the death of Ramins. We kill most of them."

"He masquerades as the Lord Ferris," Frost said, "but in fact he is no man at all. Within exists a Demon Prince of great powers, a threat to all peoples in all lands, including the leshys and Golemesk. Soon the Ferris demon will rule these lands as he rules Ariman. All this will be his. *You* will be his, and the Demon Blade, you may trust, will be his as well."

"So you say," Ergris answered.

"It is true," Madia said, speaking up, almost pleading. "The Blade may be our only hope against Ferris and the growing armies he commands. Armies that will come upon you like a plague if you do not yield!"

"And so you say as well," Ergris repeated.

"Come here, to the water," Frost said. "See what is reflected there." And with that he turned and went to the mossy edge of the wet bog. He took his staff in both hands and spoke silently over it, concentrating for a time, then he wavered, touched by a wash of mounting fatigue as he called the spell to life. He drew a long, slow breath. "Clear a spot," he told Madia, pointing to the thick green blanket of algae that floated on the waters. She used her boot to splash the green slime aside, producing a rough circle of black tea-water perhaps two paces across. Before the algae could flow back, Frost plunged the tip of his staff into the middle of the circle.

Ergris, other leshys crowding close behind, came cautiously forward, pressing in along with Jaran and his men, their hostility momentarily forgotten. As the ripples quieted, the reflections of trees and brush and Frost and leshy formed clearly on the surface, then these began to fade. In their place, new images took shape. In the silence even Frost was aware of a sudden, rising clatter and scrape behind him.

All eyes turned momentarily to find the disassembled army of dead Holan warriors now almost fully reassembled everywhere around the living. As each creature formed it raised its sword once more, prepared to take up the battle again, though as yet, none had.

"Come," Frost said, looking into their empty dead eyes, letting them see what was in his mind. "You too must share in this." He signaled Rosivok and the others to ease back a bit. This they did, though with great hesitation. The barrow-wights came slowly near, then hung in the air above the ground and the water, clutching their weapons clumsily now, as if they had come to weigh far too much.

Frost looked them over carefully, then motioned with just a finger. One of the dead floated nearer and came to rest on the ground between Frost and Rosivok, this one bearing a long pleated tunic unlike the others and the blackened remnants of what had been a massive silk hat, worn instead of a helmet.

"Watch, Tiesh," Frost said, calling the dead mage by his name. "And know the truth."

Frost turned back to the water. He finished the incantation, animating the scene that had formed clearly now on the water's surface. Great armies came in a time when the trees and ground of Golemesk were bare; they swept over the land led by a creature that was human in shape but clearly a demon in appearance, a crimson, blackened yet glowing thing with eyes that burned dull white and a mouth that gaped, revealing jagged bone where teeth might have been.

Leshys fought the invaders, striking from what little cover there was, but the army was too vast, and quick to set fire to tangles and holes wherever the leshys fled. The human and demon forces reached the bog, and the demon breathed upon the frozen waters until they melted, then began to boil, filling the air with steam. When this cleared, nothing remained but the rotting barrows and the mud and decayed debris of the bog's bottom.

One by one the barrows were smashed and the spirits cast out into the sunlight. Those who survived the sun and the swords of the soldiers, Tiesh clear among them, were left to face the demon prince. In a brief, final moment, the spirits of the dead were seized and consumed. Then the demon strode among the wreckage of barrows, and in one, digging briefly, it seemed to find something.

Frost withdrew his staff. Reflections of man and leshy and the floating dead stared up from the dark waters, then these too disappeared as the surface covered over again with green.

"You might make anything appear there," Ergris said, though the edge was now gone from his voice.

"You have enough sense of these things," Frost replied. "As do you," he added, turning to Tiesh. "The images are not mine. Both of you know this."

Ergris said nothing for a time, though there was communication of a kind between Tiesh and the leshy king, a silent exchange.

"Give the Blade to Frost," Madia said, sounding almost frightened. "You must. If we are successful, perhaps I will rule Ariman. I give you my word that I will seek the allegiance of the northern kings and defend the sovereignty of Golemesk."

Jaran cleared his throat. Madia turned to him with a fierce look. He raised his eyebrows incredulously, but said not a word.

Ergris nodded to Tiesh and received a nod in return. The dead sorcerer rose up and drifted out over the waters, then over the cluster of mounds poking up everywhere. Near the center of the pond he descended into the waters and was gone. Soon enough the surface churned gently, and Tiesh emerged again, carrying a weapon that was neither large enough to call a sword, nor small enough to call a dagger. The hilt was thick and black and bore a gold knuckle bow; the blade was straight and tapered, with no false edge and only a single groove cut along its center from hilt to point. Tiesh drifted to a stop as he reached the shore and gave the weapon over to Ergris.

The leshy king held the Blade tenderly, looking it over as he ran one dark finger along an edge. He glanced about as if drawing a consensus from the other leshys; none seemed willing to comment. Finally Ergris turned to Frost and offered the weapon over, using his left hand, as its makers had intended. Frost nodded graciously and reached with his own left hand to accept the Blade.

His eyes went suddenly wide. He opened his mouth, and he began to scream.

The Blade lay nestled in the moss at Frost's feet, exactly where he had dropped it. He held his left forearm with his right hand, trying to comfort the flesh, rubbing to bring warmth back into it. He had no doubt whatever as to what had happened, no trouble understanding the intense, exotic pain that still radiated up into his shoulder. His left hand had a thinned, almost bony look, as did the arm.

In a way the mistake was obvious, now that he thought about it. He had anticipated the moment for so long and with such intensity that his passion had overruled his wits. Like a man long of thirst he had tried to drink too deeply, had unconsciously fused with the Blade with nearly every available resource, desperate for some slight reaction. But something quite unexpected had happened—though Frost had no idea exactly what.

Every form of energy his body and spirit possessed had been diminished to some degree, instantly. He had no clear sense even now of the Blade's powers or his encounter with them. What strange manner of magic did this weapon possess? What were its limits? its controls?

He needed to know all the secrets that had been lost with the ages and the death of Ramins. *Perhaps this is how he died,* Frost thought; for such an old, frail man, skinny as Aphan, the slightest use of such a weapon would be fatal. He looked down at the Blade, unable even to consider reaching for it again, at least just now, and he wondered if the weapon's promise had been forever lost with Ramins. He wanted nothing more than to unravel its mysteries, its magic, its powers. *But not every question has an answer, even for me. . . .*

Madia touched his good hand and he met her gaze.

"I am all right," he said, answering the unspoken question. "Or I will be."

"The weapon is cursed," Rosivok said. He stepped around in front of the others, heels in the water, and reexamined the Blade from that angle, then Frost's depleted arm.

"No curse," Ergris exclaimed, fidgeting. "We would know of such. Leshys would hurt, too, but we do not." He proved his words by picking up the Blade himself and waving it about in the air, then feinting a forward strike.

"You are right, Ergris," Frost said. "I have long supposed that the Blade was somehow able to amplify the powers of the ancient wizards, that it and its user could become one. I tried to make it so. But something else happened."

"There is a pull, it is true," Ergris said, laying the Blade back down. "I have felt it and resisted. Leshys have little to give."

"Look at his arm," Prince Jaran said, standing now between Frost and Madia. "Look how withered it has already become. What good is a weapon that eats a man alive? It must think *you* a demon, Frost."

"Perhaps that is its secret," Madia said. "One simply tricks a demon into taking the Blade and using it in battle, and the Blade consumes him?"

"Not impossible," Frost said, though he felt fairly certain that was not true. There was nothing to indicate that the weapon was capable of distinguishing demons from leshys, or wizards from peasants. The "flavor" of its powers seemed endlessly complex and exotic, but not completely unfamiliar. "There are, I think, many answers," he suggested.

"Let me," Rosivok said. Abruptly he bent down and took up the Blade. He stood there holding it, examining its shimmering steel, the beads of moisture rolling off of it. After a moment he shrugged. "Nothing," he said.

"No," Frost agreed. "There should not be." He took a very deep breath—deciding he would have to use his right hand, the left simply did not have the strength—and reached toward the Subartan. "Let me try once more."

Rosivok held the Blade out. Briefly, Frost closed his eyes. He pushed all thoughts of the Blade's powers, as well as his own ideas about them, out of his mind, then spoke a minor spell to himself, one to keep his magical energies turned inward, turned off, for now. He looked at the Blade again and reached, and touched it. This time, after a moment, he gently smiled.

The tree stretched up to the high leafy canopy that hid the sky above the bogs; its trunk was massive, as big around as a dozen men. At its base Rosivok had built a tiny fire of twigs. Frost raised the Blade in his left hand, a hand still weak, but partly recovered during three nights and four days of rest among the leshys. He mouthed a brief spell and pointed the weapon, and the tree burst into a pillar of flames. Man and leshy alike quickly fell back several steps and shielded their eyes as the heat reached them. Then Frost spoke once more and the fires were gone, the tree apparently untouched.

Slowly, a handful of leshys made their way to the tree and looked it over, followed by Jaran and Madia. No sign of the bright, intense fires could be found.

"I have learned something," Frost announced. He had spent the past few days cautiously experimenting with the weapon, bringing a lifetime of amassed knowledge of magic and its working to bear, a lifetime of curiosity. The results were not ideal. "I have gained a basic control of the Blade, though it is not what I expected."

"And your arm?" Sharryl asked, looking at it.

"Well," Frost said. "I will try to explain. There are limits to how much power can be utilized by anyone at any one time. No matter now much rest and size and talent I might come by, I can only channel energy just so fast. With the Blade, however, this limit is . . . removed. I can call upon any amount of energy I possess and direct it through the Blade, all in a single instant, for any single purpose I choose. It is as if one of you knew a way to run with unlimited speed, but only until all your strength and energy was consumed."

"And if we ran too far?" Madia asked skeptically.

"You would die," Jaran answered, looking to Frost.

"Yes," Frost said. "Control is the greatest problem, though the pain is formidable as well. The Blade seems capable of absorbing my energy and directing its release, but I am still the focal point of the spell. My test on the tree went well; that spell would otherwise have taken much more time to finish, and nearly as long to undo. Instead, I was able to have my wish instantly. My arm is well because I let the Blade draw from all of me, so no part was severely injured, though I felt the shock throughout my body, and pain, briefly, of a sort I have never known."

Madia stood close to him now, looking at him as though she expected him to go on. When he did not, she said, "There is only one question, Frost: Can you use the weapon against Lord Ferris?"

"He withstood many of my best efforts at Kamrit," Frost replied, "but I do not believe he could withstand them all at once."

"Then," Jaran said, "you can hit him so hard the first time that he won't get up again."

"Something like that. I must stop short of never getting up again myself, however, and—" He looked back to Rosivok and Sharryl first, then into the bog, to the dark green shadows beyond their camp. "And I honestly don't know if I can do that, or if I can withstand the pain the effort may require."

"If you can," Jaran said, "you are our best hope of defeating him, and still our best hope for peace. If you and Madia are willing to return to Kamrit to face him, we will ride with you." He turned to his men, and found no objections among them.

"We *must* return," Madia said. "I thought we had already agreed."

"We had," Frost said, "but that was before we knew anything about the workings of the Demon Blade."

"Then what is your answer now?" Madia pressed, scowling.

Frost scowled back. "The attempt involves a fine fool's wager, of course. Risking all hopes, yours and mine, on a single untried attempt. If I fail, there can be no other. You will all die with me."

Everyone nodded.

But I have spent my entire lifetime avoiding such situations, Frost thought, keeping it to himself. *Still,* he reminded himself again, *I lost. . . .*

"Frost, my father may still be alive," Madia said, very close to him now, speaking just above a whisper. "And Ariman is surely dying. Perhaps all the realm with it. But if you do not try, then you will lose something too, something you thought you had lost in Kamrit. You said so yourself."

"I know, but should I then rush to follow a course so ill advised? Rush to lose everything this time, finally?"

"You may lose either way," Jaran Ivran said, glancing at Madia, settling on Frost. "Your life, or yourself. One is nothing without the other."

Madia looked at him a moment, then she turned an appraising eye on Jaran, who seemed to grow uneasy.

"What?" he asked.

"You may just do," Madia said demurely, "in desperate times."

"I strive for worthiness, my lady," Jaran replied sarcastically.

"You are probably right, young Jaran," Frost said, relenting. "And we will of course accept your escort. I expect the journey will not be an easy one."

"Why not look back into the waters and learn what will

become of us?" Purcell asked, looking past his prince, glancing toward the still, green surface of the pond.

"Yes," Jaran agreed, "please do."

"No," Frost said.

Jaran furrowed his brow. "Why not?"

"I will tell you. But later."

Jaran seemed unhappy with the answer, though he said nothing more.

"If you like," Ergris spoke up, "I will give you horses to ride and pack. We have taken so many of the animals lately that they have become a bother."

"Then once more, we will help each other," Frost replied.

"And then you will go away," Ergris answered, nearly a snarl.

Frost took the king's words for what they were. So many human beings living in the heart of the swamps had made the leshys restless and irritated, no matter who those humans were. And living with leshys, so far as Frost was concerned, was somewhat unpleasant to him as well.

"Yes," Frost said, "we leave in the morning."

"Enter," Tyrr made the voice say. The door opened and Kaafk presented himself. He stood in the doorway to Tyrr's chambers, apparently hesitant, judging the mood of his sovereign. The merchant was certainly aware of the many problems facing Tyrr—from the reluctance of some of the lords scattered about Ariman to pay homage, to the growing struggles occurring in the northern fiefs, and the many loud grumblings from Neleva. Though none compared with the continued difficulties involved in obtaining the Demon Blade.

Finding it was a vital part of the planning he had so carefully done. The Blade could not be left to chance! Kaafk could never understand this, Tyrr thought. No one could. Not even Tybree.

"In the morning, we will leave," Tyrr said, maintaining a calm, steady tone, difficult though it was of late. *Do not let frustration control you,* he reminded, repeating it in his mind. *Do not lose sight of your vision!* He was not yet prepared to abandon any of his plans; rather, he was seeing them through! And that required changing the timetable slightly—moving it up, nailing things down!

"Where are we going?" Kaafk asked at length. He moved a bit closer, hands under his tunic. Tyrr made use of an augmentation spell and "felt" beneath the tunic. He found nothing but Kaafk's hands.

"The wizard, Gray, has not returned from Golemesk. Neither has our good Captain Ingram nor any from his company. I can no longer suppose any of them lives. I send soldiers and emissaries north in a constant stream and get nothing in return. There are reports, I am sure you have heard, of minor defeats in the great fiefs, of lackluster fighting, of standoffs. I hire men who die or vanish or do nothing at all! Men are worthless without guidance—constant, detailed guidance! *Worthless!*"

Tyrr felt himself edging past the brink, losing control of the shape-shifting spells that formed the construct, losing control of his anger, his balance. Again the urge to strike out and annihilate those who insisted on causing him such troubles was all but overwhelming. He made the lungs breathe, made the legs pace, made the hands touch each other in a rubbing motion as he had often seen men do when they were called before him. This helped very little.

"Many of your troops seem unreliable, I agree," Kaafk said, shrugging from the shadows. "But I am not sure I see what you hope to do about it."

"I am taking my army north to join that rabble and crush the armies of Bouren and Jasnok and Vardale and Thorun. And to lay siege to Golemesk! The Blade is there, it *must* be, and I will have it! I will destroy every living thing in that swamp if need be, but I will have the Blade!"

"Easy now, easy," Kaafk said, stepping out into the light. "Perhaps you are just too worried about that Blade. You don't need it, if you ask me. I have been thinking things over of late, thinking about the future. You already have greater armies and riches than any man this realm has ever known, and more to come. More than enough to keep the lords of the great fiefs from marching against you. In time, cut off, weakened, they will have no choice but to give you whatever you want, pay whatever we charge. So you see, there is no hurry."

Tyrr allowed the remarks. "You do not understand, Kaafk."

"But I do. You want to go riding up there and get a lot of people killed for nothing; you want to ride around some swamp for days looking for mythical weapons. Well, it is your life, my lord, but myths are nearly always just that, and the dead buy no wares, they till no fields. Do not count on me when you go."

"It was not meant as a request," Tyrr replied, gritting the teeth, losing the battle to retain his shape and his carefully cultivated state of mind. *Losing control.*

"My lord, I hardly see how you can—"

"You will go! Bring enough merchants and goods to set up trade in the region as soon as I am finished."

Kaafk had a sour look on his face, one Tyrr had never seen before. One Tyrr did not enjoy.

"That depends on the war. We may have to do all that setting up long *after* you are finished."

"I think you are mistaken," Tyrr forced the lips to say. "You would threaten your own prosperity."

"Battles threaten prosperity," Kaafk came back. "The greatest threat to my purse appears to be yourself. I think you need me as much as I need you, and I expect certain dispensations, my lord. I do not tell you how to run your empire, and you do not tell me how to run mine. I have no wish to do business with someone else . . . now."

Kaafk leaned forward slightly, squinting at Ferris. He grinned, or it was more of a scoff. "You know, you do not look well. Perhaps you should be in bed, resting."

Tyrr slipped—and let a fierce burst of energy free, let it find Kaafk with its full force almost before he realized what had happened. He began to regain control after that, determined to do so. The task was nearly beyond his reach. Already the Ferris construct had deteriorated nearly beyond restoration; he thought he might have to start over again, a process Tyrr no longer had the patience to endure.

Then he made the body sit in a chair; he began wringing the hands and slowly began to wrestle back his senses until he gained minimal stability. Finally his thoughts reformed nearly as they had been, as did the body, more or less; not so perfect anymore, he decided, but it would do.

He stood, then bent to examine the body of Kaafk, a lump of blackened flesh and clothing mixed with splinters of charred wood from the chair that had rested a few paces behind him, near the door. Frustration welled up inside Tyrr, an anger he could direct nowhere but toward himself.

I needed him. . . .

But thinking this only made things worse. He changed his thoughts again before it was too late.

Others will take Kaafk's place, he insisted, attempting relief, finding some. *They will do. The plan will evolve, will go on! Somehow. . . .*

Tyrr rose and dressed the body, then left to summon his captains.

Chapter XXII

Hoke turned his horse, walking the animal slowly through the main body of the combined forces, working toward the rear. He found Lady Anna quickly enough, settled comfortably under a stand of trees, chatting with a handful of peasants collected along the road. She looked up as Hoke approached.

"The Arimanian force has been here for many days," Anna said as Hoke dismounted. "According to the villagers the castle has been under frequent attack all summer, but every assault has been repelled. Lord Ivran conducts night raids, and does well by them, it seems. He destroys his attacker's siege engines, and twice his men have hidden in the countryside until dark, then attacked their enemies as they slept." She stood up, straightening her skirts.

"About three weeks ago the invaders were driven off completely and the people returned to their villages. This week the soldiers returned once more. From what I am told, they have not many men."

"They have no friends, either; they must take their

supplies by force and watch their backs all the time," Hoke said, looking to the villagers, peasants all. He saw a worried look in the eyes of some, though he might have expected fear. Their courage came not from themselves, though, Hoke thought, so much as from faith in Jurdef Ivran, their king.

"No, no friends, but such men never do."

"Soon there will be an end to it." Hoke turned, looking back over the army gathered all around them. "And today, I think, we will truly begin."

He started to go and Anna touched his arm. "Thank you," she said, though she'd said so already, several times. Hoke smiled as he shuffled his weight off the stiff leg. "I know," he said. He returned himself to his saddle, then rode back through the camp to join the others.

From the hill's crest, he could see the cultivated fields, thick stands of woods and many small villages that spread for miles around the city's walls. Lord Ivran's castle stood on its own small hillock near the city's southern edge, high stone walls basking in the morning sun, the largest castle north of Kamrit itself. Rich lands, these, ripe with summer crops, though Lencia's fields were unattended this day. Even at this distance Hoke could see the signs of recent neglect, the absence of movement, even on the roads. Lencia had been under siege for too long.

He turned to the other men who waited atop their mounts at the edge of the trees, Bennor of Vardale, Dorree of Jasnok, Burke of Thorun, and two others who were known only by their chosen names, Grish, the older of the two, and Marrn, court sorcerers to Dorree and Bennor. Their presence, like that of their lords, was nothing less than the best of fortune. Hoke had fully expected interest, perhaps even generosity, from the lord kings of the great northern fiefs, but the depth of their enthusiasm had surprised him. Lady Anna, of course, deserved a share in the credit. Spurred by her impassioned pleas and testimony, the lords had rallied about Hoke not only in spirit but in deed. Dorree, great lord of Jasnok, had set the tone. Unwilling to leave his lands unprotected, and with skirmishes more than plentiful everywhere in the countryside, he had left most of his regular army and commanders in place, but he had supplied Hoke first with himself and then his entire personal guard, nearly one hundred of his most elite troops. They had traveled north together, where Lord Bennor had received them well and acted in kind. Finally, Burke of Thorun had agreed to join them, offering a major compliment of his best troops as well.

The remainder of their journey through Thorun north of Golemesk had been a quiet one. Men eager for righteous battle found little resistance along the way, a few handfuls of Ferris' troops, most of them too long away from the control of their liege to face such odds. The great lords took turns, rallying their troops to fight these small battles, as eager to lead as their men were to follow. Not one among their newly allied forces had been lost in those skirmishes. Nearly five hundred strong now, they were more than ready for a good fight.

"Most of the siege troops are gathered over there, east of the castle," Lord Dorree said, pointing a gloved hand in that direction. Smoke from morning fires could be seen rising among the trees, many fires. "Our scouts say they may number two to three hundred men, though none of them are fresh."

"A tired, token force," Hoke told the great lords. "And an unwelcome one. We will ask them to go."

"I'll gladly give the order," Lord Burke declared. "My men are waiting."

Hoke watched Bennor nod agreement. He looked away again to the encamped Arimanian troops in the distance. "They are preparing to attack, I believe. Probably this afternoon. We might make our way down to that cover, this side of the woods there below us. If we move now and approach from the north we may be able to keep ourselves a secret. When those troops attempt to move against the castle, we could strike from behind."

Hoke paused for the reaction—nods all around.

"I would ask our wizards to make sure there is no magic protecting the camp. And perhaps they can help shield us against enemy eyes when we move?"

"We will do all that is possible," Grish said, and Marrn quickly agreed.

"Anna is right," Lord Dorree said, chuckling. "Kelren never should have let you retire."

"It would seem he has not," Hoke said wryly. He turned with the others to prepare for war.

Just after noon, with the sun well overhead, the forces of Ariman again attacked the castle of King Ivran, an assault led by men-at-arms and a small cavalry backed by three groups of archers and what remained of their catapults. As the main force drew nearer the castle's outer walls, they were met by return fire, a fierce barrage of armor-piercing arrows that filled the air and left several wounded and a few dead. Most, however, took cover beneath their shields and continued slowly forward.

The entire action was unremarkable, a scene that had been repeated many times, Hoke decided, watching the siege forces go about their business in an almost automatic fashion. There was no sense of excitement, only a steady determination to try once again, to gain a position near the walls so the battering rams could do real damage, so the invaders could get inside: mercenaries, the bulk of them, Hoke realized. True knights and men-at-arms, or even militia forces, would not return to fight on so methodically for weeks and against such unattractive odds. These men were being paid to stay, and likely, paid well. Victory was not apparently a requirement. They could afford to wait for Lord Ferris to send a larger force or finally call off the attacks. They had everything to gain, and only a few of each other to lose.

Though that was about to change.

Hoke watched as the great lords gave the commands, sending their foot soldiers and cavalry charging from cover to pound the attackers from the rear. Archers found their targets easily, ready clumps of men with their eyes and shields facing the other way. The forces of Ariman began to turn in circles as arrows fell on them from two directions. They broke ranks just after that, as the severity of the situation quickly became clear to even the slowest and most determined among them.

Hoke left the hill and descended into the battle below. He rode straight ahead amidst the armies of Jasnok, Thorun, and Vardale, heart pounding, blood racing. He had not ridden to war in more than a decade—the fatigue that came with age and the thought of finding himself dismounted, his leg stiff and useless beneath him, had forbidden the very idea—but now, with the rush of battle all around him and the cries of men prepared to fight and die ringing in his ears, he had no choice. He could not sit idly and watch, could not deny himself this chance.

He advanced to join the first ranks of cavalry as they reached the enemy and was quick to ride among them, then to pick out another rider, striking the man in the chest with a measured swing of his battle-ax. But the ax caught in the other man's armor and would not pull free. Hoke let it go at the risk of being pulled to the ground as the other man fell. He drew his broadsword and pushed forward again, clashing against the steel of a second rider, fending two blows, then delivering a decisive thrust.

He watched this second soldier die and was struck by the irony, by how strange it was to ride against these men, to spill the blood of those who wore the crest of

Kamrit—Andarys' crest, though it had been altered slightly, some of the colors painted over, the whites at the center done in gold and black, the "A" already replaced with an "F."

Fresh cries of another charge rang out from somewhere far ahead. Hoke looked up to find the battle being joined by riders from the castle, followed by several hundred foot soldiers. All around him now, the armies of the great fiefs were slaying the siege forces. Outnumbered and out-willed, the bodies of the mercenaries began to litter the ground. As the castle guard reached them, the remaining attackers tried desperately to flee but found no route for their escape.

Lord Ivran's legions swept onto the battlefield, and in minutes the last of Ariman's attacking forces had surrendered or been cut down. The blood of their enemies flowed at the feet of the defenders of Lencia.

"I had no idea Frost was involved in all of this," the great lord Jurdef Ivran exclaimed, breaking bread at the head of the table and tightening the many wrinkles around his dark eyes with his stare. "Or that the rumors about Grand Chamberlain Ferris were smaller than the truth about him."

"Then you agree he must be stopped," Hoke said.

"Of course! His attacks will resume on all of us in time. But the very thought of that brazen little wench Madia as queen—well, to me, this lacks any appeal."

"You know her reputation, but you do not know her," Hoke said, ready for this. All three of the other great Lords had already expressed a similar concern, and he had expected this from Jurdef as well. "She is no longer the same girl. Her journey from Kamrit has had a great effect on her, as did her long stay with me, I can assure you."

"Oh, well, of course!" Lord Ivran snorted, looking to

the other lords around the table. "I failed to consider the certain effect a stay with the great Hoke would have on the girl. Surely, every woman you have known is fit to rule this realm!" Ivran's muffled laughter was joined by the others at the table. Hoke waited for the noise to die down, then he looked at Lord Ivran with a steady, crucial eye. "Most," he said.

Laughter broke out at this. Hoke waited again, watching faces, especially that of his host. Jurdef was the greatest of the northern lords and would hold sway over many, both here and in Ariman. His support was necessary, Hoke thought, there was no question.

"I ask all of you to consider carefully the task before us," Hoke began again. "I ask that you ride with me to Kamrit to rally the people of Ariman and take back the throne from the creature that has claimed it. We must save the realm; we must save ourselves.

"As to who will come to rule in Ferris' place, that is a matter to be decided afterward, with the rightful heir to that throne present to properly defend herself, and the council of lords assembled. All shall have their say when the time comes."

Silence fell about the room as Lord Ivran slowly rose and moved away from the table. He stood with his back to the others, rubbing his jaw thoughtfully as he looked out through the arches of the hall's main window. Finally Jurdef took a deep breath and turned. "I have your word on all of this?"

Hoke bowed his head. "You do."

"Will two hundred men be enough? That is all I feel I can spare."

Hoke let a smile find his lips. He snatched his flagon from the table, then waited while Jurdef came to the table again and took up his. Hoke stood up with all the others, and they lifted their cups. "Yes, my lord, enough indeed," he said, and joined in a toast.

Chapter XXIII

"We are too near Kopeth," Madia said, squatting amid a stand of thick brush, peering through leaves tinged with the first colors of autumn. She was reminded of another time, many months ago, when she had hidden herself this way. Her haunches ached from several days' riding, and they protested as she leaned forward to lift a bothersome branch. Still, she took grim comfort from the fact that Frost could barely walk.

The wizard knelt beside her, following her gaze. "I would go there," he said.

"Why?"

"To visit once more with the old wizard, Aphan. Without the proper spells to command the Blade, I am left to sorceries of my own devising, and they are not enough. Aphan may be able to help me improve on what I have learned. And," Frost added, giving Madia a nearly apologetic look, "he knows more of demons than any other; he remembers the stories. I must learn whatever I can."

"Ferris' men will be there," Madia reminded him.

"Of course. That cannot be helped. I will leave that problem in the capable hands of my Subartans."

Frost grinned at Madia, an evil sort of grin, or a perfectly satisfying one—Madia still considered herself Frost's third Subartan, at least whenever the need arose, and this was his way of reminding her that he agreed. But having earned the title of warrior did not matter to her quite as much anymore, no more than any other part of who and what she was supposed to be. No single part of anything mattered now, only the whole.

"We still must talk, all of us," Madia said, "of a plan for when we reach Kamrit again. You act as though you have ideas in mind and confidence enough, but you say nothing we can count on. I am beginning to know you, Frost. As with any man, such confidence is easily feigned."

Frost shrugged his shoulders, then let his hands rest upon the satisfying bulge of his abdomen. "I do not have a plan, at least not a good one," he said. "And you may be right to worry—with the omens calling me 'fool' at every turn, my confidence may be undue. Yet, you'll recall, you had no plan when I followed you to Kamrit."

"So you've said, and we were nearly destroyed."

Frost chuckled, more or less.

"I am glad you find this amusing," Madia replied.

"Humor can't hurt. The future looks to be a very sad thing. Even at Kamrit I had two good plans or we would not be here, yet now I have not even one. I've never felt so foolish before. In fact, prudence requires that I change my mind and simply disappear somewhere between here and Kamrit."

"You would not do that."

"I'm glad you are so convinced."

Madia frowned—as severe an expression as she could muster. "What of Jaran's question? Why did you not stir a pond and show us the way?"

"All spells, including mine, are limited, and by many things. The talent I used in Golemesk is useful for showing a possible future, but usually one that reflects what I want it to. I do not possess a gift like Aphan's. In his fires, he creates a window that looks on truths."

"Then what you showed the leshys and Tiesh was not real?"

"Possibly."

Madia considered him a moment, then she let her gaze wander. "A pity," she said.

"Truly," Frost remarked. "You have seen enough of my limitations, and still I must show you more."

"As usual, your concern centers on yourself."

"Not entirely," Frost answered.

"There must be a way to get to Ferris without fighting his entire army," Madia said, trying her best to move on. "Or some way to trick him into placing himself at our mercy, perhaps—a way to flush him out?"

"And then what?" Frost asked. "What do I do with him once I have him? Again we need two plans, and we have not one."

"But you spoke of attacking him with a single blow, using the Blade."

Another shrug, less cavalier. "I intend to try."

"Then you do not think such an attack will defeat him?"

"I have no idea, and that is the problem. I would enjoy a few years' practice with the Blade, time to learn more of its ways and how best to control them. And time to consult with others like Aphan about the weaknesses of demons, but we don't have that kind of time."

Frost turned to Jaran and his men, then Rosivok and Sharryl, who stood patiently waiting together behind him, holding the horses. No one said a word. "Come closer," he told the Subartans, then went about building false glamours for both of them, as well as for Madia and himself. When he was finished, they each took to their mounts and started toward the road.

"Strange," Jaran said, nudging his own horse in between Frost's and Madia's as they began. He looked at Madia from several angles. "Somehow, you seem easier to take when you look like this. My compliments, sir," he said, grinning at Frost.

"Accepted," Frost replied with a graceful bow.

Madia kicked at her horse and rode on ahead.

The streets of Kopeth were not so busy as they had been in spring, and merchants were not as plentiful. Many market stalls stood empty or nearly so, though a few, Frost noticed, were brimming with wares. Like the shops they had seen, some thrived, while others languished. In one of the market squares, he observed that soldiers, as they passed, only stopped to hassle certain traders, generally the poorest ones. Merchandise was insulted, merchants were taken aside for questioning. Yet other stalls, those best supplied, seemed to go unmolested. Fair trade, it was obvious, was another casualty of Lord Ferris' new realm.

Which would benefit a few for now and no one in time, Frost thought, once Ferris' greed exceeded the bounty of these lands and people.

Though that would not be the end of it. Such a creature as Ferris would only usurp new lands, whatever the cost. Finally no land would go untouched; nowhere Frost went would he be free of the demon, of what it had done to him, of what he would always fear it would still do. The choices before him were maddeningly few, and none of them allowed for sanity. Though in a way, that made an impossible decision just slightly more possible.

They reached the narrow streets of the city's western section, moving on foot, having left the horses outside the town. The buildings above hung out over the streets at perilous angles, and the sewage, for lack of rain, lay deep in the gutters and scattered onto the walk. As Frost led the others through a small intersection, a handful of soldiers wandered by at the end of the street, and one of them paused to peer down the way. After a moment, he moved on.

Since entering the city they had stayed mostly out of sight, and no one had yet taken them to task. As they continued, Frost felt a nagging at the back of his neck. A few houses more and he turned—to catch just a glimpse of someone taking to the cover of a doorway several houses back. He called to Rosivok and explained, and the warrior nodded.

Just beyond a small inn, they turned a corner and kept walking while Rosivok pressed his back to the inn's wall. Frost led the others a few feet further and paused, signaling them to prepare for trouble. There was no need.

Two soldiers, guards from Kamrit Castle, darted around the corner a moment later only to find Rosivok suddenly between them. Their eyes widened as he raised his subarta blade, then both men tried to draw their weapons as they stepped back. Rosivok was already driving forward, his powerful arm moving much too swiftly to allow a proper defense. In an instant both men lay mortally wounded, bleeding at Rosivok's feet. Sharryl and two of Jaran's men rushed up to help drag the soldiers from the street.

"There will be more," Jaran said. "Bouren soldiers walking the streets of Kopeth do nothing but invite trouble."

"We will make our stay a brief one," Frost replied. They moved quickly on, making their way to the tiny home of Aphan, where Frost asked the others to wait outside.

"You can't change the way we look, too?" Jaran asked.

"It would take time and energy, and I have very few glamours that work well. If you all looked alike, would that not draw attention as well?"

"Then see if he'll mind the lot of us in there," Jaran asked, moving nearer Frost, nearer the door. He glanced up and down the worn, cobbled way. "We'll be better off."

"That's one opinion," Madia remarked, batting her eyes at the prince when he looked. Jaran's jaw tensed, but to his credit he made no reply, simply shook his head. Their constant dueling seemed to lack the intensity it had, Frost thought, and the venom. Too much had been shared between them now.

"Aphan will not mind," Frost said, nodding to the prince. He didn't particularly want an audience, since he wasn't sure the old wizard could help him, and he wasn't even sure what questions he would ask. But Jaran was right.

He turned and knocked, but no one answered. He pressed the door open and peered inside. The hearth fire was cold and only one lamp remained lit. Aphan sat at his table, his head down, his body still.

"Too late?" Jaran whispered, leaning in.

Frost opened the door a bit further and stepped inside. "I don't think so. I sense something of his presence."

With that Frost went to the table and put his hands on the old man, then began a quiet chant, reciting a whispered phrase several times until the body began to stir. Soon enough, Aphan raised his head and took a deep breath, then let it out and opened his eyes. Frost examined the other man's face and decided he looked rather well, considering.

Aphan blinked blind eyes several times, then reached out with a timid hand and touched Frost's tunic. "My friend," Aphan said, "one day you must show me how you do that."

"There is much you must teach me as well." Frost opened his cloak and retrieved the Demon Blade, then laid it on the table. Aphan shivered momentarily, a chill that raked his wiry frame. He reached out, moving his fingers until they rested just over the Blade, then a sigh passed his lips. "You have it," Aphan said, a breathy voice, old vocal cords growing weak. "The Blade is yours!" He continued to shake. Frost leaned across the table and placed his hands on the old man's arms, calming him. "Yes," he said.

"You were meant to have it, Frost, at least for a time. I have seen this in the flames. All this was shown."

"One can only hope," Frost said.

"You will use it to destroy the thing that masquerades as Ferris?"

"I will try."

"You know it is a left-handed blade," Aphan said, not a question, more a spontaneous review.

"I know."

"You can feel its pull?"

"Yes."

Aphan shook again. "Then you have learned its powers? You know how to use the Blade to destroy the demon?"

"I am not sure," Frost replied, and he felt Aphan's body settle. "That is why I came here," he went on. "I have learned to use the Blade to direct my own power, to use all my energies in great concentration, but I am sure there is more—something that escapes me, no matter how I try—though perhaps it is only valor."

"I have so few words for you, my friend," Aphan said, his voice heavier now, losing its slight energy. "I am sorry."

"You knew Ramins."

"For a time, years ago. I have not seen him since he came to be the keeper of the Blade. Since that time he was intent on living in isolation; he even lived without guardsmen of any kind. To limit attempts to take the Blade from him, I've always thought, though surely one so powerful as he had little to fear from ordinary men. I would have kept a small, carefully groomed army about me."

"He may simply have preferred solitude," Frost suggested. Aphan only shrugged. Frost sat motionless, the silence of the room filling the air about him. He could still sense Madia and the Subartans behind him, as well as Jaran and his men. They made no sound, intent on allowing Frost every courtesy; intently hopeful, too, that Frost would gather from Aphan the knowledge he had come for.

"What do the flames tell you of the battle to come? Of my ways with the Blade?" Frost asked.

"What I have seen makes little sense. My eyes have faded these past few weeks, as have the flames I would conjure. I've lost the talent since last you were here. I cannot help you."

"Then tell me who was named Ramins' successor by the last council."

"There are few who know. Ramins knew, of course, as it was told to him. I know of no one else, though I'm sure they exist. The council members had protegés, and some had descendants, of course, who may have been told. But Ramins himself learned that he had been chosen only when an ailing Wentesh sought him out and gave it to him."

"Of course," Frost replied. "I will find no comfort, I'm afraid. From the omens, I should have known."

For a time he simply sat, arms across the table, still touching the aged sorcerer. Then he turned to Rosivok and motioned toward the door. "Check outside," he said. "I think we will go."

Rosivok opened the door to find a group of local

soldiers, perhaps a dozen or more, running by in the little street with their swords drawn and their voices raised in shouts of panic. They continued down the way, never pausing, never looking back. Madia stood with the others as they gathered at the door.

"They act like frightened game," Rosivok remarked.

Madia leaned out, looking about. "What would frighten such men?"

Frost rose to join them. "Quiet, and listen," he said. In the distance now they could hear the sounds of many more men shouting, a ragged chorus that rose over the clatter of steel against steel. The sounds of battle.

"We outnumber them at least three to one," Hoke told the great lords, his voice bouncing as his horse began to trot. They rode through the wall and into the city flanked by cavalry and archers and soldiers on foot. A squad of men on armored mounts, wearing the crest of Lord Ferris, broke lines at a hard gallop and came straight for them. Hoke rode out to meet them, drawing his sword, reining in his horse just as the first of the opponents came within striking distance. He moved quickly, relying again on old instincts still well remembered, and avoided the first blow. He countered with a sound wallop to the back that swept the other man off his horse as he turned.

The other lords showed their spirit as well, wading into the fray and cutting down two other men. Then the five of them found themselves bystanders as the main body of their attack force, some five hundred men, flowed past all around them. Hoke watched at least thirty of the city's guard rush in from a nearby square to meet them, saw them butchered almost at once.

Two hundred additional cavalry waited in reserve beyond the city's walls, but already Hoke saw they would not be needed. He rode forward again with the others, watching smaller groups of the city's guard attack from adjoining streets only to die in brief battles, or turn and run the other way. The lords of the great fiefs toured the second greatest city in all Ariman, the key to trade north of the wide waters, in triumph. The victory was largely one of commerce, but it was symbolic as well, and something this new and valiant army could take pride in.

Hoke turned his mount and rode back to find the others. Lady Anna met him near the wall. Mauro and Umblic were still with her as personal escorts, all on horseback. She looked on with apparent satisfaction.

"A shame you are too old for all of this, isn't it?" she said coyly.

"I *am* too old," Hoke replied. "I am simply too foolish to refuse the likes of you."

"I thought you listened to me because you'd grown wise with your years."

"Is that what it is?"

"I assure you."

Hoke shook his head, then the two of them started back into the city. When they had gotten only a few yards, Hoke looked up to find a Bouren soldier riding toward him at a full gallop. The man drew up just in front of Hoke and Anna, breathless. "Lord Ivran said to bring you at once!" the rider exclaimed.

"What has happened?" Hoke demanded, already beginning to follow the man.

"My lord will explain."

He glanced at Anna, an unspoken invitation, then kicked his mount into a gallop again. She followed in kind, with Mauro and Umblic trailing. They rushed through squares and down a brief maze of streets, passing many of their own men and a few captured guards, and townsfolk who had already begun to come out of their homes and shops and halls, until they reached a particularly narrow way. Here they came to a sudden stop.

Lord Jurdef Ivran stood in the street, a strange, pleased look on his face. "My son, Jaran," he said, grinning then, and he put his arm around a young man who could only have been his own. Behind the prince a very large man stood worrying over those grouped about him—already, their appearances had begun to change.

Hoke sat absolutely still, unable just then to say or do anything as he looked down at the people in the street before him. Anna, however, paused just long enough to gasp. Then she jumped down from her horse and rushed ahead to throw her arms around another who ran to meet her, calling the other's name as she did: "Madia!"

Dinner was the work of guild merchants and city officials, all of whom seemed altogether grateful to the men who had, at least for now, freed Kopeth's markets. On their way to the town hall, Frost had passed through the same market square he had seen earlier, this time to find nearly all of the occasional rich, overflowing stalls being emptied out, and the merchants who had tended them conspicuously absent. Many of the smaller booths seemed to have gained from other merchants' losses.

He stopped here and there, and the merchants had made offers of gifts to Madia and Anna, then included Sharryl as well, though they seemed less certain of what to offer her.

As they strolled further, the town's gentry met them along the way, bowing to Madia, making introductions. Just minding their business, Frost knew, as were the merchants and the city's fathers, though Madia seemed to sense this well enough on her own. Dinner had followed.

Madia said little during the meal, letting squires and nobles, merchants and town officials fill her ears as well as those of their other guests with tales of the past year, the hardships they had suffered, the oppression, the fear of Lord Ferris they each still harbored. The mayor, a balding, rather troubled man, with thick face and hands, and dressed to indicate an even thicker purse, lent many of the most woeful accounts himself.

"My own brother!" he whined. "Cast out of his shop because of 'owed taxes'—none of which he owed, I can assure you! They simply wanted his shop closed. He sold silks, you see, and so did the new shop the soldiers helped set up."

"And what has each of you done about all this?" Madia asked at last, looking around the great table, finding each man one by one. No replies were forthcoming.

"What, then, do you plan to do now?" she pressed. Though again, no one spoke.

Frost noticed the northern lords discreetly calling his attention, a signal that he was to speak their minds for them. He and Madia had talked with Hoke and the great Lords at length about allegiance—though this seemed a hopelessly mired subject at present—and about Kopeth, but only briefly had they discussed details of what would come tomorrow, or the day after. Still, it seemed there was a feeling of general agreement, a basic premise that did not require much debate. This was what the others wanted Frost to tell the people of Kopeth. He nodded, then leaned to whisper a word in Madia's ear. Madia listened, and quickly nodded.

"Then you will give supplies to the great army that has saved you this day, so that we may ride on to Kamrit," Frost said, "to reclaim the throne."

"If we are successful," Madia told them, "you will have nothing to fear from the throne of Kamrit, and all Ariman will long remember the generosity of the citizens of Kopeth."

There was a momentary pause as the men in question looked to each other. Then in unison, all around the table, glasses were raised.

"We live to serve you," the mayor replied. The servants came then, laden with trays of food, a welcome sight.

The meal itself was splendid, a hearty vegetable and broth soup followed by roasted pork and fresh oat bread, all doused with a plentiful supply of good red wine. By dinner's end, many wishful plans had been made, and not the slightest disagreement seemed to remain among those in attendance. But even now there was little talk of Madia's place in the scheme of things, and no true admission of her sovereignty. Madia, for her part, did not bring it up; like a hidden cave, she had found the entrance to her future but was afraid to enter.

As talk settled into rambling chatter, Madia felt the strain of the day and the glow of the wine begin to overcome her. She leaned back and fought with what seemed an endless yawn and found Hoke looking at her as she recovered.

"I know the innkeeper in the main square," Hoke said as the hour drew late enough. "And we'll need a place for the night. Perhaps—"

"Of course!" the mayor said. "A fine place, it is. We will put all of you up there, and as many of your men as we can."

Jaran yawned then, and Madia yawned again, helpless.

"Our men have set up camps outside the city," Hoke said. "I would stay with them. But these lords and ladies, I am sure, will find the inn a comfort."

"My Subartans and I look forward to it," Frost replied. "We have not slept indoors in weeks."

"Walk with us," the mayor asked them, getting to his feet, then leading the way. "We'll go at once." Madia watched Frost gather with Grish and Marrn, the first time she had seen him truly speak to the two court wizards from the northern fiefs, and she wondered how he viewed them, whether he already knew them. Both men seemed sincere and competent, and their lords, Dorree and Bennor, apparently had every confidence in them, but Madia had seen court wizards in her youth, at Kamrit and neighboring manors. None compared to Frost.

They must know that, she thought, *as must he.*

As they entered the street, Madia found Jaran striding beside her. He waited until she looked at him.

"We must talk, you and I."

"Of what?"

"I know my father and the other lords much better than anyone in Ariman. If you plan to ask for their allegiance, you must first tell them what you expect, and what they can expect from you. And you must listen to what they have to say. No one knows you, or exactly what you want. Except myself, of course."

"You?"

Jaran nodded.

"Then you tell me what I want."

"You have decided to rule as your father did, of course, at least lately you have. And I think you are nothing like the Madia Andarys these others have in their minds; if you were, I would not have come with you this far, nor would Frost, for he follows you as much as you follow him.

"But I would tell you that your father was the much-praised and long-respected son of Hual Andarys, and a man of great strength and honor. He maintained the peace with ease. The same is not true of his daughter, and might never be. To most you are but a young girl, untested, unknown. . . ."

"I know," Madia said, shuddering as she did.

"They talk, Madia. They see you in an . . . unfavorable light."

"I have heard enough, thank you."

Jaran shook his head. "I simply meant—"

"You needn't say."

Directly they turned a corner and the inn stood before them, and they were ushered inside. The mayor took prompt care of the arrangements, and in a moment they were being led upstairs to their rooms. Jaran was let into one of the first doors they came to. He paused and looked at Madia as he entered, a different look, Madia noticed, difficult to read—bearing a touch of concern, perhaps, or quiet despair. She walked on, entering her own room, then fell on the bed and lay there awhile, letting her thoughts spin in her mind. Fatigue nagged at every muscle, but she could not sleep.

Damn him, she fumed at last, seeing no sense to leaving things so unfinished yet again. She had to know where she stood, no matter what. She got up and headed out into the hall. She tried the door and found that it was unlocked, so she pushed it open and stood staring at Jaran, who seemed to have nearly completed the task of getting undressed for bed.

"All right," she said, "unfavorable how, exactly?"

Jaran pulled his trousers back on, then paused to tie them before speaking. "Very well," he said. "You are known to these men as an irresponsible tart, a girl without respect for her own heritage and therefore the heritage of others. They have been told differently by Hoke and Anna, and they have spoken with you enough to know that there is some truth to what your friends say, but there remains much doubt in their minds. If they are ever to pay even symbolic homage to you, they must be shown good reason to do so."

"And you say you do not agree with the other lords?" Madia asked, looking at him differently now, unable to ignore him physically, even though she wanted to resist the idea. He was making sense, and being honest, like the Prince he had been raised to be. . . .

"I know a different Madia."

"Truly?" She kept her expression still.

He crossed the room toward her slowly, until finally he stood very close, his stockinged toes nearly touching the tips of her boots. "You may just do," he said, "in desperate times."

Madia barely smiled as Prince Jaran leaned closer. She stood fast, feeling an urge to close her eyes; she kept them open, waiting for Jaran to make his intentions clear. Then she watched a smile spread across his face, and hers broadened. He kept still, apparently sensing the moment exactly as she did. For a long time they simply looked into each other's eyes.

"Good night," he said then, softly, rocking back a bit.

"In the morning," Madia replied, softer still. She turned and started up the hall, heard him gently closed the door behind her. For many things, she thought, there would come a time.

Madia could feel the eyes of the great lords keenly upon her as she and Lady Anna walked out into the late morning sun. When she reached her mount, she glanced up at the others. *Yes,* she saw, *it is as Jaran said.* The others looked away as her gaze found them, but they had been watching her, she knew, considering her, passing judgment on her—talking about her when she was not there.

They would see what they wanted, think as they had always thought, say whatever pleased them no matter what she said or did. At least, for a while they would. She needed to erase what had been and convince them of who she was now, of what could be, or she would never be a Queen in their eyes. She simply didn't know how.

But as she mounted her horse, she noticed not only the lords but *everyone* else looking at her: Hoke and Mauro and Umblic, Frost and Rosivok and Sharryl, a dozen captains that stood before their ready forces, and nearly eight hundred fighting men, those from the northern fiefs as well as the militia they had attracted in Kopeth. Waiting for her, she saw, *for me.* . . .

And for the first time in her life, she felt the full weight of her heritage touch her shoulders. She had been so caught up in redefining herself and struggling to reach her goals that she had never stopped to think about what it would be like to obtain them, what her life would be like afterward.

She looked about again as she settled atop her mount. *So many eyes, and these only the first,* she thought. *So many people, all of them wondering who I am.* Yet even now, or perhaps especially now, she felt a fleeting urge to count herself among them.

"The higher ground west of the river will be our best route," Hoke recommended to all. "There are many open fields where an army might find easy passage."

"I agree," Jaran said. "The road from Kopeth is a better one, but it is still too narrow, and we would be too vulnerable in so predictable a line."

"Aye," Dorree agreed. "We've stayed to the fields so far. And so good."

Madia watched as everyone chimed agreement, noting that now none of the nobleman seemed to be looking to her anymore, except Jaran, whose eyes seemed never to stray too far. His expression was almost too understanding. She said nothing, waiting while the conversation around her found its own end, then she solemnly followed the great lords as they turned and called to their captains to march.

A great enthusiasm filled the air as the armies spread out, loosening ranks, cavalry and footmen finding their way across the road and into the fields and woods. Villagers at work in the countryside along the way waved and some even cheered, and many were quick to offer a share of their noontime ale. And a string of local land barons turned out to greet the passing army, to offer supplies and even a few men-at-arms, and to stare at the young princess. . . .

Madia found many of the peasants she encountered aware of who she was, rumors having spread ahead of the march. And for the first time since leaving home, the people of Ariman bowed in her presence. Few said anything to her, and many seemed more curious than genuine in their attention, a curiosity of scandal and power, of course, but she did not mind the attention even so.

Still, these waiting friends meant that Kamrit would know of their approach long before they reached the city, that the beast that was Lord Ferris would have ample time to prepare his defenses. There had not been nearly enough talk of battle plans. The collective forces of the great fiefs had been unstoppable, and certainly blessed by the Greater Gods in their quest thus far. Decisions made on the spur of the moment had produced perfectly good results. These blessings, Madia thought, might not be enough in the battle that lay ahead. She maneuvered her horse close to Hoke's, near the front of the march, and told him of her concerns.

"You are right, of course," he said. "Tonight, when we make camp, we must discuss our plans."

"What have the others said?" she asked, sitting back in the saddle as the horses trudged up a long, low rise. "You must know something of their desires. Surely they do not expect to ride up to Kamrit's main gates and ask for the head of Lord Ferris."

"No, but you are not far off. They are buoyed by the magic of Frost and his Demon Blade, and by our quick successes. They feel that straightforward assault will work. They may be right."

"You were not there when Frost faced Lord Ferris the first time. I fear these men will die, most of them, Blade or no." The horses were slowing, finally reaching the top of the rise. "We may all die."

"I'm sure each of them knows that."

"But this must not be a sacrifice. I—"

"Madia!" Hoke yelled suddenly as he thrust an arm out in front of her. She reigned her horse to a stop beside his at the crest of the hill. The others riding the point had stopped as well. Out ahead lay a wide cultivated basin—ponds near its center, small clumps of trees, many acres of barley and beans and hay and grazing pastures. Beyond the valley lay another row of low, rolling hills covered mostly by forest on either side but cleared along a wide piece of the ridge straight across the way. There, atop the ridge, stood a waiting army of several thousand men.

Chapter XXIV

"There are so many," Madia whispered, mesmerized.

"They do not move," Hoke said, shading his eyes with one hand.

"They wait," Lord Ivran agreed. "They must have learned of our approach."

"Could they have come from Kamrit so quickly?" Lord Dorree asked, moving near. "Would Lord Ferris be with them?"

"No one else could mount such a force," Lord Bennor said, a bleak endorsement. "There must be three thousand of them."

"But why would Ferris assemble such a force and bring them so far north, if not to go to war with all of us?" Jurdef Ivran mused, examining the lines more carefully. "There was not time to mount a response like this; it must have already been planned. I would have called every man in the countryside had I known!"

"Very well, what should we do?" Bennor asked, looking particularly afflicted. There was no immediate reply.

Madia studied the other lords now gathered tightly about, the grim looks on their faces.

"I'll tell you the first thing we're going to do," Madia muttered. She turned in her saddle and faced back down the slope, then cupped her hands around her mouth and shouted, "Frost!"

A long moment passed while the sorcerer and his Subartans left the company of the two court wizards, Grish and Marrn, and made their way up to the cluster of nobles. He acknowledged Madia, then stared out across the shallow valley at the great army gathered on the other side. As he watched the far hill his mood seemed to grow very dark; Madia had never seen him so since they had fled Kamrit Castle.

"We need a means to better the odds," Madia said. "There are far too many of them."

"I will do what I can," Frost replied coldly, a tone that matched his features. Madia frowned at him. "I know how you feel," she said, leaning toward him, "but you must help us."

"He is there," Frost replied, colder still.

"Ferris? You see him?"

"I sense him, somewhere, perhaps there among the trees, just out of the sun. He will attempt to counter anything I do."

"And you will counter whatever he tries," Hoke said in a hopeful tone.

Frost lowered his voice and turned to Madia. "I will do what I can, but the omens . . . " He paused, taking a breath. "The pebbles tell of certain doom, a pattern of chaos, and the wind has come round to our backs, betraying us to our enemies, and only last night as we sat near the fire, a beetle crawled across my boot, a sure sign of death."

"Probably the same one I crushed," Madia said.

Frost's face bunched up into a grimace. "Oh, no," he said. "Then the bad luck was increased manyfold."

Madia wrinkled her nose at him. "And that wind omen has to do with hunting game."

"Perhaps," Frost grumbled.

"I am not interested in bugs or breezes, Frost, only in what you plan to do right now. We need help!"

Frost looked up and sighed, then nodded. "I have prepared a twinning spell that should work well enough. It will take time, and—and more, if I am to do the lot of you."

"What kind of spell?" Lord Bennor asked, overhearing.

"How much time?" Hoke asked impatiently. "They may charge at any moment."

Frost shrugged. "I cannot say. I have never tried the spell on such a scale before."

"What difference does it make?" Madia said. "Please, Frost, begin."

The sorcerer nodded, then turned and asked the lords to gather their men on the grassy slope. They each moved off without question and began calling out the orders. As the armies came together, Frost faced his palms toward them, then started at his left and began moving slowly right, repeating a lengthy chant as he went. As he spoke, Madia saw the men and horses begin to blur as if she were crossing her eyes. She blinked reflexively, but the blurring only worsened. Then the soldiers first affected gradually clarified, and where there had been one, now there were two.

She kept following Frost's hands until he finished, then waited another moment as the last of the troops became clear. Frost slumped briefly, breathing deeply; his arms seemed limp, but then he straightened just a bit, and his eyes rose to the others again.

"Two armies," Jurdef Ivran said softly, still gaping at the sight before him.

Frost cleared his throat. "Each man will go into battle

with another of himself, though these others have no substance. They are simply reflections on the air. And like any reflection, they will mimic the movements of the genuine soldier exactly. The effect is . . . interesting."

"Sounds confusing," Lord Dorree said, squinting at the field of men.

"Yes, exactly!" Hoke answered. "Confusing for any man trying to attack one of us. It is difficult to fight a swordsman that strikes from two directions at once."

"Ah, splendid," Lord Burke said, grinning widely. "A confusion we can truly use!"

Madia turned her gaze again to the armies that awaited them. *Still more than two to one, even when the doubled images are counted—still a hopeless battle,* she thought, *though now, at least, not entirely.* Then she saw the men on the far hilltop begin to move.

The calls of captains reached Madia's ears an instant later, followed by the clatter of armor and the shrill whinny of horses wheeled into motion as ranks formed behind her.

"You still need a plan of attack," Frost said, and Madia realized he was leaning toward her, speaking so the others would not hear. "And they need a leader to carry it forth. Disorder will be Ferris' ally."

Madia saw the look on his face and could almost feel his thoughts pressing in on her mind. "A—agreed," she said, some part of her convinced that every eye was glaring at her, waiting for her, expecting . . . *something.*

She tried not to say it, but part of her let it slip. "Me?" she heard herself ask.

"If you are ever to be ruler of Ariman, my young queen, you must be that woman now, or the moment will pass you by."

It struck her that he had never called her "queen" before. She felt an almost overwhelming sense of pride

as the thought swelled within her, a sense of victory—
and indelible rightness—over a foe that was both within
her and without. *But they will not let me,* she thought
then, the glow of achievement fading too quickly. The
great lords and their men and militia would not all follow
her, not now, perhaps never, even though she was . . .

"You will try," Frost told her, almost as if her thoughts
had somehow strayed to him. "You must. I was not sure,
once, whether you should ever be allowed to sit on your
father's throne, on Hual's throne. I journeyed with you
for many reasons, Madia, to fight, perhaps, but also to
study your character. I was prepared to prevent you from
gaining control, unless you convinced me I should not."

"I know that," Madia confided. "I kept trying not to
think about it. I had no question I was worthy—at the
time. Now, I am not so sure. . . . "

"Yes, you are."

She stared at him, eyes locked, their minds nearly
touching. Frost turned abruptly and coaxed his mount
down the hill a few paces, rejoining Rosivok and Sharryl.
Madia looked about to find the others muttering nervously among themselves and gesturing at the
approaching legions. Hoke seemed to be taking up the
role of moderator, a job that was already proving itself to
be nearly impossible.

She needed to say something—to prove herself somehow to these great men that even Hoke could not fully
control. *The battle,* she thought, straining to bring her
mind to bear. If it must be fought, she could at least use
it to her advantage. Use it to take her rightful place.

During the many lessons she had endured
throughout her youth, much history had been thrust
upon her. She had promptly forgotten most of it, but
war, like most tales of other lands or other times, had
always fascinated her. The details still escaped her, the
names of many cities and their rulers, but what had

happened remained clear enough. She remembered one action in particular. . . .

She took a breath and raised herself up in her saddle. "Brave lords! You will recall the Battle of Kaya-Thai. We will divide our forces into two groups. Jurdef, you and Lord Dorree will ride with me to meet the approaching forces. Lords Burke and Bennor, you will gather all the archers to back the main attack, then divide the remainder of our forces and attack from either flank. If we must break off from the battle, tell your men to disperse, then regroup here."

Well, she thought, *they are staring at me now.*

She waited out their silence, avoiding their eyes by turning to check on the approach of the enemy's forces—which were nearly a third of the way across the shallow valley, and nearly at what she thought would be an optimal striking position. She turned to the lords again and glared at them. "Now!" she said. "There is no time to tarry!"

Still, not one lord moved; they sat looking from one another to the young princess giving them orders. But as Madia found Hoke's eyes, she saw a look in them that lent her strength. *He knows,* she thought. *He understands.* Hoke prodded his horse to turn until he faced the great lords, a position that put him squarely beside Madia.

"My liege," he said, bowing to her, "I pledge my sword to you."

She noticed more movement then, and saw that it was Frost, followed by Rosivok and Sharryl, coming toward her again. The three of them gathered just behind her.

"We await your needs," Frost said, using a loud voice, one Madia was quite familiar with. She saw that the look on his face had changed for the better; some of the glow she remembered had returned.

"I, too, pledge my sword," another voice called out.

Prince Jaran came from among the other lords, followed by Purcell and the men who had made the journey with them from Bouren.

Madia felt the urge to proceed quickly now, while it was possible. "Would we wait until they are upon us?" she shouted, drawing her sword. She turned toward the valley. Behind her, she heard the satisfying sounds of many more swords being drawn.

"I heed," Jurdef Ivran replied as he broke away from the others and rode toward his captains, shouting them to readiness.

"And I," Lord Burke echoed, and turned out as well. Dorree and Bennor quickly followed. Within minutes, the lines had formed across the hilltop. Archers took up their positions at the crest of the knoll and waited to open fire as the main force gave way to them. Madia waited until the flanking cavalry was in position.

"For the realm!" she shouted, and a rousing cry went up all around her. She raised her hand, and the roar of voices rose and held as nearly four hundred men—eight hundred to the eye—joined her, rushing down the hill.

Frost stood with the archers as they drew back their long bow strings and loosed their first arrows. Again and again they fired, taking a growing toll on the advancing enemy below until the two lines of soldiers came together amid the bodies of the fallen. The archers moved off down the hill, hoping to find the range of the cavalry reserve near the base of the far hills, ready to draw swords and join the others if they were needed. Frost remained behind, gathered still with Grish and Marrn and his two Subartans, and a handful of guards.

The fighting appeared to go well at first. Though the enemy enjoyed superior numbers, their advance was stopped cold by the legions of the great lords—an army that somehow managed two bodies for every man. Frost continued to watch, monitoring the spell he had cast and listening to the echoed cries for blood and victory that rose not from the attackers but from friendly forces, from men defending their homes.

Soon the battle was joined by flanking cavalry, a hundred men—two hundred images—on either side, who charged in led by Lords Burke and Bennor. For a moment the tide seemed almost to turn as some of the offenders, caught between three charging forces, lost their confidence and bearings and turned, ready to retreat. But a moment later, Ferris' own cavalry reserve came charging forward and entered into the fray, several hundred strong.

The armies of the north held their ground. Then Frost suddenly felt his spell begin to lapse, each reflective image dissolving like so many bricks of mud in a heavy rain. Grish and Marrn each tapped him on the sleeve at the same time. Frost looked high on the far hills again and saw a figure there, just a small dot, surrounded by men and horses—the grand chamberlain, he knew: the demon prince.

Madia had seen several of her own troops fall, but many more of the enemy. Each time a thrust was aimed at her mirror image, she found it almost too easy to run her sword through the muddled attacker, and she realized that each of her fellow warriors had discovered this same good fortune. She struck yet another man down, then another, and an uncontrollable grin spread across her face. Most of Ferris' men wore partial plating and mail, their faces exposed. Madia recognized only a few of them: some weak men of Ariman, those who had paid homage to Lord Ferris in her father's absence. But most were the hired mercenaries she had hoped they were, and those that were not would be . . . remembered.

The idea rested easily in her mind. She had not made

fealty to Ferris, nor had Anna or Hoke or the great lords and the many men who fought with her now. Everyone here had made their choices, and they would live, or die, by them.

She dodged a fresh assault, then watched her target duck low in his saddle as she swung her sword about, away from him, causing her second image to swing toward him. As he came up to block the false blow, she was ready. She batted his blade aside as he raised it, then ran him through and watched with an almost shameful glee as he slipped to the grassy ground.

She looked up to find Burke and Bennor arriving from either side, their cavalry sweeping into the ranks of Kamrit's mercenary army. They quickly learned the methods Madia and the others were already perfecting, and the battle began to turn. Then suddenly, the double images faded and were gone.

The fighting nearly stopped momentarily as foot soldiers from both sides watched in wonder while half an army vanished—then a captain in Kamrit's legions barked at his men to attack, and the sound of clashing steel filled the air once more. This time, however, Madia saw the enemy's greater numbers weigh heavily in their favor. Her people began to die. The battle was quickly being lost.

"We must withdraw!" she shouted to Hoke, who was nearby, battling two men on foot from his horse. She moved closer and nearly beheaded one of the men. Hoke managed to cut off the other man's sword hand, a blow that concluded the challenge.

"Withdraw!" he yelled, joining Madia as she shouted it again. Captains echoed their words across the battlefield, and soldiers began to scatter in all directions. Madia and Hoke broke left, riding as fast as their horses would carry them, away from the screams of the dying left behind.

*   *   *

"They flee, my lord," the captain said; a new captain—Tyrr had not yet entirely bothered remembering his name, though he thought it might be Rinaud. He was an older man, well experienced, a veteran of other wars in other lands who came highly recommended and similarly priced. But already Tyrr had begun to tire of his confidence, warranted or otherwise. He was too much like Kaafk—who had forced Tyrr's hand, had made Tyrr destroy him against his wishes and better judgment! Cursed Kaafk! Cursed captain! Cursed human beings!

He felt the body shudder again. *Soon*, he allowed, *I will be only Tyrr. Once the armies of the north are defeated and Neleva lies within easy grasp. Soon, I will finally let go. . . .*

"I expect them to regroup," Rinaud added, sucking his lower lip through a space where a front tooth had once been. "Probably on the hill again. I will call another charge as soon as our scouts find them. You have defeated their magic, my liege. They will not attack us in force again, I am certain."

Frost's magic, thought Tyrr, sensing the other's presence in the spell he had dismantled, in the very air between them, by the faint resonance of the other's mind. The spell the sorcerer had placed upon the charging legions was an intriguing one, something Tyrr had never quite seen the like of, at least not on such a scale. And the troops themselves seemed well trained and well led; a fine strategist in command, no doubt, one of the northern lords. . . .

"You misjudge your adversary," Tyrr grumbled imagining what this captain might look like with no lower lip at all. *Calm*, he cautioned himself anew. *Consider the larger goals, and dismiss these annoyances.*

But the task was becoming a less savory one, the world was annoying him at every turn, Kaafk was annoying him—*no, Rinaud. . . .*

It is the strain of maintaining human form, he thought, shaking the notion from his mind, *not the events.* In fact, there had been problems and setbacks, but overall he had many reasons to be pleased. *If only I can remember them!*

"I judge that they are beaten, my lord," Rinaud persisted.

"As you wish, Captain," Tyrr replied simply, mentally preening himself for the accomplishment. "When you are satisfied that there is no viable force left, we will examine the dead. I wish to know who no longer stands against me, and who may."

His forces had been warned of the northern army's approach, and rumors that all four of the great lords were riding with them, as well as the girl many claimed was the Princess Madia, had been plentiful. But Tyrr found this altogether too fortunate—unless planning and patience was truly paying off on a very grand scale!

Tybree was so very wrong!

I was so right!

He watched Rinaud wander off to give new orders. Riders sped away to the troops below, and slowly Tyrr's forces pulled back nearer the base of the hill to regroup. Tyrr looked up, away to the far hills again. He used a simple yet most effective spell that lent great vision to his demon eyes and saw that Rinaud's instincts had been false. The enemy was regrouping as well, just where they had been before the battle. Rinaud's scouts were riding back this way, riding hard across the valley, bringing the news.

Tyrr decided to let Rinaud find out for himself, then to let him go about aligning his troops for a fresh assault. At present something much more provocative seemed to be occurring, a friction in the air barely yards ahead of Tyrr's massed forces, a gathering of ethereal energies that had already begun to form a faint glitter just above the ground. The phenomenon stretched from left to right across half the battlefield, and Tyrr felt a certain relief. He could meet any challenge, he was sure, but waiting to learn what that challenge might be held no appeal at all.

"Yes," he said, made the lips murmur aloud. *Interesting*, he thought. This Frost fellow seemed never to learn a lesson—at least, not until it no longer mattered.

Tyrr felt buoyed by this unexpected gift the wizard seemed to be sending him, and he went about preparing to unwrap it.

Chapter XXV

"Enough for now," Frost said, relaxing the effort, speaking to the two other wizards that stood with him. He paused to reexamine their collective handiwork. All along the flat terrain just in front of Ferris' great army, the air had taken on a bright, shimmering look as waves of heat radiated upwards, dissipating as they rose to the skies. The heat formed a vaguely transparent wall. The earth at its base glowed like the sun, and the grasses had already begun to smolder. Almost no detail was visible beyond the waves of heat, but as the moments passed, it was clear no man among the enemy's numbers seemed ready to breach the line.

"Wonderful work!" Madia declared genuinely. "This will give us time to ready another plan of attack."

Hoke and the great lords stood with her, their faces weary from battle, yet each one seemed to rally now and vowed again to lend her their full allegiance.

You were right about at least one thing, Madia, Frost reflected as he watched the young princess, listening to her, *you were right about yourself.* But she was wrong to think she and her able compatriots stood any chance now. He could let them go as they willed—do what his instincts and the damnable omens told him he must do and simply leave, simply run away. A fool's wager, this; discouraging odds and limited options—limited to one.

He turned to Madia, then placed one hand gently on her shoulder. "No," he said. "You have done well, but another assault will only bring your deaths."

"You can't know that," Jaran said, but the conviction in his voice was lacking.

"Even without Lord Ferris' great powers, the odds are nearly hopeless by any measure," Frost persisted. "You all know this to be true. But you face not only men, you face a beast as well. It is the beast that I must take. Pray I can succeed against him."

"We have agreed to assist Frost," Grish said of Marrn and himself. "We may better Frost's chances. We all agree the Blade might function better if more minds and strengths are applied to the spell Frost must use."

"You have learned something new?" Madia asked, hopeful.

"No," Frost said. "Only . . . an idea. We have the knowledge that the ancients always used the weapon as a group. We will work together to do as much harm as possible."

"But still you are not sure you can win," Madia said in a low voice, but not low enough that the others wouldn't hear.

"It is not a task I relish," Frost replied. "I am nearly willing to let you talk me out of it."

"Then wait," she urged him. "We can retreat back to Bouren and the other fiefs and gather more men."

"No," Frost said. "I have always been the one to offer such counsel, but I have never known a task on such a scale as this. Today, Madia, you have shown that you are the woman this world has always required you to be.

Distasteful as it may be, I fear that now I must prove myself, too."

He turned and began on foot down the hill, with Rosivok, Sharryl, Grish, and Marrn following close behind.

"May the Greater Gods go with him!" Lord Bennor said, as they watched the small party descend.

"The Greater Gods for one," Madia replied, turning, handing the reins of her horse to Prince Jaran. "But Frost has three Subartans."

Before anyone could speak, she was already off, bolting after the others down the hill.

As they neared the center of the valley, the wall of heat began to cool, a countering spell cast quickly enough by the demon Ferris. Frost stopped and called upon the other sorcerers to help him restore the fading energy. The effort weighed heavily on all three men, but finally, the wall of heat remained—for the most part.

"Ferris has allowed us this small victory," Frost stated, deciding it must be so. "He forces us to weaken ourselves."

"He makes a game of us," Grish replied.

"Do not allow it," said a younger voice, Madia's. Frost did not turn. He had heard someone behind them, legs brushing through the tall grasses, and guessed it must be her. He expected as much, though it did not please him.

"You could at least have come on your horse," Frost told her. "They are useful for hasty retreats."

"Thank you," Madia said. "Next time, I will."

Frost fixed his eyes on the hill before them, focusing on the dark figure poised at its crest. Close enough now to gather details, he could see the colors of the grand chamberlain's elaborate clothing and, just barely, the many faces of his waiting reserve troops. *We are alone here*, Frost thought, fixing it in his mind, *so near to our enemies, so far from our own forces—there is no turning back for any of us.* He looked at the other two men of magic beside him and nodded. In turn, they each stood ready.

"We will need to get his attention," Frost said dryly. He concentrated again up the hill, fixing his eyes on the figure, then whispered the proper words. He could barely discern the changes as they occurred: the face contorting, clothing becoming rumpled and torn as the creature's shape-shifting spell lost its grip and the demon that had hidden itself within slowly appeared. A hideous beast, larger than the image of Ferris would have implied, made of dark, ruddy flesh, and displaying great bright bony teeth that showed clearly even at a distance as the beast opened its mouth. The demon howled as it lost the struggle to retain its construct, a bitter sound that echoed down the slope to Frost's ears, a monstrous child screaming over a stolen toy.

"His rage is our fortune," Frost said. "But it will not last long."

The others stood close beside him and raised their hands toward the hill. They began at once, attacking the beast with the spells they had constructed while Frost drew the Demon Blade from beneath his tunic, held it in both hands, and commenced reciting the lengthy spell that would blend with the other two and call upon the Blade itself. Already he could feel the demon finding its bearings, shaking free of its tantrum, focusing on the sudden attack. The beast howled skyward once more, then bore down on its three challengers and let loose a searing blast of dark ethereal energy.

Frost felt his warding spells pale against the assault, sensed their limits already near, and knew too well that the others with him would suffer the same fate. He centered the Blade, bracing himself, and with the final phrase let go a violent shriek of green and blue-white power, all the energy he could find inside himself, all the energies the Blade petitioned, the intensity of a thousand lightning storms all gathered at once into a crackling stream—a blast so bright it brought darkness to the world around it.

Then his thoughts were overwhelmed by the sudden rush of pain that drove through every part of his body and mind at once, the pain of all the life energies he possessed being torn from him in one great, insatiable gulp, an agony no living being had ever been meant to endure. He had expected some of this from his first contact with the weapon, but what was happening to him now was more intense than anything he had considered. Through the blur of the pain, he realized that there was no limit to this weapon's draining powers—that, once empowered, the Blade was capable of consuming all the energy available to it.

All the life!

With a last effort, Frost reversed the spell's final phrase, and the stream of power vanished. The pain remained, ten thousand knives stabbing through his flesh and his bones, cutting their way out from everywhere inside him. There could be no end to it, he thought, other than death. No escape. No peace. Then the pain began to fade.

A flood of exhaustion came rushing in to replace some of the knives. He felt himself falling, then realized he was lying in a heap on the ground. The Blade had slipped from his hand, and lay just beyond his outstretched fingers.

For a time he simply lay there, his left cheek pressed against the ground, his right eye straining through pain to focus on objects and sky. Muscles flared into agony again as he tried to use them. His vision was clouded; pain stopped him. He closed his eyes and waited for the worst to subside again, then tried once more. This time the pain wasn't quite so bad, and his vision seemed less overcast. He rested, still, breathing as deeply as his present arrangement and burning chest would allow. Then he bore down and pushed up until he had propped himself on one elbow.

A bony elbow, he realized, no padding at all. He felt tentatively about—first his side, then his abdomen—and found a body nearly as insubstantial as Aphan's.

The pain was still easing, or he was getting used to it—he wasn't sure. Remarkably, he stayed propped up, and attempted a look around. From such a low perspective, he could not see over the distortion of the heated wall of air just ahead, could not see the place where Ferris had stood. He thought to dissolve the wall, but he had no strength, not just now. Soon the spell would run out of energy in any case, and there was no hope of doing anything about it.

Slowly he turned his head toward the others. He found both Grish and Marrn in similar situations, both of them alive but lying on the ground, gasping for relief, their faces and hands white and whithered, loose flesh hanging on bones far more pronounced than they had been a moment ago—*just as I am. . . .*

They had used themselves up, Frost thought, though he did not understand how, not in so short a space of time. Unless, standing so close, working together as they were, the Blade had somehow drawn energies from them as well? Frost looked more closely at his own emaciated body. *I should have stopped sooner,* he thought, almost humbly; *next time . . . have to remember to that.*

He looked at the others again and was reminded of Aphan's words, spoken as they had talked in the spring, of the Blade and its keepers: "I am told Ramins was even thinner than I, nothing but bones, as if his magic alone was all that kept him alive," the old sorcerer had said. "How he could have ever summoned enough power to use the Blade, or withstood its force, I cannot imagine. One assumes he never did."

It must be true, for how could he? Frost wondered now, seeing himself, feeling his bones, feeling the pain that still filled his head and wracked his insides. Ramins may have known the spells that worked the Blade's great magic, but with no fat to consume, and no muscle after that . . .

No, he thought. If Ramins had tried to use the Blade, even for an instant, he would have perished. *Which makes no sense. . . .*

Frost took another breath, gritting his teeth, and managed a sitting position—and was surprised to find Madia lying on the ground behind him along with Rosivok and Sharryl, surprised to see each one of them nearly as gaunt and pallid as himself and the two court wizards.

He got gradually to his haunches and tried to stretch tense discomfort from his body, and felt the snapping off of a thousand pointy knife blades. He waited again, taking time to gather what little remained of himself, then he got to his knees. The effort left him so dizzy that he lost his sight momentarily, then slowly the light returned. He breathed again, held it, and pushed himself up onto his feet.

A terribly shaky proposition, he found, swaying as if bothered by a stormy wind. But for the moment, he did not fall. With a careful effort, he turned just enough to see the far hill, and he tried to focus. Blinking he saw a figure on the hill where the beast had been. He blinked again. *Where the beast remains!*

The pain that lingered throughout his mind and body seemed to explode again with the realization. *There is no hope then,* he thought, *no choice.*

"Get up," he said, rasping at the others as he found his voice. "Get up, now!"

"What is happening?" Madia asked, barely a whisper.

"I was right," Frost told her dryly, straining to clear his throat. "I should have taken my own advice."

"Why?" she asked, attempting to sit up. "What?"

"I have given everything, you see, wagered all that I had on a fool's chance, and I have lost. The omens were true. I should have heeded them. I am a fool!"

He turned his head again toward the hill, then glanced down at the Demon Blade. A fresh pang of regret made his chest tighten. His head was pounding now, more than it had been. *Why?* he thought, furious with himself, growing equally as furious with the Blade itself, with the wizards who had used it. *Why have we failed? Why so long ago did others triumph?*

His mind was running on ahead, desperate for the answers, searching back through a lifetime of fascination with the magical arts. His powers stirred within him like the last cold winds of a dying summer storm—*useless!*

He could very nearly explain what had happened to the other two sorcerers, but as he reconsidered the condition of his Subartans, and Madia, the rest still made no sense.

Again Frost thought of Ramins, the one mind in all the world who had known the truth, and he tried to imagine an old wizard of skin and bones attempting to use the Demon Blade. . . .

How could he have defended the Blade if others had come for it? *How could he?* . . .

And then a thought occurred to him, the only possible truth, as he finally turned the puzzle full around and tried to fit the missing piece—as he saw that there was no other answer left but the one that was rushing suddenly, clearly to his mind!

"We await your word, my lord!"

Tyrr wavered, feet apart, digging easily into the hard ground with the talons on his toes, his arms held out for

balance; he remained upright. *Captain Rinaud,* Tyrr
realized, diverting attention momentarily from assessing
his own condition. Frost's attack had utterly surprised
him. The exhaustion that had drenched him like a sudden downpour still soaked him to the core. He had
managed to rally against the attack, then hold his ground
against it, but he had felt the limits of his efforts—the
end approaching! Suddenly, though, the attack had subsided, and he had begun to recover.

Tyrr fathomed the look on the captain's face, a look of
intense concern, a look of consternation. Then Tyrr
recalled that he no longer wore the construct of the grand
chamberlain, that he was now the demon prince, Tyrr, to
human eyes—which also explained the unusual distance
the captain was maintaining between the two of them.

"You do not run?" Tyrr asked the soldier, watching him.

"No, my lord. We . . . well, most of us . . . that is . . . "

"You suspected something like this?" Tyrr asked him.
The captain nodded.

"That is wonderful," Tyrr exclaimed. "Perhaps I owe
you credit! I never should have wasted so much time and
energy on the construct, it seems. If only I had known!"
Then the thought brought an added twinge of humor: to
his knowledge, this was the first time a demon, prince or
otherwise, had acted foolishly for the sake of caution!

"Tell me what has happened below." He pointed one
long, taloned finger in the direction of the small group of
attackers still gathered just beyond his own forces, near
the center of the little valley.

"No one can be sure," Rinaud said, "but I think they
are badly wounded. And some may be dead. We have
seen almost no movement."

"How much movement?" Tyrr asked, taking several
steps forward as he did, finding his balance.

"One of them has risen; the others still have not,"
Rinaud stated.

Tyrr peered down at his enemies—at Frost and the small cluster of fools that had fallen with him. The wall of heat still stood, more or less, though he could sense it quickly fading now, since there remained no one to renew the strange spell. When Frost's powerful attack abruptly lost its force, Tyrr had found it a simple matter to crush the efforts of the two conjurers with him; so simple, in fact, it was as though the job had already been done for him. They were beaten, surely, but they were the ones who might still be alive, somehow.

No, he thought, concentrating, nearly certain he could sense the mind of Frost in the one he saw standing. But the energy of this wizard's presence was weak, nearly extinguished.

"They will pose no more threat," Tyrr assured the captain. "Any of them. Prepare our forces for another assault."

"The burning wind still blocks our path," Rinaud said in an apologetic tone. "We must go around to the south."

Tyrr turned inward for a moment and worked to smooth his appearance slightly, shifting the shape of outer flesh just enough to make it more palatable to those less flexible than Captain Rinaud.

"I will remove that obstacle," Tyrr said, coming out of his brief trance, still amazed that the heat anomaly remained at all. *The spell must be a good one,* he thought, *to maintain itself so long, to find its own energy without being fed.* Frost possessed a very great talent, indeed, though that would no longer be a concern.

No obstacle was.

"Even as you speak, it is so!" Rinaud exclaimed, looking down the hill. Tyrr saw the waves of heat suddenly vanish completely, the grass fires suddenly snuffed out. *But I have done nothing yet. . . .*

The captain bowed once and went to join his men.

What, Tyrr wondered, *is happening?*

* * *

"The barrier dies!" Madia said, pointing toward the stirring ranks of Ferris' forces now clearly visible in the sudden absence of the heated air.

"I know," Frost said. "I have removed the spell."

Madia looked at him soberly, standing now, using her sword like a cane. "We will be overrun," she said evenly.

To her credit, Frost thought, admiring her a moment, this child turned sovereign nearly overnight was still able to control her fear, weakened though she was, and to deem him worthy of trust even in the face of defeat and death. *You will yet sit on the throne of Ariman, if only I am right. . . .*

"Now, get away all of you, quickly," Frost commanded. "Even you," he insisted, speaking to Rosivok and Sharryl. The Subartans only stared. They were each standing now, gaunt, bent, and wobbly like Madia and the other wizards, but standing.

"We will never leave," Sharryl said. "We cannot."

"You will because I have asked you to. You will if you truly serve me. I may require your services in times to come, but you must preserve yourselves to fulfill that duty."

"What will you do?" Madia asked. "You are as weak as we are. You *were* right, Frost. It was a fool's wager, and one we lost. He is too powerful, too clever. Look at yourself, look at what he has done to us. There is nothing we can do."

"It is possible," Frost said, breathing deeply again, stretching tentatively, "that *I* may have done all this."

Madia looked sidelong at him. "What?"

"I'm not sure, but I believe it's true. I intend to try something, but unless you all get away from me, you will not live through it."

"I need to know your plan," Madia insisted.

"It is a simple one. Another fool's wager, in fact." He smiled at her as best he could. "My last."

He waited for her eyes to let him go.

"Perhaps the omens lied?" he added. He saw a calm in her eyes, a depth that surprised him even now.

"But are you lying, Frost?" she asked. "Now?"

"No."

She nodded once, slowly. "With me, then," Madia said, beckoning to the others. She took Grish and Marrn by one arm each and set off with them, bent slightly forward, the three of them holding each other upright, loping to making good time as they retreated toward the hills behind them.

"You will not die?" Rosivok said evenly, leaning close to his master. Frost shook his head. "I may not," Frost said, saying what Rosivok needed to hear, "as long as I am right, and . . . *good* enough. Now, follow her."

The Subartans turned slowly and went after Madia, the depth of their endurance showing through as they finally managed an awkward jog.

Frost took the Demon Blade in both hands, faced forward again, and began his chants. The spell was a bent concoction of phrases culled in part from those he and the other wizards had already used, but mixed with further embellishments, bits of spells from the far corners of his mind. He used a spell that had allowed the wall of heat to draw energy from the earth and air, a spell commonly used for sensing the thoughts of others, a spell of deflection turned inside out, and finally a new spell to combine the others and to add the missing focusing aspects—a spell formed from a lifetime of spells learned and adapted to uncounted uses.

Then he waited while the legions of the enemy began to march, waited until they were nearly upon him—until those he had sent away were likely far enough behind him, hopefully safe.

The beast was descending the hill; there was no more time to wait. Frost raised the Blade and braced himself. He focused his mind on the demon's presence, then he made himself aware of the mortal legions drawing near, and finished the spell's last phrase.

Again the fires lashed out from the Blade, white-hot at first, then turning a blinding blue-white almost instantly, until they began to take on strange florid hues as the force intensified even further—a blaze Frost's own mind could barely imagine, even at this moment. His eyes saw only the stream of fire that blinded him before he could look away, but he could sense the trueness of his aim, the contact with the demon creature. He sensed the beast fighting back as well, drawing on all the vastness of the forces at its command. But already, as he gained control and willed the new concoction of spells into a finer arrangement, Frost knew that the beast's attempts would not be enough.

The savage heat of the energy leaping from the Blade threatened to burn the exposed flesh of Frost's hands and face as the pain from everywhere within began again, crackling along each fiber of muscle and biting at his flesh as it rose to the surface—though it was different this time, somehow less severe, almost bearable. Within him nothing burned, no damage occurred, no flesh dissolved, so far as he could tell. *Otherwise, I would already be dead,* he thought. He closed his eyes and kept his concentration on the spell as its intensity remained at levels he could barely comprehend. He felt the pain increasing gradually, a thing he could hold for now, but growing bigger, heavier, large enough to crush him under its weight if he waited too long—much longer at all. The heat was truly beginning to burn his skin.

Then he heard the beast scream somewhere beyond the range of mortal ears, a sound that echoed through

Frost like thunder through a mountain pass, and with that a distant feeling of terrible hunger and limitless pain—pain beyond anything Frost had so far endured, a final diatribe that flared for just an instant, and then was gone.

Frost thought to end the attack, but he was reluctant to believe in his own success. He could not let go of his fear, his passion, his intoxication with the power he controlled—until suddenly the pain within him exploded.

As he felt his body wither again, he lowered the Blade and broke off the spell, then he fell to his knees, leaning on the Blade, and waited for the agony to subside, for the glowing images in his eyes to darken. Slowly he began to recover. He waited for a long time, then he cautiously opened his eyes. . . .

Such a sight, Frost was certain, had not greeted anyone for more than a thousand years—not since the time of the Demon Wars. Nearly three thousand men lay still on the ground before him in horribly gaunt and twisted heaps, staring at death with hollow eyes, their armor and bloodless dried flesh hanging on their protruding bones, white-bone knuckles clutching at spears and swords, axes and bows. Utterly vanquished, Frost saw; no slight trace of life remained among them.

The Blade had become the true focus of the spell, had consumed all the energy Frost had found to give it, energy directed by Frost's concocted vampire spells, but gathered by the Blade itself from every living thing it found. And when that source was gone, it had come after him again. On the hillside beyond the dead army, a burnt and gaping hole in the earth marked the site where the beast had stood. Of the beast itself, there was no trace.

Frost slowly stood. He held the Blade away from him as it continued to cool, so the heat would not burn him even more. His hands and face stung—bright red, he saw, looking down. He turned and found the others coming toward him again, Madia and Rosivok and Sharryl, followed by Grish and Marrn, and behind them the great lords and their armies—several hundred running, cheering men.

Chapter XXVI

"This way," Anna said, hurrying ahead of the others down the dim stone corridor. She reached the corner and paused. "Down there," she said, her finger pointing around the corner. Madia nodded, then stepped past her, followed by Prince Jaran, Purcell, and a dozen other men. On the left, they found two guards seated at the little table at the head of the wide, dark stairwell opening. Both jumped up at the commotion and drew their swords.

Purcell took his men forward as Jaran and Madia jogged right, snatching a torch from the wall before heading down the stairs. Madia heard one guard scream as he died, then heard the other shouting surrender as she reached the bottom. Here she went right, letting Jaran take the left, and they began banging on the steel faces of the aged dungeon doors, shouting her father's name as they went. The smell of mold and rotting straw and worse filled her nose with every breath. The torchlight seemed to die in the blackness beyond the bars of the cell doors as she held it up to look inside each one.

After more than a dozen doors, Madia heard a faint voice calling back to her. She found the door, then held the torch up and peered in. A dark figure sat on the floor resting tight against the far corner. Jaran brought the keys in a moment and quickly opened the door. As Madia entered she held the torch up, then moved slowly closer as Anna came in just behind her.

"It is him," Anna said, kneeling down beside the silent, staring figure. Madia went to her knees as well, still inspecting the filthy, ailing old man who sat slumped before her. His eyes were nearly empty, unfocussed, unseeing. His limbs hung limply at his sides and his cheeks lay hollow against the bones and teeth behind them. The hair was thin and matted and filthy, but white, she decided, pure white. A man who looked at least a hundred years old. And yet, *it was him!*

"Father," Madia said, finding that her own eyes were suddenly burning, an enormous weight suddenly pressing on her chest. "Father," she repeated, "I am home."

Frost leaned back in his chair and patted the roundness of his belly. Sated smiles graced many faces all around the great table, with the exception of Rosivok and Sharryl, who seemed to insist on their usual strict expressions. Sharryl sat at Frost's side, unusually attentive these past few days, for a Subartan. Frost smiled at them all. A new third Subartan would be needed eventually, he mused, though perhaps this time he could find someone with at least some slight sense of humor, just to round things out. Perhaps someone more like . . . *Madia.*

"To your liking?" Madia asked as he glanced toward her.

"Few tables are set any finer," Frost replied. "It is good to know the hospitality of Kamrit Castle is again worthwhile. Always, I will return."

She raised her brow. "To return, one must leave."

"Come spring," Frost said. "You will have the honor of my presence for another few months."

Madia nodded and seemed to let it go at that. He had never stayed any one place for long in his life, not since leaving Lagareth so many years ago; he had never been content with what he already knew, what he had already done. Madia knew this, he thought, and she knew something of the Demon Blade. She had seen the power of its touch: three thousand dried-twig corpses strewn about the battle field at Kopeth. She had asked him how it had happened, of course. Partly, he had told her.

By now all the people of the realm had heard of the rediscovery of the Demon Blade, of its fearsome powers, and its new keeper. They would come, of course, those who wanted Frost to use the Blade in their employ, or those who wished to own such a weapon for themselves; the Blade was not something one could easily give away, yet it was no doubt harder to keep. Frost understood old Ramins perfectly now.

His eyes came to rest on Madia's father: a dry, placid old face, a quiet, frail form. Kelren was aware now, and much of his memory had returned—he was able to recognize everyone, including Frost, and owing to some spells from Grish and Marrn, and a great deal of love and kindness from Madia and Anna, he had regained some of his color and grown rather talkative in recent weeks. But the damage lingered, a grave legacy of all the beast had done to the aging sovereign. He considered himself fortunate, as fortunate as Ariman was to have a strong queen.

"Of course you will stay until after the ceremony," Jaran said, putting his arm around Madia, grinning like a young boy. "I would not allow you to miss it."

"I don't recall being notified of such an event," Lord Dorree protested, which brought a quick chorus of "here!" from Lords Burke and Bennor. Jaran's father leaned toward the three of them, winking one eye, and raised his flagon as if to toast. "I have heard it is more than just rumor," he said.

"Jaran and I have not agreed on any such thing yet, I assure you," Madia scolded them all, but the smile in her voice as she spoke of Jaran gave much away.

Jaran called to Frost. "If it were so," he said, coddling, "would you stay?"

"A fool's wager," Madia cautioned, pointing at Frost almost accusingly.

"And one I accept," Frost answered.

"Really," Madia scolded, "you ought to be more careful."

Frost nodded graciously, then he began to laugh.

There Are Elves Out There

An excerpt from

Mercedes Lackey
Larry Dixon

The main bay was eerily quiet. There were no
screams of grinders, no buzz of technical talk or
rapping of wrenches. There was no whine of test
engines on dynos coming through the walls.
Instead, there was a dull-bladed tension amid all
the machinery, generated by the humans and the
Sidhe gathered there.

Tannim laid the envelope on the rear deck of
the only fully-operated GTP car that Fairgrove had
built to date, the one that Donal had spent his
waking hours building, and Conal had spent track-
testing. He'd designed it for beauty and power in
equal measure, and had given its key to Conal, its
elected driver, in the same brother's-gift ceremony
used to present an elvensteed. Conal now sat on

its sculpted door, and absently traced a slender finger along an air intake, glowering at the envelope.

Tannim finished his magical tests, and asked for a knife. An even dozen were offered, but Dottie's Leatherman was accepted. Keighvin stood a little apart from the group, hand on his short knife. His eyes glittered with suppressed anger, and he appeared less human than usual, Tannim noticed. Something was bound to break soon.

Tannim folded out the knifeblade, slit the envelope open, and then unfolded the Leatherman's pliers. With them he withdrew six Polaroids of Tania and two others, unconscious, each bound at the wrists and neck. Their silver chains were held by some-*things* from the Realm of the Unseleighe—inside a limo. And, out of focus through the limo's windows, was a stretch of flat tarmac, and large buildings—

Tannim dropped the Leatherman, his fingers gone numb. It clattered twice before wedging into the cockpit's fresh-air vent. Keighvin took one startled step forward, then halted as the magical alarms at Fairgrove's perimeter flared around them all. Tannim's hand went into a jacket pocket, and he threw down the letter from the P.I. He saw Conal pick up the photographs, blanch, then snatch the letter up.

Tannim had already turned by then, and was sprinting for the office door, and the parking lot beyond.

Behind him, he could hear startled questions directed at him, but all he could answer before disappearing into the offices was "Airport!" His bad leg was slowing him down, and screamed at him like a sharp rock grinding into his bones. There was some kind of attack beginning, but he had no time for that.

Have to get to the airport, have to save Tania

from Vidal Dhu, the bastard, the son of a bitch, the—

Tannim rounded a corner and banged his left knee into a file cabinet. He went down hard, hands instinctively clutching at his over-damaged leg. His eyes swam with a private galaxy of red stars, and he struggled while his eyes refocused.

Son of a bitch son of a bitch son of a bitch. . . .

Behind him he heard the sounds of a war-party, and above it all, the banshee wail of a high-performance engine. He pulled himself up, holding the bleeding knee, and limp-ran towards the parking lot, to the Mustang, and Thunder Road.

Vidal Dhu stood in full armor before the gates of Fairgrove, laughing, lashing out with levin-bolts to set off its alarms. It was easy for Vidal to imagine what must be going on inside—easy to picture that smug, orphaned witling Keighvin Silverhair barking orders to weak mortals, marshaling them to fight. Let him rally them, Vidal thought—it will do him no good. None at all. He may have won before, but ultimately, the mortals will have damned him.

It has been so many centuries, Silverhair. I swore I'd kill your entire lineage, and I shall. I shall!

Vidal prepared to open the gate to Underhill. Through that gate all the Court would watch as Keighvin was destroyed—Aurilia's plan be hanged! Vidal's blood sang with triumph—he had driven Silverhair into a winless position at last! And when he accepted the Challenge, before the whole Court, none of his human-world tricks would benefit him—theirs would be a purely magical combat, one Sidhe to another.

To the death.

* * *

Keighvin Silverhair recognized the scent of the magic at Fairgrove's gates—he had smelled it for centuries. It reeked of obsession and fear, hatred and lust. It was born of pain inflicted without consideration of repercussions. It was the magic of one who had stalked innocents and stolen their last breaths.

He recognized, too, the rhythm that was being beaten against the walls of Fairgrove.

So be it, murderer. I will suffer your stench no more.

"They will expect us to dither and delay; the sooner we act, the more likely it is that we will catch them unprepared. They do not know how well we work together."

Around him, the humans and Sidhe of his home sprang into action, taking up arms with such speed he'd have thought them possessed. Conal had thrown down the letter after reading it, and barked, "Hangar 2A at Savannah Regional; they've got children as hostages!" The doors of the bay began rolling open, and outside, elvensteeds stamped and reared, eyes glowing, anxious for battle. Conal looked to him, then, for orders.

Keighvin met his eyes for one long moment, and said, "Go, Conal. I shall deal with our attacker for the last time. If naught else, the barrier at the gates can act as a trap to hold him until we can deal with him as he deserves." He did not add what he was thinking—that he only hoped it would hold Vidal. The Unseleighe was a strong mage; he might escape even a trap laid with death metal, if he were clever enough. Then, with the swiftness of a falcon, he was astride his elvensteed Rosaleen Dhu, headed for the perimeter of Fairgrove.

He was out there, all right, and had begun laying a spell outside the fences, like a snare. Perhaps in his sickening arrogance he'd forgotten that Keighvin could see such things. Perhaps in his insanity, he no longer cared.

Rosaleen tore across the grounds as fast as a stroke of lightning, and cleared the fence in a soaring leap. She landed a few yards from the laughing, mad Vidal Dhu, on the roadside, with him between Keighvin and the gates. He stopped lashing his mocking bolts at the gates of Fairgrove and turned to face Keighvin.

"So, you've come to face me alone, at last? No walls or mortals to hide behind, as usual, coward? So sad that you've chosen *now* to change, within minutes of your death, traitor."

"Vidal Dhu," Keighvin said, trying to sound unimpressed despite the heat of his blood, "if you wish to duel me, I shall accept. But before I accept, you must release the children you hold."

The Unseleighe laughed bitterly. "It's your concern for these mortals that raised you that have *made* you a traitor, boy. Those children do not matter." Vidal lifted his lip in a sneer as Keighvin struggled to maintain his composure. "Oh, I will do more than duel you, Silverhair. I wish to Challenge you before the Court, and kill you as they watch."

That was what Keighvin had noted—it was the initial layout of a Gate to the High Court Underhill. Vidal was serious about this Challenge—already the Court would be assembling to judge the battle. Keighvin sat atop Rosaleen, who snorted and stamped, enraged by the other's tauntings. Vidal's pitted face twisted in a maniacal smirk.

"How long must I wait for you to show courage, witling?"

Keighvin's mind swam for a moment, before he remembered the full protocols of a formal Challenge. It had been so long since he'd even seen one. . . .

Once accepted, the Gate activates, and all the Court watches as the two battle with blade and magic. Only one leaves the field; the Court is bound to slay anyone who runs. So it had always been. Vidal would not Challenge unless he were confident of winning, and Keighvin was still tired from the last battle—which Vidal had not even been at. . . .

But Vidal must die. That much Keighvin knew.

From Born to Run *by Mercedes Lackey & Larry Dixon.*

✳   ✳   ✳

Watch for more from the SERRAted Edge:

Wheels of Fire by Mercedes Lackey & Mark Shepherd

When the Bough Breaks by Mercedes Lackey & Holly Lisle

GRAND ADVENTURE
IN GAME-BASED UNIVERSES

THE BARD'S TALE™
Join the Dark Elf Naitachal and his apprentices in
bardic magic as they explore the mysteries of the
world of The Bard's Tale.

WING COMMANDER™

The computer game which supplies the background world for these novels is a current all-time bestseller. Fly with the best the Confederation of Earth has to offer against the ferocious catlike alien Kilrathi!

Freedom Flight by Mercedes Lackey & Ellen Guon
72145-3 * 304 pages * $4.99   _____
End Run
by Christopher Stasheff & William R. Forstchen
72200-X * 320 pages * $4.99   _____
Fleet Action by William R. Forstchen
72211-5 * 368 pages * $4.99   _____

STARFIRE™

See this strategy game come to explosive life in these grand space adventures!

Insurrection by David Weber & Steve White
72024-4 * 416 pages * $4.99   _____
Crusade by David Weber & Steve White
72111-9 * 432 pages * $4.99   _____

- -

If not available at your local bookstore, fill out this coupon and send a check or money order for the combined cover prices to Baen Books, Dept. BA, P.O. Box 1403, Riverdale, NY 10471.

NAME:_____

ADDRESS: _____

_____

I have enclosed a check or money order in the amount of $_____.

Paksenarrion, a simple sheepfarmer's daughter, yearns for a life of adventure and glory, such as the heroes in songs and story. At age seventeen she runs away from home to join a mercenary company, and begins her epic life . . .

ELIZABETH MOON

THE DEED OF PAKSENARRION

"This is the first work of high heroic fantasy I've seen, that has taken the work of Tolkien, assimilated it totally and deeply and absolutely, and produced something altogether new and yet incontestably based on the master. . . . This is the real thing. Worldbuilding in the grand tradition, background thought out to the last detail, by someone who knows absolutely whereof she speaks. . . . Her military knowledge is impressive, her picture of life in a mercenary company most convincing."—**Judith Tarr**

About the author: Elizabeth Moon joined the U.S. Marine Corps in 1968 and completed both Officers Candidate School and Basic School, reaching the rank of 1st Lieutenant during active duty. Her background in military training and discipline imbue The Deed of Paksenarrion *with a gritty realism that is all too rare in most current fantasy.*

"I thoroughly enjoyed *Deed of Paksenarrion*. A most engrossing highly readable work."

—Anne McCaffrey

"For once the promises are borne out. *Sheepfarmer's Daughter* is an advance in realism. . . . I can only say that I eagerly await whatever Elizabeth Moon chooses to write next."

—Taras Wolansky, *Lan's Lantern*

*   *   *

Volume One: Sheepfarmer's Daughter—Paks is trained as a mercenary, blooded, and introduced to the life of a soldier . . . and to the followers of Gird, the soldier's god.

Volume Two: Divided Allegiance—Paks leaves the Duke's company to follow the path of Gird alone—and on her lonely quests encounters the other sentient races of her world.

Volume Three: Oath of Gold—Paks the warrior must learn to live with Paks the human. She undertakes a holy quest for a lost elven prince that brings the gods' wrath down on her and tests her very limits.

*   *   *   *   *

These books are available at your local bookstore, or you can fill out the coupon and return it to Baen Books, at the address below.